ASHES
IN THE
WIND

Christopher Bland is a former Chairman of the BBC,
BT and the Royal Shakespeare Company.
He is Anglo-Irish and married with a son and
four stepchildren. This is his first novel.

ASHES
IN THE
WIND

Christopher Bland

ISBN (HB) 978-1-78185-933-9
ISBN (XTPB) 978-1-78185-934-6
ISBN (E) 978-1-78185-932-2

Typeset by e-type

Printed and bound in Germany by GGP Media GmbH, Pössneck

Head of Zeus Ltd
Clerkenwell House
45-47 Clerkenwell Green
London EC1R 0HT

WWW.HEADOFZEUS.COM

For Jennie

The land of scholars and saints:
Scholars and saints my eye, the land of ambush,
Purblind manifestos, never-ending complaints,
The born martyr and the gallant ninny;
The grocer drunk with the drum,
The land-owner shot in his bed, the angry voices
Piercing the broken fanlight in the slum.

Louis MacNeice, Autumn Journal

Romantic Ireland's dead and gone,
It's with O'Leary in the grave.

W. B. Yeats, 'September 1913'

THE MAN AND the boy are members of a dying tribe. In the foreground of the photograph they sit on a rocky outcrop that slopes down to the sea. There are trees on the right-hand side, a Victorian castle in the distance. Between these two and the castle there is a natural harbour, with the curved arm of a stone pier protecting a small boat from the onshore wind.

The man, in his early thirties, looks at the camera, left hand on hip, right hand on knee. He is wearing a round hat with a broad brim, tweed trousers and a sleeveless jerkin. The castle in the background is his, and the small boy is his son. The man looks confident; the small boy is smiling.

At first glance this could be anywhere in the British Isles, but the boat has a curved prow and rides high in the water; it is a currach, tarred canvas stretched over a wooden frame, light enough for two men to carry and one to row. This is a boat of the West and South-West of Ireland. In the bottom right-hand corner of the photograph you can read in white ink, 'Derriquin Castle, County Kerry, 1908', and on a second line, 'Lawrence Collection, National Library of Ireland, No. 5284'.

The Anglo-Irish, their tribe, are dying like the Cheyenne or the Arapaho on the Great Plains of America at the end of the nineteenth century. They will go without a struggle, unlamented. Their names and their places, Butler of Waterville, Roche of The Island, Dease of Rath House, Gore-Booth of Lissadell, Bowen of Bowen's Court, Gregory of Coole Park, and these two, Burkes of Derriquin, are lost on the wind.

I.
Ireland
1908–1924

1.

JOHN BURKE WANTS to be Tomas Sullivan. John wants Tomas's worn brown boots, the scabs on his knees, his green jersey darned with whatever coloured wool had come to his mother's hand. He wants to talk like Tomas. Soon enough he does, though his accent changes back when he gets home.

They are eight years old when they meet on their first day at the elementary school in Drimnamore. The two boys are the same height, but John is lean and fair, clean and tidy, Tomas stocky with dark red, curly hair, his face and hands freckled.

To Tomas, John Burke is a creature from another world. John is dropped off at school every morning in a pony and trap. It is five miles to Drimnamore from the Sullivan farm at Ardsheelan, and Tomas walks to school like all the other children, apart from the gypsy boy from along the coast road who trots up on a piebald pony with no saddle and a rope bridle, most days.

John is unsettled on his first day at school, aware that his accent, his clothes, his scrubbed pink cheeks, mark him out as different. He doesn't feel at home in the classroom, where he speaks only when asked a question, in a low, nervous voice, aware of the contrast with the strong Kerry accents around him. He is even less at home in the playground, where he is pushed and jostled, not unkindly, in the puppy-like mêlée of a dozen eight-year-olds.

His heart sinks when they decide to organize themselves into teams; he stands against the wall with the other boys, knowing he will be the last to be picked. So when Tomas, who has appointed himself one of the captains, says early on in the selection process, 'I'll take Sean,' John is staring at the rough surface of the playground and doesn't move until the boy next to him pokes him in the ribs and says, 'That's you.' This endorsement is enough for the rest of the boys, and Tomas is John's friend and protector throughout his time at the elementary school.

Tomas is a force in the playground. He doesn't pick fights, but doesn't avoid them, and there is a dangerous glint in his green eyes. He accepts John's homage with outward indifference. He knows John's father used to be everybody's landlord and the Burkes still own most of Drimnamore village. The six acres of Ardsheelan that provide the Sullivans with their hard-earned living are barely one-twentieth of the Derriquin Castle demesne and home farm.

For four years Tomas and John ride and fish and sail together. John is the better horseman, Tomas knows how and where to fish. John's father Henry teaches them how to sail the Burkes' wooden dinghy round Rossdohan Island half a mile from the Derriquin harbour, and soon no longer feels the need to watch them all the way. They catch mackerel in the Kenmare River and cook and eat them half raw on Rossdohan, they chase hares on their ponies over the mountain, they swim in the peat-browned waters of Lough Dromtine and Lough Lomanagh.

One warm summer afternoon they walk out along the coast road and camp at Staigue Fort, an ancient dry-stone ring fort seven miles from Drimnamore. John shows Tomas the souterrain.

'My great-grandfather found it, it's an escape tunnel.'

They are standing in the corner of the fort, looking at the overgrown entrance.

'Let's see where it comes out,' says Tomas, who crouches and goes in without waiting for an answer. John follows, and the pair of them crawl along the low, black tunnel, its walls never more than a few inches away on either side, until Tomas shouts back,

'I can see a light ahead,' and they emerge, blinking, in a little copse a hundred yards above the fort.

John laughs.

'Look at you, mud from top to bottom. Annie'll skin you.'

'You're no better. It'll brush off. I'm glad we did it.' They shake hands, grinning.

Tomas shows John how to catch a salmon in the Drimnamore River, how to trot a bunch of worms downstream when the water is high, how to let the fish play with the worms for minute after agonizing minute, then feel the fish swallow the bait, then strike. It is understood that when they catch a salmon it goes to Tomas's mother Annie at Ardsheelan, although Tomas says, 'It's hard to poach your own river.'

John is welcome in Annie Sullivan's kitchen. Tomas is equally welcome in the kitchen at Derriquin, although he won't go beyond the green baize door into the main house. Eileen Burke sits with them there, practises her Gaelic with Tomas and encourages John, who never becomes fluent, to join in.

'Don't you think those two spend too much time together?' says Henry Burke to Eileen. 'Shouldn't he meet Charlie Butler, or the Herbert twins?'

'They live miles away, it's an expedition to go there for a cup of tea, and the boys never leave the drawing room,' replied Eileen. 'Tomas is good for John. If he's going to live in Kerry, he needs some real Kerry men for friends, not just the gentry.'

When they are twelve, everything changes. John leaves to go to school in Dublin, Tomas leaves to help Annie on the farm. In the school holidays Tomas is busy up at Ardsheelan; John helps to save the Sullivans' turf in the summer, but their old expeditions on foot and on horseback and in the dinghy are a thing of the past.

John is taught to cast a fly for salmon by Ambrose O'Halloran, the Derriquin keeper, and he tries to wean Tomas off the worm. Tomas has no time for fly-fishing.

'You want to catch fish for sport,' he says. 'I want them for the kitchen. The worm's the thing in a spate river. The Drimnamore's good for the fly three weeks in the year, the rest of the time it's too high or too low.'

John smiles and doesn't argue.

Both young men are gradually overtaken by an awareness of what the world expects of them. At the elementary school they had thought only about each other and the rivers, lakes and mountains of County Kerry. Their physical separation, John to Dublin, Tomas to the farm at Ardsheelan, is accompanied by a growing knowledge of where each belongs in an Irish hierarchy defined by religion and race. Their old friendship has been stretched and thinned. So they meet less often, have an occasional drink in a Drimnamore bar on Fair days, but the evenings together in the Ardsheelan and Derriquin kitchens are over.

John's mother was born Eileen Brodrick; her family had owned land between Cork and Youghal since 1541. Henry Burke met Eileen when her father asked him to stay for a week's hunting with the Duhallow in County Cork. Middleton Park was intimidating, a perfectly proportioned Georgian mansion, its three-storey central block connected by curved and colonnaded arcades to a two-storey pavilion on each side. The landscape was flatter, softer, grassier than Kerry, the park, its trees carefully placed, sloping down to the River Lee half a mile below the house. A little Grecian temple topped a knoll in the middle distance.

Henry thought in comparison that Derriquin hardly deserved to be called a castle. On his arrival at Middleton Park his luggage was taken away. Shown later to a bedroom with a bright fire, he found his clothes neatly unpacked and his dinner jacket laid out, studs and cuff links in his evening shirt.

Every night they dressed for dinner, held in a long dining room with rococo plasterwork on the ceiling and Italianate landscapes painted on the walls. 'By Zuccarelli,' said Lord Middleton proudly. Henry nodded and said nothing. The silver, the candelabra, the half-dozen liveried footmen standing behind the seated guests, the smart young men from London, Etonians all, rendered Henry silent, incapable of easy conversation with Eileen and her sister Agnes.

Over dinner the conversation flowed around and over Henry, until one of the Etonians suggested that the Irish should be grateful for their civilizing English landlords.

'We aren't English, we're Anglo-Irish,' said Henry. 'We belong here, those of us who aren't absentees. Ireland's been patronized and exploited since the Act of Union. It's not surprising that most of us want Home Rule.'

'Us? Us?' said Lord Middleton, frowning. 'I'm a Unionist and proud of it.'

There was a long silence, broken by Eileen who turned to Henry with a smile.

'You're the brave boyo, talking Home Rule in this Unionist fortress. Good for you.'

Henry blushed, and said little for the rest of dinner.

In the hunting field Henry was a different man, a bold horseman. Eileen, just as fearless, rode side-saddle in a dark blue habit and a veil. On the second day's hunting, after an exhilarating twelve-mile point across banks, ditches, big blackthorns and stone walls, they took the last double bank together, up over the ditch, a long stride on the top as wide as a cottage, then out and down over the ditch on the other side. There were only seven survivors of a field of fifty. Breathless, tired, muddy, by now dismounted, they stood next to each other as the huntsman lifted the dead fox out of the mêlée of hounds. Eileen's veil had torn away; as he helped her remount, holding her bent knee for what seemed like an age, Henry decided that this was the girl he would marry. They hacked slowly home side by side as the light faded, their legs touching most of the way.

That night at the Duhallow Hunt Ball, Henry asked for Eileen's programme the moment they arrived and pencilled in 'HB' for every alternate dance, for supper and for the last waltz.

Henry was a better rider than a dancer, but tall enough to make a good partner for Eileen. She was nineteen, Henry was twenty.

There was a fierce argument when Eileen told her father that she wanted to marry Henry Burke.

'The Burkes are Williamite adventurers, and Derriquin is twenty thousand acres of bog and rock with a rent roll of two and a half thousand pounds. Half of it uncollected. Mortgaged to the hilt, I shouldn't wonder,' said Middleton.

'Well, I'm not marrying him for his money, that's sure,' said Eileen.

'And there's a dangerous religious streak in that family.'

'Deans of Ardfert and Archdeacons of Aghadoe over three generations? Those livings kept the estate afloat. Besides, I thought you were a pillar of the Church of Ireland.'

Middleton, not sure he was winning the argument, stoked the fire noisily and poured himself a glass of sherry.

'That's not what I meant at all. Henry's grandfather, High Sheriff of Kerry at the time, converted when the Revival came to the South-West. Joined the Plymouth Brethren and wound up preaching the Gospel in Weston-super-Mare. Why Weston-super-Mare, for heaven's sake? Sent me a copy of his book, he did, *Twenty-One Prophetic Papers*. Couldn't make head nor tail of it. Said I could be a brand plucked from the burning.'

'That was meant as a compliment. Henry's not like that, and he's certainly no Plym. We agree on lots of things. I like him, and for more than his looks. And he's asked me – that is, he's asked to come and talk to you. You knew his father, you invited him to stay for the hunt ball, you loaned him a horse.'

'I asked the young men for you and your sister Agnes to dance with, but not necessarily to marry. You could have the pick of County Cork. And this one's lukewarm about the Union.'

'So am I,' said Eileen.

Eileen married Henry Burke despite her father. She understood enough about the Famine, for there were many still alive to give her first-hand accounts of its toll on the Irish countryside, to convince her that Home Rule for Ireland was inevitable. Her views enlivened and disrupted many Kerry dinner parties; several of her Ascendancy neighbours thought her a traitor to her class and her country.

2.

J OHN BURKE'S TRAIN is armoured. Slabs of steel have been bolted to the sides of the engine and the top of the cab, where the narrow slits are barely wide enough for the engine driver to see ahead. On the platform are two large wicker baskets, the source of a warm murmur that contrasts with the clatter of the station. Three or four grey and blue and white heads poke out and as quickly withdraw. A large brown tag on each basket says, 'Ballsbridge Racing Pigeon Society; please release at Mallow.' The crowd on the platform waits patiently; train timetables are a pre-war luxury.

Kingsbridge Station, an Italianate palazzo with Corinthian columns, carved swags and urns and twin campaniles, looks out of place in Dublin's reluctant sunlight. The building appears embarrassed by the railway tracks, engines and ticket offices that hide behind its imperial façade. Bullet holes scar the columns and the walls, and the little dome that tops the left-hand campanile has been given a rakish tilt by an artillery shell. Dublin is danger-ous but alive; not a day passes without news of a shooting, an abduction, an escape, a Black and Tan outrage, an IRA ambush. Ireland, an angry beehive without a queen, already has two Parliaments, Dáil Éireann and Westminster, and will soon add a third at Stormont.

John, a country cousin in Dublin, is leaving the front line. He has none of the war stories that some of his older Trinity College contemporaries tell of the Easter Rising – the battles for the

General Post Office, the Four Courts, Jacob's Factory, St Stephen's Green, the failed attempt to take over Trinity. So he is pleased when his train is stopped and searched twice on the long journey to the South-West, once at Kildare Station by the British Army, once by the IRA five hours later beyond Mallow. He is travelling in a second-class carriage among the bank managers, land agents, racehorse trainers, clergymen and nuns. First class is for the Protestant Ascendancy and Roman Catholic bishops. Third class has hard wooden benches for small farmers, their wives and their livestock.

The British Army search is silent; no questions are asked. A man from the adjacent carriage is taken away, protesting angrily.

'At least it's not the bloody Black and Tans,' says a farmer as the train is waved on.

The priest is asked by a small wiry fellow, a jockey with a lightweight racing saddle strapped to his bag on the rack above, what he thinks of the IRA.

'I understand where they're at,' he says. 'But there's no absolution for murder.'

'Have you ever been asked?' says the jockey. There is no reply.

By the time they reach Mallow the carriage is full of cigarette smoke. Over the years the framed photographs of Irish landmarks on the walls, Howth Head, Killarney, the Cliffs of Moher, have turned to a yellowish brown. The jockey is asked what he's riding.

'I'm on two of Dinny MacShane's tomorrow, one in the novice hurdle, one in the three-mile chase. Hopeful Colleen in the chase has a chance at the weights.'

The priest scribbles down the name on a scrap of paper, but when the jockey gets out at Mallow the farmer says, 'Save your money, Father. That Mick Malone's still a chalk jockey after seven years, and it'll be another seven before he gets his name painted on a board. He never gets a decent ride, no harm to him.'

The priest smiles, puts away his piece of paper.

'Ah, well.'

Beyond Mallow the train is stopped again in the middle of the country, this time by a dozen IRA Volunteers in a cobbled-together variety of uniforms. They are mostly fresh-faced farmers' boys in their twenties; one of them looks no older than John. They ask the passengers in each carriage to open their bags. The priest points to his dog-collar and gets an abashed, 'Sorry, Father,' in response. After half an hour and no weapons the train sets off again and by the time they reach Kenmare the two-hundred-mile journey has taken six hours. John spends the night with his Herbert cousins at Muckross Abbey.

The next afternoon he is met by William McKelvey in the Humber. William, a taciturn Ulsterman, delivered the car, the first in Kerry, from Belfast in 1912, keeping it going for seven bone-shaking years over bog and mountain roads with an ingenuity that triumphed over the absence of spare parts. It is a long drive over the twisting mountain roads; as they reach the top of the pass the sun comes out and the Kenmare estuary spreads out before them in a dazzling mixture of colours – the colours, John thinks, of his mother's watercolour box, Ultramarine, Cerulean, Indigo, Cobalt Blue. And for the land, Burnt Umber, Siena, Hooker's Green.

As they get closer to Drimnamore they are stopped.

'It's a Shinners roadblock,' says William. 'You'd best do the talking – they'll no care for my accent.'

There are four Volunteers; after looking in the boot they wave the car on.

As the castle comes into view in the fading evening light, John, in spite of his reluctant departure from Dublin, feels a returned affection for the rough grey stone, the absurd battlements, the long view down the mile-wide estuary of the Kenmare River stretching towards America. Three little islands, the Bull, the Cow and the Calf, punctuate with the smallest of dots the wide expanse of the Atlantic. The sky is grey, matching the stones of Derriquin, turning almost black out to sea where sheets of rain slant in towards the land.

His mother rises as he comes into the library. Eileen Burke is a tall, handsome, fair-haired woman whose figure is concealed by several layers of sweaters to keep out the cold. A fire smoulders in the grate, the bitter-sweet smell of the turf smoke telling John that he is properly at home.

The library, its four tall windows shuttered against the winter gales every evening, looks out on the terrace and the Kenmare River. The shelves are full of leather-bound Dublin editions collected by past Deans of Ardfert and Archdeacons of Aghadoe, the novels of Somerville and Ross the only concessions to the twentieth century. Eileen keeps her Irish dictionary and texts in the old schoolroom. John strokes the faded green leather on the round estate table with its six lettered drawers; twenty-seven people come here every Friday to be paid. The table is covered with papers and letters. Bills are stacked high on a single spike. On the end wall, unrolled from its long mahogany case, hangs a large map of the estate, holding by holding, townland by townland.

Eileen gives John an affectionate embrace. He is a head taller than his mother, lean, with her fair hair and his father's strong features.

'You're the image of Henry,' she says, 'I'm glad you're back safe. Things have got a lot worse here since the summer. But it's bad enough in Dublin.'

'Not so bad. Exciting, dangerous only if you're a soldier or a policeman. William and I were stopped on the way here by four Volunteers. One of them looked like Tomas Sullivan. I haven't seen him for a while, he was at the back of the group, didn't say anything.'

'You recognized nobody,' replies his mother sharply.

John goes up via a winding staircase to his room at the top of the tower. There he can see the broad sweep of the estuary, over the trees to Drimnamore village and the Coomakista Pass, and back across the demesne to the wild bare heights of MacGillycuddy's Reeks. In the summer he sometimes climbs the pull-down ladder to the trapdoor that takes him out to the roof. He has a battered telescope with which he has tried to look, guiltily but unsuccessfully, into the upstairs rooms of the Great Southern Hotel two miles away. The hotel's summer dances are John's meeting ground for girls, Dublin girls from substantial Catholic families living in Rathmines or Ballsbridge, intrigued by John but armoured against his inexperienced advances by impenetrable underclothes and fear of hell-fire.

All his treasures are in his room – his shotgun, which has hung inside a pair of trousers in his wardrobe since The Troubles, his collection of birds' eggs, an old paper kite that his father made on his tenth birthday, two fishing rods, his books, his matriculation photograph taken at Trinity. In a silver frame he has a picture of his parents on their wedding day on the steps of St Fin Barre's Cathedral in Cork.

The next day John wanders around the outbuildings and the farmyard. He goes down to the sea-water pool where whiting, bream and haddock are kept for the table. He has taken some bread to feed the tame mullet, now five or six pounds, that escaped selection for the kitchen and has earned a permanent reprieve. He walks on to Oysterbed Pier, where a consignment of spats from Arcachon has just arrived. The rest of the afternoon he is up to his waist in the cold water of the estuary with the two Doyle brothers, who give him a pair of chest waders from the oyster shed. The three of them lay the spats out in the ambulances, the wooden boxes on trestles that keep the young oysters clear of silt and starfish. Big spring tides, rising and falling fifteen feet, and the clean water of the Atlantic make the Kenmare River an ideal site for the oyster parc which John's great-great-grandfather had established a hundred years earlier.

'It'll be a good year, this,' says Jim Doyle. 'As long as we're spared the disease.' He makes a sign with his right hand and spits over his left shoulder to ward off *Haplosporidium nelsoni*.

'Here you are, Sean,' he says, opening his clasp knife and shucking a mature oyster. 'Taste the good on that one.'

John takes it, feels the plump, firm, slippery texture, chews for a second and swallows, the taste of the sea on his lips. He spits and smiles. 'All right, I'd say.' The mother-of-pearl on the inside of the shell gleams in the spring sunshine.

He goes for long walks around the Derriquin estate, sometimes with the keeper, Ambrose O'Halloran, more often on his own.

'Don't go to the north of the road,' says Ambrose. 'You never know who you'd meet up the mountain.'

When Henry Burke came back from France for a week's leave over Christmas 1915, John and Eileen met him at Kenmare, a tall, gaunt, exhausted figure in a khaki greatcoat, a major's badges of rank on his sleeves. Henry spent forty-eight hours in bed, then took John shooting for the first time. John, who had been out several times with Ambrose, but always with an empty gun, was excited at this promotion, at doing something for the first time with Henry.

Father, son and gamekeeper quartered the big bogs with a riot of spaniels on a typical Kerry winter's day, overcast, scudding clouds, sharp bursts of rain, occasional redemptive sun. 'A great man for the snipe, the major,' said Ambrose to John as Henry strode thigh-deep in water and clinging peat to the far end of Reenaferrara before bringing it back with the dogs. Henry killed three snipe with seven shots on his way through; John missed everything, hurried, anxious, until instinct took over and he brought down a high, twisting bird with a shot that was over before he had time to think.

'Good shot,' said Henry, and John smiled with pleasure.

'*Mionnan aerach*, the child of the air, we call the snipe,' said Ambrose.

'Let's pick the bird,' said Henry. 'They're the devil to find unless you mark them to the inch.'

They spent five minutes searching until John's springer, the wildest of them all, found the snipe and laid it at John's feet. On the way back the dogs flushed a woodcock out of the rhododendrons in the demesne, and John killed it cleanly.

'Another good shot,' said Henry as he picked up the bird, showing John the browns and dark greys of its feathers. He took out the pin feathers and stuck one in his own cap and one in John's, 'I don't shoot woodcock any more. They're too beautiful. Look at those eyes and the long beak.'

Two days later they returned Henry to Kenmare and the long journey back to France. At the station four days earlier, Henry and John had shaken hands; now Henry held his son in a tight embrace before kissing Eileen goodbye. It was the only time his father hugged John. The rough cloth of the greatcoat scratched his cheek, his father's chin rested on the top of his head; they were both afraid to let go. Henry kissed Eileen, murmured something in her ear and boarded the train.

'What did Dad say?' asked John.

'Most of it none of your business,' said Eileen. 'But he did say we weren't to worry, that he would come back.'

Years later John read the War Diary of the Royal Irish Dragoons, which described the morning of 1 July 1916 in a few lines.

The regiment advanced in good order at 0730 hours. When the Allied barrage lifted we were instantly fired on by the enemy's machine guns and snipers. The fire was so intense that the advance was checked; A Squadron, under Major Burke, managed to make progress on the right flank, and by 1130 had reached the first line of German trenches, followed by B and C Squadrons. By noon our first objective had been secured. On our right the Queen's Victoria Rifles had been held up, and on the left flank a determined attack by the Inniskilling Fusiliers was checked. As a result the German counter-attack on both flanks was intense, and after fierce fighting for two hours, and many casualties, including the commanding officer, the second in command,

16

A and C squadron leaders and the adjutant, the regiment was ordered to withdraw. 360 out of 542 men were killed or wounded.

A contemporary German account said, 'In the valley leading to Thiepval the bodies lay like a blanket.' Henry's corps commander General Congreve wrote in a letter to his wife, 'I am proud of my splendid fighting troops. A perfect day.'

On Friday John walks the two miles into Drimnamore village to collect *The Kerryman* and the post. It is the last Friday in the month, market day, and Drimnamore is busy. Cattle, pigs and chickens are bought and sold, horses trotted up and down on the green, bargains are struck with a spit and a handshake, notes watchfully counted out, the luck-penny handed back. Women in shawls are selling yellow, salty butter in willow baskets. Small groups of men stand around smoking and holding glasses of stout. There is a fortune-teller in a little brown tent doing good business as long as Father Michael isn't around. John catches a piebald with a dangling halter that canters past him and hands it back to its breathless owner, who at once tries to convince John, 'This is the horse you've been wanting all your life. Didn't he pick you out of the crowd?'

John laughs, shakes his head, moves on, nods to Tomas Sullivan, who is talking to several older men, strangers to John. Tomas nods back.

There are several Kerry cows for sale, the offspring of Eileen's Kerry bull Cúchulain. Eileen is a crusader for the breed, threatened by bigger animals from lowland Scotland. The Kerry cow is a grand doer on the poor grazing of the South-West, good for beef and milk, hardy, doesn't mind the rain.

There are more men about than usual, and more Cork accents. John has a glass of stout in O'Hara's smoky bar where he recognizes less than half of the dozen men in the crowded room. He tells his mother on his return.

'Maybe there's something on,' she says. 'More than just searches and roadblocks. The Black and Tans are in Waterville now, and the Kerry Brigade may be pushed into doing something about them. The Cork boys are much harder and maybe that's why they're here. I'll ask around. Someone will know.'

Lunch at Derriquin the next day is a sombre affair. Their near neighbours, the Butlers, have come over from Waterville, their distrust of Eileen's Home Rule sympathies outweighed by the certainty of excellent Kerry beef and a dozen oysters each from the Derriquin oyster beds. After all, Arthur Butler reminds his wife, 'She is Middleton's daughter, and he's sound all right on the Union.'

At lunch he wants vigorous action. 'They've destroyed the police station in Tralee, ambushed and killed two policemen in Cahirciveen, burned Ardfert Abbey and Renvyle. We've been raided three times in the last month, our shotguns and cartridges taken. Kerry needs more troops, more Black and Tans.'

Eileen is scornful.

'More Black and Tans? They're the dregs of the British Army; they shot a woman in Kiltartan last week sitting on her lawn. Twenty-four years old, leaving three children without a mother.'

'Of course that's a tragedy. But Home Rule won't ever work. Look at your people. They're as feckless and as priest-ridden as ours. The Irish need a firm and fatherly hand if there is to be any future for this island. The Black and Tans will sort out the Shinners soon enough once we have enough of them.'

John looks out of the window at the rough November waves in the estuary, daydreaming of his rooms back at Trinity. It's an odd father that needs the police and the army to control his children, he thinks, sees the surprised look on Arthur Butler's face, and realizes he has spoken out loud. There is a long silence. John's mother smiles and rings the bell for coffee.

That afternoon Eileen is driven into Drimnamore to see Josephine. Josephine Burke lives in the end cottage at the entrance to the village, where she teaches at the elementary school. Josephine and Eileen are close. It is Eileen who arranged for Josephine's education by the nuns in Kenmare, who asks her regularly to the castle, who ensures that she sits in the Burke pew, who insists that Josephine calls herself Josephine Burke, not Josephine Doyle.

'It's not down to you that Henry's Uncle Arthur was too cowardly to marry your mother,' says Eileen. 'It's he was the bastard, not you.' Josephine smiles at the frank language. Eileen is Josephine's marriage broker, persistent in spite of Josephine's diffidence.

'Sure, who'd have me? I'm thirty-two, illegitimate, a Protestant into the bargain.'

'A lucky man, that's who. You know what they say – marry a teacher or a nurse and you've got a laying hen.'

Josephine laughs. She teaches Gaelic to Eileen, a good and eager pupil, who is fluent enough to say, when her younger sister Agnes elopes with John Fuller after a long and clandestine courtship, '*Sciob an fiolar togha mo schicini*' – 'The eagle has taken the pick of our chickens.'

Eileen and Josephine are together for an hour on Sunday evening in Josephine's front room. On the way back to Derriquin, Eileen calls on Father Michael. It is her first visit to the parish priest's house, a substantial brick building close to the Roman Catholic church. Father Michael has always been friendly enough, but guards his flock closely. He has been told how Henry's father tried to convert the Derriquin tenants during the Famine years.

Eileen is shown in by the housekeeper and sits on a straight-backed chair in the austere parlour, bare but for a small table, a second chair and a large crucifix on one wall. A recently lit fire struggles to warm the room.

The housekeeper brings in a pot of tea and two cups on a tray; as she leaves the room Father Michael comes in and sits down. He is much younger than Eileen, not yet thirty, and the authority of his position sits a little uneasily on his shoulders.

'I'm sorry we've no biscuits,' he says. 'I don't do much entertaining. But you'll have a cup of tea?'

'I will, thank you. I'm sorry to arrive unexpectedly, but I've heard from Josephine that the IRA are planning to move men up to Staigue Fort to attack the army convoy from Kenmare. If it happens it'll be more than a skirmish, it'll be a real battle. You and I should warn both sides, get the IRA to call the ambush off.'

Father Michael looks uneasy. 'I'm not sure what I can do, whether the Cork men will listen to me.'

'They will if you tell them the army have been warned,' says Eileen. 'We both of us should try.'

'It's been quiet enough around Drimnamore so far,' says Father Michael, getting up and poking the fire. 'I suppose we should do our best to keep it that way.'

That evening Eileen talks to John. 'Father Michael is going to warn the IRA, I'll speak to the army this evening. The last thing we need is a battle.'

John makes no attempt to dissuade her. Later, watching from his room in the tower, he sees Eileen walking along the terrace that separates Derriquin from the sea, running her hand slowly across, down, across, up the waist-high battlemented wall.

Eileen telephones General Strickland in Kenmare; the army ignores her advice to delay their convoy and instead plans an ambush of its own.

Frank O'Gowan, the captain of the Cork detachment of the IRA, is determined to go ahead. He has been sent to galvanize the Kerry Brigade, still tainted by their failure to rescue Roger Casement from the Tralee barracks in 1916. He distrusts Father Michael's warning; the Drimnamore parish priest makes no distinction from his pulpit between IRA and British killing.

'They'll be expecting two Kerrymen and a dog,' Frank says later to Tomas Sullivan. 'Not twenty of us.'

3.

THE ANCIENT DRY-STONE ring of Staigue Fort stands in an amphitheatre of hills open to the south half a mile above the coast road. On Wednesday evening, twenty IRA Volunteers move into the fort in ones and twos off the mountain. They shelter in the old guardroom built into the side of the wall, lighting a turf fire that offers more comfort than warmth. The men from Cork are quiet; the Kerrymen, who have never fired their rifles in anger, are full of nervous questions. They get short answers.

'You'll find out soon enough in the morning,' says Frank O'Gowan, yawning. 'Jesus, I could sleep on a harrow.'

'Did you see the priest Sunday?' says Patrick O'Mahony to Tomas Sullivan. He is moving a small rosary nervously between his fingers.

'Indeed I did,' says Tomas. 'I had little enough to tell him. It's hard to find an occasion of sin in Drimnamore.'

'What got you in? The farm, was it?' says Patrick.

'Not land any more. My grandfather took the grazing of five cows from the Burkes for three lives, but my da bought it out in '96.'

'So?'

'My grandfather was a member of the IRB, a proper Fenian – and his grandfather fought in 1798. It's time this country was ours, high time we had a Republic. What got you here?'

'A bit of excitement.'

'You'll have your fill of that in the morning,' says Frank.

'What about you, Captain?' says Tomas.

'The Christian Brothers and the Connaught Rangers.' He doesn't elaborate.

Frank O'Gowan was half English; he had been christened Francis Xavier Smith, reflecting his mother's hope that she had borne a priest. Her English husband had a small draper's shop on the Cork Quays. When it collapsed and her husband disappeared, she changed their name to O'Gowan and enrolled her hope in the Christian Brothers School, a grim building in Cork City as forbidding and uncomfortable as the County Jail. On his first day, standing uncertainly in a dank hall smelling of disinfectant and of boys, Frank was suddenly lifted off his feet by a massive hand that grabbed jacket, collar and vest in a single twisted bunch.

'What's your name, boy?' said the unseen owner of the hand.

'Frank – it's Frank,' said Francis Xavier O'Gowan, rechristening himself in an instant.

'I've no Frank on my list. What's your last name?'

'O'Gowan.'

'No, it isn't. It's O'Gowan, Brother Malachy. Hold out your hand.'

Frank turned around, held out his hand, was grabbed by the wrist and given three heavy welts from Brother Malachy's leather tawse.

'That will teach you your name. And mine.'

This was his introduction to the Christian Brothers. His contemporaries soon found out about his name change, teased him for his rudimentary Gaelic, and called him 'The English'; Frank tolerated this until he became big enough to clout anyone who used the nickname. He developed a talent for the kick, gouge and butt of playground fighting; he began to enjoy the fierce scuffles and seek them out. The frequent and sanctioned violence from the Brothers and among the boys made Frank a convinced atheist.

The Connaught Rangers made him a soldier, taught him to strip, clean and assemble a rifle, familiarized him with the idiosyncrasies of the Mills bomb and promoted him to sergeant. A gas attack took him out of the trenches just before the Somme; he was convalescing in a Dublin hospital during the Easter Rising, and was still in bed when he heard the news of the execution of fifteen of the Rising's leaders at the beginning of May. One of the fifteen, Michael O'Hanrahan, was his cousin. On his discharge from hospital he went home to Cork, overstayed his leave, was posted as a deserter and joined the Cork Brigade of the IRA.

Frank takes a particular pleasure in using his British Army skills against his former teachers.

'Easy with the bombs, boys,' he says as he hands them out. 'They're each to knock over three Black and Tans. And you, Patrick, stop fiddling with that ring or you'll blow us all to kingdom come.'

They clean their rifles, British Army Lee-Enfields and long-barrelled single-shot Mausers, share out the ammunition, eat their bread and cheese. It is a long night. They wake, stiff and cold, to a wild spring morning, low grey clouds, violent rain squalls, almost no sun.

The road convoy never arrives. Instead, a column of the Manchester Regiment comes over the mountain from Kenmare and down on the fort from behind. A sentry spots the column, but the Volunteers have no time to withdraw. The soldiers have brought a Lewis gun and ammunition on the back of a mule. They lay down a heavy covering fire on the fort as Frank moves his men to the northern ramparts.

The machine-gunner is accurate; Seamus O'Connell, a forty-year-old farmer from Derrynane, tries to return the fire and is caught by a burst that tears his face apart and throws him down, spread-eagled, on the grass. A pool of blood makes a red halo around his head. Patrick and Tomas look down with horror, then Patrick starts to cry.

'Get a hold of yourself, man,' says Frank. 'You'll have a chance at a wake later. If you're lucky.'

Terrified by the firing, the soldiers' mule breaks loose and bolts, braying, towards the fort. It is shot by one of the Volunteers.

'Any road, he'll not carry the gun back to Kenmare,' says Frank. 'But we're banjaxed, we're all dead men unless we can stop the machine gun.'

'We could get at them through the souterrain,' says Tomas and, seeing the blank looks, says, 'The souterrain, the tunnel. It starts from the north corner, goes up the hill on the slant.'

'Show me the way,' says Frank, and they crawl through the tunnel, dry in spite of the rain. They emerge in a small copse a hundred yards up the hill, move in a crouching run under the lee of a stone wall towards the machine gun and stop when they are twenty feet away. Frank and Tomas stand up and hurl four bombs. Two fail to explode, but the other two are enough to do the job. Three soldiers are killed outright and the gun destroyed. Frank shoots the fourth as he crawls away.

This makes the odds better, although the Volunteers are still outnumbered three to one. The British soldiers are experienced, but exhausted after the long climb, and demoralized by the loss of the Lewis gun. The Kerrymen know the fort, the irregular small fields and their stone walls very well. The fighting is intermittent; early on the British soldiers try an assault across the field in front of the fort. Without the machine gun their covering fire is inadequate, and they lose three men before retreating.

'You'd have thought they'd have learned better in France,' says Frank.

The Volunteers keep down below the ramparts; a couple of men are posted to watch out for a second attack. During a heavy squall Frank leads out a small group round the right flank of the British.

'You joined up for excitement; now's your chance,' says Frank to Patrick O'Mahony.

Using the banks and walls as cover, they succeed in picking off four soldiers before they withdraw. As they re-enter the fort

Patrick O'Mahony is hit by a bullet that shatters his knee; Tomas piggy-backs him, groaning, into the safety of the walls. Frank O'Gowan tosses a dressing to Tomas, who does his best to plug the gaping hole and stem the flow of blood. Patrick, half conscious, is muttering, 'O my God, I am heartily sorry for having offended you. I detest all my sins . . .'

Patrick grips Tomas's hand tightly as they say the Act of Contrition together. Tomas is frightened at what is happening, shocked at seeing dead men for the first time and by the smashed white bones and blood of Patrick's knee. And at the same time he is excited and determined to survive.

By three o'clock Frank realizes the fort will be taken once the Manchesters organize their covering fire. Five of his men are dead and their ammunition is down to eight rounds a man. The three wounded men, Patrick by now unconscious, are left in the guardroom; the bodies of the dead Volunteers are laid out on the grass. Frank breaks the survivors up into two groups.

'You've done well, boys, as well as could be. Now make your way home.'

The first group head down towards the road. There a section of the Black and Tans is waiting. Only three Volunteers make it across to the coast, escaping to the Derrynane caves. The first soldier who follows them down the narrow track to the caves is killed; the rest retreat to the cliff-top and wait till morning. At dawn they smoke the Volunteers out, dropping lighted barrels of tar down to the mouth of the cave. Two Volunteers come out with their hands up, waving white handkerchiefs. Both men are shot. The third dives into the rough sea and gets away from the bullets. His body is washed up a week later.

Back at Staigue Fort they wait until a strong squall driving in from the Atlantic blots out the sun for half an hour. Frank O'Gowan, Tomas Sullivan and the rest of the Volunteers escape up the mountain through the souterrain.

*

Father Michael hears gunfire out to the west all through the morning; by the time he arrives below Staigue Fort the fighting is over. Thirty or more British soldiers from the Manchester Regiment and the Black and Tans are standing by three lorries, smoking or sitting on the bank beside the road. One of the Tans points his rifle at Father Michael, laughs when he flinches, then shoulders arms.

The bodies of five Volunteers are piled in a heap on the road, all men that Father Michael knew well. He touches each cold forehead with a drop of holy oil. Seven more Volunteers are sitting in the back of one of the lorries, wrists and ankles bound, three of them badly wounded. He gives the wounded men the Last Rites, then seeks out the officer who appears in charge.

'Where are you taking them?' he asks. 'Three of them need a doctor.'

'They should have thought of that before they came out here,' is the reply. 'They'll see a firing squad before a doctor.'

The captured Volunteers are taken to Kenmare; tried a fortnight later, they refuse to recognize the court. Two are found not guilty and five are condemned to death.

After the battle Frank, Tomas and the remaining survivors spend the night in a cattle-shed on the high ground well above Drimnamore.

'Could we stay at Ardsheelan?' asks Frank.

'It's the first place they'll look,' says Tomas.

'Then we're in for a few cold, wet nights.'

They move on at first light; looking down at the village they see two lorry-loads of Black and Tans arriving, hear shots being fired, see two cottages burning.

'Bastards,' says Frank. 'Too many to take on. But we'll settle the score.'

*

Posters offering a thousand pounds' reward for Frank O'Gowan go up all over Kerry. They describe him as: 'Age thirty-two, dark complexion, dark hair, grey eyes, short cocked nose, weight about twelve stone; looks like a blacksmith coming from work; wears cap pulled well down over face.'

The posters are torn down almost as soon as they are put up.

4.

O N SUNDAY, WILLIAM drives Eileen and John to St Peter's in Drimnamore past the Roman Catholic church on the edge of the village. Father Michael's congregation are standing outside in little knots, men and women separate, dark suits, dark dresses, dark shawls. No one waves. Josephine meets them in the porch.

'There's three boys from the parish killed at Staigue,' she says. 'Seven more taken and likely to be shot, two from Drimnamore. Seamus O'Connell from Derrynane is dead. Brought his heifers to the bull, paid in eggs. There's only a daughter left to work the farm now.'

'I heard two Volunteers were killed trying to surrender at the Derrynane caves and another drowned. Father Michael and I made it worse,' says Eileen.

They talk to the other members of the small congregation. Arthur Butler from Waterville is there without his wife.

'Winifred was too frightened to come. You can still see blood on the road below Staigue. A sad business altogether.'

Inside the church there are a dozen memorials in brass and stone, whose phrases, 'generous and upright', 'sincerely lamented', 'devoted father and improving landlord', stamp seals of approval on Henry, followed by John followed by James in a two-hundred-year-long procession. Most of the pews have a brass plate engraved with the names not of the families but the houses – Askive, Glashnacree, Drimina, Derriquin at the back with its own fireplace. Since John's sixteenth birthday, at Eileen's insistence, he has read the lesson in his father's place. Standing at the brass eagle that holds the Bible, John feels the full weight of Derriquin.

Eileen watches John with a nervous pride during the lesson. Just like his father, she thinks, recognizing with a pang that John is softer, less certain, still unformed. She goes over her conversations with Father Michael and General Strickland again and again during a sermon to which she pays no heed.

They return to Derriquin after church, their mood quiet. On the road beyond Burke's Bridge the Humber's way is barred by a Crossley Tender and five Volunteers. William McKelvey brakes sixty yards from the roadblock and starts to reverse. The Volunteers shout; one of them drops on one knee, levels his rifle at the car and fires. The warning shot passes overhead. William stops the car.

'Better drive on slowly towards them,' says Eileen. 'It's only one of their routine searches for guns, and ours are long gone.'

William does as he is told, stopping the car ten feet away from the Crossley Tender. John recognizes Tomas Sullivan among the Volunteers; their captain, a heavy-set man in his mid-thirties, speaks with a strong Cork accent. Josephine and John are shoved roughly out of the car.

'You must be the Doyle bastard,' says the captain to Josephine. 'You and the young squireen can walk home for a change. We need the Orangeman to drive the car.'

John hears his mother, who looks calm, say in Gaelic to Tomas Sullivan, 'Shame on you, Tomas, taking orders from a foulmouthed Cork corner-boy.'

'Speak English,' says the captain. 'Speak English, you bitch.'

One Volunteer gets in the back with Eileen and Tomas Sullivan sits in the front beside William. Each has a drawn revolver. As the car accelerates away, John's mother turns and looks back at him until the car passes out of sight.

John and Josephine walk back to Derriquin, trying to come to terms with what has happened. 'They'll not keep them long, surely,' says Josephine. Once home, John tries to call Kenmare, but the telephone wires have been cut.

*

The little convoy drives along the road for several miles, then heads up a rough *boreen* as far as the car can manage. The Volunteers abandon the car and walk their hostages at gunpoint across rough, boggy country, slanting up the mountain to a small farmhouse, which Eileen doesn't recognize. They are many miles from Derriquin. Locked in a room with two small beds and a bentwood chair, they are escorted out to the privy each morning and evening by their guards. A frightened woman in a long black dress and grey shawl brings food; she does not speak and avoids catching their eye.

After two days they move, walking further up and across the mountain. In the middle of their journey they hear the drone of a biplane flying from Kenmare. Eileen and William are man-handled into a ditch by their escorts while the plane quarters the mountain for half an hour, then turns and vanishes.

Several hours later they arrive at a tumbledown cabin and are pushed into a bare, windowless room. The walls are rough stone covered with flaking whitewash; where the mortar has gone turf has been pushed into the gaps. The sharp smell of the farmyard stains the air. A disused fireplace at the end of the room still holds a small mound of ash. Above the fireplace is a calendar, the months long ago torn away, with a picture of Jesus, a crimson sacred heart on his left breast radiating golden beams. There is a single oil lamp, a blanket each and straw on a stone bench that runs the length of one wall.

Eileen and William are held in an uncomfortable intimacy, squatting over a bucket while the other turns politely away, eating a meagre ration of bread, potatoes and soup from the same plate, washing in cold water and sharing a grimy towel. Next door their guards play cards, talking in low tones and now and again opening the top half of the connecting door to check on the hostages.

'This place isn't fit to wash a rat in,' says Eileen.

'Now you can see how your tenants live,' says Frank O'Gowan. 'There isn't a cottage on the Derriquin estate that isn't built of stone with a slate roof and a decent privy,' replies Eileen.

Eileen and William talk in hurried whispers; longer conversations are cut short by the guards. There are always two Volunteers on duty. When one of the younger men tries to look at Eileen on the bucket, Frank O'Gowan clouts him ferociously across the head.

'Get away out of that, you dirty little devil,' he shouts.

John spends several futile and dangerous days searching for Eileen with only his dog for company. He finds the burned-out carcase of the Humber where the Volunteers have left it at the top of the *boreen,* and goes on up the mountain to Ardsheelan where Tomas Sullivan lives with his mother. The cottage and farmyard feel deserted; John knocks on the door, knocks again, and is turning away when the door opens. Annie Sullivan stands there, recognizes John, crosses herself.

'Master John . . .' she says, her voice trailing away.

'Is Tomas here?' says John. 'Do you know where he is? Was he at Staigue?'

'I don't know, indeed I don't. He's been away these fifteen days since market day, and I'm sick with worry. And I know your mother is missing, God help her. But Tomas wouldn't harm a hair on her head.'

Annie Sullivan crosses herself again and stands there, her shaking hands hanging down by her apron. John, who has been in the cottage many times, is not invited in. Behind her on the far wall he can see the red glow of the little lamp in front of the blue, white and gold statue of the Virgin Mary. He looks at Annie for a long moment, whistles to his dog, then turns away down the mountain to Derriquin.

'God keep you and save you,' she says as John leaves.

*

Several days later Eileen and William are told of the Kenmare trial. If the captured Volunteers are shot they will both be executed. Frank O'Gowan orders Eileen to write to the British commander.

'I doubt it will have much effect,' says Eileen. 'General Strickland will never believe the IRA would shoot a widow woman and an innocent man. I presume you'll have to shoot Father Michael for good measure?'

'This isn't a religious war we're fighting. Any road, madam, I'm already excommunicated by the bishop of Cork. I'd shoot Father Michael just as soon as I'd shoot you.'

Eileen writes the letter.

Dear General Strickland,
I have been told that five of the prisoners taken at Staigue
Fort are to be executed on Monday and I write to ask you to
reprieve them. As you will know, I and William McKelvey,
my chauffeur, are prisoners. If these men are executed, our
lives will be forfeited, as my kidnappers believe that I was
the direct cause of their comrades' capture. I ask you to
spare these men, for their sake and for ours.
    Yours very truly,
    Eileen Burke

A covering letter is attached:

To General Strickland,
Third Battalion Headquarters,
Victoria Barracks,
Kenmare
We are holding Mrs Eileen Burke and her chauffeur William
McKelvey as hostages. They have been convicted of spying
and are under sentence of death. If the five Volunteers taken

at Staigue Fort are executed, the two hostages will be shot.
Irish Republican Army

On the following night William waits until the guards next door
are asleep, and forces a hole through the rotten thatch in the
corner of the room. Frank O'Gowan comes in to check at dawn,
sees the hole, and shouts, 'Where the devil's he got to? Get after
him, get down to the Kenmare road.'

'You should let him go,' says Eileen. 'He wasn't involved at
all.'

'That's as may be, but he knows our faces and our names. The
world won't hurt for one less Orangeman.'

In the evening they bring William back. He is almost unrecognizable, covered in bog mud, his right eye closed and bleeding,
one arm dangling limply. There is little Eileen can do to console
or nurse him.

'I got as far the Kenmare road. But I looked like a *banshee*, all
covered in mud. The first two cars wouldn't dare stop – and the
third one along was them in their truck. I was past running; I
couldn't thole it,' says William.

'They may shoot us, you know. I'm sorry,' says Eileen.

'I know that,' says William.

That night William, in pain from his broken arm, cannot
sleep. Eileen, ashamed of how little she knows of him, asks about
his family in the North.

'Three children, me and two sisters,' says William. 'I started
at Harland and Wolff's alongside of my da. He was a foreman
welder, and I qualified after five years. Worked on all the big
ships, so we did, the *Olympic*, the *Titanic*, the *Britannic*.
Welders were the big men in the shipyard. Hard work, good
money.'

'So why did you leave?'

'My da was a heavy drinker, a hard man altogether. Always
spoiling for a fight. Used to knock my mother about. Did it once

too often, and I near killed him. Next time I would have done, so I had to go.'

'Do you ever hear from them?'

'I send my ma a little money now and then. She's not much for the writing, but I got a postcard last year saying both the girls were married. And my father had a stroke – best thing for both of them, maybe. I doubt I'll see them again.'

Eileen doesn't reply. She has kept the pen she used for the letter to General Strickland, but there is no paper. Later that night she takes down the calendar above the fireplace and on its back writes to John in the dim light of the oil lamp, a long outpouring of regret and hope, then replaces the calendar on the wall.

A week later the five condemned Volunteers are shot at dawn in Kenmare Barracks. The oldest is twenty-six.

Outside the barracks a small group stand close together. They have just heard the rifle shots, two volleys separated by ten minutes, that tell them their sons are dead. Three of the women are crying quietly, arms crossed and clasping their shoulders, rocking to and fro. Two girls are saying aloud, 'Mother of Perpetual Succour, help us; Mother of Perpetual Succour, help us'. Their men are still and stony-faced, save one who stamps up and down and curses. He stops when Father Michael, who has heard the condemned men's confessions, comes out of the barracks.

'They won't release the bodies; they're all to be buried in the barracks,' says Father Michael. He doesn't add that the officer in charge of the firing squad has told him that they will be thrown into a pit full of quicklime, 'like Roger Casement in Pentonville'.

Father Michael blesses the group, some of whom kneel; they stand together for a moment and then travel back on the long road to Drimnamore.

One of the Drimnamore boys, Patrick O'Mahony, has given a letter for his mother to Father Michael.

Dear Mother,
I write you this letter to keep you in good heart. My
sentence is confirmed, and I am to be put to death by being
shot. All the other boys the same. If the government thinks
by shooting a few young fellows like us they will break
down the spirit of the Irish nation I think Strickland's
imagination imbecile.

You have no need to be crying or downhearted when I am
gone, but take courage and be proud when you know you
have given one to God and Ireland.

From your son,
Pat

When John hears the news of the executions he goes into St
Peter's church, open and empty, and kneels down. 'God, please
get my mother back safe,' he says out loud, then guiltily adds,
'and William,' wondering whether he should be offering anything in return. Instead he says the Lord's Prayer. He gets up and
walks back towards Derriquin, pauses outside the Catholic
church on the outskirts of the village and goes in for the first time
in his life. It is a large, dark building, three times the size of the
Protestant church. John finds it difficult to believe that the same
God is worshipped here. The darkness, the strong smell of
incense, the crude paintings of the Stations of the Cross along the
side walls, all seem to belong to a different, older, darker religion,
one that has more in common with the little shrines to Celtic
gods against which Father Michael has long preached than with
the lukewarm faith of the Church of Ireland.

Three women, all in black shawls, are praying at the front of
the nave. He kneels and repeats his prayer, silently this time; as
he walks out he sees a row of votive candles flickering in iron
brackets at the back of the pews. Boxes of different-sized candles
lie on a table, a penny, threepence and sixpence depending on
their size. He buys two sixpenny candles, lights them from one
already burning and sticks them in vacant holders. He is about

to leave when he sees the confessional box and a pair of black shoes showing under the curtain on the priest's side. Father Michael is the only priest in Drimnamore. John goes in, kneels down and says into the grille, 'Father Michael, I need you to tell me where my mother is held prisoner.'

John waits, hears Father Michael clear his throat.

'This is a confessional. And if I had been told anything useful I would be unable to pass it on. But I don't know where Eileen Burke is; my only contact with the Volunteers was with the dead and the prisoners below Staigue Fort.'

John does not reply. As he opens the door to leave the church he looks back up the aisle and sees the candles guttering in the draught.

Word from Kenmare comes to the cabin, brought by three men, one of them Tomas Sullivan.

'*Tomas mo chara . . .*' begins Eileen, and then stops.

'I don't suppose you'll want the priest,' says Frank O'Gowan.

'It's you that has need of him,' says Eileen.

Eileen takes William's hand as they are led out into the farmyard. William begins to shake and a dark stain runs down the inside of his trouser leg.

'He's the first – stand him over by the wall, so,' says Frank O'Gowan to the three new arrivals, each carrying a rifle. William's legs give way and he curls up on the ground as though the foetal position might somehow save him. Tomas Sullivan crosses himself; then the three men fire. William lies there, uncurled and groaning in a pool of blood, until Frank O'Gowan shoots him once more with his revolver. Eileen has turned her head away.

'You're next, madam. Stand closer and aim for her heart, boys.'

They reload; Tomas drops two bullets in the mud and has to wipe them clean.

'Shoot, damn you,' says Frank O'Gowan, and the three men fire for the second time. Afterwards Tomas Sullivan, sickened by the smell of human excrement and blood, vomits again and again as the others wait. They take the bodies in a hand-cart to a deserted quarry, the quarry from which the grey stone of Derriquin had come, and leave them under a pile of stones and rubble.

John spends several more days on the mountain and in the village. No one in Drimnamore knows anything. No one speaks to Josephine. Ten days after the executions of the five Volunteers in Kenmare he stops looking.

He relives, morning and night, the moment the car was stopped on the way back from church. Different versions elbow reality to one side. He tells William to accelerate, they drive around the roadblock, the car teeters on two wheels over the ditch, crashes back onto the road, they escape to the barracks at Kenmare. Or he grabs the pistol out of Frank O'Gowan's hand and shoots two Volunteers. Is one of them Tomas? He isn't sure. Or he says, 'Leave my mother alone. Take me instead,' and they do. And in the end, he and Josephine are still standing on the road, watching the Humber and the Crossley Tender disappear up the road towards Kenmare.

5.

DERRIQUIN CASTLE IS raided six weeks after the abduction. Josephine has moved in to give John some company in the evenings; they watch together as the Volunteers fill the drawing room with petrol-soaked straw, setting a trail to the front porch and lighting it as they leave. The Volunteers help themselves to food but nothing else; they have drained the sea-water pool and taken the fish. John's spaniel lies in the hall, shot on the way in. John picks up the warm, bloody body and cradles it as he and Josephine are escorted outside past the bull Cúchulain lying dead in the farmyard. The horses, terrified by the smoke and flames, have broken out of their stalls and galloped off into the dark.

John and Josephine stand on the oak-studded knoll in the demesne a hundred yards away from Derriquin, feeling the heat of the fire. Tears stream down Josephine's cheeks; John is dry-eyed. They watch for a while, then walk slowly back to Drimnamore. On the path through the rhododendrons John sees a pair of eyes gleaming and realizes it is a woodcock sitting unafraid in their way.

'It's Henry Burke,' says Josephine, fearful, holding John's arm.

John takes two paces forward and reaches down to pick up the bird. It rises, and John feels the beat of its wings as it zigzags away towards the burning house. They walk on past the Great Southern Hotel, where they can see half a dozen faces of the winter staff pressed against the dining-room window, watching the flames and the smoke. They spend the night in Josephine's cottage in Drimnamore.

Derriquin takes a long time to burn. Floor after floor crashes down, glass splinters and breaks, sofas and chairs flare up, oil paintings catch suddenly and disintegrate in minutes, two hundred years of estate records char slowly, the ashes caught by the wind and whirled out to sea. The stone walls are strong and the skeleton of the building, gaunt and windowless, still stands two days later, so that from a distance Derriquin seems intact.

The bodies of Eileen and William are found in August after a tip-off, and what is left of them is buried in the Protestant graveyard. There are few mourners at the funeral, as the local Ascendancy families and the Derriquin tenants are reluctant to leave home. John's grandfather and his Aunt Agnes come over from Cork by car. Ambrose O'Halloran and the two Doyle brothers, uneasy about going into a Protestant church, listen to the service from the porch and then join John and Josephine by the graves.

After the funeral John goes to Cork with his grandfather and aunt. He has never been to Middleton Park; the war and Middleton's attitude to Henry and Eileen's marriage put paid to any social visits between the Burkes and the Brodricks.

'We'll eat in the small dining room now Agnes has gone back to England,' says Middleton. 'No need to dress for dinner in these times. Would you mind exercising the horses? They aren't getting enough work now the IRA has banned hunting. Nobody has the guts to ignore the ban, though it's not even popular with their own people.'

Middleton manages to talk to John about Eileen as they walk to the stables.

'Brave woman, your mother, no doubt about that. Never agreed with me about the Union, supported Home Rule early on. Didn't do her much good in the end. You need a long spoon to sup with these people.'

'Do you think she should have done nothing?'

'I do, I do. You'd still have a mother, I'd still have my eldest daughter. She was always the headstrong one in the family.'

'I think she was right to try. We should have learned the lesson of the Easter Rising.'

'In 1916 we were in the middle of a world war, we were shooting men for desertion on the western front. Anything else would have looked like weakness.'

By now John has saddled up one of the hunters; his grandfather walks slowly back to the house as John canters off down one of the long rides in the park.

That evening Middleton is silent at dinner, drinking most of a bottle of claret himself, then talks about Ireland's future over coffee and whiskey in the smoking room.

'Look at our country now. The RIC are frightened to come out of their barracks and do their job, the courts aren't working, taxes aren't collected, men and women on both sides are being murdered every day. It's hard to see a future for the Burkes or the Brodricks if they get their Republic. And we've every right to be here.'

'By right of conquest.'

'True enough – conquest and re-conquest. Ireland has always been like that. There's been war or rebellion two or three times every century since 1690 and the Battle of the Boyne. We've had the '98, Whiteboys, Caravats, Ribbonmen, the Peep o'Day Boys, Captain Rock and Pastorini, the Terry Alts, the Rising in 1848, Land Leaguers, the Irish Republican Brotherhood. They've all come and gone. Until now we've had the will to fight – that's what we've lost.'

'How do you think it will end?'

John's grandfather takes a drink from his glass of whiskey and looks into the fire.

'Unhappily, unhappily. It's already been disastrous for Eileen, and for you, and for Derriquin. We've been outflanked by the Ulstermen, and Lloyd George will hang the Southern Unionists out to dry. John, I don't want to talk about it any more, it's too depressing. I'm off to bed. Good night to you.'

On his way out he pats John's shoulder in a rare display of affection. The next day John travels back to Drimnamore.

The sale of the Derriquin estate takes place in the ballroom of the Drimnamore Hotel: 24,929 acres, three roods, twenty-two perches, the Derriquin Oyster Fishery, three islands in the estuary, the Drimnamore River ('a spate river, seventy-one salmon in a good year'), forty-two cottages, the demesne and the home farm, all go under the hammer. As the auctioneer reads out the townlands to be sold – Derriquin, Drimnamore, Inchinaleega, Ardeen, Gortfadda, Slievenasaska, Lomanagh, Derreenavurig and Fermoyle – John, dry-eyed since the funeral, weeps again. The hotel buys the demesne and the fishing. The proceeds of the sale bring John £2,850 after the mortgages have been paid off and the creditors settled. He gives half of this to Josephine.

Below Staigue Fort on the road to Waterville an obelisk was later placed:

IN LASTING MEMORY TO THE MEMBERS OF THE SECOND
KERRY AND FIRST CORK BRIGADES KILLED OR CAPTURED
AND SUBSEQUENTLY EXECUTED AFTER ENGAGING BRITISH
FORCES AT STAIGUE FORT ON 14 APRIL 1920

And below, in Ogham script, which Eileen Burke could have translated but not Frank O'Gowan:

LAISAIR ROMHUIN A BUADH

Eileen and William each have a simple gravestone in Drimnamore churchyard. There is no mention of how they died.

6.

A FTER THE SALE John goes to the graveyard by the church in
Drimnamore, where the raw earth on Eileen's and William's
graves has not yet settled. The brown curve above the grass
presses heavily down on the bodies six feet below. There are no
flowers. He stands there for a moment, then walks to the square
to catch the horse-drawn outside car to Kenmare. He is given a
heavy leather blanket to keep out the worst of the rain; although
he is the only passenger, the elderly cob makes heavy weather of
the long pull to the top of the pass at Moll's Gap. There he asks
the driver to stop for a moment, gets out and looks back across
the bog down towards Drimnamore.

A turf line has been cut in the bog to a depth of five feet and
the black walls glisten with the rain, showing the neat cut-marks
of the slane. The drain at the bottom of the wall is half full of
water moving slowly down the hill. The dozen beehive mounds of
cut turf are drenched. They'll hardly save that, thinks John. Only
the red berries of a small rowan break the grey landscape. The
steady drizzle does not stop; a sea mist rolling up the Kenmare
estuary blots out the country that John used to feel was his.

From Kenmare John takes the train to Dublin and stays for
the inside of a week with a friend in Trinity. It is less than a year
since he left Dublin, which had then seemed alive, at the centre
of a struggle just beginning, and Kerry a backwater. Staigue Fort,
Eileen and William's capture and murder, his days of fruitless
searching, the fire and the sale had changed, changed utterly, his

perception of the war. He had been transformed from a spectator into one of the walking wounded.

Dublin is more sombre now. There is a nightly curfew from midnight to 5 a.m. Since the arrival of the Auxiliaries there are even more troops on the streets; in parts of the city groups of Volunteers openly carry weapons, no longer on the run. The balance of power is shifting. It is clear to John that the struggle will have only one ending, an ending that a year ago he would have welcomed, as would Eileen. Now he isn't sure.

He goes to see his solicitor in Leeson Street to sign some papers to complete the Derriquin sale. On the way, two troops of cavalry trot by, and he recognizes the saddlecloths of his father's old regiment, the Royal Irish Dragoons. He had last seen them at a review on The Curragh just before they embarked for France in November 1914, his father at the head of his squadron, the regiment a heady mixture of green, red and gold, bright bits jingling, horses' coats gleaming. The horses hadn't lasted long, and Henry not much longer, thinks John. He wonders whether his father could have stopped the Staigue Fort battle, whether Henry could have found Eileen or persuaded General Strickland to reprieve the five Volunteers.

These troopers are in khaki, their tin hats incongruous on horseback. The horses' coats are dull and the line is ragged. John sees the last horse has cast a shoe. As they pass, a woman on the far side of the street yells abuse and spits. A trooper in the rear rank shouts back at her.

'Don't pay any attention to that fucking Fenian bitch,' says the troop sergeant.

The man next to him on the pavement says, 'They're on their way to Kilmainham where there'll likely be a riot. They're hanging a young Volunteer at three o'clock this afternoon. He's a boy, a medical student, barely nineteen. No sense, no sense at all.'

The next morning John travels down to Queen's County and is met at the station by his father's cousin Charles. The two Burke brothers, who had arrived in Ireland at the end of the seventeenth century, had gone their separate ways, one to twenty-six thousand acres of County Kerry, the other to eight hundred acres in Queen's County an hour out of Dublin.

'Our branch of the family had the best of it,' says Charles Burke. 'It's hard to scratch a living out of bog and rock. It's a wonder you Kerry Burkes lasted as long as you did. Some would say you're well rid of the place.'

Seeing the look on John's face, he quickly adds, 'Although I wouldn't agree with them. The most beautiful county in Ireland.'

'It is,' says John quietly.

'I don't think I'm going back to Trinity,' he tells Charles later. 'I don't like the idea of Dublin any more.'

'Don't blame you. Never thought a lot of a university degree. Although, mind you, I did matriculate – got under starter's orders, fell at the first fence.'

They pull into a long drive flanked with great beech trees.

'You're always welcome here.'

At the end of the drive is Burke's Fort, a solid, handsome Georgian house in grey stone standing among rolling pastures grazed by horses and a few cattle. John walks through a hall full of an untidy clutter of boots, whips, hunting caps, odd items of saddlery, almost tripping over an elderly foxhound fast asleep in a crumbling basket.

'Cleo from the Bicester, best bitch we ever had,' says Charles.

The drawing room is dominated by an enormous oil painting of a stallion. 'Now there was a horse,' says Charles. 'Beaten once in fifteen starts, and then only because he was giving a stone and a half to the winner.'

John admires the picture, slightly distorted as it is by the artist's eighteenth-century approach to horse anatomy. He loves the stallion's bright, nervous, white-revealing eye, the star on the broad forehead, the gleaming chestnut coat. The horse is half rearing, the better to show off the powerful muscles of his hindquarters; the groom, in a bottle-green long coat and soft jockey's cap, has eyes as nervous as the horse, the halter rope at full stretch. In the background is Burke's Fort; the artist has added an extra bay to each side of the house, bays that Charles's great-great-grandfather had perhaps planned, certainly never built, but was happy to leave uncorrected. A small cartouche says,

THE ARCHDUKE, 1787–1817
Winner of fourteen races, including the
Ormonde Stakes and the St Leger.

'He's the foundation stallion for this place,' says Charles. 'All our mares trace back to him, one way or another, although after a hundred years it's a little diluted.' Charles plainly feels that a sixtieth of The Archduke's blood is enough to transform the foal of even the most modest mare.

Around the rest of the room are racing scenes from Punchestown, the names of the horses and jockeys in narrow bands below each print.

'Seventeen started, nine finished. My great-grandfather was on the winner, horse called Lisrenny out of a mare of the Filgates from County Louth. Horse never did a damn thing afterwards, but the Conyngham Cup's on the sideboard in the dining room.

'Would you like to hunt?' says Charles as he shows John upstairs to his bedroom. 'While young Charlie's away you can ride his two. One's a patent safety, the other's a little wild, but they both jump anything in the county.'

For the next two months John hunts two or three days a week, always two days with the Queen's County pack, plus a day with one of the neighbouring hunts. Occasionally they go out with the Ward Union, although Charles disapproves of hunting carted stags.

'You never have a blank day,' he says. 'But it's not natural.'

Hunting for John is the perfect distraction; up at six to get the horses ready, the long slow hack to the meet, convivial fields of ten to twenty on a Tuesday, forty or fifty on a Saturday, mostly farmers and gentry, several officers from The Curragh, a few horse-copers always on the lookout to buy or sell. Queen's County is good hunting country, its grass, hedges and banks, well-spaced and well-guarded fox coverts, coupled with no barbed wire and little shooting, all guaranteeing a run almost every day. The huntsman, a hard-bitten, hard-riding man from County Galway, knows his business. He had been lured away by Charles from the Galway Blazers with the promise of a good cottage and better horses.

'I'm not welcome in Galway any more,' says Charles. 'Worth it to have got Timmy Murphy.'

John shows so little sense of fear out hunting that Charles has to persuade him to slow down at his fences.

'It's the horses I'm worried about, not you.'

He and Charles like each other's company, happy with long periods of silence as they hack out and home, what conversation there is concentrating on horses, hounds, coverts and the run. After a deep bath and a glass of Irish whiskey, the two of them relive the run over dinner with salt cellars, pepper pots and napkin rings.

Charles's wife Cis is happy to sit quietly through dinner, occasionally answering a question about the place-names of the county, otherwise speaking only to encourage the single maid to clear the plates and bring in the next course.

'She knows our hunting country better than I do, stopped riding after a nasty fall. Now she's in love with the Lord,' Charles says in a rare moment of candour. 'I married a Papist, you know. She spends all her time with the Poor Clare Sisters, it makes her happy, and they're harmless enough. My father would have cut me off, even though she was a Dease and her brother a VC, but there wasn't anyone else to leave it to. Good thing being an only son. And in these times having an RC wife is better than an insurance policy. That and Timmy Murphy, who knows the local boys. We've never even had a visit.'

'Eileen believed in Home Rule, and much good it did her,' says John. Charles changes the subject.

7.

'WHATEVER YOU DO, don't run,' says Frank O'Gowan as they walk down Patrick Street. 'You'll not outrun a bullet. The Tans will shoot a running man first and ask questions after. Not many questions.'

Cork bewilders Tomas; Drimnamore could fit in its back pocket. Tomas has never been out of Kerry, never seen trams and buses. The steamers unloading along the Quays are enormous. The city is full of soldiers, policemen, Black and Tans, Auxiliaries.

'The Auxies are the worst. They're the ones with bandoliers and pistols on each hip, like Mexican bandits. Ex-officers who got a taste for killing out in France and signed up to do some more. Bastards, all of them, bastards.'

They spend the first two nights sharing a room in a two-up, two-down house with a privy at the end of a neglected little garden. The row of houses is next to the railway station. Maureen O'Hanrahan is Frank's cousin and an IRA widow. Her house is well placed to see who and what passes through Cork Station.

On the second day a messenger comes for Frank, and he and Maureen go out together for half an hour. Frank comes back alone.

'That one thinks because he has a felt hat and a trench coat with a turned-up collar he's Conn the Hundred Fighter. Didn't he jump a yard in the air when a car backfired alongside of us in Waterside Lane? Any road, Michael Collins, the Big Fellow himself, wants to see me, so I'd better go. And you, Tomas, clear out for the day. That one's stupid enough to have been followed.'

'Where'll I go? I don't know my way around Cork,' says Tomas.

'Kitty will take you,' says her mother. 'Best pretend you're sweethearts if the RIC stop you.'

Kitty, who is eighteen, dark-haired and serious, blushes and looks away. She is a head shorter than Tomas and Frank, who are both over six feet; she is wearing a brown dress and black stocking, black shoes. She is a girl on the edge of becoming a woman.

Kitty shows Tomas the sights of Cork – the Municipal Gallery, University College, the Quays, the statue of Father Matthew.

'He began the Temperance Movement in Ireland,' Kitty tells him.

'I don't think it got as far as Drimnamore,' says Tomas, laughing. Kitty frowns.

They climb Patrick's Hill, looking down over the city, the wishbone of the River Lee coming together and broadening out to sea. They can smell the hops and malt carried up on the wind from Beamish's brewery.

'You must be proud of your city,' says Tomas.

'I'll be prouder when it's ours.'

They go back down along Patrick Street and the Quays. Whenever a patrol goes by, Tomas takes Kitty's hand and doesn't let it drop until the patrol is well out of sight. She asks him why he's in Cork.

'I'm not sure I can tell you.'

Kitty looks offended for a moment, then laughs. 'I'm greener than a shamrock, green longer than you, I'd say. I've been a member of Cumann na mBan since I was fifteen. I was one of the two girls on bicycles, lookouts we were, at the Fermoy ambush. And the British shot my father after the Easter Rising.'

Kitty takes out a black-and-white postcard from her worn leather handbag. It is a head-and-shoulders picture of a young man with a thick moustache in an overcoat with a bunch of shamrock in his lapel. Below the photograph the caption reads:

MICHAEL O'HANRAHAN
Author of *The Swordsman of the Brigade*
Executed in Kilmainham Prison, 4 May 1916.

There is a catch in her voice as she says, 'He was a teacher, a decent man. Not yet forty. And I hardly got to know him.'

They say nothing for a while, then Tomas tells Kitty about the Staigue Fort battle, the souterrain, how Patrick had been left behind.

'His knee was destroyed – they tied him to a chair to shoot him. Like James Connolly in 1916.'

'You had no choice but to leave him. But how did you get here?'

'We hid out in the mountains, then made our way to Cork, walking across the hills and through the bogs, mostly at night. Frank O'Gowan's a Cork man.'

'Sure, he's my cousin,' says Kitty. 'A tough one, that.'

Tomas finds he cannot tell Kitty about the hostages, about the shooting of Eileen and William.

The next morning he goes out alone to find St Mary's Cathedral, cavernous and incense-heavy. Tomas finds a confession box with a priest and no queue, goes in and kneels down, resting his elbows on the flaking varnish of the sill.

'Forgive me, Father, for I have sinned . . .'

And the whole of the Staigue Fort story and the capture and killing of the hostages pours out of him; he still cannot give the hostages their names, nor say that Eileen Burke was a woman he knew well. The voice that comes from the other side of the grille is matter-of-fact with a strong Cork accent. This is the first confession Tomas has made to a priest other than Father Michael.

'My son, murder is a mortal sin, a terrible sin. The archbishop has proscribed the Volunteers. I can give you absolution only if you can perform a genuine Act of Contrition and leave the IRA.'

'O my God, I am heartily sorry for having offended thee, and I detest all my sins because I dread the loss of heaven and the pain of hell . . .'

There Tomas stops, gets up off his knees and walks out of the cathedral. Unshriven.

He goes back to the house uneasy, aware that he has crossed into a world where his old certainties are gone. There is no return. He and Patrick O'Mahony had walked across to Staigue Fort the night before the ambush for a change from the drudgery of the farm. The bloody halo round Seamus O'Connell's head and the bullet that destroyed Pat's knee had given a bitter meaning to adventure. Tomas has to wrench his mind away from the recurring images of the remote farmyard and the shooting of Eileen Burke and William McKelvey.

He turns into Station Road and goes into the front room. Frank is there with Mrs O'Hanrahan and Kitty.

'We'd best be on the move. Get your stuff and we're away.'

Getting his stuff takes no more than a moment; all his possessions are in a small carpet bag of his mother's. He shakes Mrs O'Hanrahan's hand, holds Kitty's for a long moment, who looks down, then brushes Tomas's cheek with her lips.

'There's no time for that,' says Frank, frowning, and they walk out the door. As they reach the far end of the road a lorry pulls up outside number 17 and half a dozen Auxiliaries jump out. 'Don't run,' says Frank as they turn the corner. Half an hour later they are in a small room above a bar down by the docks.

'The Queen Victoria's a great name for a Republican snug,' says Frank, pointing to the sign. 'Eamonn was for changing it. I said, better leave it alone. Call it the Wolfe Tone or the Ninety-Eight, it'll fill up with singing heroes and get raided every other night.'

In the upstairs room they are joined by a third man a little older than Tomas. He is called Denis; no last names are exchanged.

'The three of us are away to the country for a while,' says Frank. 'Michael Collins has a job for us back here when we're ready. You two need some practice.'

'Practice at what?'

'The revolver.'

Frank leaves later that evening; the next morning Michael Kelly, a fifty-year-old farmer arrives in a pony and trap and gives detailed directions to Tomas.

'It'll take the best part of the day. And go easy on Cora, on the pony. She's not one of your Kerry mares. Frank says you know horses – I hope he's right.'

'He's right enough,' says Tomas with a smile, patting Cora on the neck as she nuzzles his sleeve. He has a sudden longing for the farmyard smells of horses and cattle and hay.

He and Denis swing up onto the trap and trot off down Victoria Quay. The city is soon left behind; the Cork countryside down towards the coast is flatter and more prosperous that the boggy, rocky little fields of County Kerry. Bracken, rowan and larch mark their journey and in the distance lies the grey-blue sea. The journey passes without much conversation. Tomas extracts a couple of monosyllabic replies from Denis and then gives up, concentrating on the road and, now and again, Kitty's soft parting kiss.

Outside Ballygarvan they are stopped by an army roadblock.

'Where are you two going?' asks the sergeant, looking down at a sheet of a dozen photographs.

'Back to our farm at Lissagroom,' says Tomas. Denis looks straight ahead and says nothing. There is a perfunctory search of their bags.

'What's in the sacks?'

'Potatoes.'

The sergeant laughs, rips open the topmost sack, tumbles out a few of the potatoes, rummages about and finds nothing.

'I'd have thought you had enough of these already. And they're a bit small, no?'

'They're seed potatoes for next year.'

The sergeant holds up the sheet of photographs alongside Tomas, then Denis. Tomas sees Frank's picture in the gallery and looks away.

'You're neither of you there yet,' says the sergeant. 'Be off with you.'

They arrive at the farmhouse in the evening after a couple of wrong turnings, directions hard to come by from the cautious travellers they pass along the road. Frank is already there.

'Were you stopped along the road?' he says.

'Only the once. They'd never seen seed potatoes before.'

'Lucky they didn't look in every sack,' says Frank as he shifts the load and takes the bottom sack into the house. He opens it and unpacks three bulky packages, each revealing a shiny new Smith and Wesson .38 revolver and several boxes of ammunition.

'These'll do the business once you learn to point them. More reliable than any automatic.'

Tomas and Denis say nothing, offended that they hadn't been told.

'I'll see to the pony,' says Tomas; he goes out, unharnesses Cora and leads her into the small stable opposite the farmhouse front door. She drinks thirstily from the bucket, then sets about the hay-net while Tomas runs his hands down each leg in turn. Sound as a bell and all four shoes still on, he says to himself. Good girl, Cora.

The next morning they take the pistols up the hill to a small quarry where Frank puts up a couple of makeshift cardboard targets. Tomas is surprised at how close they stand.

'We're none of us Wild Bill Hickok,' says Frank. 'These are accurate at close range. They're revolvers, pull the trigger each time, watch the kick as you fire. Stand square on, brace your right wrist with the left hand and pull steady, don't jerk.'

Tomas gets the hang of it quickly. After a week he is putting three shots into a soup-plate-sized ring every time.

'That's fine,' says Frank. 'We're not snipers. If you have to fire from forty yards it's to frighten them off. You'll hit anything only through pure luck. Remember, close as you can, two or three to the body, one to the head to finish him off.'

Denis takes longer. Frank is patient, showing him the grip and the stance and the pull again and again.

Practice with the revolvers takes an hour a day; the rest of the time they spend in the kitchen, smoking cigarettes and reading back numbers of *Ireland's Own*, all they have to stave off boredom. On the third day the farmer returns from Cork City.

'You've looked after Cora all right,' he says. 'Better than I'd expect from a Kerry man.' This is high praise.

The farmer has brought a message from Michael Collins.

'Here's our man,' says Frank, spreading out a two-week-old copy of the *Cork Constitution.*

The picture on the front page is of a moustached figure in British Army uniform. Underneath he is quoted as saying to a group of Auxiliaries, 'If the persons approaching carry their hands in their pockets or are in any way suspicious, shoot them down. You may make mistakes occasionally and innocent persons may be shot, but that cannot be helped and you are bound to get the right persons sometimes.'

'Colonel Gerald Smyth, DSO and Bar. All the way from Banbridge in County Down to make our lives a misery in Cork. He's attached to the Auxiliaries – they're the ones who roughed up Maureen O'Hanrahan and Kitty the day we left.'

'Why didn't you tell me that before?' says Tomas angrily.

'Because I didn't want you heading off back to Cork to no purpose. It could have been worse if the Auxies hadn't been called away.'

'You should have told me.'

'Maybe. Any road, the colonel goes to the County Club every day for lunch, and reads the paper in the smoking room after. One of our boys is a waiter there. You, Tomas, are to go in and shoot him. Denis here will watch your back.'

'Go in and shoot him, do I? Just like that,' says Tomas. What a world am I in, he thinks, where I can be told to kill a total stranger.

'Just like that,' says Frank. 'You're not being asked to do anything I wouldn't do, haven't done, myself.'

'How will I recognize him?'

'Easy enough. He's only the one arm – lost the other in the war. Always in the armchair on the right of the fireplace.'

'One arm?'

'Never mind that. It's his left he's missing, and he'll use his right to shoot you if you give him half a chance. You'll be on your own, the two of you. They're on to me in Cork City.'

The next morning Tomas and Denis set off with Cora back to Cork; this time the revolvers and ammunition are in a box on the underside of the trap.

At the start of their journey they come round a corner beyond Lissagroom and run into a small good-humoured crowd, mainly men, a few women, all heading the same way.

'What's going on?'

'Road bowling,' says Denis, excited. 'Don't you have it in Kerry? Stand up in the cart and watch – we'll not get past until they're done.'

Tomas sees a man running to a mark, lifting a large ball up and back behind him, then whirling it forward with a leap in a powerful underarm throw, the ball clattering along the rough road. His opponent follows. Each throw is accompanied by a loud cheer from the spectators, who then run forward to the next marks.

'That thing is solid iron, weighs twenty-eight ounces; you'd need to be a strong fella to lift it, never mind hurl it. Look, that one's marking the best line for his man's next throw.'

'How far do they go?' says Tomas.

'Three miles or so. You win with the fewest throws. My uncle won the Cork Championship over the Knappagh course three years ago with twenty-two. You loft the ball over the corner when you get to a bend in the road.'

The bowling, which involves argument and betting as well as throwing, holds them up for an hour.

'I've not seen the like in Kerry,' says Tomas.

There are no roadblocks, although beyond Ballygarvan there is a trench, four feet deep and three across, cut into the road.

'Bloody Tans,' says Denis.

'It's most likely our people,' says Tomas.

The earlier hold-up and the long detour add two hours to their journey, and they arrive in Cork just before the nine o'clock curfew. They spend the night in the Queen Victoria. Tomas has been forbidden by Frank to visit Station Road.

'The house is watched day and night. You'll wind up inside if you go there.'

The next day Tomas and Denis walk together along the Quays and cross the north channel of the River Lee to South Mall. The County Club is a late Georgian town house in grey stone with wrought-iron balconies on the first floor. A small brass plate by the door confirms that they are studying the right building. They look at the club for a few minutes; no one enters or leaves, and there is no sign of a police guard. When a man comes out on one of the balconies they walk away to Patrick Street.

On the following morning they go back to the club by the same route. Tomas goes in first, followed by Denis; the porter at the entrance looks up and looks away. As they go into the smoking room they pull out their revolvers. The man on the right of the fireplace sees them and begins to rise out of his chair, reaching inside his jacket pocket; his left sleeve is empty. Tomas walks towards him, fires twice and the man slumps back into the chair for a moment, chest covered in blood, then gets up as Tomas fires again. He falls forward, tries to speak, lies still as blood comes from his mouth, staining the carpet a deeper red. The three other men in the room are silent and still. The shots have been violently loud in the confined space. In the sudden silence that follows, a waiter drops his coffee-cup-laden tray with a clatter.

It is all over in three minutes. Fifty yards up the street a car is waiting, and ten minutes later they are back in the Queen Victoria.

'That was easy enough,' says Denis as they walk up the stairs.

'You didn't pull the trigger,' says Tomas. He feels a sick excitement, realizing that this time killing a man had indeed been easy. The power the revolver had given him was real. That night he wonders whether he will see Kitty again and what he will say to her if they meet.

The following evening Tomas and Michael are sitting in a corner of the Queen Victoria's saloon bar, each nursing half a pint of mild.

'Stout's too bitter for me,' says Denis, and Tomas agrees. Frank O'Gowan comes in, carrying a copy of the *Cork Constitution*.

'You're headline news. "Appalling horror in Cork City – five masked men kill defenceless war hero in his chair by the club fire,"' he says. 'You did well. The air in Cork City is sweeter for the killing of Inspector Smyth.'

Frank takes them up to the bar and orders three whiskeys.

'It's a celebration,' he says, talking more loudly than usual. 'By rights it should be five whiskeys for the two of you.' He sees the look on Tomas's face. 'We're among friends tonight,' giving a little wave of his hand that pulls in the six other men standing at the bar.

Each of them nods to Frank. The tallest, a man with a strong jaw and unruly dark hair, is Michael Collins, who introduces himself in a gravelly West Cork accent and shakes hands with Tomas and Denis.

The Big Fellow is already a legend among the Volunteers. At first sight he doesn't stand out; he is wearing a dark suit, well-polished black shoes, and his grey Homburg is on the bar beside him. Tomas has seen the *Police Gazette* description.

'Clean-shaven, youthful appearance, dark brown eyes, regular nose, fresh complexion, oval face, five feet eleven inches high, about thirty years of age, dark hair. Generally wears trilby hat and fawn overcoat.'

Frank says, 'Mick wants us in Dublin, Tomas. Denis, you're to stay in Cork.'

Denis looks relieved.

'I'll need to get a letter to my mam,' says Tomas. 'She's heard nothing from me since Staigue Fort. I'm killed or captured for all she knows.'

'You do nothing, no letter-writing,' says Frank. 'We'll get a message to her, put her mind at rest.'

There'll be little rest for my mam if she knows what I've been doing, thinks Tomas.

Frank leans forward on the bar and orders another whiskey for himself and the Big Fellow. They clink glasses. To Tomas's astonishment Frank starts to sing in a sweet tenor voice. The others around him join in, the Big Fellow beating his hand on the bar in time with the tune. Frank looks at Tomas with a half-smile, then sings the second verse.

And we're off to Dublin in the green, in the green
Where the helmets glisten in the sun
Where the bayonets flash and the rifles crash
To the rattle of a Thompson gun
I'll leave aside my pick and spade, I'll leave aside my plough
I'll leave aside my horse and yoke, I no longer need them now
And I'll leave aside my Mary, she's the girl that I adore
And I wonder if she'll think of me when she hears the rifles
*   roar.*

When the song ends the little group breaks up.

'I'll be in touch,' says Frank to Tomas as he leaves. 'Denis, you can go home.'

Tomas spends the next two days wandering around Cork City. He buys a copy of the *Cork Constitution*, reading and rereading the front page, matching the lurid description of the killing to his own much briefer memory.

He knows a visit to Station Road would be too risky, and stops a barefoot boy on the Quays, gives him a shilling and careful instructions, blushing as he speaks.

'Wait till she comes out of the house, follow her to the market, and tell her to meet the Kerry man on Patrick's Hill at noon on Thursday. Come to the Queen Victoria that evening and there'll be another shilling for you. Her ma doesn't approve of me.'

The boy smiles and trots off down the Quays.

On Thursday, Tomas is waiting on Patrick's Hill, hears the cathedral clock strike twelve, and an hour later walks back down, thinking his shilling wasted. At the foot of the hill he meets Kitty walking quickly towards him. She takes his arm and they go back up the hill to the place where Kitty had pointed out the landmarks of the city three weeks before. A lifetime. They sit on the grass holding hands. Tomas leans across and kisses her on the cheek; Kitty puts her hand on the back of Tomas's neck and presses her lips against his for a long moment.

'Walk me home,' she says, and Tomas, still in the spinning moment of his first kiss, stands up and they walk together down the hill.

They are still holding hands, when Kitty asks, 'Were you involved at the Constitution Club?'

Tomas stops, turns to look at her. 'I was.'

Kitty lets go of Tomas's hand when they get close to Station Road.

'He was a bad man,' says Tomas, and echoes Frank's words, 'Cork's a better place without him.'

'That's as may be,' says Kitty. 'But Staigue Fort was a battle, soldier against soldier. This was . . .' she is about to say murder, changes her mind '. . . cold-blooded.'

'More cold-blooded than shooting your father, worse than a firing squad?'

'About the same, I'd say. Best leave me here.'

As they part, she brushes Tomas's cheek, not this time with her lips but with her fingers, and then walks swiftly away. Tomas's intense happiness at the top of the hill has been replaced by sudden, confused misery. He watches as Kitty turns the corner without looking back.

8.

Tomas thinks Dublin is to Cork as Cork is to Drimnamore; Cork is a big town, Dublin a proper city. He and Frank travel up together by train. Frank is exultant when they arrive at Kingsbridge Station.

'This is the place,' he says as they walk down Upper O'Connell Street. 'Nowhere else counts for a candle.'

Their billet is in the Summerhill Dispensary, a ramshackle building that houses a Registry of Births, Marriages and Deaths, a chemist's shop, a saddler. On the three floors above there are thirty small bedrooms sharing a bathroom and kitchen at the end of each corridor. Medical staff from the nearby Rotunda Hospital occupy most of the rooms, but it is soon clear to Tomas that there are several other Volunteers in the building.

Frank is a taciturn companion. Tomas's questions receive either a monosyllabic reply or silence, and Tomas soon gives up trying to find out what is going on. After two days a messenger arrives who has a hurried conversation with Frank in the street. He leaves two bicycles behind.

A week later they are with Michael Collins in a small room above a haberdasher's shop. Tomas notices the sign as he and Frank walk in. 'Sullivan's Gentlemens Outfitters' it reads. He nudges Frank.

'Look, must be my cousin,' and gets no reply.

Michael Collins is sitting behind a wooden table covered in papers, a revolver acting as a paperweight. Behind him is a large-scale map of Dublin inned to the whitewashed wall. Fifteen red crosses mark streets clustered around the centre of the city. The room gradually fills up as men arrive in twos and threes. Tomas recognises one face from the bar of the Queen Victoria.

Michael Collins stands up, leans forward, places his hands upon the table and looks around the room until the quiet chatter dies away.

'We're going to wipe out the British Intelligence network in a single morning. The Cairo Gang, fifteen of their best men in Dublin. Next Sunday's the day. Same day as the GAA match at Croke Park. You'll be able to disappear into the crowd. Donal will tell you your detailed instructions and timings. Nothing in writing, no notes.'

Tomas and Frank are given a name and address – Captain Newbury, 92 Lower Baggot Street, close to St Stephen's Green. Early on Sunday morning Tomas goes to Mass.

'Much good may it do you,' says Frank. 'Light a candle for me. And one for Captain Newbury.'

Tomas doesn't go to confession, doesn't take Communion. He is troubled by the thought of the morning's work – Staigue Fort and Ashtown were little battles, as Kitty had said. This was to be another . . . He cannot find a word he likes for what they are about to do.

Tomas and Frank arrive at Lower Baggot Street just before nine. When the housekeeper answers the door Frank pushes past her, asking in a whisper where the officer's rooms are. Too frightened by the grim-faced men and the drawn revolvers to speak, she points up to the first floor. They run up the stairs and burst through the door on the landing. Newbury, still in his pyjamas, is halfway to the window as both men fire. Newbury falls forward, crashing through the window glass, and hangs, half in, half out of, the room.

As the firing stops, Tomas hears a woman scream; Newbury's wife is standing in the corner of the room. She is heavily pregnant, holding up her hands as if to push them away when they leave the room.

As they leave the house, Tomas looks up and sees the woman trying to cover her husband's jack-knifed body with a blanket. They walk to the Ha'penny Bridge and drop their revolvers into the river as they cross.

'We're to make for McCarthy's boarding house in Mountjoy Street later,' says Frank. 'Dublin will be crawling with Black and Tans and Auxiliaries.'

'Did you see she was pregnant?' says Tomas. Frank does not reply.

They get to McCarthy's in the evening; most of the Apostles are already there in an upstairs room. This time Michael Collins is triumphant.

'We've killed fifteen of their best men, it's a knockout blow. They've taken McKee and Clancy, and I think Fitzpatrick is dead, God help him. The Tans and the Auxies went mad in Croke Park this afternoon, opened fire on the crowd, killed more than a dozen, two of them children. But believe me, boys, it's been worth it. Just mind how you go for the next week. They'll not be particular who they pick up.'

'Newbury's wife was pregnant,' says Tomas.

There is a long silence; as they leave the room Michael Collins pats Tomas on the shoulder. 'Newbury had to be killed,' he says.

Two days later Tomas is picked up by a patrol of the Auxiliaries on his way out of the Dispensary; Frank has already gone back to Cork. Tomas is taken to Jury's Hotel in Great Dame Street, commandeered as an Auxiliary stronghold. He is pushed into a small room by three Auxiliaries, who set about Tomas with fists, boots and blackthorn sticks without speaking. Tomas winds up on the floor, bleeding from a deep cut on his forehead, one eye completely closed, bruised all over his body.

'That'll teach you to resist arrest,' says the last one to leave, giving Tomas a parting kick.

The next day he and three other Volunteers are taken to Mountjoy Jail. They don't acknowledge each other. As they walk through an inner courtyard their guards point out bullet holes on the far wall.

'That's where we shoot rebels. Your lot'll get the noose.'

There are over a thousand men in Mountjoy; every evening a crowd collects outside the walls to shout encouragement to the prisoners. In a series of identity parades the British try to weed out the active Volunteers. Tomas can barely stand at the first parade; he is wrongly identified by a policeman as one of those involved in a murder two days before. His documents prove he was already a prisoner at Jury's.

At the second identity parade, the Baggot Street housekeeper is there. The soldiers escort her, shaking, white-faced and terrified, to the security of a sentry box with a slit cut in its back at eye level. She identifies Tomas, who is immediately put into solitary confinement. A fortnight later he is tried, found guilty of murder.

'You killed three people,' says the judge. 'You shot Captain Newbury in cold blood, and you were responsible for the death of his wife and unborn child when she miscarried the following day.'

Tomas is condemned to death. After the trial he is taken to Kilmainham Jail, where he is weighed, measured, washed and photographed. This, he is told by his escorts, is where he will be hanged.

9.

B URKE'S FORT IS insulated from the world of The Troubles. Only the *Irish Times*, arriving a day late, keeps John in touch with the turbulence that killed his mother and William, and swept him up and out of Kerry. He has pushed the horrors of a year ago to the back of his mind, until one morning over breakfast Charles, uncharacteristically reading the news pages instead of going straight to the racing section, asks John, 'Know any Sullivans from Drimnamore?'

'I do.'

'Well, they've convicted a Tomas Sullivan, one of the IRA squad who killed the Intelligence officers. They're all to hang.'

John reads the paper carefully when Charles has finished breakfast. It describes in detail the trial, conviction and sentencing of Tomas and two others, including the words of the judge as he condemned Tomas, 'not for one murder, but for three'.

John wonders what, if anything, he should do, then decides to try to see Tomas. Several days later he is in Dublin to visit his solicitor, a dusty man who tells him over lunch in the Kildare Street Club that he has two thousand pounds in the bank before lawyers' fees.

After lunch he finds his way to Kilmainham Jail; outside there is a crowd of fifty or sixty men and women, most of them, judging by the shawls of the women and the heavy nailed boots of the men, up from the country. The men are smoking and some of the women are running rosary beads through their fingers or reading from well-thumbed missals. The iron gates of the jail are studded and painted black. Above the gates a writhing five-headed monster is carved in relief.

John attracts curious glances; his clothes set him apart from the crowd. After waiting for half an hour he asks the man next to him how to get to see a prisoner.

'What does an Englishman want with a prisoner? It's a warder you'll be wanting to see, surely.'

'I'm not English, I'm from Kerry,' says John, realizing as he speaks that this is no longer true.

'Are you, so? Ask at the building over there at the end of the wall. Your voice might get you better treatment than the rest of us.'

In the administration office John joins a long queue, and after an hour in which most of those in front of him are told to go away he is asked by the sergeant in charge who he wants to see.

'Tomas Sullivan, from Drimnamore in County Kerry.'

'Sullivan, is it?' Looking up the name in a massive black ledger. 'Sullivan's to hang. Only near kin allowed to see him.'

'I'm his cousin, all he's got. His father's dead, his mother's too old for the journey.'

The sergeant looks at John sceptically, decides saying yes is easier than saying no, and tells him to come back at seven the next morning. After filling in a lengthy form and getting it stamped and counter-stamped, John goes back to Trinity for the night.

The next morning he is led through a maze of courtyards and corridors by the sergeant, searched by a warder in a small windowless room, and taken into the main wing of the jail. Three levels of cells rise up either side of a central well bridged by an iron walkway at each level. A huge skylight runs the full length of the wing and gives the place a strange symmetrical beauty, offset by a powerful smell of urine, rancid cooking oil and stale sweat. The silence is broken now and again by the clang of a cell door, a shout from a prisoner, a bellowed order from a guard. A voice begins to sing:

O my dark Rosaleen,
Do not sigh,do not weep

and stops as suddenly as it began.

At the far end of the ground floor a line of twelve cells is separated from the rest by a large door guarded by two sentries.

'This lot are all for the gallows,' says the sergeant. 'The sooner the better, including your cousin. Do you know what he did?'

John doesn't answer. He is taken to the end cell; the warder opens the door, and there is Tomas sitting on his prison cot, shackled with leg-irons.

'It's your cousin from Kerry,' announces the warder.

'I have no cousin,' says Tomas.

'How would you know in County Kerry? When you aren't shagging sheep . . .' The warder, pleased with his wit, shuts and locks the door behind John.

'Why are you here? I have nothing to say to you or your kind.'

'Kind? Kind? We were friends enough when it suited you.'

'We're on opposite sides now.'

'Were you there when my mother and William were murdered?'

'They were executed for betraying an IRA column, passing information to the British Army and causing the death of thirteen Volunteers, on a warrant from the IRA divisional commander. And I have nothing more to say. I do not recognize the court that sentenced me or the government that holds me here.'

'For God's sake, Tomas, you're to be hanged, and you're talking to me as if I was a judge. I'm Eileen's son.'

Tomas looks away. 'You know they executed five Volunteers in Kenmare. Patrick O'Mahony was twenty, taught by Josephine in Drimnamore, just like us. They had to tie him to a chair before they shot him.'

'You were all soldiers – and you'd killed a few Englishmen first. My mother killed nobody. Were you there when she was shot?'

Tomas stands up, clasps and unclasps his hands. 'Three of us brought the warrant. I was in the firing squad.'

There is a rattle on the door. 'Five minutes almost up.'

'She didn't suffer. She wasn't abused. She was a brave woman right enough. And I wish . . .' His voice trails away, and for a moment he closes his eyes.

'I wish,' says John, 'I wish I had died in her place. I wish you as quick a death as you say you gave my mother and William.'

The door opens, he is ushered out, but not before he sees Tomas putting a sleeve to his eyes.

10.

Two weeks after he has been visited by John in Kilmainham, Tomas's leg-irons are taken off, and Dick Teeling, another member of The Squad, is moved into his cell.

'We're the elite,' Teeling says. 'This is the Murder Row. There's only one way out, and that's over the wall.'

'Or in a coffin.'

'No coffin for the likes of us, only a pit out the back full of quicklime. We might as well try the wall. I'd as soon be shot trying to escape as die by the noose.'

The cells in Kilmainham have wooden floors and stone walls covered in flaking whitewash. High and low peepholes are cut into the door, which is secured by a massive bolt and lock on the outside. Old graffiti, a calendar with 231 days crossed out, a crude drawing of the Republican flag, an illegible name, an inscription 'A few men faithful and a deathless dream', remind Tomas that Kilmainham has been a jail since 1796. The cells are damp, unlit, lice- and flea-ridden; Tomas itches all over, but his bruises have almost gone, and he can walk. They are exercised in small groups of twenty in an outside yard for half an hour each day. Kilmainham is guarded by soldiers and the RIC; discipline has broken down, and the regime is less strict than at Mountjoy. Although the block is sealed, the cell doors are often left open unless an inspection by an officer is due. There are visitors, food parcels are allowed, and notes are smuggled in and out. It is easy enough for the prisoners to talk in the exercise yard or at Mass on Sunday.

Teeling tells him one of the soldiers is friendly.

'He's from Limerick, and I've said we'll look after him when the Republic arrives. Most of the English soldiers can't wait to get home. The Irish are scared. They know they'll have nowhere to go when this is all over. Collins and his men will try to get us out, but we'd best make plans to save ourselves. There's no knowing when the hangman will come for us.'

Tomas, for whom everything that has happened at Staigue Fort and after has seemed to take place in a strange and different world, cannot stop thinking about the hanging.

'Where do they do it? Does it take long? Do we get any warning?'

'This'll be my first time,' says Teeling, laughing. 'They've got a separate block, the hang-house. They take you there, blindfold you, put a big thick rope around your neck, open the trapdoor and that's you gone with a broken neck. It's quick enough provided they've got the drop right, otherwise you strangle. The offer of a priest an hour before is all the notice we'll get. The hangman comes over from England to do the business. We've tried to get him several times, but he's guarded more closely than the Viceroy. He'll be brought here to take a look at us through the peep-window, judge our weight for the drop.'

They make a careful note of the prison geography – there are two yards between their cell block and a gate through the wall to the outside world. The second yard is the place where the leaders of the Easter Rising had been shot, including, Tomas remembers, Michael O'Hanrahan, Kitty's father.

'I've got a message to the fourth battalion that we need bolt-cutters and a revolver. They're in touch with our Limerick man. I've told them we don't have long.'

A day later Tomas is taken to Dublin Castle.

'You're here for questioning,' the Auxiliary tells him as he is pushed roughly into his cell, a narrow room with an arched ceiling, a stone floor, no light and two bunks. He is the only occupant.

'This is the cell Dick McKee and Peadar Clancy were in. We shot them when they tried to escape, and we'll do the same to you.'

'You murdered them, and Conor Clune, in cold blood, we know that, and you'll pay,' says Tomas as the door clangs shut.

The Auxiliaries in the castle are a strange mixture – journalists, clerks, some graduates, most of them mature men. They have all seen service, in France, Mesopotamia, Gallipoli or Russia, and they are all ranked and paid as officers. There are two Military Crosses, a DSO and a DFC among their medal ribbons. Tomas is exercised on his own in the castle yard, escorted by two soldiers.

On his third day he is brought to the Intelligence Room and made to stand in front of a desk while he is interrogated by a heavy-set man in civilian clothes. Two soldiers carrying rifles stand either side of Tomas.

'I'm Inspector McTaggart, Royal Irish Constabulary. I am going to ask you some questions – the soldiers here are for my safety, you won't be hurt in this room. What's your name?' He has a strong, harsh Ulster accent.

'Tomas Sullivan.'

'Address?'

'Drimnamore, County Kerry.'

'Were you at the Staigue Fort ambush?'

'I don't know what you're talking about.'

'We know you were there. Frank O'Gowan was captured last week. He was in charge, no?'

'Why ask me if you know the answers?'

'Look, if you cooperate with me you could earn a reprieve. And go free if you give us something useful.'

'I don't think touts last long outside these walls. And I've told you I don't know anything about Staigue.'

'You know the name well enough, I notice. Who was in charge of the operation on 21 September? Was it Collins? Was it Lynch?'

'I don't know.'

'Who else was living in the Summerhill Dispensary? Was Frank O'Gowan there?'

'I don't know, but as you've captured him he'll be able to tell you.'

After half an hour the interrogator closes his notebook.

'You can go. The Auxiliaries won't be so gentle. You'll be going to your Maker soon enough. And you'll have to answer His questions.'

'What makes you think He's on your side?' says Tomas as he leaves.

The next day he is taken to a cell by four Auxiliaries and given a savage beating. The men don't bother to ask him any questions.

'This is for Captain Newbury,' one of them says. Tomas notices he has a Military Cross.

'Is there a medal for this sort of work?' Tomas asks as they set about him with truncheons. It is worse than the beating at Jury's Hotel; Tomas covers his head, hears the grunts of the Auxiliaries as they laugh and lay into him, feels his ribs crack and passes out on the floor.

Back in his own cell he lies in a pool of blood, urine and excrement for three days before he recovers enough to stand up and to walk to the foul-smelling latrines. He is escorted there by one of the two soldiers outside his cell; they take pleasure in pretending not to hear him ask. At night the gas lights in the cells go out at ten. The silence is regularly interrupted by a shout from a prisoner, a roar from a guard, high-pitched swearing, a banshee wail, a sudden song that never lasts more than a verse.

Dublin Castle has become a garrison fortress rather than the seat of government. The British in Ireland are now beleaguered in castles, barracks, police stations, commandeered country houses and hotels. The IRA are moving about Dublin in daylight with a freedom unthinkable a year ago. The curfew in the city begins at midnight and ends at five. Only civilians stay indoors. It is clear from the conversations Tomas overhears that both Auxiliaries and soldiers are no longer convinced that they are on the winning side.

After two weeks in the castle, Tomas is taken back to Kilmainham.

'Can't you make your mind up where to hold me?' he says to his two escorts, both Auxiliaries.

'We don't hang people in the castle. And you've lost your chance of a reprieve.'

He is put back in his old cell, relieved to see Dick Teeling is still there.

'I didn't think we'd meet again,' Teeling says. 'I thought they'd treat you like Clancy and McKee and Clune. They still haven't brought us the stuff. They'll need to get a move on.'

Three days later the bolt-cutter and the revolver arrive in flour sacks stolen from the kitchen store, then hidden beneath a loose flagstone in their cell. The guards are two cells away, and spend their time playing cards or sleeping. That night they get past the guardroom and through the two yards easily enough, but the bolt-cutters cannot cope with the outer gate.

'We need something three times as strong – this yoke wouldn't cut through butter,' Teeling says to the soldier from Limerick. 'Tell fourth battalion to get a decent cutter, tell them to test it first on a two-inch-diameter bolt.'

In the exercise yard there are rumours that the next wave of hangings is imminent. There is also news that the tout who betrayed McKee, Clancy and Clune is dead.

'They tracked him down to the Five Lamps and plugged him while he was reading the *Independent* and drinking a bottle of stout,' says Teeling to Tomas. 'It didn't take long to avenge the boys. I hope they finished the bottle.'

The new cutter arrives in a clothing parcel uninspected by the guards. Dick Teeling looks at the two three-foot handles and the separate heavy-duty cutter head.

'These look like they'll do the business. If they don't it's the long walk and the short drop for the two of us.' Tomas cannot joke about the hangman.

On the following Friday night their cell door has been left unlocked by the Limerick man, and for the second time Tomas and Dick Teeling walk quietly along the unlit passage in stockinged feet, their boots around their necks. Teeling has a hand on Tomas's shoulder as he runs his fingers along the rough stone wall to keep his bearings in the darkness. Tomas feels sick, his heart pounding loudly at this chance of escaping the hangman.

The only light comes from the guardroom door, which is slightly open. As they pass it, the smell of beer and warmth overrides the cold prison smell of urine and shit. They go through the inner courtyard, freezing against the wall when they hear the guardroom door open and slam shut.

'They're just going for a piss,' whispers Dick. 'And that's the other way, thank God.'

Once in the outer courtyard they use the new cutter on the lock in the small postern gate, then ease the bolt open and are out and free under the prison wall. They see a single soldier, and Tomas hears the click as Dick cocks the revolver, but the soldier is wrapped around a girl and the revolver is not needed. Within five minutes they see a late tram; as they board Dick Teeling says, 'Look at the board – that's a lucky sign.'

'Nelson's Pillar and Dalkey?'

'No, you eejit, the shamrock above.'

They are not asked for their fare; they take the tram as far as the Liffey, cross on the Ha'penny Bridge and reach the safe haven of Dick's aunt's house in Heytesbury Street by midnight.

The escape of two of the men captured and condemned for the elimination of fourteen Intelligence officers enrages the British. Tomas is again headline news.

'Daring escape from Kilmainham; security arrangements to be strengthened,' says the *Irish Times*. 'Police confident that the two condemned men will be speedily rearrested.' There is a grainy photograph of Tomas and Dick below the headline.

The curfew is brought forward to ten o'clock. Both the Auxiliaries and the IRA step up their patrols, and the IRA, confident and now better armed, look for trouble rather than avoiding it. Little battles break out all over the city during the curfew; grenades, rifle and machine-gun fire regularly punctuate the darkness.

Tomas meets Michael Collins two days later.

'You and Teeling did well,' he says. 'The Brits are beginning to realize that they can't win. We're in charge now. But you're a marked man. Best get back to Cork and lie low for a while. You're Harry Meehan from Waterford from now on. Here are some papers – letters, bills, a wallet with forty pounds in it. The quartermaster will give you some clear spectacles and a different suit. Once you're back at Lissagroom you'll be safe enough. The Tans and Auxies daren't stick their noses out of Cork City.'

Tomas can hardly recognize his bespectacled new self in the mirror. Prison life has made him gaunt; he looks like a man of thirty-five. Perhaps he has indeed become Harry Meehan. The train journey to Cork is slow and uneventful , although the train is stopped and searched twice, both times by the IRA. At Cork Station he thinks about going to see Kitty in Station Road, but there are Tans and policemen around the station, so he goes directly to the Queen Victoria on the Quays.

11.

TWO DAYS LATER he is in Lissagroom.
'I'm glad to see you back and living,' says Michael Kelly.
'Dead heroes are no use to man or beast, and there's work for three here right enough. You'll earn your bed and board.' This is a long speech for Michael Kelly, who asks no questions and speaks only to give Tomas his tasks for the day.

Tomas is happy to have hard work to distract him from the turmoil of the past year. Life in Cork and Dublin and the prison diet have softened his muscles and the first couple of weeks are exhausting.

Michael Kelly has bought three neighbouring fields from a widow woman who has given up her farm. 'The stone walls are destroyed altogether,' says Michael. 'You'd not hold cattle in any of the fields.'

It is over a month before the walls are rebuilt, a month in which Tomas works from dawn till dusk, finding stones the right size, moving them into position, breaking them into manageable pieces, building each wall up to four feet high. 'Anything lower and my cows will be in County Kerry,' says Michael Kelly.

The old bedsteads and odd timber are replaced by proper gates that Tomas puts together in the farmyard and hangs on long-disused iron gateposts. Michael is pleased. 'These fields are fit for the King of Connaught,' he says. 'O'Brien will be looking down from heaven at the wonder of it. Fair play to the man, he was crippled with the arthritis in his last years. Now for the drains.'

Now for the drains. Digging diagonal trenches across each field, laying in the drainage pipes, then covering them over, is only a little less back-breaking than stone-walling. Tomas's hands blister at first, then heal and harden. In the smallest field he is set to digging a lazy-bed for potatoes. As he plants the seed potatoes he remembers his first trip from Cork to Lissagroom with Denis, and the British sergeant who had stopped them on their way. And Frank O'Gowan, who hadn't told them of the pistols and ammunition at the bottom of the last sack. Frank had left Dublin immediately after the killing of Captain Newbury. As far as Tomas knew he hadn't been taken, but the *Skibbereen Echo* once a week was the only source of news at the farm. Michael Kelly goes into the village to Mass every Sunday. Tomas stays behind.

Although he is tired after each day's work, Tomas finds it hard to sleep. He has nightmares – Staigue Fort, the destroyed face of Seamus O'Connell, Patrick O'Mahony's shattered knee, William McKelvey curled up and groaning in the farmyard. Worst of all is Captain Newbury's screaming, pregnant wife, who as she turns towards him has Eileen Burke's face.

After his first month at the farm he starts to go into the village in the evening. The Lissagroom bar doubles as the Post Office and general store, and he is often the only man drinking in the back room. There is a wooden bench along one wall, a table with four bentwood chairs, sawdust on the floor and Guinness and Beamish posters on the walls. A small turf fire throws out little heat; this is a place not for conversation but for drinking. Soon Tomas is drinking six or seven pints of stout every evening, and after a month of scrutiny by the landlord he is offered a glass from the bottle of poteen that is kept hidden underneath the counter. This does the work of several pints. By eleven each night Tomas is only just able to make the journey back up the road to the farm, where he slumps onto his bed fully clothed. The drink banishes the dreams, at least during the night-time.

The news of the Truce in the middle of 1921 is followed by Dáil Éireann's approval of the Treaty. Early in the following year Tomas gets a message telling him he can become Tomas Sullivan again, and that he is to go to the Queen Victoria in Cork. Michael Kelly drives him into the city, Cora pulling the trap, the journey this time uninterrupted by broken bridges and trenched roads. Outside the Queen Victoria Michael Kelly shakes his hand and says, 'You're a real worker. Cora will miss you.'

'Goodbye,' says Tomas, 'I'm sorry we didn't finish the last drain,' and goes into the pub. He is given a room for the night and told to report to the Imperial Hotel the next day.

The Imperial Hotel is the temporary headquarters of the Free State Army's Southern Command. There are two sentries outside the grand entrance; Tomas is shown upstairs by a young woman wearing the badge of Cumann na mBan.

'We don't take over Victoria barracks for a few months,' she says. 'You'll find the commander-in-chief and his people in here.'

In the room Michael Collins is sitting at a table drinking a cup of tea, almost unrecognizable in the uniform of the Irish Army. Tomas can't take his eyes off the gleaming brown boots, the Sam Browne belt, the peaked cap, the holstered revolver. Collins sees the look and laughs.

'You'd better get used to it. We need to show the world we can be as smart as the British, that we're not just a bunch of hobble-dehoys. Now the Tan War is won, we're a real army and you need to join it.'

He pauses, takes a mouthful of tea and continues, 'It's not clear the fighting is over. There are enough Volunteers who hate the Treaty, hate the oath, to cause trouble.'

Tomas nods – his relief at the Truce and the Treaty has left no room for worrying about the fine print of documents he has never seen.

'Good man. You'll be part of the Cork No. 1 Brigade, a lieutenant in the second battalion. We'll teach you what that means; go to the barracks at Ballincollig in the morning. Donal here, you'll remember him from Dublin, is the adjutant. He'll sort you out and find you a uniform. Don't worry, this is strange country for all of us.'

Strange country indeed. The same evening Tomas goes round to the O'Hanrahan house with a bunch of flowers and knocks on the door. Kitty opens it. 'Tomas,' she says, putting her hand over her mouth; she steps back as Tomas tries to embrace her and starts to cry.

'We thought you were dead. Frank told us you were taken and going to be hanged.'

'Two of us escaped from Kilmainham. I've been out at Lissagroom ever since. Now I'm covered by the amnesty. It wouldn't have been safe to come here before.'

Tomas follows Kitty into the front room where they sit facing each other on two stiff-backed, velvet-upholstered chairs. The fire is unlit. Kitty reaches for a box of matches, changes her mind. In the corner of the room Tomas notices a shrine to Kitty's father. Michael O'Hanrahan is looking out of a silver frame, the picture an enlarged version of the postcard Kitty had shown him on the hill above Cork City. In front there is a statue of the Virgin Mary, a votive lamp, two books and an unfamiliar half-furled flag.

'Those are his two stories, and that's the Plough and the Stars that flew over Jacob's Factory during the Rising. He was there with MacDonagh and MacBride.'

Tomas looks at her directly; she is prettier than he had remembered, still serious, but a young woman now, not a girl.

'It was terrible for your mother and you to lose him,' he says. 'I've thought about you often. Even at the worst times. And now the Tan War is over, it's won.'

'Is it, so? I'm not sure. We've not got our Republic.'

'We've got our freedom, and that's enough to be getting on with. The rest will come soon enough.'

There is a long, awkward silence. Kitty has stopped crying, but is twisting and untwisting her fingers. She finds it hard to look at Tomas, then suddenly says, 'There's something I must tell you. I've been seeing Frank O'Gowan. He's asked me to marry him and I've said yes.'

'Marry Frank O'Gowan? Jesus, Kitty, he's fifteen years older than you. And he's . . .' Tomas stops, then continues, 'He's not the man for you.'

'You don't have to swear. I've not seen you nor heard a word from you for three years. It's not for you to tell me who to marry.' Kitty stands up and holds out her hand. 'We can still be friends.'

'That's not enough for me,' says Tomas. 'When we kissed it felt like there was something good between us, something that I've been holding onto. I see I was mistaken.' He puts the bunch of flowers on the table and stands up, keeping his hands by his side. 'Good luck with Frank O'Gowan.'

Kitty takes a step towards Tomas, stops, then sits back down in her chair and starts to cry quietly. Tomas walks out of the house and down the Quays along the north channel of the River Lee. The river is high, brown and roiling, trying to escape its confining banks. Back at the Queen Victoria he starts drinking, sitting alone in the corner of the saloon bar. Denis comes in; Tomas hasn't seen him since the shooting of Colonel Smyth in the Constitution Club.

'How the devil are you?' says Denis, pumping Tomas's reluctant hand. 'I hear you did the business in Dublin all right. I've joined the Free State Army; they'll be wanting you, surely.'

Tomas grunts a reply, rebuffs the invitation to join Denis and his friends at the bar and continues to drink alone. His parting from Kitty two years before had been hard enough, and he'd been unsure of his reception, but the news that she is engaged to Frank O'Gowan is unbearable. Had she really thought he was dead? Hadn't the news of the escape from Kilmainham been in the Cork newspapers? Frank must have known he was still alive. The questions come and go in his head, the answers blurred by the drink, until at midnight he has to be helped upstairs and put to bed by the landlord.

The next morning he reports to the barracks at Ballincollig

with a blinding headache, swears allegiance to the Irish Free State and is given a typewritten commission as a lieutenant. Donal congratulates him when the short, perfunctory ceremony is over, and takes him to the quartermaster's stores, where a sergeant measures him for a uniform, makes him sign for a revolver, ammunition, boots, leggings, a Sam Browne, a greatcoat, two shirts and two ties, and tells him to come back the next day. Outside on the square two platoons are drilling; the sergeant major shouting at the men is plainly a former British Army soldier.

'We'll teach you the drill in the officers' squad once you're properly dressed. Done any drilling?' says Donal.

'I've fired a revolver, fired a Thompson gun and thrown a few grenades. Never saluted in my life.'

'That's true of most of us. It's not so hard, although some of the men resent it. They think it's aping the British. But the Big Fellow says we need to change from being fighters into soldiers. Discipline wasn't strong among the Volunteers at the best of times, and drill and turnout are important. You've been allocated a room in the Officers' Mess.'

Tomas, who has difficulty thinking of himself as an officer, gets his uniform the following day and spends the next fortnight in a squad of a dozen lieutenants, drilling in the morning and learning their duties in the afternoon. The instructors are ex-British Army and not all of them have impeccable War of Independence credentials.

'There were thirty-six of us at the Kilmichael ambush, and I've met forty-eight of them in the past three months,' says Donal.

Tomas tolerates the drilling every morning, although some of his companions have two left feet. Nevertheless there are moments when The Squad halts or presents arms as one, and Tomas admits to himself, although not to the others, that these are curiously satisfying. He stops the heavy drinking when Donal takes him to one side in the Officers' Mess.

'Tomas, I don't know the cause of your drinking and I don't care. I do know you'll be out on your ear if it goes on any longer.'

He makes a half-hearted attempt to see Kitty, watching Station Road from a safe distance early one Sunday morning in the hope of intercepting her on the way to Mass. Instead he sees Frank O'Gowan leaving the house, and the violent jealousy that overwhelms him is followed by a return of the despair that had turned him to drink. He goes back to Ballincollig, realizing that he cannot see Kitty or Frank again. He asks Donal about Frank.

'Frank O'Gowan's got a company in the second battalion. They're at Macroom,' says Donal. 'I'm not sure for how long – he's an out-and-out Republican, doesn't try to hide it. Weren't you with him at Staigue?'

'I was.' Tomas does not elaborate further, thinks that the twenty miles between Ballincollig and Macroom is distance enough.

In the second week they take it in turns to drill The Squad, and all but two are deemed competent to take on their new roles as platoon commanders. Tomas's platoon, three sections of ten men each headed by a corporal, is slightly below full strength. His sergeant, James O'Connor, is a Connaught Rangers veteran who had fought in the Boer War and survived the German spring offensive in 1918. Tomas and he have a careful respect for each other. Tomas knows O'Connor has been a proper soldier, O'Connor knows Tomas has been one of The Squad.

Most of Tomas's platoon have seen, or claimed to have seen, some action in the many skirmishes and ambushes of the War of Independence. Once the novelty of their new uniforms, regular meals and a sound roof overhead wears off they are easily bored. Tomas's and Sergeant O'Connor's solution is ceaseless activity. Drilling, a ten-mile route march once a week, weapons training, firing practice, Gaelic football and hurling are the best possible substitute for war. There is no time for disaffection. The Ballincollig bar is off limits, and the prohibition is strictly observed after two members of No. 3 Platoon are caught there and sent home.

Tomas finds the transition to lieutenant difficult, sustainable only by acting the role, a role largely improvised with few stage

directions and a brief script. It is reassuring that his brother officers clearly feel the same. Only Donal seems entirely comfortable.

'He's one of nature's adjutants,' Tomas says to O'Connor. 'He
does it all without breaking sweat.'

In the Officers' Mess the play-acting is at its most pronounced.
They are waited on by women from the village, they eat off
plates bearing the crossed lances of a departed British cavalry
regiment with the King's broad arrow underneath, and they
stand to drink the health of the Irish Free State at a formal dinner
once a week. Unease is added to the unreality Tomas has felt ever
since leaving Drimnamore for Staigue Fort.

'You're doing great,' says Donal. 'O'Connor's a good man,
and he doesn't want your job. The men like you well enough,
they do what you tell them, and they all know what you've done
during the war.'

'How do they know that?'

'I told them.'

After a month at Ballincollig, Tomas's platoon wins the battalion hurling competition. Tomas feels this is a good moment to
ask for a week's leave and uses the time to go back to County
Kerry.

Returning to Drimnamore is an ordeal, made no easier by his
mother's joy at seeing him. Annie Sullivan cries, hugs him, cries
again.

'It's thanks to the Blessed Virgin Mary you're back,' she says,
crossing herself. 'We thought you dead until Father Michael read
that you had escaped. The Tans came looking for you here several
times, but I told them I knew nothing. As indeed I did.'

'I couldn't send a message. I'm sorry for the worry I caused
you,' and Tomas wraps his arms around Annie, who is sobbing
and smiling.

'You'll stay here now surely,' she says anxiously.

'Ah no, I'm in the army now, and there's still work to be done.
But I'll be back to help with the harvest later on, and you'd better
set me to work.'

Tomas spends three days doing the jobs that were too heavy for Annie, planting out the seed potatoes, repairing the fences and re-laying half a dozen slates that had been dislodged by the winter gales. He strips and repairs the water pump in the yard, oils and sharpens the scythes and the axe, and puts a new shaft on the slane. He goes out to the old turf line above the house, digs out the drain and takes the thick four-inch layer of fibrous grass off the top to expose the rich chocolate brown. He has always enjoyed the work; with a sharpened slane it is surprisingly easy once the top is clear and in two afternoons he cuts and stacks enough to see Annie through the rest of the year.

In the evenings they sit and talk over the fire in the kitchen. Tomas gives his mother an exact account of the battle at Staigue Fort, but is much vaguer about his life on the run in Cork and in Dublin.

Late one evening she says, 'John Burke came looking for his mother and asked me if I knew where she might be, and where you were. I said I didn't know, that you wouldn't harm a hair on her head.'

On Saturday Tomas walks out to Staigue Fort, the sun gleaming on the Kenmare River, the hedges red with fuchsia in full bloom. He stands on top of the fort wall, looking up at the pass where the Manchester Regiment had first appeared, then goes to the souterrain and crawls along it until it surfaces in the little wood. He looks at the site of the Lewis gun where he and Frank had killed three men. There are still empty cartridge cases lying half hidden in the grass. He picks one up and puts it in his pocket, plucks a fuchsia flower from the hedge and slips it between the pages of his missal, the bright red of the petals the colour of the blood around Seamus O'Connell's head. He walks back down to the fort, which looks impregnable.

'They'd never have driven us out if we'd had a machine gun and a few more men,' he says out loud.

He ducks inside the low entrance and stops where Seamus O'Connell and Patrick O'Mahony had both lain on the grass, one dead, the other with a shattered knee. He tries to remember the Prayer for the Dead.

'Eternal rest grant unto them, O Lord, and let perpetual light shine upon them.' He has forgotten the final line, and ends, 'Rest in peace, Seamus, Patrick, Michael . . .'

He walks back into Drimnamore, where a much-reduced Fair Day is in progress on the green. Father Michael is there.

'Welcome back,' he says. 'I'll see you in church tomorrow. There'll be plenty there glad to see you back.'

'Thank you, Father,' says Tomas, and walks on to the O'Mahony cottage, which looks out on the green. Mrs O'Mahony's reaction to seeing Tomas is like his mother's. He is taken into the front room; in the corner there is a shrine to Patrick almost identical to the one he had seen in the O'Hanrahan house. Only the flag is different; it is the new green, white and orange of the Free State.

Tomas picks up the Mass card.

IN THE MOST HOLY NAME OF JESUS
Patrick O'Mahony
Who gave his life for Ireland at Staigue Fort
On 14 April 1920
RIP
O Immense Passion! O Profound Wounds! O Profusion of
Blood! O Sweetness Above All Sweetness! O Most Bitter
Death! Grant Him Eternal Rest.
Amen – 400 days Indulgence.

Tomas thinks the words strange, finds it hard to believe they offer any comfort. He puts the card back in its place.

'God help us, we miss him,' says Mrs O'Mahony. John O'Mahony, who has come in off the green, nods but cannot trust himself to speak.

'He was a good boy, a good boy,' says Mrs O'Mahony.

'He was a brave soldier. And he fought in a war that we've won. I wish he'd been here to see the end of it.'

ASHES IN THE WIND

Tomas puts on his uniform to go to church the next morning; this is the first time Drimnamore has seen the olive-green of the Free State Army. Tomas doesn't go to confession and doesn't take Communion. This is noticed by Father Michael, who takes Tomas to one side after the service.

'You can't stay away from God for ever,' he says. 'You carry a heavy burden. You should have the faith to share it.'

Tomas nods, shakes Father Michael's hand, moves away and is quickly surrounded by a small circle of admirers. Some are the parents of the men who fell at Staigue Fort or who were executed later. He enjoys this sudden celebrity, and the pleasure it gives his mother, but he no longer feels at home in Drimnamore. Too much has happened to him in and after Staigue Fort, in Cork and in Dublin – these are things he cannot share and cannot leave behind. He makes arrangements with one of the Doyles to help his mother with the heavy work on the farm, says goodbye to a tearful Annie, promises to return soon, and makes the long journey back to the barracks at Ballincollig.

He sees Donal the next morning.

'I've the great job for you,' he says to Tomas. 'You're to march your platoon to Kinsale and take over Charles Fort from the British Army. They're ready to leave as soon as you get there.'

'It's the best part of twenty miles,' says Tomas.

'It'll be good for your men. There's too much talk in the barracks about the IRA. We need to remind ourselves we're the Free State Army now. There's no need and no room for anything else.'

During his week's leave in Drimnamore, Tomas has lost two men from his platoon. One has gone back to his farm in Kilkenny, the other has joined the Republican group in Macroom. To Tomas's surprise his men are happy to leave the barracks, even for a twenty-mile march. He and Sergeant O'Connor drill them hard for an hour the night before.

'You'll be on show, boys,' says O'Connor. 'It's a bit of a detour, but we're going through Cork City and on down through

85

Fivemilebridge. So make sure your boots and brasses are shining bright.'

They set off after an early breakfast the next day. North of the city they give a smart eyes right to the flag of the Free State flying above the Victoria barracks; through Cork City the cheers and clapping put a spring in their step. There are no British soldiers, no Tans, no Auxiliaries, a few policemen in the new uniforms of the Garda.

They reach Charles Fort in the middle of the afternoon. Tomas finds the British captain, salutes him and gets a reluctant salute in return.

'There's accommodation for you and your men in C Block,' he tells Tomas, pointing across the central square. 'Food in the cookhouse next door. Best if you eat tonight and tomorrow after my men have finished. We'll be gone by noon.'

Tomas is taken aback by the size and strength of Charles Fort. It sits on the top of the bluff a mile outside Kinsale, an enormous star-shaped stronghold with two bastions facing the sea, three more on the landward side, containing buildings enough for a small village within its walls, a powerful reminder of the strength and bloody-minded will behind the British domination of Ireland over seven hundred years.

He walks around the grassy ramparts in the evening with Sergeant O'Connor.

'You could house a brigade in this place,' says O'Connor.

'And most of Drimnamore. The twenty of us will rattle around like three peas in a tin bucket. It makes you realize just what we've pulled off. The Brits built this place two hundred and fifty years ago, and now they're off without a shot being fired.'

'We never sent for them in the first place. They'll be little enough missed.'

The next morning Tomas walks around the main rooms with the British captain, who is carrying a lengthy checklist. After three hours of 'Twenty beds, men's, single. Forks, two hundred. Blankets, grey, fifty. Mugs, enamel, seventy-five,' Tomas stops the captain.

'Look, I'll sign and trust you for the rest. The Free State will survive if we're short a few forks. There's more than we could ever use, and any road we haven't paid for the stuff.'

The captain looks shocked for a moment, then laughs. 'It's up to you. Sign at the bottom of each page, you keep a copy, and we'll be off. And the best of luck.'

They shake hands. Tomas brings his platoon out onto the parade ground, the Irish flag is hoisted, and the British soldiers climb into their truck and drive away. There are no cheers, no jeers, the British soldiers silenced by their defeat, the Irishmen by their immense victory. Tomas stoops down and picks a clover leaf from the parade ground grass, puts it in the lining of his cap for luck, then walks back with Sergeant O'Connor to C Block.

12.

Back at Burke's Fort a few weeks after his visit to Kilmainham, the hunting season over, John is sitting at breakfast in the morning room when Charles says in a worried tone, 'Sean was badly kicked by The Elector yesterday – got between him and the back wall of the stable, the damn fool. Leg's broken in three places, he won't be out of Navan Hospital for a month, and then he'll be in plaster for heaven knows how long. Doubt he'll want to be our stallion man any more.'

'You're not young enough to hold him,' says Cis. 'John's good with the horses, and he's strong. It'll give him something useful to do.'

'I've never dealt with stallions, only geldings and mares,' says John. 'But I've helped with the foaling at home.'

'There's no one else. I'd be grateful if you'd take it on,' says Charles. 'You'll learn soon enough.'

Sean never comes back to the stallion yard, and John does learn soon enough. His new life revolves around The Elector, the mares and their foals, and the visiting mares who come to be covered.

The stallion looks like his ancestor The Archduke, lacking only the star on his forehead to be a living replica of the painting in the drawing room. He is a five-year-old, with the powerful muscled neck of a mature entire horse, and although not vicious – he never bites his handler or his mares – he needs care, particularly in the stable. John loves the horse, treating him with affectionate caution, taking him out to the paddock every day in the winter for an hour's exercise, watching him canter off once released from his head-collar, neck curved, tail raised, bucking a couple of times for the joy of being free from his stable.

He spends an hour every afternoon rubbing the stallion down with a thick wisp of hay, hissing in imitation of the bedridden Sean, who has told him it soothes the horse. He enjoys the warm smell of the bright chestnut coat, and when the grooming is finished runs his hand along the powerful neck to stroke each ear until The Elector, wanting his evening feed, turns and pushes him away.

'He loves his work,' says Charles. 'Eighty-five per cent fertility, and not many needing a second cover. He could handle eighty mares a year easily if we could get them.'

Charles talks John through his first half-dozen covers – the teaser stallion to excite the visiting mare, the twitch on the upper lip of the mare to help the groom to hold her steady, tail bandaged at the top and tied forward out of the way, vulva swabbed clean, a heavy leather blanket across the mare's quarters to prevent any damage from The Elector's forelegs as, whinnying in excitement, he mounts the mare, the massive penis – 'You're lucky, some horses need to be helped in. He knows what to do' – the brief, shuddering moment as the stallion does his work.

Eleven months later the foals arrive. John brings the mares into the foaling box as soon as they wax up, and spends many nights in the cubbyhole next door waiting for the waters to break. He helps the foal out, feet first if he's lucky, watches the foal dive into the world. John is moved by the moment when the mare turns around to lick the foal clean, the afterbirth hanging down behind her until he ties it off and cleans her up. And within the hour the foal is up on long unstable legs, nuzzling the mare to find the milk.

A new range of seasons frames John's life. Hunting between October and March, foaling and covering in the first three months of the year, point-to-points between February and May, racing all the year round. The mares come into their stables in the autumn and are turned out in the spring onto the rich grassland, so rich that it has to be grazed by sheep before the horses can be allowed on it. The big sales are in October on The Curragh and at Ballsbridge during the Dublin Shows, the spring show in April, the main show in August.

After a probationary month looking after The Elector, John has become the stallion man. The stables are a mile from the house, three sides of a square with boxes on each side, a cobbled yard, red-painted stable doors, two large water troughs with a handpump each, a mounting block that Charles now has to use. The plain wall on the fourth side of the square is broken by a curved archway

The tack room to the left of the archway smells of leather, saddle soap and neat's-foot oil. Down one wall hang the saddles, halters and bridles, on the opposite wall in a glass case are the yellow, blue and red rosettes from twenty years of horse shows up and down the country. There are photographs of winners being led in or jumping the last fence – a dozen horseshoes are nailed up, each marking a Classic success.

'That's Dublin,' says Charles, pointing to a large red, white and blue rosette. 'Champion Heavyweight Hunter in 1902. Long time since we had a horse as good. But we might enter The Elector once we see how you both get on.'

Behind the main stable block is the smaller stallion yard – a generous box for The Elector, smaller boxes for the visiting mares and the teaser, and a derelict two-up, two-down cottage in the corner. John asks if he can move in to be closer to the horses.

'Fine by me, but you'll need to make it habitable first. I'll get the builder in from the village to help you out. It's got electricity on the ground floor and water, but you'll need a bathroom. The last man to live there used the pump in the big yard.'

Once he has moved in, he realizes that John Burke Esquire, formerly of Derriquin Castle, has become John, the stallion man at Burke's Fort. He is happy about the no-man's-land he inhabits; he still lunches with his cousins in the Big House every Sunday but drinks with the other grooms in the village snug most Saturday nights. He wears strong boots, dark brown corduroy trousers and a broad leather belt, a striped shirt with a collar stud and no collar or tie, a rough tweed jacket and a peaked cap, all bought from the haberdasher's shop in Maryborough. He has two voices, one for Sunday lunch, one for the rest of the week.

Young Charlie Burke, his own age, is friendly enough when he comes back for the holidays from agricultural college, but has difficulty placing John in his ordered, hierarchical view of the world. The three Burkes go out hunting together, but on their return Charles and Charlie hand their horses over to the grooms, while John waters and feeds his mare, makes sure she's dry and sound, and cleans the saddles and bridles with Michael and Sean in the tack room before going back to his cottage.

He goes to the occasional hunt ball with Charlie, almost always because a spare man is needed. The mothers of the girls he meets are cautious in their welcome. John understands this; in a universe of young men who are either at Trinity or in the army, he enjoys the look of surprise when he says, 'I'm the stallion man at Burke's Fort.' The mothers don't enquire further.

Most of the daughters are curious enough to ask for a detailed explanation of what he does; several find it exciting that John has carried the stable-yard into the ballroom. John sounds the same as the other young men, but looks different. He is tall, lean, with his mother's fair hair and his father's strong features, and his hands and face are tanned. He has a strength and independence that is attractive and, to ambitious mothers, dangerous.

Hunting, racing, dancing and tennis appear to be a subordinate but important part of the campaign to keep Ireland within the Empire. At a tennis party at Kilkee Castle, John, who is an erratic but occasionally brilliant player, is paired with the daughter of the house. He'd met Nesta Fitzmaurice, a small, energetic, fair-haired girl, at a dance a month before, where she had shown a healthy interest in John's explanation of how the covering of the mares was organized.

'You mean the teaser stallion never gets the mare? What kind of a life is that?'

'It's the only one they know.'

'I'd not settle for it.'

After their narrow defeat in the final of the tennis, Nesta takes John down to the lake to look at the black swans. The swans are gone; she makes up for their absence by showing John the summer house, where she advances John's sexual education by several important and enjoyable steps. A few weeks later they meet again at a garden party at Ballybrittas. When John sees Nesta take an older ex-soldier to look at the orchid house, he realizes she is not going to advance his education any further.

It is not only John's occupation that marks him out. The story of the kidnapping and killing of Eileen is widely known but never discussed. When John first arrived at Burke's Fort, Charles and Cis had offered a few sympathetic words but never referred to Eileen again. He no longer relives the kidnapping. His visit to Kilmainham Jail and the brushing of the sleeve across Tomas's eyes have convinced John that his worst fears about his mother's end – torture, rape – are unfounded. What remains is bad enough, but easier to escape through his long working days with the horses.

In the stallion yard he is insulated from the outside world. He has stopped reading the *Irish Times* and begins his day with the *Sporting Life*. He hears about the Truce in the middle of 1921 from Sean, recently returned from hospital with a pronounced limp and no desire to look after The Elector again, happy to be working with the hunters alongside Michael. Many months later he learns of the general amnesty, but he never attempts to find out whether Tomas was either pardoned or hanged.

Over lunch early in 1923, Charles asks John to get The Elector ready for the Dublin Show at Ballsbridge.

'We need another big rosette. We need to show him off, bring in more mares. Only thirty-five last year, and a lot of them wouldn't pay the full thirty pounds.'

'We'll need to build him up, change his feed, give him more exercise.'

The stallion can't be ridden, but takes kindly to trotting and cantering around the large paddock on the end of a lunging rein. He gets an extra ration of oats, linseed and a secret preparation from Michael guaranteed 'to put a shine on the coat of an undertaker'.

There is a preliminary outing to the show at Abbeyleix, where The Elector wins his class, from, it is true, only four other stallions. By the time of the show he looks magnificent. There is a slow journey up to Dublin in the horsebox, a converted army truck. The Elector takes an hour to be convinced to walk up the ramp; John has renewed the padding inside and barred off a space at the front where he can stand and steady the stallion.

It is John's first visit to Dublin since he went to see Tomas in Kilmainham Jail. The city is still full of soldiers, but ones who wear the unfamiliar uniforms of the newly formed Irish Army. The Royal Irish Constabulary have been disbanded and replaced by the Garda Síochána. Both are full of former rebels who are now on the side of law and order.

There are three elements of the Dublin Show; the showjumping, which attracts teams from all over Europe; the serious judging of horseflesh, from Connemara ponies to heavyweight hunters; and the riotous dances in the big hotels every evening. The stallion competition is on the Thursday and has twenty-seven entries.

'They're judged on conformation, and that means looks,' says Charles. 'How he behaves in the ring will count. And some of the others will already have won at bigger shows than our fellow.'

John is uncertain how his horse will react to the crowds, the noise and the other stallions – the mares are kept well away from the stallion ring. The day brings out the showman in The Elector, who arches his neck and strides out around the ring, coat gleaming, hooves oiled and polished, mane plaited and tail combed. He is one of five called in from the original twenty-seven. The judges – sombre men in bowler hats, breeches, boots and hacking jackets, notebooks in hand – take an age to winnow two from the last five. The Elector is one; both horses are asked to stand while a judge runs a careful hand down each foreleg. The Elector takes this well, but his rival, a beautiful four-year-old grey from the Mount Juliet stud, backs away. The judges consult their notebooks, talk in low voices in the middle of the ring, ask for a further trot towards them and away, and after an age announce The Elector as the winner of the stallion Supreme Championship.

John trots his stallion around the ring in a lap of honour, the large rosette flapping against The Elector's head-collar, while the small crowd clap respectfully. Charles comes up to John afterwards, beaming, and presses fifty pounds into his pocket.

'Best day of my life, best day of my life. We'll have a queue of mares after this.'

'He's come on a lot since Abbeyleix,' says John. 'And he made the most of himself, liked showing off to the crowd. Michael's mixture did the business.'

Several complete strangers insist on shaking John's hand. One of them, a small, sharp-featured man with a weathered face, says, 'It's good to see Burke's Fort in the prize-money again. And you showed him off well in the ring. You've been feeding him right, I'd say.'

Later Charles tells John that this is Desmond Curran, the Master of the Limerick, 'Best eye for a horse in Ireland'. John travels home in the back of the horsebox, smiling with pleasure all the way. He stops stroking The Elector only to look at the red, white and blue rosette and the Champion's silver salver.

13.

Raising the green, white and gold flag over Charles Fort is the high point of the War of Independence for Tomas; it is also the moment that Ireland begins to break apart. Tomas is recalled to Ballincollig, leaving Sergeant O'Connor in charge.

'There's little enough for the men to do here,' says O'Connor, 'except talk about the Treaty and the Republic. Some of the boys might run, especially the hard ones who liked the fighting. Jimsy Malone and Con O'Donnell, for two. I could be left with the johnny-come-latelys, the ones who've never fired a shot.'

'Keep them as busy as you can, and let them go down into Kinsale only on a Saturday,' says Tomas. 'I expect I'll be back soon enough.'

Passing through Cork, he avoids Station Road but calls in on Victoria barracks, where he receives a frosty welcome from the guard at the barracks gate.

'All of us here are for the Republic. We owe our allegiance to the Executive in the Four Courts. If you're one of Collins's men there's no place for you here.'

Tomas doesn't argue. Back at Ballincollig he tells Donal.

'We've known that for a while now,' says Donal. 'It's a stand-off at the moment; no one wants to bring it to a fight, though that's the way we're heading. People change sides and back again every week. The Commander-in-Chief wants you in Dublin as his ADC. You're a captain from today. Congratulations.'

'What does an ADC do?'

'It's French for dogsbody. You go wherever Michael Collins goes and you do whatever he tells you.'

'That's it?'

'That's it. But you'll know what's going on, that is if anyone does, and you'll be at the centre of things. It's not a soft job. There are plenty of hardline Republicans who'd like to kill Michael Collins and not mind about taking you with him.'

'They'd never kill Michael Collins, surely to God?'

'He's our commander-in-chief, not theirs. The way they see it, he's the man who gave away the Republic, who agreed to the oath, who lost the Six Counties. It's all changed. Changed utterly, as your man Yeats wrote.'

Back in Dublin, the city he left with a price on his head and in disguise, Tomas reports to Michael Collins in Beggars Bush barracks. Collins returns his salute with a bear-hug.

'Good to have you here. My last man got the vapours, couldn't stand the pace. I hope you're made of sterner stuff. But you'll need to smarten up your leather and your cap badge – we're on display all the time. What's good enough in Ballincollig won't pass muster here.'

Tomas mutters an apology, which Michael Collins cuts short.

'We've work to do. The country's in a bloody mess, and we can't blame the British any more. The Republicans are holding General O'Connell as a hostage in the Four Courts. At the moment we can count on seven out of sixteen divisions; we'll have to sort the rest out. We've come to the end of talking.'

Two days later Tomas is sent to the Four Courts with a message, which he delivers to Rory O'Connor, the commander of the Four Courts Republicans.

The Officer in Charge,
Four Courts

I, acting under the order of the Government, hereby order you to evacuate the buildings of the Four Courts and to parade

*your men under arrest, without arms, on that portion of the
Quays immediately in front of the Four Courts by 4 a.m.*
   *Failing compliance with this order, the building will be
taken by force, and you and all concerned with you will be
held responsible for any life lost or any damage done.*
   By order
   Thomas Ennis
   O/C 2nd Eastern Division

O'Connor reads it and laughs.

'We'd take you as a hostage alongside Ginger O'Connell,
but you're not senior enough. Off with you now, sonny, and
tell Tom Ennis and the Big Fellow they'll have to come and get
us.'

During the following day National Army troops occupy
buildings around the Four Courts. The Republicans are under
orders not to fire first and make no attempt to prevent the en-
circlement. Emmet Dalton is sent to collect two borrowed
eighteen-pounders from disgruntled British gunners in Phoenix
Park. Dalton, who joined the British Army in 1914 and ended the
war as a major in the Dublin Fusiliers, sometimes wears his
Military Cross on his major general's uniform.

The British Royal Artillery major looks at Dalton with resentment, sees the blue and white ribbon. 'Where did you get that
MC? Off the body of some poor bastard you ambushed?'

Dalton enjoys the question. 'George V pinned it on me at
Buckingham Palace. I commanded a company of the Dubs when
we took Ginchy during the battle of the Somme. I don't remember seeing you there. Perhaps I'd only recognize your back view.'

The major takes a step towards Dalton, thinks the better of it,
checks the paperwork and hands over the guns.

The next day the attack on the Four Courts begins. Tomas is
an onlooker from the comparative safety of Merchants' Quay on
the other side of the river, watching in disbelief. Until this moment
he had thought that the split would heal itself, and would never

end in Irishmen firing on Irishmen. Several members of The Squad are on the Republican side.

After three days of intense fighting a huge explosion destroys the western wing of the Four Courts and the Public Records Office, and what is left of the buildings catches fire, although Gandon's great dome still stands. When the Republicans surrender, Tomas sees one hundred and eighty men, his former fellow Volunteers, march out into the street without their weapons to be escorted by soldiers of the Free State Army to Jameson's Distillery.

The road in front of the Four Courts is covered in rubble, beams, spent ammunition, tangled tram wires, plaster. The head of one of the Corinthian columns, its acanthus leaves and scrolls still intact, lies upside down on the edge of the embankment. Someone has scrawled 'WE HAVE NO TIME FOR TRUCERS' on the side of the abandoned armoured car.

Inside the building the surrendering Republicans have left piles of disabled rifles and revolvers, ammunition boxes, mattresses and blankets, discarded clothing, stale and mouldy food. There are papers and documents from the Public Records Office scattered all over Dublin on the wind of the fire – wills, census returns, writs, judgments, some black, some grey, some white. Tomas picks up a half-burned ledger detailing government expenditure on victuals, ammunition and horses in the year 1798. We lost that one, he thinks, but what kind of victory is this?

On his way back to headquarters he walks down O'Connell Street where the fighting has been fierce. Shops, offices, pubs and hotels are all closed, many of them badly damaged. When he brings the news of the Four Courts' surrender, Collins is exultant. 'That should put an end to it,' he says, beating his hand on the table. 'The others won't last long.'

Michael Collins plans a trip to the South against the advice of his staff. 'They'll not shoot me in my own county,' he says.

'You're running short of lives,' says Tomas. 'The British nearly got you a dozen times, your car was blown up two weeks ago when by chance you weren't in it, and you're not exactly in disguise any more.'

'Never mind that, the devil looks after his own. I won't need you tonight – I'm off to Kilteragh to dine with Horace Plunkett.'

'You'll need an escort, sure.'

'No, and that's an end of it.'

Tomas asks another staff officer what's going on.

'He's got his escort sure enough – it's Hazel Lavery, his Friday wife.'

'I thought he was engaged to Kitty Kiernan,' says Tomas, shocked.

'So he is, but the Big Fellow is generous with himself, and he makes his own rules, you should know that by now.'

Two days later they set off for the South. They arrive in Cork City late, delayed by blown bridges and blocked roads, but dinner in the Imperial Hotel sees Collins relaxed, expansive, playful. Donal Ryan has come from Ballincollig at Collins's invitation to join them for dinner and Emmet Dalton is also there. Donal fights the battle of Kilmichael with peppers, salts, glasses and cups on the dinner table.

'Kilmichael helped to turn the tide,' says Collins. 'The Brits had never seen us turn out in force, and we killed, how many?'

'Seventeen Auxiliaries, captured a lot of ammunition, and lost only three Volunteers.'

'The other turning point was taking out the Cairo Gang. Tomas here was part of The Squad. Different altogether, but after that the Brits hardly dared to poke their noses out of Dublin Castle,' says Collins, looking at Tomas as he speaks. Tomas realizes he is getting a blessing and nods.

'I hear de Valera's in Cork County, but where I don't know,' says Emmet Dalton. 'Our intelligence isn't as good as it should be, isn't as good as theirs.'

'I don't think there's much point in trying for a meeting. He's a brilliant man right enough, a spoiled cardinal if ever I saw one, but you never know what he's thinking, except it's not what he's saying. Lloyd George told me that dealing with him was like trying to pick up quicksilver with a fork,' says Michael Collins. 'Dev could have a compromise tomorrow – he could have had one six months ago. But when he said, "The IRA would have to wade through the blood of the soldiers of the Irish government" – that's all of us here – those weren't the words of a man we could do business with.'

They talk of the motives of the anti-Treaty leaders, and then Dalton lightens the mood by asking Collins to tell the story of the dog show. This is a set piece, one that the Big Fellow has told many times before.

'Ah, that was something else entirely. You know I love the Kerry Blue terrier? Tomas here is going to get one, they're from his county.'

'I'm not sure I'm man enough. Your dog won't do a thing I tell him,' says Tomas.

'Anyhow, it was a strange moment, like the truce in the trenches over Christmas 1914. We held a breed show in Langrish Place in the middle of October 1920. Con O'Herlihy and Dan Nolan from Kerry were the judges. The curfew was on, but there we were, Kerry Blue lovers all, the Under-Secretary, Sir James McMahon, Captain Wyndham Quinn from Vice-Regal Lodge, who gave the cup, and lots of Kerry Blues. My good dog won, entered under the name of Convict 224, my Frongoch number. Dawn of Freedom came second and McMahon's bitch third.'

'Did they know who you were?'

'It wasn't too hard to guess, given the names of the dogs – Trotsky, Markiewicz, Munster Fusilier. I had a moustache then, they didn't have a good photograph of me, and besides we outnumbered them by five to one. But it was a real truce. Both sides suspended belief because they loved the Kerry Blue.'

After dinner Collins strips off his tunic for 'a bit of ear', wrestling with the commandant and anyone else who will take him on. Tomas doesn't join in; he hasn't got used to the sight of his chief rolling about on the floor, even though the bouts are good-humoured enough, with Collins usually ending up on top.

At breakfast the next morning the mood is different; Collins is subdued. 'I had the news late last night that they hanged our two men in Wandsworth Jail.'

'They could have blown the Treaty sky-high,' says Emmet Dalton.

Collins doesn't answer directly. 'We tried hard enough to get them out, but the Brits weren't going to let the killing of their CIGS go unpunished.'

After breakfast the small convoy, a motorcycle scout, two Crossley Tenders each with ten soldiers, an open Leyland tourer with Collins and Dalton in the back and Tomas alongside the driver, sets off for Bandon, Clonakilty, Rosscarbery, Skibbereen, Sam's Cross. A Rolls-Royce armoured car, the Slievenamon, brings up the rear. It is part triumphal procession, part armed patrol; in the towns and villages they feel safe enough, but the country roads are dangerous.

They stop at Woodfield, opposite the house where Michael Collins's mother was born, and go into the bar, the Four Alls.

'The king, who rules all, the priest, who prays for all, the soldier, who fights for all, and the peasant, who pays for all,' says Emmet Dalton.

Tomas laughs. 'They've forgotten the Cork farmer, who drinks for all.'

From the outside the Four Alls looks like a prosperous farmer's cottage, whitewashed, slate roofed, windows red-painted. Inside, a long room, its stone floor sprinkled with sawdust, runs the full length of the building. The bar is crowded; word had got round that Michael Collins was due, and some of the drinkers had been there since noon. They are mostly farmers – weathered, reddening faces with a day or two's stubble above collarless shirts closed by a single stud, thick tweed jackets, dark corduroy trousers held up by a wide black belt or binder twine, the boots heavy and cracked. There are two or three shopkeepers or bank clerks from Rosscarbery in suits and ties, and in one corner the parish priest keeping a watchful eye on the hard drinkers. There is a warm, damp smell of spilled beer, wet sawdust, drying tweed and sweat.

Collins buys a barrel of the local beer, Clonakilty Wrastler, which he hoists onto the bar. He sends Tomas out to bring the soldiers in, Tomas insisting that four remain to guard the vehicles. They stay in the Four Alls for almost an hour. Tomas listens to the strong Cork accents, the passionate exchanges, and thinks these are good men. They may not be heroes or poets, not Cúchulains nor Blind Rafterys, but these are the ones we've been fighting for. As the conversation flows with the beer, Tomas contrasts their faces with those of the Anglo-Irish men and women he had seen coming out of the Protestant church in Drimnamore of a Sunday. The Prod faces were leaner, more elegant, but they never looked as though they belonged in the land around them. The gentry have flat ears and beaky noses and they don't have curly hair, his mother used to say.

Tomas looks at Michael Collins's reflection in the big Guinness mirror behind the bar, the square face, the strong, slightly fleshy, jaw, the thick dark hair, the generous mouth, the bright eyes, and notes the way in which those around him defer to him even when he is silent. He's our Commander-in-Chief all right, thinks Tomas, he doesn't look like a bank manager any more.

Just before they leave, Michael Collins jumps up onto the bar, his head almost brushing the ceiling. He shakes the thick lock of black hair out of his eyes, stamps his foot on the bar for silence. 'I know I am among friends – I'm related to the half of you in this room. Not all of you are on the side of the Free State. I'm one of the men who signed the Treaty. Some of those who sent us to London called us incompetent amateurs . . .'

'De Valera and Brugha,' whispers Emmet to Tomas.

'. . . tricked by a wily Welshman. Well, Lloyd George tricked us by withdrawing his troops from Ireland, he tricked us into victory.

'Now listen. We are free to get back all that was taken from us, the freedom that was dreamed of by Wolfe Tone, the freedom that was foreseen by Thomas Davis. The Brits are going at last; they'd be gone already if Dev and his friends would let them leave. We will have our Republic, we will bring in the North, but only if we stop tearing ourselves apart. John O'Leary said, "There are things a man ought not to do to save his country," and that includes Irishmen killing Irishmen.' Michael Collins smacks his fist into his palm. 'We've won our war; let's show we deserve our peace. Let's show we can use what we've earned by force of arms, what the Treaty gives us, the freedom to be free.'

He jumps down from the bar to cheers and is carried out to the car.

'I've never seen him do that,' says Tomas.

'He's a force of nature all right,' says Dalton. 'He has them eating out of his hand. But if Dev were to turn up tomorrow, and tear into Mick and the Treaty the way he can, there'd be more than a few would have changed sides by the time Dev was out the door.'

Three miles outside Clonakilty the road is blocked, and it takes half an hour to move the fallen trees out of the way. Michael Collins takes off his tunic and joins in clearing the road, ignoring Tomas's suggestion that he should wait in the armoured car.

'Show me that axe,' Collins says to one of the soldiers. 'It's not the first time I've used one.'

Tomas and Emmet Dalton argue strongly for a different return journey from Bandon to Cork. They stop on the road and send out the motorcycle scout to check the two alternative routes. Both have been blocked. The road back alternates between open stretches of flat, boggy farmland and enclosed green tunnels where the roadside trees meet overhead. The verges are covered in ferns, cow parsley, yellow gorse, rushes, occasional clumps of purple foxgloves. They reach the valley of Béal na mBláth, the

Mouth of Flowers, where the road is overlooked by low hills matching the curve of the valley. As the motorcyclist disappears round the corner, a volley of shots shatter the windscreen of the Leyland and ricochet off the armoured car with an angry whine.

'Drive like hell,' shouts Dalton.

'Stay where you are. We'll take them on,' says Collins.

Grabbing his rifle, he jumps out of the car, waving to the men in the tenders to dismount. At first it is hard to see where the shots are coming from. Three or four men appear and disappear behind a high bank up the hill to the left; the machine gun in the convoy's armoured car opens up and tears great chunks of earth from the top of the bank, jams and is silent for fifteen minutes, then starts firing again. The skirmish lasts no more than an hour – sporadic firing from the hill, returning fire from the soldiers on the road using their vehicles for cover. Tomas is alongside the Commander in Chief most of the time. Michael Collins is behaving like a Volunteer enjoying his first battle, dashing between the armoured car and the tender to encourage the men, trying to pick out the elusive targets of the men on the hill. He pays no attention to Tomas's attempts to keep him down behind the armoured car.

The firing dies away, and suddenly flares up again as the men on the hill are seen to be retreating. Tomas sees a kneeling Collins, who has moved into the middle of the road, aim his rifle, then suddenly spin round and fall back. Tomas runs across; Emmet Dalton is already cradling Collins's head, the back shot away, blood and brains staining his uniform and the road.

'The bastards, they've done for him,' says Dalton.

Collins's eyes are still open, his lips move, then all is still. Dalton and Tomas, both in tears, say an Act of Contrition. Together they lift the heavy body into the back of the car. On the way back they stop in Crookstown. Dalton finds the parish priest, who blesses Collins's body. Five minutes later the armoured car arrives.

'We killed two of them,' says the commandant.

'Lay their bodies out. They can have the priest too,' says Dalton.

Tomas recognizes one of the dead men; it is Frank O'Gowan, face undamaged, body disfigured by several bullet wounds. Tomas closes Frank O'Gowan's grey eyes, the skin of the eyelids still warm. He crosses himself and thinks of Kitty O'Hanrahan. How can I tell her? Who fired the shots that killed him?

One of the soldiers nudges Frank's body with his boot.

'Get away out of that,' says Tomas. 'They were men as good as you.'

He helps to lift the bodies back into the tender when the priest has finished. Frank is half the weight of Michael Collins. The rest of the journey back is a nightmare; the bridge over the Cork–Macroom road has been blown up, and they have to cross fields to get back on the Cork road. The wheels of the Crossley Tender spin in the mud, and they make a carpet of blankets and coats to give the wheels purchase. It is after midnight when they unload the bodies at the Shanakiel Hospital in Cork. Tomas sees that Frank's eyes are open again, staring up and past him to the dark evening sky.

The next day Tomas and Dalton go back to Dublin, accompanying Collins's body. They travel by sea, as the land journey is no longer safe. Tomas feels this is the end of everything – the end of Michael Collins, the end of the Treaty, the end of Irish unity. In Cork the night before, burdened with sorrow and guilt, he hadn't been able to call on Kitty and tell her the news about Frank.

Michael Collins lies in state for three days in Dublin's City Hall. Tens of thousands file past the open coffin, and in Kilmainham Jail Republican prisoners kneel and say a rosary for the man they had abandoned as their leader. There is a funeral Mass at Dublin's Pro-Cathedral, and thousands line the streets and fill the cemetery at Glasnevin. Tomas sees Kitty Kiernan in widow's weeds holding a single lily at the graveside, and watches

Hazel Lavery throw her rosary beads on the coffin as it is lowered into the ground.

Michael Collins is succeeded as commander-in-chief by Dick Mulcahy; on the walls of Dublin someone has scrawled, 'MOVE OVER MICK. MAKE ROOM FOR DICK.'

14.

AFTER HIS DUBLIN triumph, The Elector has plenty of breeders eager to send their mares and his book is soon full for the following year.

'And that's after putting the price up to fifty pounds – they're not getting that at Mount Juliet,' says Charles. 'Sixty mares will do us – we don't want to wear him out. You'll need another pair of hands in the stallion yard, and we'll call you the stud manager from now on.'

On the strength of this promotion and a salary of six pounds a week John buys his first car, an old Morris Oxford with a starting handle that kicks like a mule and a top speed downhill of forty miles an hour. He paints his car dark blue, and it is second only to The Elector in his affections.

Since the beginning of the new season John has begun to ride in point-to-points, at first on young Charles's hunter, on whom he wins a couple of Adjacent Hunt races and finishes third in the big Open at the Ward Union in April. After these results he begins to pick up a few rides from other owners, not without risk. After a crashing fall and a mild concussion on a chance ride he becomes more selective.

The thrill of seeing a stride, the crackle of the birch as the horses brush through the top of the fence, the shouts of the jockeys, 'Give me room, damn you, give me room,' the hard-bitten, leathery semi-professionals a sharp contrast to the Anglo-Irish amateurs, the *craic* in the dressing-room tent, the noise of the bookies calling out the odds, the comments of the crowd, 'That one would be better off between the shafts of a turf-cart,' it all makes the blood flow faster through John's veins. He enjoys the danger and learns the darker arts quickly enough; he tries to come up on the inside of one of the hard men, who puts him through the wings of the fence rather than giving way.

'You'll not try that again in a hurry' is his rival's unsympathetic comment as they weigh in after the race.

John is a natural horseman, a good judge of pace, relaxed enough to leave an experienced horse alone, able to sit tight when he hits a fence hard. He can do eleven stone only by watching his weight during the season, and he can't ride much of a finish, but he is soon in demand by owners with decent horses who want a sympathetic jockey.

He starts to ride out in the early morning with a local trainer, Paddy Brennan, who has a racing yard and a string of thirty point-to-pointers, hurdlers and chasers at Ballyroan about ten miles away from Burke's Fort. His car is just man enough for the journey, and once the covering season is over he is able to get up early, drive over to Ballyroan, ride out his two on the gallops and get back to Burke's Fort in time to lead The Elector out for his morning exercise.

The Elector shows no signs of exhaustion from his increased workload. By the summer he has come into his coat and looks as good as he did in the Dublin ring. Only John handles him – the other grooms, to whom Sean's limp is a useful warning, are more than happy to deal with the mares, the foals and the geldings.

John comes back one morning after riding out to find a tall, dark-haired girl waiting in the stallion yard.

'I'm Grania Mannion,' she says. 'You must be the stallion man.'

'I am that,' says John.

'I am that! I am that! Come on now, I hear that's not the way you always speak. I'd like to see The Elector, please.'

John smiles and says in his Sunday voice, 'I'll show you the horse,' taking her over to the box.

He leads the stallion out and stands him in the yard while Grania studies both of them with a critical eye.

'Plenty of bone,' says Grania. 'Can you trot him up while I look at him head on?'

John does so.

'Is he quite correct?'

'The Dublin judges thought so,' says John, then sees the smile on Grania's face and realizes he is being teased again.

'We've two mares he would do nicely. We're over at Collinstown, three miles away.'

'You'll need to get in the queue. He's due to go out now to the paddock. You'll see him move there.'

They walk to the paddock, John leading The Elector.

'He's quiet enough.'

'He is with me.'

They lean on the gate and watch the stallion first trot, then canter around the field. The Elector plays to his little gallery, gives a couple of spirited bucks, then comes up to the gate and nuzzles John for a carrot.

'He's beautiful. He's the real thing,' says Grania. 'I can see you're in love with him all right.' She puts her hand on John's forearm for a moment. 'I hope my mares pass the test.'

'I hope so too,' says John, turning to smile at her. She has green eyes, arched eyebrows, a straight nose, full lips.

'You're looking at me as if I was in the show ring,' says Grania. 'Is my conformation all right? Do I get a rosette?'

'You do,' says John, and thinks, she's beautiful, she's the real thing. As they walk back to the yard he surprises himself by asking if he can drive her home.

'Only if you can fit my cob in the boot of your car. He's in a stable in your big yard – Michael said that would be all right.'

In the big yard Grania takes her horse out of the box and stands there, leg bent at the knee, until John, transfixed, gives her a leg up.

'Sorry.'

'What for? Come over to check out my two mares on Thursday; my father's away buying hay. He doesn't like Englishmen.'

'I'm not English. I'm a Kerry man,' says John.

She smiles and trots out of the yard.

John has managed to banish Eileen, Drimnamore, Derriquin and Kerry to a remote and unvisited corner of his mind. He has had one short letter from Josephine, thanking him for her share of the money from the sale, and sent a reply describing his new life at Burke's Fort. Neither letter mentioned the terrible weeks they had lived through together.

When he receives a letter with a Kerry postmark towards the end of April, he recognizes Josephine's neat schoolmistress's copperplate and remembers her insistence on a Waverley pen and Stephen's blue-black ink. Even her crossings-out, two exactly parallel lines, are neat.

> Driminabeg,
> Drimnamore,
> County Kerry

Dear John,

I am sorry to have been so long in writing, but the post has been almost non-existent this past two years, and I can only hope you get this letter in due course. We have been isolated in Drimnamore for many, many months. No post, no telegrams, no newspapers (plenty of rumours), roads trenched, railways and bridges blown up. We get an occasional visit from a coastal steamer with much needed supplies, but most of us live on what we can grow or exchange.

Since you left, Askive, Derreen and Dromquinna have been burned. Anyone with a car has had it commandeered by one side or the other. The Stokes, the Butlers and the Hartleys have gone to England; there are not more than six or seven of us in church of a Sunday, and we get a curate from Kenmare once a month, and then only if travel conditions permit.

Most of Kerry seems to be opposed to the Treaty. It has split several families, not least the Doyles. Mikey has joined the Free State Army, Donal is with the Republicans in Listowel. If the Treaty hadn't been so identified with Michael Collins and the Cork men, I believe Kerry men would have found it easy to approve. Terrible things have been done by both sides. Most recently the Free Staters made ten captured Republicans stand over a land-mine at Ballyseedy Cross, which they then detonated, killing all but one. This in reprisal for the death of five of their own men at Knocknagoshel. And so it goes on.

The school continues although attendance is ragged owing to the state of the roads. None of us have been paid by the state for over a year, and we don't know where to ask. Father Michael is friendly enough, but all save a few in Drimnamore avoid me if they can. I told anyone who would listen that your mother tried to save lives, as did Father Michael, but the preferred version is different.

Farm money is very low, as there is no means of getting anything to market, and one farm convoy guarded by Staters was ambushed by Republicans on the way to Kenmare and a soldier killed and a farmer from Waterville wounded and his horse dead.

I am sorry to sound so gloomy, but that is how things are, never to be the same again. I wish all was as before, but as your mother used to say, 'Beggars would ride'.

Thank you again for the money, which has been a great help. Ambrose O'Halloran is keeping well, and tells me to tell you he remembers your first snipe as if it were yesterday.

Your affectionate cousin,
Josephine Deborah

John smiles at Josephine's use of both her Christian names. The letter brings back the memories that he had successfully banished and it is two or three days before he can write a reply.

He posts the letter in Maryborough, and on the way back calls on Mannion's farm to see the mares and Grania. The farm is a long, low building with a handsome Georgian fanlight over a central door leading straight into the kitchen.

'We've horses, cattle, sheep, and you can see the chickens,' says Grania as she comes out, shooing away a brown hen who tries to follow John in.

The kitchen is a surprise to John; two of the walls are solid bookshelves, the books well used. John picks out a book at random, a copy of Daniel O'Connell's speeches.

'That's one of Mannion's,' says Grania as she gives him a cup of tea. 'The politics are his, the poetry and the novels are mine.'

They talk about horses and bloodlines for a couple of minutes, long enough for John to realize that Grania knows more about breeding than he does. They go to the nearby paddock where her two mares are out at grass. They are both strong half-breds sired by decent thoroughbred stallions.

'Middle-weight hunters, that's what we're after. What do you think?'

'They'll do. They'll be suited by The Elector.'

'Is there a special price for local farmers? Fifty's a bit steep.'

'You'll get a hundred and fifty each for their yearlings,' says John, laughing. 'I told you we have a waiting list.'

'Ninety pounds for the two – cash in your hand now,' says Grania, who goes into the kitchen and comes back with a handful of notes. 'No foal, no fee.'

John takes the money, and as he goes to put it in his back pocket Grania takes him by the hand.

'Call yourself a Kerry man? You're forgetting the luck-penny,' she says, taking a ten-pound note back. 'I'll have a kiss as well,' and kisses John on the cheek. 'There, that's done. I'll bring the mares over as soon as they're in season,' she says, and goes back into the farmhouse.

15.

THAT NIGHT JOHN doesn't sleep well. He is twenty-three and the cautious kisses with Dublin girls at the Drimnamore Hotel, the more adventurous kisses in Big House gardens at hunt balls, the time in the summer house with Nesta Fitzmaurice, have not prepared him for the sudden strength of his feelings for Grania.

Grania had kissed him. Perhaps it was only the luck-penny. She'd put her hand on his arm. Perhaps it was only the beauty of The Elector. He falls asleep thinking of her green eyes, her black hair, her lips on his cheek, her long fingers lying on his sleeve, the feel of her knee when he boosted her onto her cob. He dreams of her clothed, half clothed, naked, coming to him, turning him away.

Three days later he has a ride at Punchestown in a novice chase; Paddy Brennan is putting him up on Hunting Cap, a promising five-year-old point-to-pointer.

'He's ready to cope with those fences; he's a careful jumper, so he is. You qualified him with the hounds, you've ridden him out often enough. He needs a jockey who won't nag at him, won't keep telling him when to take off. And you've schooled him over our banks and stone walls.'

Schooling is one thing, taking those fences at racing pace quite another, thinks John. He walks around the course twice on the morning of the race, looking carefully at the unique mixture of obstacles, two regulation brush fences, all the rest stone walls or banks. The stone walls are solid blocks of stone up to three feet, then a dividing layer of turf, then a foot of rounded stones each no bigger than a fist.

'They'll rattle through these all right,' says Brennan, picking up a stone and hefting it, then putting it back.

They come to the big double bank – five feet high, six feet six across, with a six-foot ditch on take-off and a four-foot ditch on landing.

'You'll need to check him into the bank, give him time to take a full stride on the top. I've seen too many horses treat it like a single bank and wind up in the ditch on the far side. The water jump's like any other, and the single banks are all on and off, though I've seen a bold jumper fly a single and get away with it. Not recommended. Watch out for the plain drop – there's no fence in front of it, only a white pole on the ground to tell you there's a five-foot drop on the other side.'

There are two thousand or more people in the Punchestown crowd and an army of bookmakers, a third of them from Dublin. John's is the third race; he watches the first out in the country by the banks and the stone walls. He comes back past the grandstand, a ramshackle affair of concrete steps, no seats, a curved tin roof and a crowded bar at the rear, still a big step up from the carts, carriages and cars that carry the spectators at point-to-points. The three-card-trick men, the trick-of-the-loop men and the thimble-riggers with their vanishing peas are doing good business. Above them the green, white and orange flag of the new Free State flutters bravely in the breeze alongside the flag of the Kildare Hunt, whose meeting this is. In the enclosure are many of the British soldiers who made up a substantial part of the race-going and race-riding crowd all over Ireland, but since the Treaty they are in civilian clothes. There are men in uniform, but these are Irishmen in the new green serge, brown boots, leggings and harp buttons of the Irish Free State's National Army.

He buys a racecard for the pleasure of seeing his name in print; 'Mr John Burke', it says, opposite 'Hunting Cap'. On the cover, 'Ladies are requested not to wear native fox furs.' The bookies have Hunting Cap as second favourite at five to two.

'Lough Corrib at even money is the one to watch; the bookies have got this right for once. Hunt our boy round on the first circuit, stay out of trouble, and take close order with Lough Corrib three out. He's in the green and red silks. But you and Hunting Cap will work it out. Races aren't often won by trainers' instructions.'

John has a hollow feeling in his stomach as he changes into his racing silks with the other jockeys. They are all amateurs, and he recognizes and says hello to one or two from the point-to-point circuit. No one talks much. In the parade ring he and Paddy Brennan are joined by Charles, who seems to know everyone inside and outside the ring. To John's surprise and pleasure Cis is with him.

'Take care,' she says, crossing herself as she speaks.

John checks the girth and the stirrups, swings up into the saddle and leaves the ring. As he starts to canter down to the start he sees Grania by the rails; she gives him a smile and a wave. Who is she with, John wonders, and then the race blots everything else out of his mind.

It is a small field of only nine horses. The starter has some difficulty getting them into line, and John and Hunting Cap are left two or three lengths behind. They take the first circuit steadily, avoiding trouble on the outside of the field. Hunting Cap is unaffected by the rattle of flying stones as they take the walls and pricks up his ears at the noise of the crowd when they pass the grandstand for the first time. As they go out into the country, John has a double handful and is beginning to enjoy himself. By this stage there are only four in with a chance.

At the big double there is a near disaster; the horse two lengths in front falls on landing and sprawls to his right, unshipping his jockey, and only a quick pick-up by John and clever footwork by Hunting Cap prevent them being brought down. They lose a good three lengths, and John resigns himself to finishing second or third. But two fences out the rank outsider alongside the favourite falls, and the green and red colours of Lough Corrib start to come back. As the two horses go into the last fence together John asks Hunting Cap to stand back and reach for the fence, which he does. They land half a length clear of Lough Corrib and hold the advantage to the winning post. In a daze of mud-spattered, exhausted glory he trots back to the winner's enclosure, where he is slapped on the back by an overjoyed Paddy Brennan, congratulated by Charles and hugged by Cis. He weighs in and three minutes later hears the confirmation over the loudspeaker, 'Winner All Right'.

He leaves the tent through a cheerful, back-slapping crowd and is making his way to his car when Grania comes up and hugs him.

'My money was on you; I can afford the stud fee now.'

John smiles.

'You can't have bet that much, surely?'

'Twenty-five pounds, and I got on early at four to one.'

'I'm glad I didn't know before.'

'I've always liked the horse – he's the type for banks and walls, and I hoped you'd be smart enough to let him do the business. Fair play to you, you drove him into the last fence hard, and that was the race over. And you did well at the big double. Will I see you at the dance tonight?'

'I haven't been asked.'

'Asked? It's not one of your hunt balls. You just turn up and buy a ticket.'

John drives home via the yard and checks Hunting Cap over with Paddy Brennan.

'He'll be stiff in the morning. He's a small cut on the near fore, but he's eaten up well and drunk a river dry. Here, you take the cup – I've got the prize money. And the stable had a good bet.'

John goes home, falls asleep in the bath and again over supper up at the Fort.

'Off to bed with you,' says Cis.

John walks slowly back to his cottage and looks in on The Elector. It's a long drive to Kildare, he thinks, and then remembers Grania's bright eyes. He changes into his dinner jacket, drives slowly over to Kildare, buys a ticket and goes into the Leinster Arms. On his way to the ballroom John has to pass through the long, busy bar, and is immediately embraced by the jockey who fell in front of him at the big double.

'We had you beat barring the fall,' he says. 'Any road, let me buy you a drink.'

There are many happy gamblers to help him celebrate his win. Paddy Brennan is holding court at one end of the bar; he beckons John over and insists on another bottle of champagne.

'Big win for the stable,' he says, his face red with the warmth of the room and the drink, his voice hoarse and only a little slurred. Paddy smiles at the circle around him, all happy to relive the story of the race any number of times as long as the drink keeps flowing.

John leaves the bar to look for Grania in the ballroom of the hotel. This is past its glory days, decorated, but not recently, in gold and red; heavy velvet curtains are drawn across its tall windows. A ten-piece dance band is playing quicksteps, waltzes and foxtrots from a gallery set above the dance floor. The royal arms – not for much longer, thinks John – are the only ornament on the wall. The room is filled with a noisy, cheerful crowd, many of whom have spilled over directly from the racecourse. Half the guests are in dinner jackets, half in tweeds or corduroys.

He eventually finds Grania in a large party around a table on the far side of the dance floor. She is wearing a dark green dress that shows off her white shoulders, her black hair gathered by a tortoiseshell comb, her lips red. She stands up, takes his hand and says to her table, 'This is John, stallion man at Burke's Fort and winner of the third race. He's made me a rich woman, and I owe him a dance.'

They push their way onto the crowded floor, where luckily there isn't enough room to test John's quickstep. The band is playing 'My Blue Heaven'. Grania is almost as tall as John; he holds her close, her hand on his shoulder. Their cheeks touch and stay together. Her fingers gently stroke the back of his neck. The dance is over all too soon for John.

'I must go back to my table,' says Grania. 'Eamonn thinks he's my beau. I'll be over to see you with Tess next week.'

Is Eamonn her beau? wonders John as she walks back to her table. As he leaves the dance floor he is pulled into the bar by an insistent Paddy Brennan.

'Just one for the road,' he says, speaking slowly and deliberately. He is swaying a little. John sips a glass of Guinness.

'We've drunk them dry of champagne,' says Paddy.

The last waltz is played; John can't see Grania on the crowded dance floor. The music finishes, there is a roll of drums and the Master of Ceremonies announces, 'The National Anthem – The Soldiers' Song'. There is one quickly silenced boo as the band strikes up the unfamiliar tune. Although the bar is quiet, it is clear not everyone knows the words; some are singing in Gaelic, some in English. John misses the beginning, hears,

> *... Sworn to be free,*
> *No more our ancient sireland*
> *Shall shelter the despot or the slave.*

As he drives carefully home he remembers Grania's fingers stroking the back of his neck.

Three days later she rides over in the morning on her cob, leading her mare.

'She's been ready for twenty-four hours, but I couldn't leave the farm yesterday.'

'We've no teaser stallion. We'll have to leave it to The Elector to excite Tess. I'll get Sean to come and hold her. You can have a cup of tea in the cottage if you like.'

'I don't like. She's not Sean's mare. I'll hold her,' and, seeing the look on John's face, adds, 'I *am* a farmer's daughter.'

They take Tess into the covering stall, and John gets her ready, bandaging her tail, tying it forward, covering her quarters with the heavy leather blanket. As he swabs the mare clean, Grania, impressed, says, 'She's used to being turned out in the field with the stallion and told to get on with it.'

John puts on the bitted head-collar and leads The Elector out of his box into the yard.

'Come on now, be a good boy, don't let us down,' he whispers.

And The Elector is a good boy, whinnying softly, circling and sniffing Tess for a few minutes. Tess is skittish at first, moving away from the stallion and pulling hard. John is surprised that Grania is able to keep hold of her. They take the mare into the covering stall, where Grania talks to Tess in a soothing voice and strokes her neck. After a first failed attempt, The Elector rises up and shudders violently into the mare.

'That's a good cover. You did well to steady her. We'll put her in the visitors' box and cover her again tomorrow to make sure. I'll fork some hay down for her.'

They put the two horses away, and John climbs up the outside ladder to the hayloft. He pushes a double armful of hay down into the manger below, and turns to find Grania standing beside him. His heart leaps; he puts his arms around her and kisses her ears, her nose, her cheeks, her mouth. 'Like this,' she says, parting his lips with hers and pulling him down to the soft pile of hay. Her skin smells of lavender; John presses his mouth against her neck. 'This might be more comfortable,' says Grania, and it is more comfortable, more comforting than anything John has ever known. She runs her hand down to loosen John's belt, and holds him, then strokes him to a climax. He touches her in return and she says, 'There, just there,' and closes around his hand. They lie together, holding each other, until Grania says, 'Mannion'll come looking if I'm not back soon,' and they climb back down the ladder.

This time John knows to give her a leg up into the saddle.

'Thank you, Sean, my dear one. And I misled you – I've never seen a covering before, it's not thought suitable for young Catholic virgins. And they're right.' Grania smiles, leans down and kisses the top of John's head and trots out of the yard.

16.

Tess is covered for the second time on the following day, not out of necessity but because John wanted to be sure of seeing Grania again. He goes up to the Fort to hand over the eighty pounds to Charles.

'Where's this come from? They'll be late enough foals.'

'Two decent mares from Mannion's. They don't mind a late foal, they're not for racing. Hunters is what they're after. Mannion's daughter brought the first mare over the day before yesterday.'

'Saw her at the races. She's a handsome girl, I'd say. I hear she's about to get engaged to a lawyer in Maryborough. Did you see her at the dance in Kildare?'

News travels fast in the County, thinks John.

'I did. She was well escorted, but I had a dance.'

'One dance is probably enough with Johnnie Mannion's daughter. He was at Boland's Mill during the Easter Rising, and then became the IRA's battalion commander round here. Bought his farm off the Nugents only three years since; two hundred acres for three thousand pounds. Nugent told me he paid cash.'

'Where did he get the money?'

'I doubt he got it from dealing in cattle. Boasted in the Dáil that he'd robbed twelve Post Offices in a fortnight. He's an out-and-out Shinner, hates the Treaty. He'd have burned the Fort down long ago if it wasn't for Cis. By the by, shouldn't it be a hundred?'

'Ninety for the two. And she took a ten-pound luck-penny.'

'That sounds like a Mannion.'

John walks back to the cottage, his head full of Grania in the green dress, Grania's luck-penny kiss, Grania in the hayloft, Grania kissing the top of his head. And of the lawyer from Maryborough.

The next day he comes into the stallion yard after putting The Elector out in his paddock, and sees a short, heavy-set man leading Tess out of her box.

'What are you up to with the mare?'

'Up to? I'm from Mannion's. I've been sent to collect her. McCarthy's the name.' He doesn't hold out his hand.

'Have you indeed? I know nothing about it.'

'Well, you know now. I'll be riding her back; I walked over with the bridle, but I'd like to borrow a saddle.'

John is about to tell him to go to blazes, and then remembers the saddle will need to be collected.

'I'll find one in the tack room.'

They go into the main yard, not speaking; McCarthy saddles the mare and rides her away.

Two days later he rides over to Mannion's in the morning to collect the saddle. When Grania comes to the front door John takes her by the shoulders and kisses her on the mouth. After a moment she pushes him away.

'He'll kill us both if he sees us carrying on – he's only up in the long field, he'll be back in a minute.'

'Carrying on? Is that what we've been doing? It meant more to me than that, the dance and the hayloft.'

The look on Grania's face softens. 'And to me. Take the saddle and be off with you before he comes back. Meet me at the Trafalgar Folly at around ten next Thursday. He'll be away to the market at Maryborough all morning. And I dare say he has other business there.'

She goes back into the house, hands over the saddle and looks around before giving him a quick kiss on the cheek. They're making a bogey-man out of Mannion, he thinks. We're both adults, we can choose what we do and who we see. It's the twentieth century, not the eighteenth.

John has ridden past the Folly but never been inside.

'The Folly was built by my great-grandfather to mark the battle of Trafalgar,' Charles tells him. 'He was one of Nelson's band of brothers, captained the *Bellerophon*, seventy-four guns, at Trafalgar. Lucky with the prize-money, spent most of it enlarging the estate and building the Folly. There was a story that he used it to entertain a woman from the village. We used to go there for picnics when we were young. Cis won't go near the place, thinks it's a house of ill repute.'

John visits the Folly the day after returning with the saddle. Hidden away in a wooded dell, it has the feeling of a grand doll's house, two rooms, one above the other, each a perfect twelve-foot cube, with a single-storey cube on each side linked to the main house by a four-foot-high wall. There is an external double staircase curving left and right up to a door on the first floor. Above the door is carved 'TRAFALGAR 1805' and on the linking walls are the names of the ships at the battle – *Victory, Mars, Temeraire, Bellerophon, Ajax, Revenge* . . . John reads the sonorous names out loud, stops when he realizes his mare is the only audience.

The upstairs room is dry and bare, well lit on each side by two windows. John organizes a bunch of birch twigs into a makeshift broom, sweeps the floor into the fireplace, and lays and lights a fire. The wood burns quickly and there is a sudden roar as generations of rooks' nests in the chimney catch fire. Alarmed, John runs outside, but the nests soon burn out, and there isn't enough soot to set the chimney alight.

The room below is almost as bare except for a collection of old cushions, badly holed by moths, left there by past picnickers. In one corner there is an iron water pump and a Belfast sink. After a few wheezes the pump yields up first brown and then clear water. John waits until the fire dies out, collects up more wood and re-lays it, and goes home well pleased with his work.

On Thursday morning he is up early, takes The Elector out to his paddock, checks the mares and foals, and saddles up his own mare. He straps a tight roll of three blankets behind the saddle and rides over to the Folly, where he is sitting outside the first-floor front door, legs dangling, when Grania arrives. She ties up her horse and runs up the stairs to meet him; they hold each other in a long embrace.

'Look what I've done,' he says, leading her into the room. He has made a bed out of the cushions and blankets, put some honeysuckle in a white enamelled tin mug on the mantelpiece, and the fire is lit.

She laughs. 'You've been the busy one. And it's clear what you have in mind. They say that one of the Burkes used the Folly to meet his fancy woman from the village. Is that what I am?' dropping his hand suddenly. 'Your fancy woman from the village?'

'No, it is not. You're my girl, you're my only girl. I . . .' And Grania silences him with a kiss before he can say any more.

Later, when they are lying on the blankets and the cushions, John asks her about her father.

'He's IRA all right, and a hard man, a leader. He's killed men, I'm sure, but so have most soldiers, and he wanted to see Ireland free. He doesn't think we've got there yet. He hates the Oath, hates the Six Counties separated from us, doesn't believe in the Free State, he's a de Valera man. When I was at university in Dublin, he was on the run – he'd turn up unannounced every now and then, take some money and some food, and then be off again. I'd hoped all that was over. And now it's Irishmen killing Irishmen.'

'You were at Trinity?'

'You should know by now Trinity's not for us Papists, on pain of excommunication. I was at University College, Irish Literature.'

'I've not read much, a bit of Swift and Yeats.'

'That's Anglo-Irish literature. I mean poetry and prose written in Gaelic. It's an undiscovered world – you should visit it. Have you any Gaelic?'

'A little. My mother was fluent.'

'Good for her. It's a wonderful language for poetry; it translates pretty well.'

She looks steadily into John's eyes, and says in a soft voice,

> *I thought, O my love! you were so –*
> *As the moon is, or sun on a fountain*
> *And I thought after that you were snow,*
> *The bright snow on top of the mountain;*
> *And I thought after that, you were more*
> *Like God's lamp shining to find me,*
> *Or the bright star of knowledge before,*
> *And the star of knowledge behind me.*

That's from 'The Love Songs of Connacht'. Douglas Hyde translated it; he's a Prod, God help him. It's even better in the original.'

'It's lovely. *As the moon is, or sun on a fountain.* It's how I feel about you.' He kisses her.

'Is it indeed?' Grania looks happy, jumps up, straightens her clothes and heads for the door.

'Next Thursday?' says John.

'Next Thursday.'

For John these stolen mornings are a source of anticipation for most of the week, delight for two or three hours, and a sharp sense of loss as he rides away.

He finds a Dun Emer Press edition of *The Love Songs of Connacht* in a second-hand bookshop in Maryborough and gives it to Grania when they next meet at the Folly.

'It's in English and Irish,' he says as he gives it to her, and she reads out the poem she had first recited in both languages.

'You don't have to choose,' she tells him.

Later he tells Grania about the murder of his mother and William, his fruitless search, the fire, the visit to Tomas in Kilmainham.

'It's a terrible story. I'm sorry about it, sorry for us all,' Grania says, and holds him tight. 'And Mannion would have done that sort of thing in his day.'

'I thought I was a Kerry man, even after the killing and the fire. Right up to the day I left I thought we belonged there. I'd spent most of my life in Kerry. I knew every inch of the Drimnamore River. Tomas and I used to poach it with worms, although he used to say you can't poach your own river, so what's the fun in that? I knew all the bogs, knew when the snipe and the woodcock would be in. I could sail around Garinish Island and Rossdohan blindfolded.'

He blows his nose hard.

'I knew everyone in Drimnamore. We employed twenty-seven men and women on the estate – what's become of them? What's happening to the oyster beds? They'll need to be order-ing the spats from France now. Kerry's such a beautiful county, rain or shine – wild, big, not calm and contented like Queen's County.'

Grania gives him a little dig in the ribs.

'I know, Queen's County is better in many ways. The Famine here was bad enough, but it was far worse in the South-West. You pass roofless cabins every couple of miles along the Kerry roads. But you don't have the mountains, the estuaries, the big waves of the Atlantic. One day we'll go there together.'

Grania doesn't reply, kisses him instead.

'Grania,' says John, stroking her cheek. 'It's a great name. I love the sound of it.'

'She was the daughter of Cormac mac Art, high king in Tara. You're my Diarmuid.' She kisses John again, and goes on, 'Grania was promised by her father to Fionn, the leader of the Fianna, even though Fionn was far too old for her. So there's a great feast in Tara before the wedding, and Grania, pale and silent, suddenly sees the handsome Diarmuid among the guests. She takes the loving cup to him, whispers, "My heart is filled with longing for you," and lays a *geis* on him, a spell of obligation. Diarmuid has no choice but to go with her, even though he owes loyalty to Fionn. So that night while the guests are asleep they steal away. They are pursued for a year and a day by Fionn and his two hounds, Brann and Sgeolan, but Fionn never lays eyes on the lovers. After many narrow escapes Fionn and Cormac allow them to live in peace. They have four handsome sons.'

'That's a happy enough ending.'

'But it's not the ending. Fionn and a small band of the Fianna visit Diarmuid, and they decide to go hunting around Ben Bulben. Rash of Diarmuid, as another *geis* had been laid on him years before, forbidding him to hunt the boar. Perhaps he forgot. Anyhow, during the hunt Diarmuid kills a huge boar, but not before it gives him a terrible gash in the thigh. The boar is his half-brother, by the way. Fionn finds Diarmuid dying. Although he has the power of healing, his old resentment is still strong, so he returns with the healing water too late and Diarmuid dies. Years later, Grania's hatred of Fionn fades away and she marries him and goes to live in Kildare.'

'I like the beginning, and the four handsome sons. I'm not so happy about the boar, and the way she marries Fionn,' says John.

Grania smiles and jumps up. 'Enough legends. There are no boars in Ireland any more, so you're safe enough. And perhaps it's you that have laid the *geis* on me.'

John kisses her and she rides away.

The Folly is becoming more comfortable; in one of the side buildings John finds a wooden table, a couple of serviceable chairs and some more cushions. He brings over a dark red carriage rug that he bought in Abbeyleix.

'It looks like a Turkish seraglio now,' says Grania, adding as she sees the crestfallen look on John's face, 'I've always wanted to be the only woman in the harem.' She pulls him down onto the rug.

They are never together more than a couple of hours, barely long enough to talk, barely long enough to give each other pleasure. When John tries to go further, Grania pushes him away and sits up.

'I want you too, properly,' she says. 'I dream about you, about having you inside me. It's not hell-fire I'm worried about, although when I go to confession I don't tell the priest everything, just the sins of pride and envy, and that gives him enough to be getting on with. If I told him about us I'd be saying Hail Marys until Christmas. But I can't risk getting pregnant. Mannion would kill the both of us. And I like what we do, even if it's getting off at Rathmines.'

'Rathmines?'

'That's what we convent girls call not going all the way. It's the last station before Dublin. I'd like to go there with you again, please.'

The next Thursday Grania brings lunch, hot soup in a thermos, slices of ham, some cheese, a couple of apples, two bottles of Guinness. They sit at the little table, drinking Guinness out of tin mugs. John plucks up his courage and asks about Eamonn, not certain he wants to hear the answer.

'Charles says you're about to get engaged to a lawyer in Maryborough.'

'It's none of his business, and I'm not sure it's any of yours. They're all well ahead of themselves. They don't have enough to think about. You saw Eamonn at the dance. He's decent, good-looking, rather dull. He's a Pioneer, and that counts against a man in my book. He never touches a drop, not even this stuff.'

Grania takes a sip of her Guinness.

'Mannion would like me to marry him sure enough, see me settled with a professional man and surrounded by Catholic children. Funny, that, when you think about his life – farm labourer, gunman, didn't have a feather to fly with until three years ago. Scrimped to send me to a convent school, thrilled when I went to university, likes the fact that I speak Gaelic better than he does. And now he's a member of Dáil Éireann, although he followed Dev out and hasn't been back.'

She takes another sip of her Guinness.

'I'll tell you something else. He's enjoyed the war, God help him. Commanding the IRA round here, and the revolver in his pocket, means that he's respected and feared. People look up to you Ascendancy Prods automatically. I don't mean you, my dear one, but you've got a confidence you were born with. Which I like, because it hasn't turned to arrogance. Mannion's earned his respect. He doesn't have to touch his cap to anyone.'

'Do you love him?'

'Of course I do,' she says, and pauses. 'Although he's not easy. He gets angry, and takes it out on whoever's handy.'

She pauses, rubs the back of her neck, then goes on.

'I'm a little afraid of him, if I'm honest. He's thought about raising his hand to me once or twice, but never done it. He sees everything in black and white, or green against red, white and blue.'

'I meant Eamonn. Have you ever . . .' and John's mouth goes dry before he can finish.

'You needn't worry; I don't love him, and Eamonn would faint if I opened my mouth for a kiss. Here, let me show you something else he and I haven't done together.'

She pulls him down onto the rug, loosens his belt, grazes her cheek along his stomach, and takes him in her mouth. Then she says, 'And you can kiss me there too,' and shows him how and where.

'Glory,' she says when he has stopped. 'That took me well beyond Rathmines.'

Later John watches as she trots away down the ride. He sets off for his cottage, passes a wild apple tree, plucks a branch of blossom, turns around and canters after Grania. When he catches her up she has dropped the reins and her horse is ambling along; she is singing quietly to herself, 'O my dark Rosaleen, Do not sigh, do not weep.'

John pulls up beside her, kisses her and gives her the white and pink branch.

'Sean, you're my dear one,' she says. They ride along slowly, knees touching and holding hands, until they reach the top of the little hill looking down on the Mannion farm.

'Be off with you now,' and Grania leans across for a final kiss.

The next time they meet they leave the horses tied up outside the Folly and walk slowly through the woods, holding hands, stopping to kiss each other. Grania picks a bunch of primroses, which she puts in the tin mug above the fireplace. When they have finished lunch, John stands up, holds her hand and takes a step towards the cushions. Grania shakes her head.

'The English have landed, it's the wrong time of the month,' she says, and John is happy at the reason for the morning's celibacy. He sits down again and asks Grania about her mother.

'She walked out on Mannion after the Easter Rising. She couldn't stand the coming and going in the middle of the night, not knowing where the next meal was coming from. I went with her at first to Mountrath, but then my sister got married and I moved to the farm to look after Mannion and the horses. I go over there once or twice a month. She's a teacher in the elementary school, teaches Gaelic. She got me going on the language, sent me away to summer school every year in the Gaeltacht, in Connemara. I love it there, it's maybe as beautiful as Kerry. Wild enough, and it has those big Atlantic waves.'

'You won't go there this year, surely.'

'Ah, my dear one, I will, I must. I speak no Gaelic when I'm here, read little enough, and I still have work to do on my MA thesis. It has a grand title, "The impact of *The Lament for Art O'Leary* on the poetry and politics of modern Ireland".'

'Art O'Leary?'

'Shame on you, Sean, and it written by a Kerry woman from Derrynane, just down the road from Derriquin. Eileen O'Connell, aunt of the Liberator. Her husband, Art O'Leary, was murdered by one of yours – all right, by an Englishman – who wanted his horse. It sounds best in Irish:

Mo ghrá go daingean tu!
Lá dá bhfaca tu
Ag ceann tí an mhargaidh,
Thug mo shúil aire dhuit . . .

'I know Mo ghrá, and mo mhuirnin. My love, my darling, I'll find eight weeks without you hard.'

'I will send postcards, although they won't be very loving, as they all get read and passed around at the Post Office. And when I come back . . .'

She doesn't finish.

'And when you come back?'

'Then we'll see. I'll not be here next Thursday; I spend most of next week with my mother. I go to Connemara two days after I get back from Mountrath.'

They hold each other for a long time outside. Grania's face is wet with tears, which John kisses away.

A day later John goes to take The Elector out to his paddock and finds him lying down in his box. He doesn't get up until John gets Mick to help him.

'Looks like colic,' says Mick.

'I looked in on him last night and he was fine. And he's only getting a peck of hay, no oats.'

'It'll walk off, sure.'

They take the horse up to the paddock; his eyes are dull, his head heavy. Once through the gate he stands still where he normally canters away.

'He's not himself at all. I'll get Charles to come, see what he thinks.'

Charles comes and looks worried. 'If it's colic it's bad – best get the big vet over from the Curragh. He's your man for a real problem. I'll phone him from the house. You take the horse back to the box and stay with him.'

The big vet doesn't come until the afternoon. The Elector is back in his box, head lowered and swinging from side to side, clearly in pain. Now and again he makes a low harsh groan, a sound John has never heard from a horse.

'If it's colic it should be better by the morning. See if he'll take this in a bucket of water. Keep him on his feet if you can, but if he goes down, leave him be.'

By the evening The Elector is down again. John spends the night in the box, watching for any signs of recovery. There are none. The vet comes back, looks the horse over, takes his temperature, and says, 'It's not colic, more's the pity. It's grass sickness.'

'Grass sickness? We've the best grass in the county, and there's no ragwort in our paddocks.'

'It's not the grass, it's a virus and we don't know much about it. I've only ever seen half a dozen cases.'

'What's the cure?'

The vet looks first at John, then at The Elector and says, 'There is no cure. It kills a horse in forty-eight hours or less. The kindest thing . . .'

John turns his head away; he doesn't want to hear the kindest thing.

'He's in great pain, you can see that, hear it in his breathing. And it'll get worse.'

Charles comes down ten minutes later. 'We had a case here six years ago,' he says to John. 'The first and I hoped the last. It's nothing you've done, or not done.'

'Best do it out in the yard if you can get him up,' says the vet.

John, in a daze, scarcely believing what is happening, gets The Elector out in the yard with Mick and Sean.

'You hold his head up, and mind you stand clear when he goes.'

The vet holds the bolt gun to The Elector's forehead, there is a sharp crack, and the stallion goes down sideways onto the cobbles, twitches and lies still.

'I'll get Timmy to come tomorrow and take him away for the hounds,' Charles says, sees the look on John's face and adds, 'We'll bury his heart by the big oak alongside The Archduke.'

John, unable to hold back his tears, walks over to his cottage.

The next day John watches as Timmy, Mick and Sean haul The Elector's body up onto a trailer and drive away to the kennels. By now the dead stallion's legs are stiff and straight like a child's horse that has fallen over. He tries to remember The Elector proud and gleaming in the Dublin Show ring, but terrible images of the stallion being cut up and used to feed the hounds are hard to force away. Cis comes and knocks on his door in the evening, but he doesn't answer.

John spends the next day looking for ragwort in the paddock. He wants to be sure that it is a virus that has killed The Elector, and not carelessness on his part. The paddock grass is clear. All day he is unable to rid his mind of the stiff dead body of the stallion. He goes to bed early, and is lying awake when he hears a horse come into the yard; a few minutes later Grania comes into his bedroom. He jumps out of bed and she holds him, his head buried in her shoulder. After a minute or two John lights the oil lamp.

'We've never been naked,' says Grania.

She undresses quickly, and they stand together in the lamp-light, looking at each other, touching each other. John bends down, runs his hands from her heels to her calves, the backs of her thighs, her buttocks, strokes the channel of her back, then lifts her into bed. A few moments later Grania gives a little cry, and says, 'That's where you belong.' She stays until morning.

'You'll be all right now?' she says as she leaves.

'We'll be all right.'

17.

JOHN SPENDS THE next three months working around the stud, repairing fences, painting gates, replacing old water troughs and cleaning every saddle, bridle and bit until they are almost worn away. Charles and he go to look at possible replacements for The Elector, but don't see anything they like. Charles will consider only a stallion from The Archduke's bloodline.

'That two-year-old up in the home paddock might do,' says Charles. 'He's by The Elector out of a good mare, and he looks the part. But he'll have to do something on the racecourse first. He'll go into training next month.'

John continues to ride out most mornings at Paddy Brennan's yard. He wins another hunter chase and is placed a couple of times on Hunting Cap, but the horse pulls up lame after a race at Naas and is put away for the season.

John wants to forget The Elector; he wants to remember his night with Grania. He gets only a single unsigned postcard from Connemara, a view of the Atlantic and the Cliffs of Moher; on it Grania has written, 'Passion or conquest, wander where they will, Attend upon them still.'

The words make John happy; he is not sure what the Post Office will make of them.

Towards the end of July he is called up to Dublin to see his solicitor in Leeson Street.

'We're making good progress with the claim. You're entitled to compensation for the burning of Derriquin and its contents; we've asked for twenty thousand, and you might wind up with ten. Your mother was a careful woman; she maintained a detailed inventory of all the pictures, silver, books and furniture in the castle, and all the livestock and farm machinery.'

John is shown the ledger, bound in dark green cloth, with 'Derriquin' in gold letters on its cover. Seeing Eileen's neat writing brings back memories of his mother at her desk in the Derriquin library, her face illuminated by the soft light of the oil lamp, her fingers brushing a loose strand of hair from her cheek. John has to blink hard to avoid tears. He stands up, walks over to the window, looks at the busy street below for a moment.

'How long will the claim take to settle?'

'Probably a year or two. They're snowed under with claims. We can arrange an advance against the final payment if that would help.'

John declines the offer, but he goes away pleased. He's never felt he needed more money, but he has started to think about Grania's return.

Two days later John is cleaning out the visitors' stables when Mick comes into the yard looking worried.

'He'd like to see you up at the Fort now.'

John walks up to the house and sees an unfamiliar car standing outside the front door; he recognizes the driver, the man McCarthy who had come to collect Grania's mare. He has a moment of elation, followed by a feeling of unease when he sees Mary the kitchen maid. She is not normally on duty at the front door.

'They're all in the dining room,' she says.

At one end of the mahogany dining table, below the full-length portrait of Nathaniel Burke in the full wig and red robes of a judge of the Prerogative Court, next to Grania, is a man he has never seen before. Johnnie Mannion is strongly built, with dark hair, bushy eyebrows, brown eyes, big hands that he opens and closes on the table in front of him. The knuckles and backs of his hands are covered in black hair. Grania has been crying and there is a bruise on her cheekbone, which she hides with her hand. She looks at John for a moment, then looks away. At the other end of the table are Charles and Cis.

John goes towards Grania and is pulled back by Charles. 'Better sit with us and hear what Mannion has to say.'

'It's Mister Mannion. And I won't take long. Grania's pregnant, and it's down to you, Mister John Burke.'

John looks astonished, then smiles.

'It's no laughing matter. You seduced my daughter.'

Grania looks up, manages a little smile of her own, and says, 'That's not . . .' John notices that her lower lip is cut and swollen.

'That's enough. I'm doing the talking. I know all about the love nest at the Folly, and it's not the first time that it's been used by a Burke for this sort of carry-on. You are never to see her again. And you'd better leave Ireland, else I won't answer for the safety of this house nor anyone in it.'

'There's no need for that kind of threatening talk, Mister Mannion,' says Cis.

'I'll marry Grania. I love her.' John stands up, and Charles puts a restraining hand on his shoulder.

Grania begins to cry quietly and holds her face in her hands.

'I'll see you both dead first,' says Mannion. 'You're an English Protestant, the son of an informer. Your mother was responsible for the death of thirteen Volunteers, all good men. Grania's to marry Eamonn McCann next week, and she's lucky he'll take her and your bastard. I want you to hear it from her.'

Grania takes her hands away from her face, looks at John, says, 'It's true. It's what will happen. Else you'll be killed and this house burned.' She buries her face in her hands again.

'She wouldn't say this if you hadn't beaten and browbeaten her. What kind of man are you to knock your own daughter about, bullying her into marriage? Grania, I love you, you know that. I meant what I said.'

'I meant what I said,' replies Mannion. 'Stallion man, is it? More a pony boy, I'd say.'

He gets up, one hand around Grania's elbow, the other in the small of her back. John looks at her stomach, still flat, not showing. As they push past John he reaches for Grania's hand, but she pulls away, and they leave the room.

Charles holds him back. 'It's a youthful infatuation and you'll get over it soon enough, you're only twenty-three, for heaven's sake. The girl's better off with her lawyer. But you can't stay here; Mannion means what he says, and I'm not having Burke's Fort go the way of Derriquin. Besides, we've no stallion now.'

John says nothing more. He remembers how he had been slow to react when Eileen and William had been kidnapped by the IRA Volunteers; he is not going to make the same mistake again. He is determined to talk to Grania, confident that he can persuade her to come to him. Mannion's a loud-mouthed bully, he thinks to himself. It's our child she's having, not Mannion's to give away to Eamonn McCann. Our child, he says out loud, our child.

John walks over to Mannion's farm after dark. As he comes into the farmyard a dog starts to bark. He hears a noise behind him, turns and is knocked over by a powerful blow to the head. Half conscious on the ground, he curls up into a ball to avoid a series of kicks to the ribs and groin and head until he blacks out.

Charles and Cis find him, more dead than alive, dumped on the front steps of Burke's Fort the next morning. He is still unconscious, his face bloody and bruised, his jaw and nose broken, both eyes completely closed, one leg at an impossible angle. The ambulance is called and takes him straight to hospital in Dublin.

For five weeks John lies in a coma. He wakes up to find Cis beside his bed.

'I thought you were gone, gone beyond my prayers and the Poor Clares. Thanks be to God you're back.'

John, through a splitting headache, says only one word. 'Grania.'

'She's married, she's Mrs McCann now, and that's for the best. They burned the Folly the day you were dumped on our doorstep; Mannion has said Burke's Fort will go the same way if you come back to Queen's County.'

John turns his battered face into the pillow.

II.
England and Ireland
1924–1936

18.

A WEEK LATER John is moved to a convalescent home, a handsome Italianate villa in Howth with a view of the Irish Sea. There are only twenty-four patients; one other civilian, a lawyer injured when the Four Courts were blown up, the rest British Army soldiers wounded during the War of Independence. These are men who have lost legs, whose arms have been amputated at the elbow or shoulder, one man blinded, several with bad burns. The home is kept going by a charitable trust set up by public subscription just after the Great War. Charles Burke pulled some strings.

'He's a war casualty,' Charles argued without going into unnecessary detail. 'His father was a major in the Royal Irish Dragoons. Won the MC, killed in 1916 on the Somme.'

It is the regimental connection that clinches John's place. Questioned by the other patients about his injuries, he gives non-committal replies. By now his face has recovered its normal shape; there has been no permanent damage to his eyes. His broken nose and jaw have healed, although his nose has set at a crooked angle.

'You look like a boxer,' says one of the nurses, who has taken a fancy to him. 'Not a very successful one, I must say.'

His right leg is the problem, broken at the ankle and in two more places below the knee. When finally the plaster comes off, John is shocked at the shrunken, bleached, scarred leg that emerges. It throbs continuously, and he cannot put any weight on it for more than a few seconds.

'Will it ever come good?' he asks.

'Only if you do the exercises. Some of the men here would be glad of a leg like that,' says an unsympathetic doctor.

John, chastened, takes his regime seriously. He abandons his crutches, swims every day in the small sea-water pool, and lifts weights attached to his ankle every morning and evening to build up his muscles.

He has too much time to think. Images of his night with Grania, her body in the lamplight, her last kiss as she left in the morning, the meeting with Mannion at Burke's Fort, the bruise on her cheek, her last words to him as she left, 'It's what will happen,' shuttle through his brain in an agonizing slideshow. Thoughts of Grania with Eamonn are impossible to banish. He plans a trip to Maryborough and then realizes he has no idea what to say or do if he meets her again. Is she still pregnant? Could that child ever be mine? He torments himself with unanswered, unanswerable questions until he thinks he will go mad.

Cis comes to see him and is a comfort, although he cannot share her faith that everything is God's will and must be borne. She prays for him, and smiles when he says he is a lost cause. She gives him a little book of prayers, in the front of which she has written, 'To John from Cis Burke, in the hope that he will come to God through all his troubles'. Although he cannot pray any more – he had prayed for Eileen's life, and was unanswered – one of Cis's prayers, *Mother of God, Star of the Sea, Home of the Wanderer, Pray for me,*' sticks in his mind, and he says this in spite of himself.

When his leg is healed he takes long walks along the sea, often pushing a captain from the Lancashire Fusiliers who has lost both legs above the knee.

'I survived three years on the Western Front, and then get blown up when they attacked our armoured car in Leeson Street. I hate this country, hate the bloody Irish. Now they've finished killing us they've started on each other.'

John doesn't argue, and it is true that his own feelings about his country and those he thought of as his countrymen have changed. They killed my mother, burned my house down and one of them nearly killed me. I might as well have been English, or a staunch Unionist, a Black and Tan even, for all the good feeling Irish, being Irish, has done me.

Charles visits him ten days before he is due to be discharged.

'I've put a thousand pounds in your account in the Bank of Ireland to tide you over.' As John protests, he says, 'It's a loan until you get compensation for Derriquin. But you can't come back to the Fort, even Cis agrees that. There's no law or police to protect the likes of us against the Mannions who control the new Ireland. You could go back to Trinity, I suppose, though that'd be risky. The Royal Irish Dragoons would have you if they've got any room in the peacetime army.'

'I'm done with Trinity, and I doubt the army's for me.'

'Fair enough. I could speak to Tom O'Brien in Lambourn. He's from Queen's County – Laois we have to call it now – a good trainer of jumpers. He'd give you a job in his yard. It'd be a place to go, and you need to get out of Ireland for a while.'

Although John still thinks about going to find Grania, somehow taking her away from Eamonn McCann, he knows he needs a cure. He thanks Charles and is cut short.

'Listen, there's a lot of self-preservation in this – if I was a braver man I'd say to hell with all of them, and get Mannion prosecuted for attempted murder. Lambourn solves my problems as well as yours. I'll tell O'Brien to expect you next week. We'll send on a trunk with your stuff.'

'Would young Charlie like my Morris Oxford?'

'Good idea. Teach him car mechanics the hard way.'

Looking out from the back of the steamer to the Liverpool ferry as it steams out of Dun Laoghaire, which used to be Kingstown, John thinks about what he is leaving behind. Eileen, Josephine, Charles, Cis, Grania. He is leaving behind these people, County

Kerry, Ireland, and his identity with them. 'I'm a Kerry man' becomes 'We used to live in County Kerry', and when he arrives in Lambourn he has to add, 'It's in the South-West of Ireland.'

Tom O'Brien's yard is bustling, a courtyard of forty boxes, all full, with the trainer's house in one corner. Tom is small, wiry, bow-legged, a man of few words.

'Charles told me about you,' he says. 'You'll do your two here, and if you're any good we'll get you the odd ride. I'm not paying you, so you can ride as a gentleman. Start off in the dormitory with the other lads. Is your leg better? Charles said it was a nasty fall.'

'It's fine,' says John, and moves into the dormitory, which he shares with the other lads, lads ranging from sixteen to fifty. The long room is spartan, twelve narrow beds, tall army surplus lockers, a bathroom and lavatory at each end. The room smells of cigarettes and sweat; there is a shout of protest when John opens the window above his bed.

'Shut the bloody window for Christ's sake, you'll blow out what little heat we've got,' and it is true that the solitary black stove in the middle of the room warms only the six beds closest to it.

The work is hard, much harder than at Burke's Fort. Morning stables start sharp at six in the summer, seven when it gets dark; the first lot of fifteen horses and riders walk round in the yard with Tom O'Brien in the middle giving instructions.

'Jimmy, take Duchess in a steady canter alongside The Trader. George, yours needs a gallop; keep him back to the end and give him a good workout. John, Blaeberry's running on Saturday, she just needs to stretch her legs . . .'

And the first lot trots through the village and up onto the downs, where Tom is waiting on his hack to watch them, two by two, come up the mile of downland turf that they use every day. Then back to the yard, unsaddle, walk round to cool down, rug up and into the loose-box to fresh water and the first feed of rolled oats and a net of hay. Then the same again with the second lot at eight. At ten, a giant breakfast cooked by Tom's wife Maeve, eggs, bacon, fried bread, tea, bread, butter and jam that vanishes as quickly as it is produced. Then mucking out, dung and straw delivered in a steaming heap onto the wagon in the middle of the yard, fresh straw once a week in every box. Then cleaning the tack, a job John likes for the smell of the leather and the saddle soap and the oil; the webbing girths, damp with sweat, are washed and dried every day.

Tom is strict. At the end of every morning, each horse and loose-box is checked with the lad standing by. Tom has a keen eye for an oversight; if he picks up a hoof it is sure to be the one that hasn't been cleaned out. If he runs his hand down a foreleg and finds some unreported heat, the tongue-lashing that follows is to be avoided. John is not exempt; a sweat-stain still on one of his horse's quarters gets him his first dressing-down, for which he is ribbed at breakfast. And when his second horse, startled by a dog, dumps him on his back and canters away, luckily coming to no harm, he is ribbed again. John feels chastened; he is also beginning to feel part of the group.

19.

THERE ARE A dozen jumping yards like Tom O'Brien's in Lambourn, all competing at the racecourse and for good horses, generous owners and competent jockeys. At the same time, while there are some long-running feuds between a few trainers, there is a camaraderie bred out of the danger and the excitement of steeplechasing and hurdling. When a Lambourn trainer wins a Gold Cup or a Grand National, the whole village, not just the winning yard, celebrates putting one over the Northern trainers or the Irish.

There are eight pubs where most of the lads' meagre wages go every Saturday night. Tom O'Brien's lads like The Bell; it's a hundred yards away, which makes walking home easier, and it's one of only three pubs in Lambourn that stock Guinness. It's in The Bell that the lads swap yard gossip and try to extract reliable information about other yards and other horses without parting with too much in exchange. Betting coups are planned there, and sometimes brought off. The small bets placed by O'Brien's lads aren't enough to move the market or produce spectacular returns, so elaborate doubles, trebles and Yankees are the preferred roads to fortune. By Tuesday or Wednesday most of the stable pockets are empty.

John fits easily into this new world of riding two, mucking out, cleaning tack, the pub and bed by ten o'clock. He is a good horseman and soon is given horses that need sympathetic handling. Early on he is told to ride Blaeberry, an unraced and difficult five-year-old mare, partly to test him, partly because three experienced lads have already tried and failed to handle her. No one else is eager to take her on. When she whips round at the bottom of the gallops and puts John on the floor, there is an ironic cheer. But he manages to hold on to the reins, remounts, gives her two sharp cracks with his whip behind the saddle and sits tight through the three or four outraged bucks that follow. He never hits her again. She goes sweetly up the gallops at a steady canter, her stride lengthening all the way, holding her own with the good gelding alongside her.

'She'll be a racehorse yet,' says Tom as they hack back to the yard. And when she goes on to win her second bumper with John up, and subsequently scores in two maiden hurdles ridden by the O'Brien stable jockey, John's reputation is established.

As a horseman, but not as a race rider. John has real difficulty doing less than eleven stone seven pounds, and he still can't ride a strong finish. He gets a dozen rides in his first year in amateur steeplechases, and wins a couple, is placed in three and gets round safely every time. It is the same pattern in the following two years. His best result is a respectable fourth in the Foxhunters at Aintree.

After a year in the dormitory, John rents a former keeper's cottage on an estate just outside Lambourn. A two up, two down, running water heated by an explosive gas geyser that singes John's hair on several occasions, it has no electricity but a long view over the Berkshire downs. From time to time he shares the cottage with another amateur from the O'Brien yard, but they come and go. Most of the time he is on his own. One of the owners sells him a cocker spaniel bitch, Bella, that keeps him company. Bella goes everywhere with John, except to the races, and comes to an early understanding with Tom's Jack Russells in the yard office that they are the top dogs.

This combination of hard physical activity and a solitary life in the evenings, broken only by a weekly visit to The Bell on Saturday night, suits John well. He is a man in exile; the few friends he has are left behind in Ireland. He tries hard to forget Grania, but she appears too often in tortured dreams, sometimes as a succubus, sometimes in the arms of the Maryborough lawyer. He is unable to imagine or dream of the child.

Why, he asks himself, didn't she talk to me before Mannion? Just as he had so often relived and altered the kidnapping of Eileen, so his night visit to Mannion's farm becomes a meeting with Grania at the Trafalgar Folly, an elopement to England, marriage, until these imaginings dissolve into the harsh memory of the attack in the farmyard and the blackout from which he often wishes he had never emerged. Sometimes, when he is pushing down fresh hay from the loft into the basket below, the memory of that first embrace with Grania comes to him so strongly that he has to lean against the wall, his head against his arms, his body shaking.

Encounters with girls are few and far between. His mother's sister Agnes had married a successful barrister with a house in London and Dorset. She makes valiant efforts to introduce John to eligible young women, with little success. He goes to a few coming-out dances in London, but white ties, tails and debutantes are not for him. When he fails to write effusive bread-and-butter letters, the invitations peter out.

He is still in occasional contact with Charles and Cis. He gets the first tranche of the Derriquin compensation, three thousand pounds, and uses some of this to buy a couple of horses from Charles that he brings over and puts into training with Tom O'Brien. One of these, a five-year-old gelding, is by The Elector, and John wins two good races with him before selling him on at a decent profit. And he buys a car, an Alvis, that is much admired by the other lads in the yard.

He remains alone and apart, still thinking from time to time about Grania, still reliving his encounter with Mannion in the dining room at Burke's Fort. And his leg continues to hurt in cold weather.

*

After he has been in the yard four years, Tom calls John into the office, an untidy room cluttered with terriers, form books, old copies of the *Sporting Life*, photographs of past triumphs and a stack of bills and letters. Only the owners' racing silks are hung up in anything resembling order in a long cupboard leading off the room.

'I'd like you to be my assistant trainer,' says Tom. 'We're up to sixty horses now, and I'm run off my feet. Whenever we have runners at different meetings on the same day I have to choose. And any owner that gets George feels short-changed.'

George is the travelling head lad, drives one of the horseboxes and has been with Tom for twenty years.

'How will George take it?'

'He'll be fine. He knows what he can and can't do. He'd run a mile from the paperwork.'

He points to the mess on his desk.

'You can see we need to sort ourselves out. And you're good with the owners. Five hundred a year – you'll no longer be an amateur rider.'

John asks for a day to think it over and then accepts.

His days in the new job are just as long, but he no longer rides out and does his two. Instead, he takes out the first and third lots to the gallops and spends the rest of the morning sorting through letters and bills. He and Tom spend an hour every afternoon going through the available races over the following three months, planning their campaigns horse by horse.

The yard's strike rate improves when John suggests that the stable jockey, who is spending too much time in The Bell and is having difficulty doing the weight, is replaced.

'Danny's lost his nerve. He's drinking too much, and it's only a matter of time before he starts betting against himself,' says John. 'We could get Michael Molloy over from Ireland, I reckon, see if he suits us. He can do ten seven if he has to, powerful in a finish. He's had twenty winners in Ireland so far this season, and he's not often out of the frame when he's on a decent horse.

Danny can drive one of the horseboxes – provided he gives up the drink.'

'Will Molloy come?'

He does come, he does suit, and rides forty winners in his first season. And he rides Dunkerron, the stable's first winner at Cheltenham, for Billy Vincent, O'Brien's biggest owner, who immediately sends him six more horses.

'We shouldn't have more than sixty altogether,' says John. 'Or at least not for long. Let's cull the weak performers, and send them back to point-to-pointing or hunting where they belong. We'll be doing our owners a favour.'

20.

'THIS IS MRS Vincent. She'd like us to find her a chaser.'
John shakes hands with Mrs Vincent; she is fair-haired, in her mid-thirties, John guesses.

'It's my birthday present from Billy. All you've got to do is find me one as good as Dunkerron,' says Mrs Vincent, smiling.

'Do you think we should try the Newmarket sales?' says Tom.

'Only if we want a hurdler. Up there they've all got flat-racing pedigrees and prices to match. If we want a staying jumper, one that will get three miles, Ireland's a better bet. I'll ask my uncle, he bought me a couple of decent horses last year. He'll have some suggestions. I need some idea about price.'

'Billy says I can spend up to fifteen hundred,' says Mrs Vincent.

'We may not need all of that. There's no point in buying the finished article. You'll have a lot more fun watching your horse make progress – provided he does. It's a chancy business, steeple-chasing. A lot can go wrong.'

'I'll not be put off,' she says with another smile.

She shakes Tom's and John's hands and goes out of the yard. Tom looks relieved as she leaves.

'Were you trying to put her off altogether? You're not much of a salesman, I'd say. Vincent's our biggest owner by a long chalk.'

'At least she has some idea what she's in for. As long as she doesn't expect a winner at Cheltenham or Aintree in her first season.'

He rings Charles at the weekend.

'I'll talk to the Filgates in County Louth,' Charles says. 'They've always got something to sell. I hear they have some decent young point-to-pointers in their yard. What sort of money?'

'The right sort of money for a good five-year-old gelding with a bit of jumping form, and sound in wind and limb. Has to be a stayer, needn't be a thoroughbred.'

'Fair enough,' says Charles. 'And tell your owner in advance that I take five per cent of the sale price. Young Charlie tells me I have to be more businesslike now farm prices have gone to blazes. That apart, things are much more settled here since you went away. You should come over.'

John doesn't reply to the suggestion and says goodbye. Went away, he thinks; banished, more like it, run out of my own country by a gunman. The thought of Ireland is unsettling.

Ten days later he gets a long letter from Charles, which to his relief is only about horses. Charles has taken his horse-coping role seriously.

I've looked at seventeen horses in all, and narrowed it down to two. A seven-year-old chaser, won three times last year, but doesn't get a yard more than three miles on good ground. Takes a liberty with his fences every now and again, he's fallen twice in seven starts. Four hundred and fifty pounds plus the cost of getting him to Lambourn from Tipperary. The other is a five-year-old with the Filgates. Three Open wins as a pointer, plus a good bumper and a novice chase. Unbeaten in five starts. I didn't dare ask the price. He's got a smidgen of The Archduke in him through Likely Lad, his dam's sire.

John talks to Tom, rings Charles again, then calls Sammy Filgate.

'Best horse I've had through my hands in twenty years. Bought him out of a field in Galway. I schooled him myself.

Brave as a lion, stays for ever, never puts a foot wrong out hunting or over fences. Can't let him go for less than a thousand pounds.'

John whistles. 'Call it nine hundred after the luck-penny and you're on.'

'Luck-penny? I'm selling horses, not cattle at the Athlone fair. I'll take nine-fifty as Charles is a friend of the family and that's it.'

After a brief conversation with Tom and Billy Vincent, that is it. A fortnight later the horse arrives, none the worse for wear after the long journey by boat and train. Tom and John look with a critical eye at Knocknarea, a seventeen-hands-high iron-grey gelding.

'Bit over at the knee. And he isn't quite straight – dishes a bit with the near fore.'

'For goodness' sake, John, he's not for the show ring. Look at his chest, look at those quarters. He looks worth the money, even though we've never paid as much for a horse. Mrs Vincent should be pleased.'

Mrs Vincent arrives the next day to inspect her present.

'He's very handsome. Looks strong, and I love greys. What shall I call him?'

'He's named already. Knocknarea, after a Sligo mountain. The Filgates bought him out of a field in the West of Ireland as an unbroken two-year-old,' says John.

'Can't I change the name?'

'Terrible unlucky thing to do,' says Tom. 'He's won five times already as Knocknarea. It's a winner's name all right.'

Knocknarea remains Knocknarea. He is given time to recover from his journey, and runs in his first race a month later.

'You take him to Kempton,' says Tom. 'You bought him, you've schooled him, he's in your first lot.'

Knocknarea makes his purchase look a bargain, winning a novice chase at Kempton Park by an easy three lengths.

'He could have gone round again,' says Michael Molloy as he

dismounts. 'Never put a foot wrong, and he can fiddle a fence when he has to.'

Mrs Vincent, who has watched the first half of the race through her fingers, clutching John's arm before each fence, is delighted. She hugs the jockey, hugs John, tips the jockey, tries to tip John, apologizes, hugs everyone again.

'It was so exciting, he did do well,' she says, running her hand down Knocknarea's neck, still dark with sweat. 'Billy will be sorry he isn't here.'

'He's got real potential, Mrs Vincent. Here, your hands are covered with him – use this.'

John produces a large blue handkerchief and Mrs Vincent wipes her hands.

'My name is Chantal,' says Mrs Vincent, sees the look on John's face, and says again, 'Chantal. It's French, like my mother. I'll keep this and bring it back clean.'

'No need for that,' says John, but she pockets the handkerchief anyhow. 'It's a lovely name.'

'Terrible unlucky thing to change a name,' she says, in a good imitation of Tom O'Brien's accent. 'What next for Knocknarea?'

'We'll see how he is in the morning – he looks sound enough now. He's a star in the making, we don't want to rush him.'

Knocknarea eats up when he gets home and trots up sound the next day.

'This is a very good horse,' says John to Tom in the office. 'Maybe the best in the yard. He could win at Cheltenham, maybe even at Aintree.'

'Michael agrees, says he's not sat on a better. But let's not get ahead of ourselves. Aintree is best kept on the long finger. He's still a baby. There's a race at Chepstow in three weeks might suit him, though he'll carry seven pounds extra for yesterday's win. We'll think about the novice chase at Cheltenham when we see how he does next time out.'

A week later at Warwick, John is waiting outside the parade ring for the runners in the third race to arrive – he is interested in one of them, a potential rival to Knocknarea if he runs at Cheltenham – when he is greeted warmly by someone from his Irish past.

'You don't remember me, do you? Robert Keen, next door to you in Botany Bay at Trinity,' says the not-stranger, shaking him warmly by the hand. John does remember him now, a clever historian from County Clare who, unusually at Unionist Trinity, shared John's view about Home Rule.

'Never knew you were a racing man,' says John. 'Where are you now? Still at Trinity?'

'Couldn't wait to leave Ireland the minute I graduated. I'm a history don at Christ Church. I teach mediaeval history; I'm your man for manorial rolls. But I get to go racing often enough. I see you're a trainer,' looking at John's badge. 'Any useful runners today?'

'We've one in the fifth race, but it's her first time out. You could do worse than back our novice, Knocknarea, when he next runs.'

'I'll watch out for him. How do I get hold of you? Come over and have dinner – Lambourn's pretty close to Oxford.'

John is glad to see Robert, but wary of any reconnection to Ireland. Nevertheless, when a stiff little card embossed with a cardinal's red hat arrives at the yard, inviting him to dinner at Christ Church, he accepts by return.

He meets Robert in his rooms in Peckwater Quad for a drink before dinner. John has never been inside an Oxford College; Christ Church seems almost as large as Trinity.

'They look after the Fellows very well,' says Robert. 'Until they get married. Then we're chucked out to north Oxford squalor and domestic bliss and nappies. It's an incentive to stay celibate or become queer. I haven't decided which way to go yet. You're next to me at dinner, and you'll have our Senior Tutor, David Allingham, on your left. He's a philosopher and deaf, so you'll have to shout.'

Christ Church hall is magnificent, candlelit, with portraits of past deans, benefactors and distinguished graduates rank upon rank on the walls. There is a sonorous Latin grace from one of the scholars, followed by the clatter of chairs and benches as three hundred undergraduates and dons sit down to dine.

This is far removed from John's world. He has spent the years since he left Ireland thinking only about horses, handicaps, breeding, jockeys, courses and other trainers. The philosopher on his right has scant interest in John's daily life and switches the subject at once to Irish politics. John is shocked by his own ignorance. He feels he has lived through a revolution without any real understanding of what was going on outside his own narrow, violent experience. Luckily Robert and the Senior Tutor have a lively argument about the Treaty and about Lloyd George, and John can restrict himself to the occasional comment.

'A republic is inevitable,' says Robert. 'They'll simply announce it in a few years' time and that will be that.'

'They'd be crazy to leave the Commonwealth,' says the Senior Tutor. 'Economics always triumphs over ideology.'

And later in the Senior Common Room over port the Betting Book is called for and '*Robert Keen bets David Allingham five pounds that Ireland is no longer a member of the Commonwealth in five years' time*' is solemnly entered and signed.

'Only hope he is still alive for me to collect,' says Robert as he sees John to his car.

As John drives the Alvis home late that night he is dismayed by how insulated he has become in the cocoon of the racing world. 'I'm a bore,' he says to Bella, stroking her ears as she jumps up to greet him. 'I know you don't think so, but I am.'

The next day he buys a radio, orders *The Times* and takes out a subscription to the *Spectator* and the *New Statesman*.

'Don't know why you bother with *The Times*,' says Tom. 'It hasn't tipped a winner for years.'

'I've the *Sporting Life* to keep me straight on racing. I need *The Times* to keep me straight on the rest of the world.'

Tom returns with a grunt to the runners and riders at Uttoxeter.

Knocknarea continues to make progress. Chantal Vincent comes to watch her horse on the gallops early one morning.

'Can we go by car? I've not ridden much.'

'Never in this world,' says John. 'We'll put you on Pinky. He's a patent-safety, seventeen years old, slow, steady as a rock. Only fourteen hands, closer to the ground if you fall off,' and adds, seeing Chantal's nervous look, 'No one's ever fallen off Pinky. I'll put him on a leading rein until you're happy.'

It's a cold, bright sunny day on the Downs; steam comes from the horses' nostrils as they canter up the gallops.

'There's your husband's Cheltenham winner,' he says as two come into view. 'He's alongside Bay Tree, new in the yard last week, the one with the star. They're both moving well.'

'How can you tell them apart?'

'I have only thirty horses to remember, Mrs Vincent, and I see them every day. I look at them up here, check them over in the stables, feel their legs, watch their feed. I can tell the moment they're out of sorts. I don't know thirty people anything like as well. Here comes Knocknarea and The Preacher. Look at the lovely stride of your horse.'

'It's Chantal, Mr Burke. And you don't know thirty people? That's a shame.'

After John's string have finished their work they trot back to the yard; by now Chantal no longer needs the leading rein.

'Pinky's just perfect,' she says, her eyes bright, her cheeks pink. 'It was such a treat to see what goes on between the races, and to see you in your kingdom.'

John sees her to her car. As she says goodbye she adds, 'You must come to dinner. We're this side of Oxford. Knowing more horses than people is something I'm going to put right.'

John is worried about the etiquette of dining with an owner and consults Tom.

'Of course you must go if she asks you,' says Tom. 'The Vincents are our biggest owners by far. She's taken a shine to you.'

The invitation does arrive, and John goes out to dinner for the second time in three years; his dinner jacket hasn't had such use since his rapid exit from the London season. The Vincents live in an Elizabethan manor house deep in the Oxfordshire countryside. Breweries are doing well, thinks John, as he is shown into a large hall with a blazing log fire. He takes a drink from a waiter. Chantal greets him warmly and introduces him to her husband, whom John has met once before at Cheltenham. Billy Vincent is tall, thin, with a fierce profile and a strong handshake. He is distinguished in his dinner jacket and looks ten years older than his wife. He asks John about his horses; John, realizing that Billy isn't a man for detail, gives him a quick summary. Billy has soon had enough horse talk and Chantal moves John away to meet the other guests.

'This is Robert Keen.'

'We know each other. We were at Trinity together, Trinity College, Dublin,' says John.

'Good. So I've only twenty-nine to go.'

John looks puzzled for a moment, then laughs. At dinner he is next to Chantal; she is a careful hostess, talks for half the time to the Yeomanry brigadier on her left, while John talks horses and hunting to the MFH's wife on his other side. Then Chantal turns her direct gaze and her bright smile on John.

'I was so happy on Pinky that morning watching Knocknarea,' she says. 'May I come again?'

'Of course. But you picked your day well. It's different altogether when it's driving sleet and muddy under foot.'

'Different altogether? You do have an Irish turn of phrase. You're halfway to Tom O'Brien some of the time. What took you away from Ireland? I asked Robert, but he wasn't sure.'

John takes a deep breath, thinks for a moment about a one-sentence, mind-your-own-business reply, and then tells Chantal half his story. He tells her about Eileen, William, Derriquin, Tomas, leaving Kerry. He doesn't talk about Grania. His voice is steady as he finishes by describing his visit to Tomas in Kilmainham.

Chantal keeps her eyes on his as he talks, squeezes his hand for a moment at the end and says, 'I'm sorry I was so inquisitive. I'm glad you told me.'

After dinner, the men move to the library and talk politics and business. Robert and John have a quiet conversation about the future of Unionists in the Free State.

'There's not much victor's magnanimity about,' says Robert. 'It's become a strange, repressed society, dominated by the Catholic Church. Don't underestimate the power of the hierarchy in the new Ireland. All the politicians are terrified of a bishop or a cardinal. And the boycott of Protestant shopkeepers has had a terrible effect. My family's gone from Clare, like yours from Kerry. My older brother is listed in *Burke's Irish Landed Gentry* as Keen, formerly of Ballykeen House, Keen's Cross, now PO Box 1221, Nairobi, Kenya. He grows coffee.'

'It's not surprising there's a Catholic backlash. It's their turn after years of repression, years of famine, years of paying tithes to a church they didn't belong to. We've only ourselves to blame.'

'Perhaps, but I don't have to admire the result. You know there's an extended Dublin version of the Papal Index, and *Ulysses* is on it.'

'*Ulysses*?'

'James Joyce's *Ulysses*. The most important novel of the twentieth century. I'll send you a copy.'

As the guests leave, Chantal holds John's hand for a moment. 'I enjoyed sitting next to you. Can I come over again soon?'

'Of course.'

Ulysses adds another dimension to John's self-improvement. He finds the book bewildering at first, perseveres and is picked up and carried along on the torrent of Joyce's language, almost a foreign language, against the background of a Dublin he knew well. And he understands why the Dublin hierarchy banned the book.

Spurred on by Robert, he becomes more adventurous in his choice of reading. He finds in 'The Wild Swans at Coole' the two lines Grania sent him on a postcard from the Gaeltacht: *Passion or conquest, wander where they will, Attend upon them still.*

He still has the postcard tucked away in his wallet. The Cliffs of Moher have faded. This is his only tangible reminder of Grania Mannion, other than a dull ache in his right leg when it gets cold and a crooked nose. A faded postcard, an ache and a broken nose seem little enough to have left of such an intensity of feeling. The dreams and the nightmares both have gone.

Every Friday, two books arrive from Harrods in a cardboard box, in which the two that arrived the week before are returned. Only *The Critique of Pure Reason*, a suggestion of the Senior Tutor's, goes back unfinished.

John spends at least one afternoon a fortnight in Oxford. Robert has become a good friend; they are drawn to each other by the common bonds of literature, racing and Ireland. Robert urges John to drop into Peckwater any evening, and this becomes part of John's Oxford routine. He spends a lot of time buying books in Blackwell's, and persuades his way into all the great Oxford libraries, Duke Humfrey's in the Bodleian, the Radcliffe Camera, the Codrington in All Souls and the Upper Library in the Queen's College.

'They're all wonderful,' he says. 'But Trinity is even better, and we have the Book of Kells.'

'I wish my pupils were half as dedicated,' says Robert. 'We'll make a scholar of you yet.'

'On the same day that you become a racehorse trainer.'

They are talking over a drink in the Mitre Hotel.

'I like it here,' says Robert. 'No undergraduates, not like the pubs. How's my horse getting on?'

In spite of John's attempts to put him off, Robert has bought a horse and put him into training in the O'Brien yard.

'Picked him out myself – second in a selling hurdle at Stratford. Only paid two hundred pounds for him. The owner didn't seem to mind seeing the horse go. He should make a chaser, don't you think?'

The horse is a flashy chestnut with little else to recommend him beyond his colour.

'He'll need a fair bit of schooling,' says John.

'Just like you.'

John laughs. 'Fair enough. But he isn't going to win a Gold Cup.'

Christmas in the yard is merry; half the lads can't or won't afford the fare back to Ireland, Scotland or the North, and the owners' contribution to the staff fund is spent on a mammoth lunch that begins at noon and ends well after midnight when the last lad lurches into the dormitory.

'We've three runners tomorrow,' says Tom. 'Actually, it's now today. You roust out the lads and get the horses ready. I'll take Sandown, you take Huntingdon.'

Robert's horse is having his first run over fences at Huntingdon. It is a modest novice chase with only seven runners. In spite of taking diabolical liberties with four of the twelve fences, the O'Brien apprentice sits tight and finishes third. Robert is delighted.

'First time out and in the frame. I'll get my money back in no time.'

'Twenty pounds for third place. And you ought to give a fiver to Liam. Not many jockeys would have stayed in the saddle after the way your fellow uprooted the last fence.'

'He'd have won if he'd jumped better – only ten lengths off the winner.'

Robert parts willingly with the fiver for Liam and spends the rest of the prize money on dinner with John at the Randolph in Oxford.

'I wish all owners were as realistic and as easy to please,' John says to Tom the next morning.

'So do I. We've lost eight horses in the last month, owners either taking them to cheaper stables or else selling out altogether. The slump is beginning to hit racing, all right. Let's hope Billy

Vincent's brewery holds up. Mrs V. telephoned to say she'd like to come over to see Knocknarea Saturday.'

Saturday is cold, overcast, with driving rain that now and again turns into sleet.

'It's the devil of a day,' says John to Chantal Vincent. 'You'd be better off with a cup of coffee in front of the office fire, and I can report back.'

'You'll do no reporting back, thank you very much. I've not got up at five-thirty and driven twenty miles for a cup of your rotten coffee. If Pinky can cope, so can I.'

Up on the downs there is no escaping the wind and the almost horizontal rain. There is barely a dawn, and it is hard to distinguish the horses as they come up the gallops out of the murk. They both dismount and stand in the lee of their horses. Chantal is soon wet and shivering; John puts a wing of his large poncho around her over her useless, elegant mackintosh.

'I'm freezing,' she says, holding out her hands, and he rubs them together between his own. Her head comes just below his chin. He is conscious of the softness of her shoulder and the smell of her hair.

As the last two come by, John says, 'That's Knocknarea, three lengths clear of a good seven-year-old, both giving it their all. He'll be ready for Chepstow in ten days.'

Soaked through, they canter back to the yard and go into the office. There is a good fire. Chantal takes off her coat, jacket and sweater as John gives her a cup of coffee.

'It'll take me half an hour to dry out. I've a skirt and shirt in my bag, but everything else is damp. Do you mind?'

'Of course not. You'll have the office to yourself; Tom's out with the second string. I'll go and see Knocknarea rubbed down, talk to his lad. You can lock the door so you won't be disturbed.'

Knocknarea, dried off and rugged up, is looking a good deal more comfortable than his owner.

'He was hardly blowing at all at the top of the gallops,' says his lad. 'And the going was heavy.'

'Give him some bran with his oats,' says John, and goes out to check on the other horses.

After twenty minutes he goes back to the office, knocks twice, hears nothing and goes in. Chantal is by the fire in a cream slip that stops just above her knees; she turns her back to the door, but not before John sees the darkness of her nipples and pubic hair.

'I'm nearly decent,' she says, putting on her shirt and a wrap-around skirt with her back to John. She turns around, smiling. 'I'm dry enough now for the drive home and a hot bath. How was the horse?'

'I'm sorry, I did knock. Knocknarea worked well up the hill,' the lad says. 'He's ready for Chepstow, but that'll be a real test against some good novices.'

'I'll be there,' and she goes past John, who is still standing by the door, pats him on the cheek and says, 'Thank you for looking after me.'

21.

JOHN IS CONFUSED and excited by holding Chantal's hands on the gallops, the picture of her in her slip in front of the office fire never far from his mind. He talks to Robert when they meet in the week.

'I'm hardly the man to ask,' he says. 'I'm a celibate history don. But there are two clear alternatives. Either she thinks of you as a son . . .'

'Hold on, she's not old enough to be my mother.'

'All right, then as a friend. Or she's attracted to you, and was very happy for you to see her naked in front of the fire.'

'She wasn't naked.'

'She might as well have been in view of the effect it's had on you. Anyhow, there's only one way to find out. What's the worst that can happen? "Mr Burke, I'm a respectable married woman."' This last in a high-pitched indignant voice as he slaps his own cheek.

John laughs. 'Thank you for the rigorous analysis. You're like the tipster in a two-horse race that tells me either of them can win.'

'Here's to the spirit of discovery,' says Robert, and they clink glasses.

The big race at Chepstow takes place the following Friday. John travels down in the horsebox with George, unwilling to risk the Alvis on such a long journey. It is a cold clear day, and there has been a sharp frost, though not enough to call off the day's racing. He meets Chantal in the owners' and trainers' bar, crowded and fuggy with cigarette smoke and damp tweed overcoats, the Welsh voices reminding John that he has crossed the Severn.

'Anything to eat?' he asks.

'A brandy might calm my nerves.'

John produces the brandy.

'Have you ever watched by a fence?' he asks. 'You get a completely different impression close up.'

'Never. This is only the fourth race meeting I've been to.'

They watch the next race beside the big open ditch. The noise of fifteen horses thundering into the fence, the shouts of two or three jockeys at their mounts or their rivals, the long arc of the horses that stand back and jump big, the noise as some of them go through the top foot of the fence, leaves Chantal wide-eyed.

'You were right, it is completely different from up there,' she says, pointing to the stands. 'Much more dangerous than I'd realized, much more exciting.'

In the parade ring, Chantal listens as John talks to Michael Molloy.

'The going is good, slippery in places. The pace will be hot, so you can't afford to lie out of your ground. He's up against two good horses. We'd like to win.'

Michael Molloy nods, touches his cap to Chantal, is jumped up into the saddle by John and trots off with the other runners out of the parade ring.

'Knocknarea looks wonderful. It must be that gallop in the rain. Oh, I do hope he wins.'

'He's ready all right, and we'll see how good he is. I saw Maltese Cross win at Warwick. He's a decent horse, and he's got a good jockey aboard.'

They watch from the top of the stand. Chantal grabs John's hand in hers and holds it tightly through the race. Knocknarea jumps well, barring a slight slip on landing four out, when Chantal buries her face in John's shoulder for a moment. Three horses come together at the last. Michael Molloy sees a stride and asks Knocknarea to stand back. He lands level with Maltese Cross as the horse between them hits the top of the fence hard and loses two lengths. Knocknarea and Maltese Cross drive together for the line; Michael Molloy has the whip out, and at the finishing post it is Knocknarea by a head.

'He did win, didn't he?' says Chantal, who has been shouting her horse home from the last fence.

'A near thing, but I think he got up,' and when the announcer confirms Knocknarea as the winner John is rewarded with a kiss on the cheek and a warm hug. He doesn't try to hide his own pleasure and relief.

Knocknarea returns to the winner's enclosure, flanks heaving, nostrils flaring red, the marks of Michael's whip visible on his quarters.

'He looks exhausted,' says Chantal.

'George, go you and get him a bucket of water. I'll walk him around. He's had a real race, you can see that. But he won, and beat a couple of good ones. We'll see how he is tomorrow morning.'

'His jumping was perfect again,' says Michael Molloy, face spattered with mud. He looks only a little less exhausted than Knocknarea. 'I've not ridden many better.'

Chantal collects the winner's silver cup and says to John, 'We're going to celebrate. I'll give you a lift and we'll have dinner on the way, if George'll be all right taking the horse back on his own?'

'George'll be fine if he leaves now – it's starting to snow.'

A few flakes have fallen and settled on the ground; the sky to the north is a level iron-grey.

'I'll put Knocknarea into the horsebox and meet you at the entrance.'

John sees the horse off; when Chantal pulls up outside the entrance to the racecourse she gets out of the car, tosses the keys to John and says, 'Would you mind driving? I'm still too excited to concentrate. We'll have an early dinner at the Rose Revived at Barton and beat the snow home.'

On the journey Chantal relives the race several times over. 'Wasn't that a fantastic jump at the last fence? He's a strong jockey, Michael.'

'It had to be if he was going to win – Maltese Cross matched him in the air. Knocknarea's a Cheltenham prospect if he's sound in the morning.'

As they park outside the Rose Revived, it has started to snow in earnest.

'We'll need to be quick over dinner; the snow's definitely settling.'

'Don't be an old woman. I'm not going to let the weather spoil our celebration.'

She doesn't; they share half a bottle of champagne and a bottle of Burgundy.

'Do you mind if I order the wine? I've eaten here before. And I'm half French.'

John doesn't mind. Dinner with an older married woman, but not old enough to be his mother, he reminds himself and Robert, is a new experience.

Chantal picks John's hand up off the table, turns it over and traces the lines in his palm with her index finger. Her nail varnish is pink.

'What do I see?' she looks thoughtful and lets go of John's hand. 'A winner at Chepstow.'

'I saw that too,' says John, taking a gulp of red wine. 'Tell me how you're half French.'

'My mother was the daughter of an admiral. The French navy is very grand, you know, they've long forgotten Trafalgar, and blame the Spanish for that anyway. She met and married, beneath her, my grandmother thought; she wanted a *duc*. Daddy was in the British Embassy in Paris, a career diplomat. They're both in Berlin now. I went to school here, did some courses at the Sorbonne but didn't graduate. My mother believed in educating women.'

'So did mine,' says John. 'How did you meet Mr Vincent?' He doesn't feel on Billy terms with Mr Vincent.

'At a London dance. I did the season, and he was this older, confident man, quite different from the rest of my weedy dancing partners. And he decided to marry me, and eventually he did. He doesn't give up easily. He's a good husband. Shall we finish with a brandy?'

'Absolutely not. Look outside at the snow. We need to leave now if we're going to get back tonight.'

Two or three inches of snow have settled, and it continues to fall in big, heavy flakes. They set off, John driving with the caution that a strange car, a heavy snowfall and several glasses of wine deserve. The snow whirls in the car's headlights; there is almost no traffic on the road. The snow has already blotted out the tracks of any cars in front of them.

'I hope Knocknarea has got home safely,' says John. 'He did have a three-hour start on us. But I'm glad we celebrated. It's not often you get as good a win as that.'

'Or in as good company, you were about to say.'

'I was too nervous to say that.'

There is a long silence, and John wonders if he has been too bold. The snow is falling in thick flakes. As they pass the pub at the bottom of the steep hill that rises to the top of the Cotswold escarpment, John says, 'I'm not sure we'll make this. Look ahead. Everything's white.'

'We'd better try.'

'It's your car – I'd hate to damage it.'

John drives slowly and carefully up the beginning of the hill; the windscreen wipers are barely keeping pace with the snow. As the hill steepens, the wheels begin to lose traction and spin and John has difficulty keeping the car straight. Up ahead he sees a lorry that has skidded diagonally across the road on its way down, its lights still blazing.

'Glad we didn't meet that. We'll not get past him tonight. Best if I back slowly down to the Crown and see if they've got rooms.'

'Well, you did try. And it's my fault for lingering over dinner.'

'It takes two to linger.'

They make it in reverse back to the Crown's car park. Inside, they shake off the snow in the little lobby and go into the bar. The bar is already crowded with refugees from the snow. Steaming bodies and plenty to drink have created a cheerful atmosphere.

John asks the landlord if he has two rooms for the night.

'Only the one left,' he says. 'It's at the back at the top of the stairs. Thirty pounds, cash in advance, if you don't mind.'

John pays and tells Chantal, 'I'll find a chair in the bar.'

'Don't be silly. Look around you. Standing room only. Let's get in the queue for the phone box and then inspect the room. It may have twin beds or a sofa.'

The room has a small double bed and an armchair. There is a gas fire, unlit, coin-operated. John uses his last half-crown to get it going, and immediately the room is transformed by the reddish-orange light and the comforting hiss of the fire.

'You'll need a supply of half-crowns. I'll go down to the bar and get some change.'

'Plenty of cash tonight,' says the landlord. 'You get about an hour for two and sixpence.'

John takes twenty to be on the safe side, and then orders two glasses of brandy.

'Tumblers OK? We're out of brandy glasses.'

The coins clink in John's pocket as he goes back up the stairs, feeling suddenly brave. Chantal is sitting on the side of the bed, wearing only her slip.

'Here's the brandy we missed,' John says. 'Here's to Knocknarea.'

'Here's to the snow,' says Chantal.

They both take a long swallow. John leans across and kisses her warm, soft mouth, tasting of brandy. She reaches over, turns off the light, pulls John to his feet and helps him out of his clothes. When he is naked, she sits down on the bed, unclips and unrolls her stockings and shrugs herself out of her suspender belt and underclothes.

'It would be a waste if you spent the night in that armchair. You wouldn't get much sleep.'

It would have been a terrible waste, John thinks the next morning, although I might have got more sleep. He looks at Chantal's head on the pillow next to him, kisses her gently on the cheek. She wakes up, stretches herself, smiles and says, 'I suppose I hope the snow has gone.'

John goes to the window. It has stopped snowing, but the road is still white and unmarked. No cars have been brave enough to leave the car park.

'We'll not leave for a while,' says John. 'The snowploughs and the grit haven't reached this part of the country yet. I'll go and see if there's any breakfast about.'

'Not yet you won't,' and Chantal pulls him back into bed. 'The only sensible thing to do,' she says, and then she stops talking as John does the only sensible thing.

It begins to thaw at eleven, and by noon it has started to rain. John and Chantal leave at two, without breakfast or lunch, as the pub has run out of food. Braver drivers have left clear tracks on the still snowy road, the hill has been gritted and last night's stranded lorry has gone. The road is still treacherous and John has to concentrate to keep the car on the road. They are both thoughtful about what has happened between them, and hardly talk. After a while, Chantal's head tilts sideways onto John's shoulder and she falls asleep.

She wakes up not long before they reach the yard.

'We'd better tell the same story, I suppose,' says Chantal. 'I don't plan to make a full confession to Billy.'

'Well, they already know we were stranded and spent the night in the same pub. The sleeping arrangements . . .'

'. . . are nobody's business but yours and mine.'

They pull up outside the yard. John hands over the car keys to Chantal and tries to kiss her.

'That's not a good idea, especially here,' says Chantal, pushing him away.

John looks disappointed. 'When will I see you again?'

'I'm not sure. I've got some thinking to do.'

John goes into the yard. Was that it, he wonders, a single accidental night, thanks to the snow and a stranded lorry? In the office Tom jumps up and shakes his hand.

'A great win, a great win. George has taken me through it fence by fence. Knocknarea has trotted up sound this morning and eaten everything he's been shown. You must have had the devil of a journey. How was the pub?'

'Uncomfortable. Mrs Vincent got the last room,' says John, truthfully enough. 'The roads were pretty bad.'

'What do you think about Cheltenham?'

'He'll have a good chance. Same distance, stiffer test up that hill. Maltese Cross's connections are sure to let him run.'

John slips quickly back into the yard's routine. He hears nothing from Chantal. He tries telephoning her one evening, but hangs up when a man's voice answers.

He feels guilty – this is, after all, what the Bible and the law call adultery. Does he love Chantal? He's not sure. He loves her body, her sense of humour, her sudden, genuine passion for steeplechasing. But he doesn't feel that lacerating pull at the heart that he has felt once before in his life. Perhaps that's a relief.

A week later, still with no contact from Chantal, he meets Robert in the Mitre.

'Well done. I hear Knocknarea won, and you got snowed in with Chantal Vincent for a night at the Crown. Did anything happen?'

John goes red. 'What do you mean, anything?'

Robert says nothing, waits until John fills the silence.

'All right, I have to tell someone. There was only one room, and one bed, and it was wonderful. She's a lovely woman, but that, it seems, is that. No word for over a week.'

'Ring her to talk about the horse, you idiot. The Cheltenham plans for Knocknarea. And if that's all she wants to talk about, that's up to her.'

'I suppose you're right. Look, I could do with another drink. How are the manorial rolls?'

Robert launches into an impenetrable account of the relationship between rising rents, the price of corn and security of tenure in 1300. John is happy to let this flow over and around him.

'You haven't listened to a word, have you?'

'Of course I have. You're on to something, I can see that.'

'Ha!'

A day later John takes Robert's advice and calls. Chantal answers the phone.

'Knocknarea's very well after Chepstow; we'd like him to run at Cheltenham,' says John.

'That's good – of course I'd love him to run. Keep me posted on how he gets on. I don't know whether I'll have time to watch him on the gallops again.'

'That's a pity. Goodbye.'

'Goodbye.'

John hangs up, a sick feeling in his stomach at the stilted conversation. Why didn't I say something more, like I miss you, or I must see you again. It was the neutral, almost unfriendly tone in Chantal's voice that held him back. This, and a real fear of rejection.

You were brave enough at the Crown, he thinks, but perhaps that was the drink talking. He sits there for a few minutes, then gets up to go home, when the phone rings again.

'John? I'm glad I caught you. It's Chantal.'

'I recognized the voice.'

'Thinking it over, I'm not absolutely certain about Cheltenham. Could I talk it over with you and Tom? Tomorrow afternoon?'

'Fine. Four-thirty?'

'Four-thirty it is.'

John is even more confused by this second call. There's not much to discuss, so why does she want to come over? She was very careful to say she wanted Tom there.

Chantal arrives the following afternoon and John's heart stirs as she comes into the room. She is wearing a blue and green tweed coat and skirt and a cream polo-necked sweater, completely out of place in the scruffy office and muddy yard, but she carries it off. She's a beautiful woman, John thinks, as she shakes first Tom's hand, then his own.

The conversation about Cheltenham is short and straightforward. She wants to be reassured that Knocknarea is up to it, that it's not too soon after Chepstow, and that he will come to no harm.

'It's not too soon; he plainly belongs in that class,' says Tom. 'He's no more likely to get hurt at Cheltenham than at Chepstow. Michael will look after him.'

'Fine. We'll run. Can I see him in his box?'

To John's disappointment, Tom comes too. Knocknarea has his head in his manger when they look at him – after a couple of minutes John says, 'I'm off home. I'm glad he'll get a run,' and shakes Chantal's hand.

He goes out to his Alvis. Chantal's Rover is parked next to his car. He thinks for a moment about leaving a note, decides against it and drives slowly home.

Once inside his cottage he lights the fire; Bella jumps into his lap when he sits down. Somebody loves me, he thinks. He gets up to pour himself a drink, and hears a car outside. There is a knock on the door. He opens it and there is Chantal, holding out his blue handkerchief.

'I forgot to return this; I washed it myself.'

John puts his arms around her as she comes in, his chin on top of her head, and kisses her. He pulls up her skirt and pushes her back onto the kitchen table.

'Gently,' Chantal says, but John isn't gentle.

When he has finished he says, 'I wanted you badly,' and Chantal laughs.

'So did I, but I'm not sure you noticed.' Then she says, 'I must get home – but I want to see you again. If we can manage it. And I'm sorry I was so distant. I didn't know what to do.'

'You can always come here. No one else does, except me and Bella.'

'Bella?'

'She's my regular girl,' says John, and quickly adds, 'my cocker spaniel.'

22.

Jₒₕₙ and Cₕₐₙₜₐₗ meet in John's cottage whenever Billy Vincent is away.

'Billy's a creature of habit; he's always in London for meetings on Wednesdays or Thursdays. But I have to be back before the housekeeper comes in from the lodge at eight o'clock.'

'Won't she see you coming and going?'

'I use the back drive. There's no lodge there. And besides, she likes me, she's frightened of Billy.'

'Are you frightened of him? He seems formidable to me.'

'Formidable is right, partly because he's rich, used to getting his own way, used to people agreeing with him. If I'd agreed to marry him straightaway he'd soon have lost interest. No, he doesn't frighten me, but I don't want him to know about us. I've no idea what would happen, and I don't intend to find out.'

They are sitting over supper in John's kitchen; John has provided the food, Chantal the wine. It's her second visit to the cottage; Chantal has brought, along with the wine, a large cardboard box.

'Open it. It's a present for you, for us.'

John opens the box; inside is a new HMV gramophone.

'It's lovely. But I don't have any records.'

'The records are in the car. I'll show you there's more to music than the Light Programme.'

Chantal goes out to the car and comes back with the big brass horn that fits onto the turntable and a box of fifty records.

'All jazz and blues. I fell in love with the blues in Paris – and there's no point playing a Beethoven symphony when you have to change the record and the needle seven times. Listen to this – it's Bessie Smith singing "St Louis Blues".'

Chantal fits a needle carefully onto the arm, winds up the gramophone, and John hears the blues for the first time.

'It takes you a long way from the English countryside.'

'I first heard Josephine Baker sing "Bye, Bye, Blackbird" at Blacktop's in Paris when I was seventeen. This is her singing "Ain't Misbehavin'".'

'I suppose we are,' says John.

'We're giving pleasure to each other, and we're not hurting anyone.'

'Not Billy?'

'Not Billy. Unless he finds out, and he won't. I'm very careful.'

Chantal changes the record to 'Tishomingo Blues', and when it finishes they go upstairs.

'She always gets up at six to go back to the manor,' says John to Robert Keen a few weeks later over dinner at the Randolph.

'What are you grumbling about? You get up then anyhow to see your horses on the gallops. You don't know how lucky you are. Sex, wine, a musical education. I suppose jazz counts as music, can't see it myself. And no responsibilities. I'd love to be in your shoes – although she'd have to be out of Christ Church by ten o'clock sharp.'

'Ten o'clock?'

'No women in Oxford colleges after ten o'clock. It has been scientifically established that ten o'clock is the moment when undergraduates, and dons for that matter, become unstoppably priapic. How's my horse?'

Robert's horse has finished well down the field in two races since his third at Huntingdon.

'We think he likes heavy going. There's a little conditions race at Newton Abbot in a couple of weeks that might suit him. If it rains continuously between now and the off.'

'Excellent.'

Two weeks later they are at Cheltenham to see Knocknarea run in the Champion Novice Chase. John is too busy getting the horse ready to go to Billy Vincent's box at the top of the grandstand, and the first time he sees Chantal with her husband since they became lovers is in the parade ring. Chantal looks smart, beautiful, distant; Billy has his arm through hers. They shake hands, then John gives Michael Molloy, who doesn't need them, his riding instructions, and follows the Vincents and Tom O'Brien up to the box to watch the race.

'It's soft ground, softer than Chepstow, and this is a stiffer course,' says John.

'Four of the sixteen are in with a good chance,' says Tom.

'Including my boy?' asks Chantal.

'Including your boy. He and Maltese Cross are joint second favourites to Kilreckle, the Irish mare; she's unbeaten in five starts.'

In spite of the going, the race is run at a fast gallop from the off; there are three early fallers, including the favourite. Two out, Knocknarea and Maltese Cross are together going into the fence. Knocknarea hits the fence hard, somersaults in the air and lies still; Michael Molloy is thrown clear. Chantal cries out and buries her face in Billy Vincent's shoulder. John runs out of the box, down several flights of stairs and out onto the course to the second last fence.

Michael Molloy is sitting up, his right hand holding the top of his left shoulder.

'Collarbone,' says Michael. 'He slipped on take-off. I think he's broken his neck.'

Knocknarea is still breathing, surrounded by a little crowd that includes the course vet.

'He'd be dead already if it was the neck,' says the vet. 'We'll splash him with a couple of buckets of water, see if that brings him round.'

After two or three minutes and the water Knocknarea lifts up his head, tries to rise, falls back.

'Give him a bit more room and time,' says John, who holds the horse's head down. 'He's badly winded, but he'll be all right.'

Five long minutes go by, then with help from half a dozen men Knocknarea struggles to his feet.

'I'll take him to the box behind the stand,' says John, and they walk slowly back, Knocknarea unable to put much weight on his off-fore.

They pass the winner's enclosure, where Maltese Cross's connections are still celebrating; their trainer comes over as John walks by. 'Glad to see he's up; he's a good horse. I thought you'd lost him.'

John thanks him and they walk on; Tom is in the box, but there is no sign of the Vincents.

'She was in a terrible state, she thought they were the both of them killed. Mr Vincent has taken her home. At least Michael's not badly hurt, and the horse is alive.'

'Alive, but feel the heat and look at the swelling in his off-fore. We won't know till morning, but it's probably a tendon. We may have to fire him and turn him out for a year. Let's get him home.'

Back at Lambourn, John leads Knocknarea, still stiff and sore after the fall, into his box. Tom O'Brien runs his hand slowly down Knocknarea's leg.

'It's filled up below the knee. Stand the leg in a bucket of cold water for an hour, and again in the morning. He'll not see the racecourse again this season. Will you call the Vincents?'

John feeds Knocknarea and stays in the box for an hour to make sure that Knocknarea doesn't kick the bucket over. Then he puts a bandage soaked in cold water around the leg, straps on a leather guard and goes back to the office. He rings Chantal; the phone is answered by Billy.

'Mr Vincent, the horse is all right. Badly winded, and he took a while to get up. I'm afraid he's damaged his off-fore, and it'll be some time before he's sound again, even if all goes well. Michael Molloy's fine, apart from a broken collarbone. He'll be riding again in three weeks.'

'Thank you. I'll tell Chantal. She's very upset; she thought the horse and the jockey were goners, couldn't bear to stay. She'll be relieved – she's gone to bed, taken a sleeping pill.'

John and Chantal don't meet again for three weeks. And when Chantal next comes to the cottage John feels their relationship has shifted. They were brought together by the win at Chepstow; Knocknarea's fall at Cheltenham seems to have pushed them apart.

'We shouldn't have run him,' says Chantal. She sounds angry. 'It was too tough, that race, that course in heavy going.'

'Listen, he was alongside the winner two out, with plenty in the tank, according to Michael. He slipped on take-off. That can happen over a schooling fence. It was bad luck, and there's plenty of that in chasing. Knocknarea could have broken a leg, or his neck. You've still got a horse, and he should be back for next season.'

'I suppose you're right.'

When they meet at the cottage, they have dinner, share a bottle of wine, play some music, go upstairs and make love. They talk, but their worlds of racing and Oxfordshire society are parallel universes, and the early excitement has disappeared.

On one Thursday evening Chantal says, 'I've got a plan for next weekend. Billy's away in Amsterdam on brewery business, and our housekeeper's on holiday. Can you get away? I'll come and collect you on Saturday morning, and you can bring Bella.'

John can get away, and is excited at the thought of a weekend with Chantal.

'We're not going very far,' says Chantal; when they turn in through the gates of the Vincents' manor house, John is taken aback.

'Have you forgotten something?'

'We've the house to ourselves for two days. I couldn't face being Mr and Mrs Robinson in some suspicious hotel, or risk running into anyone we knew. It's very comfortable here, you'll see, and at least I know my way around. And you've been able to bring Bella.'

The weather is fine, and they go for a long walk after lunch with Bella and Chantal's lurcher Moss; in the evening they have dinner in a small candlelit dining room looking out over the park, and then move to the panelled library. John hasn't dined in such splendour since he stayed with his grandfather after Derriquin was burned down.

'I've looked up your grandfather's house. Middleton Park was designed by James Gandon, painted ceilings by Zuccarelli, famous Italian plasterwork. You're far more used to big houses than I am. We're new money in Oxfordshire.'

'That was a long time ago – I've been living above and around the stables ever since. I still worry I smell of horses.'

'I like the smell of horses. Come upstairs and let me show you.'

Chantal takes him up to the master bedroom, and the large four-poster bed she normally shares with Billy. On the dressing table there is a silver-framed wedding photograph of the Vincents; Chantal turns it face down. She is stimulated by the thought of making love in this bed. John is not.

'What's wrong?'

'I know you're another man's wife, but sleeping with you in this bed seems . . .'

'Look, he spends most of his time in his dressing room. It's ages since Billy and I slept together. And a week since you and I made love.'

After ten minutes Chantal says, 'Perhaps the guest bedroom would work better,' and they go down the passage to an equally handsome room, but one empty of any traces of Billy Vincent. The guest bedroom doesn't work any better, and over breakfast the next morning John apologizes.

'Don't worry. I understand,' says Chantal, although it is not clear to John that she does. They are both quiet over breakfast. Chantal has to collect Billy Vincent from the airport at lunchtime, and her kiss is perfunctory as she drops John and Bella off at the cottage.

Since leaving Ireland John has kept in touch with Charles Burke, and young Charlie has travelled over with horses and stayed with John in Lambourn. Charles has encouraged John to return in a phone call the previous month.

'Johnnie Mannion died last week of a heart attack. Big IRA funeral in Glasnevin. There's no one else who'd be interested in you, and it's all a lot calmer in Ireland now. Cis and I would love to see you again, and you'll do a better job if you pick the horses yourself.'

'You and Charlie have chosen well for this yard. But it's time I came to see you, time I came back.'

John begins his return journey in Kerry – he has written regularly to Josephine, who is still teaching in Drimnamore. She bursts into tears when he arrives at the front door of her cottage.

'I thought I'd never see you again; I thought you'd become English, that visiting Kerry and Drimnamore and Derriquin was too painful altogether.'

'Too painful not to come back, it turned out. But I don't want to see Derriquin.'

'It's still standing, it refuses to fall down. The hotel have built a little golf course in the demesne.'

'Good luck to them. Is Ambrose still alive?'

'He is, of course, and he'll be happy to see you. He knows you're the big trainer in England. Are you married yet?'

'I am not. What about you? My mother always had plans.'

'I'm on my own, happy, still teaching. I'm part of the

landscape now. I haven't been called the Doyle bastard for a long while. And Father Michael, he's still going strong. He knows I'm not trying to turn his children into Protestants.'

John calls on Ambrose and Father Michael, then visits his mother's and William McKelvey's graves, both carefully tended by Josephine. He goes to church on Sunday and is asked to read the lesson.

'That wouldn't be right,' he says to the vicar. 'I'm visiting, I'm not coming back.'

From Kerry John makes the long journey up and across Ireland to Burke's Fort, where his memories are equally strong, equally violent. He doesn't ask Charles about Grania, and avoids the burned-out folly when he goes riding with Charlie, who knows enough to make the detour.

John borrows Charlie's car to go to the sales at the Curragh and then on to County Carlow and Limerick to look at more horses. He buys an unbroken three-year-old from the Kavanaghs at Borris, spends an uncomfortable night in Limerick and in the morning goes to see three horses that Charlie has strongly recommended. He agrees a price for all three. Charlie has a good eye, able to see through the shaggy coats and muddied quarters of untried horses that are at best three-quarters thoroughbred and not in any book. Two of the horses are for Billy Vincent.

The road back from Limerick passes through Maryborough. John decides to drive straight through without stopping. Then changes his mind, parks outside the Post Office and walks around the town. He has no clear plan.

'A railway station, two jails and the old District Lunatic Asylum is about the size of it,' Charlie had said. 'And they've changed the name – it's Portlaoise now.'

'I thought Mary was a Catholic.'

'Bloody Mary was, this one was King Billy's wife.'

Maryborough is ten times the size of Drimnamore, with a narrow main street of shops, bars, offices, two hotels and the ruin of an old bastion showing above the low roof line; John goes into a little square and sits for a while on a disused cattle trough. 'Metropolitan Drinking Fountain and Cattle Trough Association' is carved into its side. He decides to go back to the Post Office. On the noticeboard there is a Mass card, the most recent among many, for Johnnie Mannion.

'Much good may it do him,' says John to himself.

John checks the telephone directory. There are two McCanns living in Maryborough, but only one Eamonn, at Cloonagh, Harpur's Lane. He dials the number, but when it is answered by a male voice he hangs up. Outside the Post Office he stands on the pavement, knowing he should go back to Burke's Fort. Instead he asks a passer-by the way to Harpur's Lane.

Cloonagh is a large double-fronted detached house, one of a group of a dozen similar houses in what looks like Maryborough's best address. John parks on the far side of the road, one house away from 'Cloonagh', sitting in the car for nearly an hour, afraid to do anything but watch. He is about to leave when the front door opens; Eamonn McCann comes out, followed by a woman and a small boy. They both wave him goodbye. The boy runs after his father, says something that John cannot hear, then runs back to his mother.

Grania is no longer the girl John knew in the Trafalgar Folly; she is a woman, still beautiful, even in a plain dress with a white kitchen apron. John feels a hollow in the pit of his stomach and turns his head away for a moment. When he looks back, the boy comes down the steps again onto the lawn, picks up a toy from the grass and goes back into the house. John can see that he is no more than three or four. Grania puts her hand on his head and closes the front door.

The boy is too young to be John's child. Perhaps Grania miscarried, perhaps their child was adopted, or handed over to the laundry nuns. John is fifty yards away from an answer to these questions. It might as well be five hundred miles. He sits in the car until his heart stops pounding, then drives slowly back to the centre of town.

He goes into the office of the *Maryborough Gazette* on the other side of the street to the Post Office. It is cluttered, part editorial, part production, desks at the front, a small printing press at the back. He does some mental arithmetic, then asks the harassed young man who comes to the counter for copies of the *Gazette* for January and February 1925. The young man looks astonished.

'Sure, we keep only the past year. The rest are thrown away. We'd have no room in the place else.'

John leaves the office, and as he turns to cross the road his eye is caught by the display of photographs in the *Gazette*'s window. They are typical of an Irish weekly – weddings, a fair, a traffic accident, the local school play. And in the middle, 'Mr and Mrs Eamonn McCann, Cathleen and Diarmuid McCann at the County Show'. John looks carefully at the photograph, the four of them in their Sunday best, smiling a little stiffly. The girl looks as though she could be five or six years old.

The girl could be his daughter. She looks like Grania, dark-haired, dark-eyed. He feels a moment of intense happiness, then wonders whether this new possibility is better than his fear of miscarriage or adoption. Much better, he decides. He goes back into the office and asks for a copy to be sent to him in England. The young man takes his money and his Lambourn address.

'He's the town lawyer, and she's Johnnie Mannion's daughter. They buried him last month, God rest his soul.' He crosses himself . 'Are you related?'

'I am,' says John, and drives back to Burke's Fort without returning to Cloonagh.

He has four horses to bring back, and catches the boat from Dun Laoghaire two days later. Seeing Grania and discovering he may have a daughter have together reawakened the passion and despair he felt when losing Grania. As he touches the lump where his right jaw had knitted badly, he is reminded of Johnnie Mannion's revenge.

Back at Lambourn he settles into the routine of the stables. Knocknarea is slowly improving, but still confined to his box; the new horses are unridden, and it is John's job to break them in. He continues to see Chantal, but they have changed after their brief weekend together. Chantal thinks John was priggish about the master bedroom; John thinks Chantal was insensitive.

And John's head and heart are still full of his morning in Maryborough. Chantal has been moved a little to the side. John has never told her about Grania, and he is not about to mention that he might have a daughter.

A few weeks later Chantal comes to the cottage in tears. She pushes John away when he kisses her.

'Whatever's the matter?'

'Everything's the matter. Billy's found out about us. And I thought I'd been very careful.'

'How does he know?'

'He's so bloody precise. He saw the mileage on the Rover. Fifty miles a week for six months adds up. I didn't have a good explanation. And then he asked me whether I was having an affair. With you. And I said yes.'

'What happens now?'

'I don't know. He's so angry, with you as well as me. He may kick me out – he hasn't spoken to me since yesterday evening. He's in London today, but coming back this evening. So I need to go home now.'

The next morning John is called into Tom's office.

'I've just had a call from Mr Vincent. The long and the short of it is he says you've got to go. Or he'll take his horses away. He didn't say why, and I didn't ask, but I can make a good guess. He owns more than a third of the horses in this yard, plus two of the four you brought back from Ireland. Sorry, but I've no choice.'

John begins to speak, realizes there is little point, shakes Tom's hand and goes out of the office to Knocknarea's box. He checks the horse's off-fore, rebandages it, gets into his car and leaves the yard for good. As he drives away, he thinks that this is the second time this has happened to him.

23.

AFTER MICHAEL COLLINS's funeral, Dick Mulcahy asks Tomas to stay on as his ADC. The Civil War continues on its confused, sporadic, violent path through the rest of 1922 and Dublin returns to the uneasy guerrilla days of the Tan War. Reprisals begin again. The Public Safety Bill is passed by the Dáil, and by the end of the year eleven Republican prisoners have been executed for the new capital offence of carrying arms.

Tomas has a fierce argument with Dick Mulcahy.

'We're no better than the British. Have we forgotten what the executions in 1916 brought on? These are our people we're killing. How can you shoot Childers for carrying the revolver Michael Collins gave him?'

'Childers is an Englishman at his core. And the rest of them only understand one thing – violence. They began the hostage-taking and the killing. Commuting their sentences would look like weakness. Michael Collins would have done the same.'

'Weakness? That's what General Macready said in 1916. It wasn't true then. It isn't true now. I believe in the Treaty, but not in what we're doing to maintain it. I have to go.'

'You can't go on as my ADC, I see that. But there's no need to resign. We've set up a new department in Oriel Street – I'll have you transferred there.'

Tomas, still uneasy, moves to Oriel Street and is assigned to the Protective Corps, responsible for guarding members of the

Provisional Government, who have been named as legitimate targets by the Republicans.

Oriel Street is full of former members of The Squad. The Protective Corps' duties are routine and straightforward, but it soon becomes clear to Tomas that the rest of the Gardai there are actively engaged in hunting down Republicans. And then killing them. When the bodies of three young Republicans are found shot in a ditch in Clondalkin, Tomas asks Timmy Lawlor, a former member of The Squad, what happened.

'I caught the three of them putting up posters,' says Lawlor. 'They were shot while trying to escape.'

'Like Clancy and McKee and Clune?'

Lawlor laughs. 'You need to catch yourself on, make up your mind which side you're on. If you don't like it, best get back to Kerry and your cows.'

Tomas thinks often of Kitty O'Hanrahan. He wonders about going to see her in Cork, but remembers their last unhappy parting. And he was at Béal na mBláth when Frank O'Gowan had been killed. Frank's wounds had been caused by rifle fire; Tomas had fired only half a dozen shots from his revolver. Nevertheless, he had been in the battle and on the opposite side to Frank. And he had shirked the task of telling Kitty the news.

Dublin is a lonely place for Tomas now. He is an outsider in the Oriel Street headquarters. In spite of his former membership of The Squad, he is thought to be unsound. Some look on him as a potential turncoat and are reluctant to share the details about planned raids. When two Garda detectives in plain clothes are shot and killed in an attack at Ellis Quay, Tomas realizes he is suspected of betraying them. There is an internal inquiry; although it is clear that Tomas knew nothing of the men's plans, he is ostracized in the mess.

He and Michael McGarry, a former Royal Irish Constabulary policeman from Kildare, are responsible for escorting Sean Hales and Padraic O'Maile, two strongly pro-Treaty members of the Dáil. Setting out for a meeting at Leinster House before their escort has arrived, Hales and O'Maile are ambushed by half a dozen Republicans on Ormonde Quay. Tomas and Michael arrive a minute later to find Hales dead and O'Maile wounded. Tomas chases after the gunmen as they run down the Quay, kills one and wounds the other. The four who are left run on down the Quay, then turn and fire at Tomas. Tomas, only thirty yards away, feels a powerful blow on his right side and another on his thigh, knocking him back on the cobbles. He hits his head as he falls and blacks out.

He wakes up the next morning in the Mater Hospital. His partner Michael is there.

'You just about saved our bacon,' he says to Tomas. 'We're in disgrace for losing Hales. They shot him dead and wounded O'Maile in the arm. But you plugged two of them, and the dead one's Tadg O'Leary, who we know killed our two boys at Ellis Quay. So we won't get medals, but we won't get the push.'

Tomas spends three weeks in the Mater; both his wounds are clean, and no bones or vital organs were damaged. The shot to his leg has destroyed his thigh muscles, and it is a full month before he can walk without a stick. While he is in hospital Tomas sends a letter, after many drafts, to Kitty.

> Mater Hospital,
> Dublin
>
> Dear Kitty,
> I was sorry indeed to hear the news about Frank. He'd been through too much to end like that, and you will feel the loss keenly. He was a real leader at Staigue Fort, and after. I will have Masses said for him at the cathedral.
>
> We live in difficult times, and finding myself on the opposite side to Frank, and I suppose you, is hard.
>
> One of the TDs we were guarding got killed in an ambush on Ormonde Quay, and I was wounded, but have made a

good recovery. It's hard to tell what the future holds, but I would like to call on you and your mother when I am next in Cork.

Yours very truly,
Tomas Sullivan

PS You can write to me if you wish, care of CID Headquarters, Oriel Street, Dublin.

When Tomas is discharged from hospital, he goes to the Pro-Cathedral and arranges for a Mass for the soul of Frank O'Gowan on the anniversary of his death for the next five years. The cost makes Tomas whistle, but for the first time in his life he has money in his pocket, even though the payments from the army are unpredictable. He is able to send money back to his mother in Drimnamore.

On his way out he passes a confession booth, goes in and kneels down. This time he doesn't walk out. He begins with Staigue Fort, continues with Eileen and William, Colonel Smyth, and Captain Newbury, and tells the priest he was condemned to death, escaped and is now covered by the amnesty.

'Are you an Irregular? Because in October last the Catholic bishops of Ireland condemned them and their guerrilla war.'

'I'm a captain in the army of the Free State.'

'And did you believe that all these terrible deeds were carried out on behalf of and at the behest of what is now the Free State?'

'I did believe that.'

'Then I can give you absolution.'

Tomas leaves the cathedral with a lighter step. His Catholic faith had been lost, and he had been unable to find it again, either in Cork or through Father Michael. He now feels cleansed, able to go to Mass and take Communion.

Several days later he goes to see Emmet Dalton, who has continued to serve under Dick Mulcahy. It is a brief and unsatisfactory conversation. Tomas begins to unburden himself, and is cut short by Dalton, who replies to Tomas very formally.

'Captain Sullivan, I cannot advise you what to do. Nor can I comment on what goes on in Oriel Street. You must address these problems to the commandant there.'

Tomas stands up and salutes. As he opens the door to leave, Dalton says, 'Maguire's Bar, Amiens Street, seven o'clock tomorrow evening. Civilian clothes.'

In Maguire's Bar, Tomas meets a different Dalton. They continue the conversation about Michael Collins that they had begun on the boat carrying the body from Cork to Dublin.

'It was a terrible waste of a great man. By God, Ireland needs him now. And I really loved him,' says Dalton.

'Why didn't he drive on?'

'Thing about Mick was that he never saw enough action. He had a small part in the GPO, he was Plunket's ADC, and Plunket was too sick to do much. Cathal Brugha in the Dáil asked whether Collins "had ever fired a shot at an enemy of Ireland". And it struck home. He doubted himself, though we never did, given the risks he took in Dublin later on. Maybe that was what all the wrestling was about. He always had to prove himself. With women too.'

'He was with Hazel Lavery the night before we went down to Cork.'

'So I heard – and the Irregulars tried to ambush the car on the return journey. That was your man all right. I would have followed him anywhere – except the boudoir, mind – but plenty hated him. Cathal Brugha, Liam Lynch, de Valera. Especially Dev. Dev knew what he was doing when he wouldn't go to London the second time to negotiate the Treaty.'

They move from Maguire's to dinner at the Standard Hotel.

'This is a temperance hotel for the Brethren, the Quakers,' says Dalton. 'We'll not see many of our brother officers here.'

Tomas talks about Oriel Street.

'The Protective Corps is all right, but the rest of them seem to be carrying on like gangsters.'

'Most of them are compensating because they were never part of The Squad.'

'I didn't like what we did in The Squad, but it had to be done. Now we're killing Irishmen, men we fought alongside. And the executions are senseless.'

'Tomas, I've tried my best. I might have persuaded Mick, although that wouldn't have been easy. He was a hard man right enough – I've always thought he organized the killing of Wilson. But I've not got within a bullock's roar of persuading Dick Mulcahy. So I'm off.'

'What do you mean, off?'

'I'm resigning my commission. They'll not try too hard to stop me. I'm a former officer in the Dublin Fusiliers, and I was in charge of the artillery when we recaptured the Four Courts. That's enough enemies for one man. And my protector is dead. They're spreading a rumour now that I killed him at Béal na mBláth.'

'For God's sake . . .'

'That's what we've become. It's a miracle we stayed united long enough to beat the British. Now we're tearing ourselves apart. Sinn Féin means Ourselves Alone – I don't have any Gaelic, but what's the word for asunder?'

' a cheile. I'm minded to resign too.'

'You'll do no such thing. You're younger than I am, and you'd be wasted on a six-acre farm in County Kerry. Oriel Street will be disbanded soon. Most of the Protective Corps will be transferred to the new Garda Síochána. They need good men, and you'd make a decent policeman.'

The two men shake hands and part. Back in his mess, Tomas decides to wait and see whether Dalton's forecast about Oriel Street is accurate. Ten days later he reads of Dalton's resignation in a footnote in the Daily Orders, a brief column in the *Irish Independent*, attributing this to Dalton's recent marriage.

24.

TOMAS THINKS HARD about resigning when thirty-four anti-Treaty prisoners are shot in January. But Liam Deasy, the commandant general of the Republicans, is captured and calls for an end to the fighting, and when Liam Lynch is killed in a skirmish in the Knockmealdown Mountains in April a ceasefire soon follows.

Oriel Street is disbanded later in 1923. Tomas is offered a job as an inspector in County Clare, based in Ennis. He has a police house, a good salary and plenty to do. Although the Civil War has ended, there has been no formal peace, and there are still thousands of Republicans in the Free State jails.

Tomas still thinks about Kitty O'Hanrahan. He remembers the touch of her lips on his cheek when he left Cork City for the first time, their gentle kiss on Patrick's Hill, her low, firm voice, her brown eyes and, guiltily, her slender legs and ankles. He is still a virgin; he has flirted with some of the Cumann na mBan girls, but Kitty remains the only girl he has ever kissed.

He has had no reply to his letter – given the erratic nature of the post it may never have arrived. Or perhaps Kitty did reply, perhaps her letter was lost. Tomas knows the only answer is to go to Cork, but he remains unsure of his reception, frightened that a confession to Kitty might not be treated in the same way as his confession in the cathedral. Had she married Frank before he was killed? Had his child? Remarried? He isn't sure he wants to know the answers.

CHRISTOPHER BLAND

He makes regular visits back to see his mother in Drimnamore.

'Tomas, it's a terrible thing, you a district inspector and not yet spoken for. You could have your pick of the Drimnamore girls if you stayed here long enough to look them over.'

'Ah, Mother, leave me be. There's time enough.'

'For you, maybe, but not for me. Perhaps I'll set the match-maker on to you.'

'You'll do no such thing,' and he silences his mother with a hug.

After this visit Tomas returns to Ennis via Mallow, where he has to change trains. He sees the Dublin–Cork train pull in, and on an impulse crosses the platform and climbs on board. An hour and a half later he is in Cork. Happy not to be in police uniform, he walks to Station Road, stops on the doorstep of the O'Hanrahan house for a long minute, then knocks hard twice. There is a delay, he hears footsteps, the door opens, and he is faced by a young man of about his own age.

Dry-mouthed, he asks, 'Is Mrs O'Hanrahan in?'

'Ah, they've been gone from here these nine months.'

'Did they leave an address?'

'They did not. We moved in two months after they left, we never saw them.'

Tomas goes next door to try and find out more, but there is nobody home, and the house on the other side is empty. Tomas's carefully rehearsed speech to Kitty dies on his tongue.

He goes back to Ennis depressed, and that evening finishes the best part of a bottle of whiskey to dampen down his mind. You're a man obsessed, he tells himself, and by what? A girl you met three times, kissed twice, and then she turned you down for a man ten years older.

His hangover the next morning is bad, but he hasn't given up. There is only one telephone directory for the whole of the Free State, and eleven O'Hanrahans in the book. He calls them all in the next week. No one can help, save for a distant cousin, who says, 'Wasn't Michael O'Hanrahan executed after the Rising?

194

The widow will be on a pension. The pension people in Dublin will know where it goes, and maybe they'll tell you.'

Tomas visits the Government Pension Office in Dublin, tries to pull rank, and when that fails confesses to the young woman in charge the romantic reason for his search.

'You'd have saved yourself a deal of trouble if you'd told me that at the start,' she says, pushing across a piece of paper. 'Here's the address, but that's only the widow. If the daughter's taken you can give me a call.' She smiles, Tomas hugs her and goes back to Ennis happy.

Tomas now knows where the O'Hanrahans live – Macroom is only thirty miles from Ennis – but he still does not know what Kitty has become since their last parting.

It takes him three days to decide to travel to Macroom. He wears his policeman's uniform – she'd best know what I'm doing from the beginning, he thinks. He arrives in Macroom and asks the way to Mafeking Street. At the top of the street he sees a woman walking towards him, and realizes at once that this is Kitty. She doesn't recognize Tomas in his uniform until she is three paces away, when she stops, putting her hand to her mouth in the same gesture that Tomas remembers from their last unhappy meeting in Cork.

'Tomas, Tomas Sullivan,' she says, holding out both hands. Tomas takes her hands in his, wants to embrace her, holds back.

'I came to Macroom to seek you and your mother out, to see how you were going on,' and adds, not entirely accurately, 'I heard you had moved here from Cork.'

'I'm on my way to the market. Walk with me and you can tell me about your uniform. And carry some vegetables back home.'

'Did you get my letter?' says Tomas.

'Indeed I did, three weeks after you sent it. I wanted to reply, but I didn't know what to say. So in the end I sent a postcard with our new address in Macroom.'

'It never caught up with me.'

They walk along side by side, each wondering where to begin.

Back from the market in Mafeking Street, Kitty says to Tomas, 'Come in for a cup of tea and say hello to my mam. She'll be back soon, she's the housekeeper to the parish priest at St Benedict's.'

They sit, still quiet, over a cup of tea in the kitchen. The silence presses heavily on both of them, until Tomas asks, his voice unsteady, 'Did you get married?'

'We did not. Our wedding was to be the month after Frank was killed. I was pregnant, and we moved away from the knowing looks and pursed lips in Cork. I'm known as Mrs O'Gowan here. But I never was.'

'And the baby's here?'

Kitty begins to cry quietly. 'There was no baby. I miscarried on the night of Béal na mBláth. Michael Collins and Frank O'Gowan weren't the only ones who died that day.'

Tomas moves to kneel beside her chair, takes her hand in his and says, 'I'm sorry, I didn't know, I had to ask.'

'That was part of the reason I took so long to write back. But you're here now, and I'm glad you came. But don't expect . . .'

'I expect nothing.'

Tomas is still kneeling beside Kitty's chair when Mrs O'Hanrahan comes into the room.

'Lord save us, is it Tomas? And what get-up is that?' she says. It is not clear how pleased she is to see Kitty's visitor.

'Mam, Tomas is a policeman now. I wrote to tell him we had moved to Macroom, and here he is to see us both. Sit down now, will you, and have a cup of tea.'

The conversation is stilted; Tomas soon gets up to go, says goodbye to Mrs O'Hanrahan, and Kitty sees him to the front door.

'May I see you again?'

'If you wish.'

'I do wish,' and with that Tomas gives Kitty a quick kiss on her cheek and makes his way back to Ennis.

On the train Tomas is happy that Kitty seemed pleased to see him, but he is confused by Kitty's story. To have become pregnant by Frank, to have slept with him before they were married, didn't match his idea of her. Had Frank forced himself on her? Was she what his mother would have called a loose woman, no better that she ought to be? He goes to bed beset by second thoughts, but by the morning he knows that he is going to see Kitty again.

Tomas visits Macroom twice a month; he and Kitty go for walks along the river, have tea with Mrs O'Hanrahan or in Driscoll's Tea Rooms, occasionally have lunch in the County Hotel in Macroom's main street.

During one of their walks along the river Tomas tells Kitty everything that he had told the priest in the Dublin Pro-Cathedral.

'I was there at Béal na mBláth,' he says. 'I saw Frank's body. I closed his eyes. He was killed instantly. I didn't kill him, I'm sure of that. But I didn't have the courage to come and tell you that night, and I was off to Dublin with Michael Collins's body the next day.'

Kitty shakes her head, says nothing as they walk to the station. When they part she says, 'I'm glad you told me. It's better to know, and it's in the past now.'

Tomas takes this as an absolution, and kisses Kitty's cheek as the train pulls into the station. 'I'll be back soon.'

25.

Tomas's courting of Kitty is slow and careful. It is difficult for him to get away from Ennis to Macroom, and it is clear Kitty does not want to be hurried.

'Tomas, I'm happy for you to come and see me. But my head's still spinning from all that's happened to us, and around us. I've lost a father, I've lost Frank, I've lost a baby.' They are sitting having tea in the County Hotel in Macroom.

'I know that,' says Tomas. 'I thought I'd lost you, and I don't plan to lose you again.'

Walks, endless cups of tea, the occasional supper and chaste kisses when they meet and part mark the slow progress of their relationship. Kitty's lips are as sweet to Tomas as when they first kissed on Patrick's Hill above Cork City.

They are both again devout Catholics; both have had to confess and seek absolution for mortal sins, Tomas for murder, Kitty for going to bed with Frank. Tomas doesn't see that they are equivalent.

'You were about to get married. It wasn't down to you that Frank was killed.'

'That's not how the Church sees it. It's done now, but I'm not letting it happen a second time.'

They are lying on the grass by the river, and Tomas, who has put his hand gently on Kitty's breast, finds it just as gently removed. There are moments when he thinks it strange that Kitty insists that he treats her like the innocent eighteen-year-old he

ASHES IN THE WIND

had first met in his mother's front room in Station Road. But such moments are rare, offset by the pleasure of being with, talking to, looking at, and kissing, however gently, Kitty O'Hanrahan.

'I'd like to take you to Kerry, to Drimnamore, to see where I come from. And to meet my mother.'

Kitty looks thoughtful. 'Tomas, that's a big step for me.'

'Perhaps it's time you took it. Did you ever meet Frank's parents?'

'It's time you put Frank behind you. I've told you that's past and gone, so don't go back there again. And just so you know, Frank's father disappeared off to England before the Great War, and his mother, may she rest in peace, was dead by the time I met Frank.'

Tomas returns to Ennis angry with himself for mishandling the idea of going to Drimnamore, and doesn't raise the question again for some time. His job as inspector involves regular visits to the police stations in his division, disciplinary hearings, promotion boards, complaints from the public, disputes between his own men. He misses, although he doesn't admit this to Kitty, the excitement and danger of the years between 1919 and 1923.

'It's well and good for you to look back on it like that,' says his mother. 'You came through alive, thanks be to God,' and she crosses herself. 'You could easily have been killed at Staigue Fort, or hanged in Kilmainham, or shot dead on the Quays. It gives me the shivers. Every time I see Brigid O'Mahony I think you could have been where Patrick lies, rotting in quicklime.'

'I know that,' says Tomas. 'I'd not speak like that to anyone but you. I'm lucky to be alive, lucky to have a decent job and a good wage. And I'm walking out with a girl from County Cork.'

'Cork, is it?' says his mother as if it were Vladivostok. 'There are plenty of good girls in Kerry.'

'Not as good as this one,' says Tomas, and gradually Annie Sullivan extracts the story of how Tomas met Kitty and how they were reunited. Tomas doesn't feel it necessary to go into detail about Kitty's relationship with Frank O'Gowan.

'She's from a Republican family all right, I'll give you that. And you say she's a good Catholic. Father Michael told me how happy he was that you took Communion this morning.'

'She's a good woman. And she's beautiful.'

'I hope she's strong.' Annie Sullivan means strong enough to cut turf, draw water, herd cattle, bear children.

'She's nearly as strong, nearly as beautiful, as you,' says Tomas, hugging his mother.

When she frees herself from his arms, she says, 'Very well, so. The sooner I see her the better.'

Back in Ennis there is a formal inspection of the division by General Eoin O'Duffy, the Commissioner of the Garda. Tomas had known O'Duffy during the War of Independence , an energetic and successful commander who became deputy chief of staff and close to Michael Collins. O'Duffy is his own man, with a flair for personal publicity and a vanity that is barely held in check.

The tour of Tomas's division goes well; afterwards they are sitting over a glass of whiskey in divisional headquarters when O'Duffy unburdens himself to Tomas.

'Fianna Fáil are out to get me, call me "Yo-Yo Duffy" and demand that I be sacked. They think I was in Cosgrave's pocket, that I hate Fianna Fáil.'

'It's down to you we've got a strong police force in this country.'

'We'll see. De Valera pays no attention when I tell him there's a real Communist threat in this country, that they're infiltrating his beloved IRA.'

Not long afterwards O'Duffy is sacked. Tomas finds the news unsettling, and wonders whether a wholesale purge will follow.

He says to Kitty one afternoon, 'I'm sick of the lot of them. I sometimes think we were better governed when the Brits were in Dublin Castle. The Civil War was bad enough – the endless bickering between Cumann na Gael and Fianna Fáil is almost worse.'

'I'd rather have inefficient Irishmen than efficient Brits. And if they were so efficient, how did they manage to lose the War of Independence?'

'They were tired, we were lucky, and we had Michael Collins. By God, I wish we had him now. He'd never have started the Economic War. It's killing the country slowly. My mother told me the Drimnamore farmers couldn't sell a single cow in Kenmare market last month, had to bring them all back.'

'Perhaps it's because we never got our Republic.'

'Kitty, I was a Volunteer in the Irish Republican Army, I took the oath. The IRA today are small-minded, trigger-happy gunmen who can't come to terms with peace. I miss the old days, right enough, but these little acts of violence make no sense. They shot John Egan last week, a former Volunteer, to what end? It's not the IRA we were part of, it's a different beast altogether.'

Tomas, depressed by the state of his country, starts drinking again heavily most weekends when he is not visiting Kitty. On one of his visits to Macroom he is still showing signs of the night before, his eyes bloodshot, his hands shaking.

'Tomas, I can still smell the drink on you. I'll not have it. What's it to be? Whiskey, or me?'

'It's you, it's you. But I hardly ever see you, and I've a lonely job in a lonely place. We're meant to be together. It's time we set a date for the wedding, became man and wife.'

Kitty kisses Tomas passionately for the first time.

'That would have been even better if it wasn't for the taste of the whiskey,' she says. 'You're right. We've courted long enough. It's time I went to Drimnamore to meet your mother.'

Back in County Clare the next day Tomas is called out to the market in Ennis. The Garda are organizing the auction of three horses for the non-payment of rates. There are a hundred and fifty farmers present, determined to stop the auction, keen to spot the government agent who is there to bid if a real bidder fails to emerge. The superintendent knocks the first two horses down for a pound apiece amid cries of 'Who's the bidder?' and 'Get the bailiff'.

When the third horse, a good half-bred by Royal Academy, is brought forward, its owner snatches the halter, saying, 'This is still mine,' smacks the horse on the rump and sends it trotting through the crowd. Someone identifies the rate collector, who is knocked to the ground and kicked. Tomas pushes forward, draws his revolver and fires three shots overhead. He pulls the frightened man to his feet and escorts him back to the safety of the main body of Garda, revolver still drawn.

Back at Divisional Headquarters, Tomas says to his deputy, 'This isn't what I joined for. I'm on the side of those farmers. Since Dev launched the Economic War there's been no market for cattle at all.'

'You can't give good beef away in Munster,' says his deputy. 'The Brits can live without selling us their coal; we can't survive without selling them our bullocks.'

'And now the government wants farmers to slaughter their cattle. Three pounds for a dead cow, thirty shillings for a dead bullock or calf. I think it's madness.'

A week later Tomas and Kitty make the trip over to Drimnamore. Annie Sullivan is lukewarm at first, but Kitty is undeterred, helps in the kitchen, praises the soda bread, and tells Annie what a good job Tomas is doing over in County Clare.

'The men like him, you can tell that,' she says. 'It's not because they can do as they wish. He's good on the discipline, and he's fair. O'Duffy said Tomas's division was the best in Munster.'

Tomas takes Kitty to meet Father Michael and the O'Mahonys, thinks about calling on Josephine, but decides against it. He wears his uniform to Mass, Kitty's arm through his, and afterwards they are surrounded by a group of Tomas's friends and relations.

'You're the big man in Drimnamore right enough,' says Kitty. Tomas laughs; he likes the welcome, enjoys being teased by Kitty.

They go to one of the bars in Drimnamore after church, where Tomas refuses a Guinness. 'Not while I'm in uniform,' he says.

'Nor at any other time,' Kitty whispers in his ear.

Afterwards they walk through the Derriquin demesne and pass the skeleton of the castle on their way back to Ardsheelan. 'Kerry is a beautiful county,' says Kitty. 'Would you ever come back to the farm?'

'That would depend on you. But not for a long time yet; I'll stick with the Garda. A well-paid job is rare enough in these times.'

Their wedding takes place a month later in Macroom. Father Michael comes over to share the duties with the parish priest, and Emmet Dalton and Michael McGarry come down from Dublin for the ceremony at noon and the long lunch that follows in the County Hotel. Emmet Dalton is best man; he's now making films in Bray, and in his speech says Kitty is pretty enough to star in his next film. Tomas agrees.

Tomas and Kitty have a four-day honeymoon at the Gresham Hotel in Dublin. Kitty has never been to Dublin, and Tomas's experience of the city was as a member of The Squad and the Protective Corps. They visit both cathedrals, Trinity College and the Guinness brewery, where Tomas refuses the free sample. They look at the ruins of the Four Courts.

'Here's where the Civil War started,' says Tomas. 'Here's where Emmet placed the big guns.'

Kitty rules out a visit to Kilmainham. 'I can't bear to think of what happened to my father there,' she says. 'And nearly to you. He's still lying there with the others. They should all be given a decent Christian burial in Glasnevin.'

Kitty goes shopping in Grafton Street, picks out a red dress and red shoes.

'Are you sure we can afford it?' she asks Tomas, shocked at Dublin prices.

'We can, of course,' says Tomas. 'I've spent little enough on you, barring a hundred cups of tea in the County Hotel. You're an inspector's wife, you need to dress the part, Kitty Sullivan.' He enjoys saying Kitty's new name.

On their last night they have dinner in the grand dining room of the Gresham, Tomas in his uniform, Kitty in her new red dress. They are confident enough to enjoy the luxury, aware they are a handsome couple. Upstairs in their room the red dress is carefully taken off by Tomas, carefully hung up in the wardrobe, and then Kitty and Tomas, almost as carefully, make love.

On the train back to Ennis the next day they read the newspapers for the first time since their wedding. The papers are full of stories about Eoin O'Duffy and the formation of the Blueshirts.

'He's a big man, O'Duffy. And maybe that's what the country needs right now.'

Kitty is less certain. 'Ireland needs fewer uniforms, fewer slogans. I don't know what the Blueshirts stand for, except for O'Duffy.'

'They're due to meet in Ennis in ten days' time, it says here. I might go along, hear what they have to say for themselves.'

'Mind, Tomas, I don't want to see you in a blue shirt,' says Kitty. 'Your Garda outfit's uniform enough for me.'

Kitty moves into the superintendent's house and transforms it. The floors are polished, the front step cleaned, the door knocker polished, there are flowers in the front room, a new radio is bought, comfortable sofas and chairs installed. And there is a proper tea when Tomas gets back from work at five-thirty.

After two years, Kitty asks if Mrs O'Hanrahan can move in with them.

'She can, of course, as long as she knows it's your house and you're in charge.'

'We'll find her a job with the parish priest. That's what keeps her out of mischief in Macroom. Besides, it'll be handy her being here when the baby comes.'

'When the baby comes?' Tomas drops his teacup with a clatter as Kitty smiles at him and kneels down beside her, his arms around her waist.

'I'm two months' pregnant. I didn't want to tell you until I was sure.'

Tomas immediately starts work on preparing a room for the baby's arrival. He washes, then paints the walls of the little boxroom next to their bedroom, and buys an old wooden rocking cradle from the junk shop in Ennis, which he strips and varnishes.

When Mrs O'Hanrahan arrives, she tells Tomas to stop fussing over Kitty.

'You'll drive her mad trying to wrap her in cotton wool. This isn't the first baby to be born in the world, and it won't be the last.'

Tomas is unrepentant; his unspoken fear is that Kitty might miscarry again. Kitty is calm and content to let her mother do the heavy housework. Mrs O'Hanrahan has found work as the relief housekeeper in the Carmelite convent.

'There's no money, but Masses for the repose of my soul, and for your father.'

'The two of you are well enough covered with prayers and candles by now. I'd say you'll skip Purgatory entirely. It's time you started to look after Tomas's and my immortal souls.'

Mrs O'Hanrahan brings back regular, lurid news from the convent.

'Mother Superior told us this morning that if the Communists take over they'll turn the Pro-Cathedral into an anti-God museum and Westland Row church into a dance hall.'

'We're a long way from that,' says Kitty. 'And I don't want you filling Tomas's head with these stories, or he'll join the Blueshirts.'

Tomas has heard O'Duffy speak at a big public rally in Ennis, a meeting interrupted by scuffles, shouts and stone-throwing. O'Duffy is a compelling speaker, but Tomas is too preoccupied with controlling the crowd to play close attention, and he comes back unconverted.

'Your man made great play of the news that W. B. Yeats has written the words for a Blueshirt anthem. I'm not sure that's enough to make me sign up.'

Tomas and Kitty lead a quiet domestic life; the red dress, which Tomas persuades Kitty to wear on Saturday nights, is soon outgrown and carefully put away. Mrs O'Hanrahan (Tomas never calls her by her first name, and she refers to him as 'Inspector') is no trouble, spending most of her time cleaning the house or with her nuns, joining Tomas and Kitty for meals only at the weekend.

Tomas is visiting a station in Corofin when Kitty's waters break. He hurries home to find the midwife looking concerned.

'It's a difficult birth, a breech, and I haven't managed to turn the baby around. I've sent for Dr Donovan, but he's an hour away in Inagh, seeing a patient with pneumonia. Mrs Sullivan's lost some blood. No, you shouldn't go and see her – make yourself a cup of tea and we'll come and get you when the baby appears.'

At noon Dr Donovan arrives, shakes Tomas's hand and goes upstairs. Tomas is left pacing up and down, hearing faint, low groans from upstairs that pierce his heart. Two hours later Dr Donovan comes down.

'Tomas, I think you should go for the priest.'

'For the baby?'

'No. Kitty's lost a lot of blood, and we can't get her into hospital now. It's gone beyond that.'

Tomas, who doesn't fully grasp what is happening, fetches the priest and they go upstairs together. Tomas sees Kitty, pale and unconscious, lying on blood-soaked sheets and blankets. Mrs O'Hanrahan is crying; the midwife is holding the baby.

'You have a beautiful boy.'

Tomas brushes the offered bundle away. He has eyes only for Kitty. The priest murmurs the last rites, anoints Kitty's forehead with oil and makes the Sign of the Cross. She gives a final gasping sigh, her eyes open for a moment, then close.

'She's gone. May she rest in peace,' says the priest, closing his prayer book.

'Gone? Gone? She can't have gone. She was having a baby, that was all,' and Tomas cradles Kitty in his arms, his cheek pressed against hers, his body shaking.

They take the baby next door; Tomas stays with Kitty until nightfall, and is finally persuaded by Mrs O'Hanrahan to come downstairs.

'It's God's will, Tomas. And you have a strong son.'

'It's my wife I want, it's Kitty I want.'

Tomas cannot bring himself to hold his new child. He doesn't leave the house for three days, unable to believe that his life has been turned inside out. He is used enough to violent death, but the disaster that has overtaken Kitty seems to belong to a different order of things. He looks at the whiskey bottle on the table for comfort and amnesia, then empties it into the sink.

Kitty is buried three days later, and two days after that his son is christened. Tomas finds it impossible to love, even to hold, his son, who seems to sense his indifference and cries the moment Mrs O'Hanrahan passes him over. She has found a wet-nurse for the baby, christened Michael after the dead martyr of the Easter Rising. Tomas shows no interest in the name.

He begins a round of ferocious inspections of the stations in his division. His reputation changes quickly from that of a reasonable disciplinarian to that of a martinet. He dismisses three Garda for relatively minor breaches of discipline, and when his decisions are reversed in Dublin he responds with an angry, intemperate letter to the commissioner. The commissioner is a supporter of Fianna Fáil, as are two of the three Garda that had been dismissed.

A month after his letter Tomas is summoned to Dublin and sacked; he doesn't fight the decision. He is given a week to move out of his house.

Tomas rents a cottage in Ennis for Mrs O'Hanrahan and Michael, and goes back to Kerry and Ardsheelan. Annie Sullivan tries to console him, to persuade him to think about his son. Tomas still thinks only of Kitty.

'We were good together,' he says to his mother. 'I've never been so happy, and I made her happy too. Now it's all gone. It's a punishment for the things I've done.' He remembers Captain Newbury, how his pregnant wife miscarried and then died.

Annie's robust. 'That's nonsense. You did what you and the others had to do. It was a war. You've confessed, you've received absolution. God has forgiven you.'

'Has he? I can't stay here for long; I may leave Ireland for a while, go to England, find work there. I've put money by for Mrs O'Hanrahan and the baby, and she has her pension.'

After Mass on Sunday, Father Michael stops Tomas on his way out of church and suggests they walk together out to Staigue Fort. Tomas hesitates, then agrees; after two silent miles Tomas unburdens himself to Father Michael, says how he feels Kitty's death was a punishment.

'God doesn't work like that,' says Father Michael. 'Or only in the Old Testament. It's hard to understand, hard to accept, but retribution it is not. You've confessed, you've received absolution, you've done penance enough one way or another.'

On the road below Staigue Fort, they stop at the *boreen* that runs up to the walls.

'I came out when I heard the firing, anointed five dead men, gave three of the wounded the last rites. And I felt responsible – I'd warned your man O'Gowan that Eileen Burke and I had agreed to tell both sides what was planned, but I wasn't persuasive enough for him to call it off. They'll be expecting two Kerrymen and a dog, he told me, not twenty Volunteers.'

'I was one of the firing squad that shot Mrs Burke. Frank O'Gowan wasn't a man you could change once his mind was set.'

'For months I felt responsible, felt guilty, but I've come to terms with it now. As you must.'

Back at Lissagroom, Annie tries to persuade Tomas to stay. 'I need you here, and your boy needs you.'

'This farm can't support the two of us.'

'It can if you want it.'

Tomas doesn't want it. He plans a trip to England; then his eye is caught by an article in the *Independent*, saying an Irish Brigade is about to leave to fight for the Church and for the Nationalists. Three days later Tomas, together with four hundred other volunteers, is on board a German boat, the SS *Urundi*, on his way to Spain.

III.
Spain, Ireland and Greece
1936–1969

26.

JOHN AND ROBERT are lying in a narrow trench below the crest of a hill in Aragon, and if they raise their heads they can see across the red, fissured earth of the steep valley to the matching ridge on the other side. The heat draws shimmering lines across the valley; scrub oak, a few stunted olive trees, a dried-up river bed, an abandoned field in which whatever had once been planted had long ago withered and died.

'They'll not attack in daylight across the valley, will they?' asks Robert. He is unshaven, dirty, his fingernails broken and grimy, his spectacles held together with wire, a crack across one of the lenses. His uniform is torn and inexpertly patched, his boots red with dust.

'Doesn't seem likely. You'd think they'd come round on the plain.' John points to the west, where the two ridges drop down to a vast red flatland. A small town, Huesca, is visible in the distance. 'It looks more like Africa than Europe.'

'The Moors must feel at home. I hope our commanders have, what's that disgusting phrase, secured our flanks.'

'I expect they're too busy rooting out informers.'

An artillery shell shrieks overhead; it lands a quarter of a mile away and fails to explode.

'Two out of five shells are duds,' says Robert. 'So our commissar told me yesterday. And he says the Moors' morale is terrible, that they all want to go home.'

'I'm right with them. This doesn't feel like a war we're winning.'

'The commissar's view is that we're on the side of the angels.' The end of the sentence is drowned by the shriek of another artillery shell.

'Perhaps we ought to dig deeper, not rely on the angels.'

Robert takes a long drink from his water bottle and begins to clean his rifle.

'How many times have you fired that bloody thing?' says John. He lights a cigarette and throws the packet over to Robert.

'Twenty or thirty times.'

'Twenty or thirty dead Fascists then.'

'It would be an unlucky Fascist that was hit by a short-sighted Oxford history don. Look, here's our lieutenant come to lower morale.'

The lieutenant, a tough Scots Communist from the Clydebank shipyard, arrives in a crouching run, says, 'We expect an attack tonight. We'll hold the hill, then counter-attack and sweep down into Huesca,' and runs on.

'If I understood Big Jimmy's dialect and dialectic right, that sounds like a good, simple plan. Maybe we'll even pull it off.'

'I wonder where Kate is now,' says John.

They had met Kate Lowell, a tall, fair-haired war correspondent for the *New York Times*, when their contingent arrived in Alicante to join the International Brigade in the spring of 1937.

'Can you two give me a story?' she asked, picking them out in the transit camp. 'I can't take another hardline Communist explaining why the real enemies are the bourgeoisie.'

'We're your men,' said Robert. 'I'm an Oxford don specializing in thirteenth-century manorial rolls and he's an Anglo-Irish racehorse trainer. Completely untypical. Eighty per cent of the International Brigade are working class, and half belong to the Party.'

'You're just what I wanted,' said Kate, and they went to the canteen where she was the only woman among sixty or seventy men. They talked over thin soup and black bread.

'What brought you here?' asked Kate, pulling out her note-book.

'We came for the food,' said Robert.

'Don't pay any attention,' said John, leaning across the table as he spoke. 'We're both here, we're all here, because we believe in the *causa* of the Republic. If we fail there'll be a war in Europe within two years.'

When Kate stood up, John looked again at her carefully, her brown eyes, her short blonde hair, her long fingers closing the notebook, locking them away in a war-free zone in his memory, then said, 'Make sure you find us if you get to the front line.'

'Of course I'll get to the front line, probably before you. I've already been shot at and shelled, which is more than either of you can say.'

'Quite right,' said Robert. 'My friend means well, he just wants to see you again.'

They met again six months later in Jarama, a town secure enough for a dozen journalists to be bussed in. John heard of their arrival and went to the Hotel Victoria, the only large hotel. He saw Kate standing in a small group of journalists outside on the pavement. They were being briefed by a smartly dressed commissar, who scowled at John as he returned his salute.

'Robert and I want to buy you a drink in the Bodega Nacional. It's just round the corner. We've become battle-hardened veterans since we saw you last.'

'I'd like that,' she said, smiling. 'I made shameless use of you after our meeting in Alicante. You were both famous for a day in New York.'

Two of the other journalists looked disappointed as Kate walked away from their group.

The cobbled square had a plane tree at each corner and a dry fountain at its centre. It seemed remote from the war. There was little food in Jarama. Bread, meat and cigarettes were rationed, there was no coffee or milk, and only wine was plentiful. Robert made Kate laugh through the long, hot evening. John, more serious, found it hard not to keep his eyes fixed on her. He persuaded a waiter, one of the collective that had taken over the bodega, to produce black olives and hard cheese, which they washed down with several jugs of rough red wine.

'It turns out,' said Robert towards the end of the evening, 'that Tolstoy was right. War is chaos and confusion. There is no connection between the plans of the generals and colonels and what actually happens on the ground. It's all a series of random events, and the most important thing to do is not to kill the enemy but to avoid being killed yourself.'

'I've had a detailed briefing with maps and statistics showing how the Government forces will defeat Franco's Nationalists within a couple of months,' said Kate.

John refilled their glasses. 'That's their reality, not ours. Our chaos is greater than Franco's. We're a patchwork army, Communists, socialists, anarchists, anarcho-syndicalists, democrats, mostly untrained, and 'as suspicious of each other as the Fascists. There's a war of initials going on – CNT, FAI, POUM, PSOE, PCE, UGT. Hard to keep up with. Although we have plenty of men, enough to shoot twenty of our own troops, including three officers and a brigadier, after the Brunete fiasco. We've got several hundred in our own concentration camp. Which is where I'll wind up if a commissar overhears me.'

Kate lit a cigarette, offered the pack to Robert and John, then asked, 'So who will win in the end?'

'The big battalions always win in the end. At the beginning, in Barcelona especially, we thought we were fighting for an idea, for a new kind of democracy. Then the commissars took over. Now we're fighting for survival.'

A militia man walked past, unshaven, dark blue boiler suit, red and black scarf, rifle slung over his shoulder. Robert gave a right-fisted salute.

'No *pasarán!*'

'No *pasarán!*'

'Anarcho-syndicalist. Surprised he didn't ask for our papers.'

'How can you tell?'

'Red and black scarf. He'll be off to a meeting. If long lectures and group discussions could win a war, we're there. They've just sent round a new directive reinstating the salute.' Robert fished a crumpled copy of 'Our Fight' out of his pocket. 'It says here, "A salute is a sign that a comrade who has been an egocentric individual in private life has adjusted to the collective way of getting things done." And listen to this bit. "A salute is proof that our brigade is on its way from being a collection of well-meaning amateurs to a steel precision instrument for eliminating Fascists."'

Ten minutes later John stood up and took Kate's hand. 'Let me walk you back to your hotel. Robert will settle the bill.'

Robert and Kate were both surprised at this sudden end to the conversation. She looked again at John, brown, lean, tall, smiling, and didn't drop his hand as they walked slowly back in the hot night. Outside the hotel, John, a little dizzy from the heat and the wine, steadied himself by putting his hands on Kate's shoulders. She laughed.

'I thought you were seeing me home.'

'You know what Horace said? "Trust not tomorrow's bough, for fruit. Pluck this, here, now." You're a pomegranate, a peach. I'm in love. I don't think I'll make it back to barracks.'

'Horace would say you'd better stay here until the morning.'

'That would be safer. Robert will tell them I haven't deserted.'

27.

Dear Mother,

I am sorry not to have written sooner, but we have been constantly on the move since we arrived in Spain, and much has happened, not all of it good, I must say.

We began badly when our lorry from Kenmare broke down and we thought we would not get to Galway in time. As luck would have it the embarkation was delayed for two days. La Bandera Irlandesa had a great send-off, with Archbishop Gilmartin leading us in prayer in the big square in Galway. We sang 'Faith of Our Fathers', feeling that we were going on a crusade. O'Duffy made a good speech.

That has been the best of it so far. Our German ship, the SS *Urundi* of fourteen thousand tons, was not allowed within the three-mile limit, so we had to board the *Aran Island* tender. On our way out the wind got up, and we sheltered under Black Head for five hours. Many of our fellows were seasick, and twenty of them could not face the rope ladders up the side of the *Urundi* and turned back. Or perhaps it was the thought of five more days at sea.

Anyhow we arrived at El Ferrol, and entrained to Caceres, where we were given uniforms and, eventually, decent rifles after we refused the single-shot Mausers. They were at least thirty years old.

We did some basic drill and training in Caceres. We are a mixed bunch, a few old soldiers, IRA or British Army, but mostly green farmers' boys. There are four companies in the Bandera. I am in No. 2 Company.

Next thing we were off to the front to take part in an attack on the Republicans (strange that our enemies are called Republicans) near Jarama. What happened was we were attacked on the way, not by the enemy, but by our own troops – Canary Islanders, who hadn't been told we were coming and opened fire on us without a warning. They killed four of our men, a Kerryman from Dingle among them. We fired back, not knowing who they were. Apparently we killed a dozen of them, but that was little consolation. It was all of an hour before we all realized our mistake; as you would expect there has been a real Donnybrook about the whole affair since.

That was over a month ago. We have seen many ruined churches and convents, and the stories of Republican outrages against the Church are not exaggerated. It is certain that four thousand priests and nuns were killed in the first weeks of the war, and many more since. At the same time our side is pretty ferocious – not many prisoners are taken, and those that surrender are treated very roughly.

The food is plentiful but most of it not my taste. There is an abundance of wine, and many of our fellows drink too much of it. I must close now, and remain,

Your loving son,
Tomas

PS Show this letter to Mrs O'Hanrahan when you next see her, as I haven't written to her yet.

Valencia, June 1937

Dear Mother,
Since I last wrote we attacked the village of Titulcia, our first proper action. It poured with rain, the attack failed, and we

lost two men. The next day we were ordered to renew the attack, and our leaders refused. They don't seem to have much of an appetite for fighting, and we've been kept in reserve ever since, not a surprise.

We saw little of O'Duffy, who spent most of his time in hotels well behind the front line. The men have started calling him 'O'Scruffy' and 'Old John Bollocks'. He was a good Commissioner of the Garda, but he is completely discredited after Titulcia.

So when our six months, which is all we signed up for, was over, we were asked whether we wanted to fight on, not that we'd done much fighting. Out of four hundred men only eight of us agreed to stay. I still believe in the cause and I've seen what the Reds can do to churches and priests and nuns. And I'm not ready to come back to Ireland yet. The eight of us are now part of the Foreign Legion and we have a new general, Yague. This is a different kettle of fish entirely, much tougher, battle hardened, well drilled and disciplined. We are more than a match for the Republicans; our air force, mainly Germans, has shot down almost all the Republican planes.

Your loving son,
Tomas

Teruel, December 1937

Dear Mother,
We are outside Teruel, a town that the Republicans kicked us out of at the end of last year. Reinforcements have arrived and the weather has improved, which means that our air force has bombed the town for three days in a row. We expect to attack on the ground very soon.

I am getting used to the Spanish food, although I avoid the wine. I look forward to coming home to a good stew. We have the other side beat, and the war will be over by the summer. Don't worry about me. It's much less dangerous here than Dublin was in 1921.

My best regards to Mrs O'Hanrahan and Father Michael.

Your loving son,

Tomas

28.

Y THE END of 1937, John and Robert's battalion is in Teruel – a different war and different weather. Teruel is a small town in harsh country; it is bitterly cold. They fight from house to house, hand-to-hand combat with bayonets, interrupted by strafing and bombing from the Nationalists' Condor Legion whenever the weather allows. The Republicans pray for snow and cloud, and for the last two weeks of December their prayers are answered, although their casualties are heavy. Robert is hit by shrapnel and has to go back to a field hospital for three days.

'You've taken Teruel while I've been away. I didn't think you could manage it without me,' he says to John on his return. He has a bloodstained bandage around his head and he looks tired and grey.

'I'm glad you're back. How do you know we've taken the town? We're still getting shelled every day.'

'It's in this morning's directive. They say the journalists are coming for tonight's concert. Perhaps your friend Kate will be there.'

'What concert?'

'God only knows.'

There is a concert on Christmas Eve; Paul Robeson sings spirituals to the battalion in the Town Hall.

'The Nationalists have got their Moors; we've got Paul Robeson,' says Robert.

'Ideologically impure, that comment. And he can sing,' says John.

Next to the stage there is a small group of journalists and brigadiers, healthy and well dressed, a sharp contrast to the four hundred ragged soldiers sitting in the well of the hall. Kate is one of two women in the group; she is wearing a dark green tunic, and looks to John like someone from a world to which he no longer belongs. He manages to catch Kate's eye and she waves. After the concert he hurries outside. The journalists are already in the bus. Kate rubs a clear space in the glass, presses her hand against the window, and is gone.

Three days later the Nationalist counter-attack begins. The weather clears, the bombing and the strafing are relentless, and the Republicans are slowly driven back to the edge of the town. Teruel is no longer pretty, much of it destroyed by grenades and dynamite in the house-to-house fighting. The bombs of the Condor Legion have completed the destruction. Only a few buildings are intact. Most are shells, their walls cracked, an occasional half-floor with a ruined bedstead or bath. In the streets, now under six inches of snow, there are abandoned carts, several burned-out tanks and the frozen bodies of dead mules and horses.

John's section is told to make their own way out and regroup when they can. They pass another section of their battalion guarding a small group of prisoners huddled on the ground. On the wall above them someone has painted, '*Teruel será la tumba del fascismo.*'

'This lot overran their advance,' says the lieutenant. 'Or else they got lost. Some of them are your countrymen, leftover Micks from the Bandera Irlandesa.'

John looks at the men sitting on the ground, looks again and sees Tomas Sullivan – gaunt, bearded, left arm in a makeshift sling, no boots and bleeding feet, the man he had last seen in Kilmainham Jail awaiting the hangman.

'Tomas,' says John, and Tomas raises his head.

'What are you going to do with them?' John asks the lieutenant.

'What do you think? We're not taking them along with us.'

'That man's mine. I've unfinished business with him.'

The lieutenant hears the intensity in John's voice, then says, 'One bullet's as good as another.'

John prods Tomas to his feet with his rifle. Tomas rises slowly, and John escorts him around the corner and into a ruined shop fifty yards away.

Tomas looks at John for the first time. 'You need to know how to do this. One shot to the heart, one to the head to finish the job.'

The guards and the prisoners hear two shots. One of the younger prisoners begins to cry, his tears leaving two pale streaks in his grimy face. An older man sitting next to him puts an arm around his shoulder. Three minutes later John comes round the corner, his rifle slung over his shoulder. His hand shakes as he lights a cigarette.

'Now you've got the hang of it, you can help us finish off the rest,' says the lieutenant.

'That was family business, an old score settled. We'll see you at the rendezvous.'

As they trot down the street Robert looks at John curiously. 'That was strange.'

'We should have stopped the executions. That boy can't have been more than seventeen.'

'Hard to do after you'd just picked one of them out and polished him off yourself. That lieutenant would have shot us if we'd tried to stop him.'

'We should have tried.'

The retreat from Teruel is disorganized and drawn out; it is several days before the battalion regroups and is reinforced. They are held in reserve until the battle of the Ebro. This last desperate attempt to win the war, a long battle of attack and counter-attack, finally ends in November with the Republicans thrown back across the river.

The International Brigade is withdrawn in October. A month later they are given a farewell parade in Barcelona past President Azaña and General Rojo. Three hundred thousand people line the streets, the women throwing flowers, many weeping, as the tired, dirty soldiers march down the Avenida Diagonal.

'La Pasionaria has told us, "We are history, we are legend, we can go proudly." I think we should go quickly,' says Robert. 'It's an odd way to celebrate defeat.'

'Let's celebrate being alive.' John looks at Robert, gaunt with dysentery, a shrapnel scar on his forehead. 'We're abandoning these people to the Nationalists. We know how bad that will be. I'm not sure they do.'

'Now what do we do? Back to manorial rolls, back to horse-coping?' says Robert.

'For as long as Hitler lets us.'

They make their way across the Pyrenees in a train crowded with refugees, and then on to Paris, where they part. John spends two days at the Paris office of the *New York Times*, trying to find Kate.

'I can't tell you where she is,' says the duty editor. 'You can see from the paper that her last despatch was from Madrid.'

Back in England John tries the London office with little more success. Kate's next piece is from Paris, and he curses his timing. He sends a hopeful telegram asking her to meet him for lunch at the Savoy in a week's time.

Against the odds Kate arrives for lunch. John watches her come down the short stairway into the restaurant; she is wearing a white dress that makes her arms and legs look very brown. John stands up and hugs her tightly. Kate is surprised for a moment at his embrace, kisses his cheek, then pushes him away to look at his face.

'God, you look tired. I'm glad you tracked me down. I've never seen you in a suit before, only your scarecrow uniform.'

They talk about the war, and then about each other. At the end of lunch John takes her hands in his over the empty glasses and says, 'I want to marry you.'

'Oh my. I thought you Englishmen were reserved.'

'I'm Anglo-Irish, and unreserved. I mean it.'

'My dear, you hardly know me. We've spent an evening and this lunch in each other's company.'

'And a night together.'

'I'm surprised you remember – you went straight to sleep the moment you got into bed, and I had to shake you awake in the morning to get you to first parade in time.'

'I remember what you looked like with no clothes on.'

'You were seeing at least two of me that night.'

'I'll make up for it. I've booked a suite here for three days. I can return your Jarama hospitality. It's a much nicer room.'

'That wouldn't be hard. But I'd like to inspect the suite.'

Kate and John don't leave the Savoy for three days, and are married ten days later by special licence. Robert Keen is their best man.

29.

JOHN AND KATE spend their brief honeymoon in the Lake District, where the rain fails to spoil their enjoyment of each other. Finding out whom they had married, after less than a week's acquaintance, is exciting. They already know they are well matched in bed, which is where they spend most of their time, but they also discover they are compatible over breakfast, on long walks even in the rain, on their fondness for dogs and dislike of cats, on their preference for whisky over gin. Each knows little enough about the other's history, and indeed about the other's country, to make discovery a pleasure. When John tells Kate he wants to train horses again in Ireland, when Kate tells John she intends to continue as a journalist for the *New York Times*, it seems a reasonable balance.

John takes Kate back to Ireland to stay at Burke's Fort, where Kate is presented to Charles and Cis. They are about to move out to the dower house on the edge of the estate, and young Charlie and his Irish wife have already moved in.

John has told Kate about Chantal. He has not told her about Grania, about the Trafalgar Folly, about the possibility that he has a daughter living a few miles away in Maryborough. He knows that Charles and Cis will have erased that part of his past from their minds.

Two days before they are due to leave for London, young Charlie says over breakfast, 'The O'Connells are selling Killowen, twenty miles away from here in County Kildare.

Forty boxes, a cobbled yard, two hundred acres, access to the Curragh gallops and a nice dry house with a fanlight. It all needs work. They're asking fourteen thousand and I hear they'll take twelve.'

John does some quick arithmetic and rings the bank. Kate thinks the house is charming.

'It's your decision, though,' she tells John. 'You're the one who is going to be living here all the time. And I'm not going to make the curtains.'

John laughs. 'I picked you out in Alicante as a real American home-maker. How could you have deceived me so?'

Forty-eight hours later the house is theirs. They decide to lock it up and ask young Charlie to find someone nearby to keep an eye on it until they return.

'And that may not be for a while – there'll be a war before the year is out,' says Kate.

'Dev's determined to keep Ireland out of it, and I think he's right. It's too soon after the War of Independence to be fighting on the same side as the British, and conscription won't work here. I hope the Republic will be friendly neutrals, though the Treaty Ports have gone,' says Charles.

'I'm still a hybrid, still Anglo-Irish,' says John. 'I feel bound to volunteer if they'll take me. I can't have Kate risking her life as a journalist while I sit at home. She's off to Berlin next week while I try to find the Royal Irish Dragoons.'

John finds the Royal Irish Dragoons in Tidworth.

'I see your father was a Dragoon,' says the commanding officer. 'Won an MC, killed on the Somme. I can make you a second lieutenant, though you're a bit long in the tooth, give you a troop, see how you get on. None of us knows anything about armoured cars as they haven't arrived yet, so you won't be at a disadvantage. At least you've been under fire, unlike the rest of our troop leaders.'

*

228

For the next six years John and Kate meet as often as they can manage, in the South of England where the Royal Irish Dragoons spend all of the Phoney War, in London on leave, in Cairo, and in Paris after the liberation. James Burke is born in Dublin, the first of his family for two hundred years not to have been born in Derriquin. Kate is combining a report on Ireland's role in the Emergency with a trip to Killowen for two months before James arrives. She cables John in Egypt, 'A nine-pound boy; both of us fine.' James spends most of the war at Burke's Fort alongside his cousin Fred, born later in the same year. When the war is over John is a stranger to his five-year-old son, who bursts into tears when he is first introduced to his father.

Back at Killowen after demobilization in 1946, John gradually restores the house and the yard, with a little help and some money from Kate. Racing in Ireland recovers quickly after the war. For some time John struggles with only a dozen mediocre horses in the yard, surviving through a number of big bets at decent odds.

'It's a risky strategy,' says Kate. 'I'm a Boston Puritan at heart, at least about money. We could always live in the house without the horses and let the land. My income from journalism is pretty steady.'

'I'll make a go of it, you'll see. I'm the first Burke to have a proper job – I'm not going to be the first to live off his wife's money.'

'What about your grandfather and Letitia Hamilton?'

'It was different then.'

John does make a go of it. He has several good wins with difficult horses, buys unbroken four-year-olds out of muddy fields in the South and the West, and passes them on to new owners at reasonable prices. Most of the new owners stay with the yard.

One day Michael Molloy turns up at the yard looking for a job.

'I'm too old now for the jumping game. I can't do the lighter weights any more, and I've broken five collarbones, three wrists and an ankle. I haven't counted the ribs. I reckon I learned enough watching you and Tom O'Brien at Lambourn to be useful to you here.'

John agrees. He has been his own head lad since he started at Killowen, and Michael proves invaluable. He is a good judge of when a horse is out of sorts, and a hard bargainer with the feed merchants. Killowen's growing prosperity is reflected in the yard. The boxes are whitewashed, the doors painted, loose slates replaced, and the tack is immaculate.

'Some of your competitors believe a smart yard puts owners off, looks expensive. They'd rather use binder twine than repair a head-collar properly,' says Willie O'Driscoll, a cattle dealer from County Louth who is one of John's biggest owners. 'I think you'll find the paint pays for itself.'

It does pay for itself. John no longer has to rely on the bank, and can afford the boarding school fees for James.

'I think it's pretty barbaric,' says Kate. 'Sending our boy away for three-quarters of the year to be looked after by cranky school-masters. I bet you half of them are queer.'

'Well, boarding school did you no harm. You're often away, and the stable routine doesn't give me a lot of time to spend with James. It's better than the Christian Brothers.'

'The Brothers aren't the only alternative.'

James goes away to school despite Kate's misgivings; the public school system is an aspect of Anglo-Irish life that she decides to accept, not least because she is away on assignment for at least half the year. She gets some satisfaction from pointing out to John the inaccuracy of the description.

'Typical of the English to describe something as public that's the exact opposite.'

John grunts and doesn't reply.

James isn't consulted, and leaves Killowen for preparatory school in Northern Ireland with a bewildered acceptance that this is the way things are. He shares a dormitory with twelve other eight-year-olds, who seem equally miserable for most of their first term. The routine and the discipline, the latter often random and supported by the final sanction of the headmaster's cane, give James a carapace of toughness that dismays Kate at the beginning of every holidays.

'It takes him a week to get used to being hugged,' she says to John. 'And just as we're getting to know each other he's off again.'

'Or you are. There'll be nobody about to hug him when he's out in the world. And he says he likes it, he's made friends there.'

James is happiest at Killowen, especially when his mother is at home. He rides out every morning with the other lads in the yard, and his father makes sure he gets his fair share of the difficult horses.

'You'll learn nothing if all you ride are the patent-safeties,' says John. 'You're strong enough for the job. Most of our lads want to ride at ten stone seven, and you can be fourteen pounds heavier in point-to-points.'

Boarding school is a kind of limbo to be endured, where James is neither happy nor unhappy, where he has no enemies but also no friends close enough to ask back to Killowen.

Years later, Kate asks him whether it was as bad as she had sometimes imagined. 'I felt guilty about sending you away to school, especially when you were only eight,' says Kate. 'But not guilty enough to keep you at home.'

'My prep-school memories are an odd jumble of Latin, ration books and Waverley pens. "They came as a boon and a blessing to men, The Pickwick, the Owl, and the Waverley Pen." You fitted the little steel pen-nib into a wooden pen-holder. The nibs were bronze-coloured, and they crossed easily, or broke. You had to dip the pen into a white porcelain inkwell that fitted into a hole in your desk. I always had blue-black fingers.'

'I remember you were ravenous when you came home from the North of Ireland.'

'You had no rationing in the Republic. We had ration books with different-coloured detachable tickets for eggs, butter, meat, sugar, milk. And sweets. The food was terrible.'

'I'm ashamed we never came to see you. Perhaps I thought if I saw you there I'd have taken you away. I never met the headmaster. Some friend of John's recommended the school.'

'The headmaster used to take the scholarship class, six of us, for extra Latin in his bedroom after supper and before lights-out on Thursdays. We were in pyjamas sitting on his bed. I suppose he was gay – queer, we would have called it then if we'd known the word – but nothing like that happened, at least not to me. And I can still remember some of the lines from the *Aeneid:* "*Quadrupedante putrem sonitu quatit ungula campum.*" It describes, and sounds like, the noise horses' hooves make on the dusty plain. I learned it years ago, and it's still stuck in some strange corner of my brain.'

Kate laughs and puts her arms around James. 'Some people would regard that as a complete justification for sending you there. I'm not convinced, but it's done now, and you don't seem badly scarred.'

'I remember at Winchester they tried to call me Paddy, to get me to speak in an Irish accent, to show them my shillelagh. It was pretty good-humoured, and I refused to answer to a nickname. They soon moved on to more rewarding targets.'

When he was fifteen James asked his father, 'Dad, what are we? English, Irish, or what?'

'We're the Formerlies,' John replied. 'Look at us in the *Irish Landed Gentry.*'

He pulled down a heavy red volume from the bookshelf and leafed through its pages. '"Burke formerly of Derriquin, Eyre formerly of Eyre Court, Kirkwood formerly of Woodbrook, Persse formerly of Roxborough, now Box 462, Aptos, California." Formerlies all.'

He poured himself a generous whiskey and a little water.

'We don't belong in England or in Ireland. We're upper class in Ireland, middle class in England if we're lucky. We stand up for "God Save the Queen", we know the words of "The Soldier's Song", but not in Gaelic, we want the Irish rugby team to beat the English and the English to beat everyone else. We send our sons to Trinity College Dublin, not Trinity College Cambridge. We talk about World War Two, but it was the Emergency in Ireland. We're happy when the Irish economy booms, we're even happier when it busts. We dislike comic stories about the Irish unless we tell them ourselves. And on the back of Swift and Burke and Sheridan and Yeats we give ourselves intellectual airs.'

John got up to refill his glass. 'Brendan Behan was close to the mark: "An Anglo-Irishman only works at riding horses, drinking whiskey and reading double-meaning books in Irish at Trinity College." I've known a few like that, your cousin Rut Uprichard, for instance. Won the Conyngham Cup at Punchestown when it was still over banks and stone walls, finished fourth in the Grand National, and drank himself to death at the age of forty-two. Though he never read a book – too busy with the women.'

'So we're Anglo-Irish then?'

'Both and neither. That'll have to do. That's what we are.'

As his father finished, James looked up to see his mother standing by the door. She smiled, walked over and ruffled James's hair. She didn't comment on the conversation until the following morning, when she and James were sitting in the kitchen having breakfast. John was out in the yard with the horses.

'Fifteen years in this country has washed the rose-tint off my glasses. This is a priest-ridden country; you can't buy a copy of *Ulysses* in Ireland thanks to our extended version of the Index. And now, God help us, the bishop of Galway has banned mixed bathing. Anyone who can raise a flicker of sexual excitement once they're up to their waist in the Irish Sea deserves a medal. The Anglo-Irish and the Irish live in parallel historical universes, they use the past to make the present halfway bearable. They've been fighting each other for seven hundred years. When the war was over in 1921, the real Irish straightaway started another between themselves. The Anglo-Irish just gave up.'

'Dad hasn't given up.'

'No, he hasn't. Surprising, given what he went through. Your father entered the Anglo-Irish world just as it began to disintegrate. His mother was executed, Derriquin burned, and he had to leave the country. God knows why he came back – except he does think, in spite of everything, that he belongs here.'

'I think that too,' said James.

The yard continues to prosper, and John, while James is away at school, begins to wonder again about Grania's daughter. He has left it too late to talk to Kate about her, and he is still unsure whether the girl is his. Would Grania tell him the truth? Has she told her daughter? And what would he do if he was the father? By now she would be a young woman, perhaps a graduate, perhaps married, perhaps a mother.

So John does nothing – until, on a rare visit to Dublin, he goes to the Periodical Library, gets a reader's ticket and asks for the copies of the *Irish Independent* for January and February 1925. In the Births column for 7th February he finds the entry he is looking for. 'To Eamonn and Grania McCann, of Cloonagh, Harpur's Lane, Maryborough, the precious gift of a daughter, Cathleen Mary. Deo Gratias.'

John copies out the entry with an unsteady hand. This new certainty gives him a disturbing combination of pleasure and pain. One barrier to action has been removed; all the others remain. Back at Killowen he puts the copied entry into an envelope that contains his Military Cross, Henry Burke's wedding ring and his will, and locks the envelope away on the top shelf of the safe.

John continues to think about going over to Maryborough, telephones Grania McCann twice, but hangs up without speaking. Instead he goes back to County Kerry to see Josephine for what may be the last time. She is still living in the same house in Drimnamore. She gives him a cup of tea and some soda bread in her front room.

'Baked it myself, so I did. Go on, try it, the blackberry jam's homemade too,' she says to John. 'I gave up teaching five years ago, so I've little to do now save bake bread and make jam. They kept me on well beyond retiring age, although I'm not sure they knew how old I was, and I wasn't about to tell them. They've a twenty-five-year-old girleen from Dublin with a teaching certificate and barely a word of Gaelic.' She sniffs her disapproval of certificates.

'Ambrose O'Halloran is long dead. I'd not know many in Drimnamore now.'

'There are less of us born here, plenty of Dubliners with holiday homes. And a few rich Germans who say that Kerry is the safest place from nuclear fallout if the Russians invade, much good may it do them. They all seem to need high walls and iron gates to feel really safe.'

'I drove past Askive on the way in. It looks like Kilmainham Jail.'

There is a pause, then Josephine, looking worried, says, 'I've a confession to make to you. I've converted.'

'You've become a Plym, like my grandfather?'

'I've gone the other way, I've become an RC, a Papist. I was never happy in St Peter's after your mother died, although it took me a long time to realize it. You're not angry?'

'Of course not, of course not.'

'Father Michael's still here, and I'm one of his flock now. He'd be glad to see you; he'll be at the match this afternoon.'

John goes to the football pitch on the outskirts of Drimnamore after lunch, arriving in time to see the last few minutes of a needle match against Tralee. There are only twenty or so spectators on the Drimnamore side of the field; a friendly neighbour explains the scoring to John while an injured Tralee player is being attended to.

'One point over the bar and between the posts. Three points for a goal in the net. And we're two points down. Come on, boys, come on,' he shouts as play starts up again.

John finds it hard to follow; in the dying moments of the match, one of the Drimnamore players gets the ball close to the touchline, takes it forward, bouncing it after every fourth step, rounds two Tralee men who fail to take the ball away, looks up and sees the goalkeeper a few yards out of his ground, and gives the ball an almighty kick. It soars, hangs in the air for a moment, then comes down behind the back-pedalling goalie and into the net.

'Three points, great kick,' says John's neighbour, hugging him with joy. 'That's Mikey Sullivan. He'll go far, that boy.'

After the match is over, John goes over to Father Michael, who is pleased with the result.

'We're now clear at the top of the Munster League,' he says. 'Michael over there is our star player, best full forward I've ever seen.'

Michael Sullivan leaves his celebrating team-mates, and comes over to Father Michael, who slaps him on the back.

'I thought they'd marked you out of the game. That was a great last goal. This is John Burke, used to live at Derriquin.'

Michael shakes John's hand; he is nearly as tall as the two men, strongly built for his age. He has his father's dark red, curly hair; his knees are muddy and there is a purple bruise on his cheek.

'Good to meet you,' he says politely, and goes to rejoin the team.

'You remember his father Tomas? He didn't come back from the Spanish Civil War, God rest his soul.'

'Tomas and I were both taught by Josephine,' says John. 'We were good friends when we were boys.'

He remembers Tomas's last words to him, 'One to the heart,

one to the head,' and is on the verge of saying more when Father Michael continues, 'You should call on Annie Sullivan; she'd be glad to see you, doesn't get many visitors.'

John makes a non-committal reply. He returns to Killowen without going up to Ardsheelan.

30.

O N HIS RETURN to Ireland from National Service, James spends two weeks with his father and mother in County Kildare; there are now forty horses in the yard.

'Though we could do with ten more – it's easy to get the no-hopers, but they don't do the yard any good in the long run, even if they cheer the bank manager up for a moment,' says his father.

They go to church on Sunday; John makes a point of asking James to come.

'Dad, since when have you become a churchgoer?'

John looks embarrassed. 'I started going again a year ago. I suppose it's a sign I'm getting closer to meeting my Maker, if he exists. And I'm beginning to think he might.'

James's mother laughs. 'He believes for the pair of us. I go along for the words and the music – there's a decent organist in St Mark's. It would be nice if you came too.'

In church, where his father reads the lesson and takes the collection plate round the sparse congregation, James notices John during prayers, kneeling upright next to him, hands clasped in front of his face, lips moving, eyes closed. He thinks how little he knows about his father, who looks much older than when James had left for the army.

The next day he and his mother are in the kitchen while John is out on the gallops. Kate looks at James as they talk; he's tall, still sunburned from Malaya, leaner than the Winchester schoolboy who'd gone off to Catterick Camp two years earlier. He's not as handsome as his father, he's got the Lowell nose, but he'll do, she tells herself. And, feeling time suddenly accelerating, he's a man now.

'We're all getting older, even you,' says Kate. 'Your father is sixty, you know. I'm not sure he should ride out any more at six in the morning, but he won't ever stop. He's had a hard life, first The Troubles, then Spain, then North Africa and Normandy.'

'He had a good war, didn't he?'

'A good war is one that you survive. He certainly did that – survived the North Africa campaign and Normandy. Finished up as a major with an MC, like his father, but lived to tell the tale. Not that he does. Most men in Ireland cling to their ranks, give themselves a promotion every ten years or so, like Colonel Kavanagh down the road, who left the British Army as an acting captain. Your father has been Mr Burke since the day he was demobbed in 1946.'

'What did Dad get the MC for?'

'Don't bother to ask him. He'll tell you they were handed out with the rum and rations. I had to get the citation to find out. He was in charge of the reconnaissance troop in Normandy, they were ambushed by a platoon of SS in a little village, and he held them off while the troop withdrew. When they went back the next day, and I remember the exact words, "There were nineteen dead Germans, all killed by Captain Burke with his Sten gun."'

'Golly. Nineteen Germans.'

'That's what they mean by a good war. Not so good for the nineteen. You know he went to Spain in 1936 as part of the International Brigade, so he was fighting for almost ten years. And Spain, which is where we met, was far worse than North Africa and Normandy. Something strange and violent happened there, in Teruel. Says it's all in the past and best forgotten. Not a typical attitude to history among the Irish, I have to say.'

'You had a pretty good war yourself, didn't you?'

'Interesting and busy, but not dangerous like the front-line war correspondents. I was kept well back until Paris was captured, covered London during the Blitz, the Battle of Britain, all that. And I went out to Cairo, where I caught up with your father, who wangled a week's leave. And where you were conceived.'

James looks embarrassed.

'I thought I'd better tell you, otherwise who knows what you'd imagine – it was one of the only times we met in six years.'

'Oh.'

'Do you know the secret of our marriage? It's absence. I love Ireland, but I don't want to live there all the time. I love your father, but I don't want to be a trainer's wife, cooking up big breakfasts for ungrateful owners. I want to go to two race meetings a year, not two a week. And I don't want to drive a horsebox except in an extreme emergency. So off I've gone to interesting places, Palestine, Moscow, Korea, Berlin, Vietnam, South Africa. But I always come back, and we're always glad to see each other.'

'You were quite exotic compared to my friends' mothers.'

'Was that a good thing? I couldn't stand the Pony Club, but I did see you ride in your first point-to-point, though my eyes were closed most of the time.'

'You did? Where did I finish?'

'First, last, who knows? I didn't care as long as you got round safely. By the way, he'd love it if you rode out with him tomorrow.'

James rides out with his father every morning for the rest of the week, which makes him feel better about leaving for Oxford so soon after his long absence in the army.

'The vacations are good,' he said as he kissed his mother and gave his father an unaccustomed hug. 'I'll be back for Christmas.'

James arrived at Worcester College, Oxford, as one of a mixed bag of freshmen – half eighteen-year-olds, happy that National Service had been abolished, half twenty-year-olds who had just finished two years in the armed forces. On his first day he was dressed as if he were still in the army, stiff white collar, regimental tie, hacking jacket, grey flannel trousers, suede chukka boots. It took him three days to change to another uniform – jeans, blue shirt, baggy sweater. The stiff collar, jacket, flannel trousers and boots were never seen again.

'Sounds ditchwater dull to me,' says Kate. 'You might as well become a chartered accountant.'

James has just told his mother that he has passed the Civil Service exam and been accepted by the Treasury.

'Not a bit. The public finances, how much tax is raised, how it's distributed, how expenditure is controlled, that's the most important part of government. No money, no public services.'

As he speaks, James realizes he is parroting the words of the Civil Service brochure. He knows the reason he chose the Treasury was that it was the hardest department to enter. 'It's for the real high-flyers, but with your degree and a Blue you should have a good chance,' his tutor had told him.

'Darling, I'm sure you know what you're doing,' says Kate. 'By the way, I have to go into Dublin on Monday. I'll be in hospital there for a few days.'

'What for? Is it serious?'

'Tests and investigations, that's all.' Kate's voice is steady, although she isn't looking at her son, picking up and polishing a silver cup as she speaks.

James is too scared to press his mother for more details. His father is equally vague when they are out together on the Curragh gallops, watching the first lot come up the hill, two horses at a time, steam coming out of their nostrils in the cold December air.

'You know as much as I do,' says John. 'Your mother isn't one to make a fuss. Look, that's Handyman alongside Touch of Class – only a four-year-old and he's not pressed to keep up with the older horse. He'll win first time out in a couple of months. You can come up to Dublin with me on Thursday to collect her if you like.'

The Dublin hospital is an old-fashioned building staffed by nursing nuns; the corridors are clean and there is an air of calm and competence. Kate is sitting up in a four-woman ward when they come in.

'You needn't both have come up to collect me,' she says, although she is clearly happy to see the two of them. 'You aren't going to have to carry me out, you know.'

'I was promised lunch at the Gresham,' says James.

'I'm hungry enough for that after three days here,' says Kate. 'Now let me get dressed and pack my things and we're off.'

On the drive back to Killowen they talk about horses and the crisis in the Congo. 'I've persuaded the *Irish Times* to send me there; there's a big Irish contingent in the UN peacekeeping force.'

'Only if the doctor says so,' says John.

'Ma, exactly what were you in hospital for? What were they testing?'

'I have a lump in my breast – the tests are to find out if it's malignant, whether it's spread. Whether I've got cancer or just a lump.'

The three of them are quiet for what seems to James a long time. He sees the whites of his father's knuckles as his hands tighten on the steering wheel, and realizes they are both hearing the word 'cancer' for the first time. The word hangs in the air for the rest of the journey.

James goes off to London to find a flat, first extracting a promise from Kate that she'll call him with the test results. A week later she speaks to him.

'The bad news is that I've got cancer. The good news is that they don't believe it's spread. So I'm going in next week for a mastectomy, and they think that and a course of chemotherapy will fix it. James, are you there?'

ASHES IN THE WIND

James cannot speak for a moment. There is a constriction in his throat and he wants to cry. He manages to get out, 'This is a terrible line,' puts the phone down and weeps. After a couple of minutes he collects himself, rings Kate back, apologizes for the bad line and says, 'When do you go into hospital?'

'We're leaving for Dublin now. They'll operate tomorrow. The sooner the better, they said. Come and see me at the end of the week when I'll be in a fit state to see you.'

A week later James flies back to Dublin, goes to the hospital and joins his father at Kate's bedside. John is holding Kate's hand; he looks up and says, 'They say they've got the worst of it, and the chemotherapy is just to make sure.'

Kate holds out her other hand to James and says, 'I'm an Amazon now. That was my nickname at St Timothy's, so life is imitating art. I can't wait to get home.'

Kate is back at Killowen in ten days' time, weakened and thin after radiotherapy. She is losing her hair. 'They say it will grow again, so I'm not bothering with a wig. I've got four fetching skullcaps, all in different colours.'

There is no more talk of going to the Congo.

James gets a month's deferment of his arrival at the Treasury and stays at Killowen. In the beginning, Kate is up and about the house, but she gets progressively weaker and has to stay in bed. It is soon clear, but unspoken, that the cancer has spread. She goes back to hospital by ambulance for more tests and is back at Killowen after two days.

'They've done all they can,' she tells John and James; they are sitting beside her bed, which has been moved downstairs into the drawing room. 'I've got you two, I've had a good life, and I'm not in any pain at the moment. Dr Donnan has plenty of morphine if it gets bad, and we'll get a nurse in when I can't manage.'

'We won't need a nurse,' says John, 'I'll look after you.'

And he does for the six weeks that Kate has left, while James and Michael Molloy deal with the horses and the owners. For her last two days Kate is unconscious; she dies quietly in bed on a sunny March morning, John and James each holding one of her hands.

The funeral five days later is in St Mark's church. Kate's older brother, a Trust lawyer, flies over from Boston for the day; the Burkes come from Queen's County; four of Kate's journalist colleagues; several owners and their wives; and all the lads from the yard. And Robert Keen is there from Oxford.

There is no eulogy. 'I'm not having some strange clergyman repeating second-hand platitudes about her,' says John.

He reads the lesson from St Paul's Epistle to the Romans, and as he begins, 'Who shall separate us from the love of Christ?' James realizes that his father believes every word.

Robert Keen stays the night at Killowen and cooks the dinner. 'If you've been a bachelor for as long as I have, you become a decent cook or starve.' After three bottles of claret between them Robert talks about Lambourn.

'You never made a decent fist of that horse of mine. I hope you've done better since.'

'Placed twice, fell four times, not bad for a no-hoper bought out of a seller for sixpence. Only a friend would have had him in his yard.'

'What was that good horse of the Vincents? Won at Chepstow, fell in the lead in the big novice chase at Cheltenham. Never did much after that.'

'Knocknarea. And I moved on soon after Cheltenham, if you remember. You know,' John says, turning to James, 'Robert and I were comrades-in-arms in Spain.'

'That's where we met your mother, in Alicante, in Jarama, in Teruel. She was gorgeous,' says Robert. 'Your dad took her away from me just as I was beginning to make an impression. She was genuinely interested in mediaeval history.'

John laughs for the first time in several weeks. 'We spent a long time drinking at a café, and I walked her back to her hotel.'

'Pretty unsteadily as I remember. Kate had a better head for the Red Infuriator than you.'

'What was the war like in Spain?' asks James.

'Hot, disorganized, not very dangerous most of the time. Cruel and violent on both sides. We never seemed to be in one place for very long. And the more they told us we were winning, the more we knew we were in trouble.'

'Teruel was bloody cold and bloody dangerous,' says Robert. 'We were lucky to get out alive. That was strange, coming across those Irishmen fighting for Franco.'

'Indeed it was. Have some more whiskey.'

Later, after Robert has gone to bed, James asks his father about the lesson in church.

'Dad, you read it well. As though you believed every word.'

'I do believe every word. "For I am persuaded, that neither death, nor life, nor angels, nor principalities, nor powers, nor things present, nor things to come, nor height, nor depth, nor any other creature, shall be able to separate us from the love of God, which is in Christ Jesus our Lord." I couldn't make any sense of this life if I didn't think there was something more, particularly since Kate's gone. I'm not sure the Church of Ireland has the answer, but the New Testament may. I'll probably go to Mount Athos again this summer when the season's done. You know I went there instead of your mother years ago. No women allowed, not even American journalists. You can imagine how angry that made her. I found it a comforting place and I need comfort right now.'

'So do I,' says James. 'Dad, I wish I could . . .' and before he finishes John stands up and the two men embrace for a long moment.

James stays with his father at Killowen for a week, then goes back to London to begin his life in the Treasury. The strangeness of this new world and the twelve-hour working days are a powerful distraction from the shock of his mother's death. And he meets Linda Armstrong again.

Linda was in the same year as James at Oxford; slim, dark-haired, she was one of a group of three clever girls from Lady Margaret Hall who would have been dismissed as bluestockings if they hadn't been so pretty. James had seen her at parties and dances during his Finals year, but they were no more than acquaintances.

They meet again almost a year later at a day's induction course for new civil servants.

'What are you doing here?'

'Women are allowed to join the Civil Service, you know. And in the administrative grade, not just as typists. I'm in the Department of Health. You're in the Department of Penny-Pinching, I suppose.'

'Sorry, I didn't mean to sound patronizing,' and at the end of the day James asks Linda out for a drink.

'Hadn't you better consult the *Handbook on Ethics*? It will look as though I'm lobbying you for an increased allocation,' says Linda, then sees the disappointed look on James's face. 'That was a joke. Don't they have jokes in the Treasury? A drink would be good.'

They go to a bar in Northumberland Avenue, and then to a restaurant off Trafalgar Square. They had last seen each other at the Worcester Commemoration Ball. Linda, in the same party as James and his Italian girlfriend, had been escorted by an undergraduate wearing the dark blue tailcoat of the Bullingdon Club, to whom James had taken an instant dislike. James had one enjoyable, decorous dance with Linda, and afterwards wished for something more.

Over coffee James asks, 'What happened to your Bullingdon Club man?'

'What happened to your sultry Italian?'

'She went back to Rome.'

'William went back to Shropshire.'

James and Linda have a leisurely courtship, the pace dictated in part by the demanding hours of their jobs. After their first serious argument, when Linda says how disgraceful the squeeze on the Health budget is, and James explains how excessive public debt is crippling the country, they agree to leave their work at the office.

They become lovers after six months.

'I'm not in a hurry to jump into bed with you or anyone else for that matter. William was a disaster. Or perhaps it was me.'

It wasn't Linda, as James discovers when they finally sleep together. Linda attributes considerable sexual experience to James because he is two years older. 'And you were in the army,' she says, as though that clinches the matter. James does his best to live up to Linda's view.

In their second summer James takes Linda to Killowen.

'We'll have the place to ourselves. Dad's gone off to Mount Athos – he goes there every summer now for a month's retreat. Michael looks after the yard while he's away.'

'I love the high ceilings and big windows. It's all very simple,' says Linda. 'Irish houses, even the grand ones, are less fussy, feel lived in.'

'Almost all our family stuff was burned in The Troubles,' says James, telling her the story of Derriquin and Eileen. They visit Burke's Fort for lunch, and afterwards Fred shows them around the stud.

'Your dad was the stallion man at the Fort when he was young, looked after our great horse, The Elector, won the big prize at the Dublin spring show with him. Never had anything as good since. He's done well with the horses at Killowen. Would you ever move back when he retires?'

'I'm not sure. I'm well on the way to becoming English – educated there, working in London. If I'd been to St Columba's and Trinity College, Dublin, it might be different.'

They walk on, and James reminds Fred of their golfing expedition to the West of Ireland.

'We were independent for the first time, driving that little Ford Prefect, staying in B&Bs, drinking in those run-down bars.

The sun shone every day, unheard of in Galway and Mayo. Do you still play?'

'Gave it up after you left for the army. I was never in your league. Didn't you get a Blue?'

That evening James and Linda have dinner on their own at Killowen. They finish a bottle of wine between them, sit in front of a turf fire, and James says, 'I think we should get engaged.'

'Engaged? You mean, "Mr and Mrs Alexander Armstrong are pleased to announce . . ." in *The Times*? Shouldn't you be on one knee?'

'I'm too comfortable. What do you think?'

'I think yes.'

James and Linda are married a year later in the chapel of Worcester College. 'It was where we first met,' says James.

'Yes. And you had an Italian beauty looking at you adoringly all evening.'

'Well, your Bullingdon beau spent the evening looking at himself every time he passed a reflective surface.'

'No wonder we got together.'

The marriage is as simple as James and Linda can negotiate with Mrs Armstrong. James heads off the suggestion that they should leave the church under an arch of Royal Irish Dragoons sabres, pointing out that the university golfing team of 1963 would be most upset if their offer of an arch of golf clubs was trumped. They leave the chapel archless, have a fortnight's honeymoon in Corfu, and begin their new life in a small house in Fulham that John Burke helps them to buy.

'There'll be little enough left when I'm gone,' he says to James. 'There's a hefty mortgage on Killowen, and the racing barely covers the interest in a good year. But the money's of most use to you now.'

31.

THE BOAT CHUGS slowly back to Ouranopolis in a cloud of diesel fumes. As John walks up the hill from the harbour at Daphne the breeze from the sea cleans away the diesel, replacing it with the scent of laurel, valerian, myrtle and oleander, leaving far behind the sharper, earthier smells of Ireland, peat, horse sweat, saddle soap, Guinness and whiskey. All he needs is in his small rucksack – two of everything, shirts, pants, socks, handkerchiefs and a single towel.

It is a four-hour walk across the island to the monastery of Stavronikita. The peak of Mount Athos is cloud-covered and the view of the coast recedes behind him as he climbs the rough road. Beyond the watershed the road is replaced by mule tracks, and John has to stop to regain his breath after each scramble out of the network of valleys separating him from the sea on the north. He passes through small woods of chestnut and oak, sees the occasional vineyard, and meets only one other pilgrim heading back to Daphne. When the buildings of the monastery come into view, his pace and his pulse quicken. He feels he has left home and is coming home.

The guest master greets him with an affectionate embrace, gives him some bread, cheese, olives and a glass of raki, and shows him to his room. It is the room he had on his previous visit – hard bed, single blanket, wooden table, jug and basin, a small window looking out over the harbour. A painted wooden cross hangs on the rough, flaking, whitewashed walls. The routine of the monastery embraces and sustains him – long services, simple meals, work in the garden, fishing, solitary contemplation and prayer.

The monks in Stavronikita are friendly but incurious – John's Greek is still patchy, and unnecessary conversation is discouraged. Meals are taken at speed against a background of a reading from a sacred text. The monks, less than thirty in a collection of buildings that once housed over a hundred, are often outnumbered by the guests, who stay one or two nights and then move on. John is one of three who have permission from the Abbot to remain longer, and he has arranged a donation to the monastery that makes the monks happy to have him there. And he is a good fisherman, going out in the boat from the harbour twice a week to net fish for the table.

John finds it difficult to make much sense of his past life, and it is too late to create an alternative. He reads the New Testament in his room, attends the numerous and chaotic services when the wooden gong calls the monks to the central church from early in the morning until late at night. The services are sung or intoned; the Abbot and his deputy have fine, deep voices. On his previous visit John had been baptized, which enabled him to go to church. Now he feels it was an important step towards a destination that he cannot yet see clearly. He is seeking clarity about the world, forgiveness for his past violence in Spain and in Normandy, and an understanding of himself and his patchwork existence. He goes to confession in his first week, and although his confessor is different his sins are the same. He needs to refresh and confirm his earlier absolution.

This is John's fourth visit to Mount Athos. His first trip was accidental. Kate had an assignment from the *New York Times* to write about the Greek monasteries and asked John to cover Mount Athos, where women were not allowed.

'Even American women war correspondents, would you believe,' she had said to John. 'I tried to persuade them to make an exception and was told I was arguing with a thousand years of history. So I gave up.'

'American women would make the monks especially nervous,' said John. 'It's not aimed at you especially. They don't allow anything female on the peninsula. No cows, no hens, no mares. I'd love to go. I haven't been out of Ireland since the war; I don't count Cheltenham.'

On his first visit he had been little more than a tourist, making copious notes, taking photographs and finishing up at the Stavronikita monastery on the north of the peninsula. After Kate's death he went back a second and a third time to Stavronikita for a month's retreat, drawing from his days there a comfort that stayed with him back in Ireland and made him eager to return.

He now spends every evening with Elder Daniel, who has been appointed his mentor by the Abbot. After he has been at the monastery for three weeks, the Elder says, 'This time I think you will stay with us, enter fully into the life here, and the life hereafter,' and John realizes he is not going to return to Ireland.

He drafts and redrafts a letter to James, knowing that sending it will be an irrevocable step.

Stavronikita,
Mount Athos,
19 July (by the Gregorian calendar)

My Dear James,

This is my third trip to Mount Athos (four, if you include my first visit as your mother's surrogate reporter), and after weeks of contemplation and prayer I have decided not to return to Killowen. I have found a way of living here at Stavronikita that suits me.

They have encouraged me to stay and given me my own permanent room. Later this month I will formally become a novice; I am already baptized. I have made myself useful in the garden, and indispensable in the fishing boat. Perhaps the need for fresh fish explains their willingness to take me on! I have started to learn bookbinding, and I hope to be allowed to work on the wonderful manuscripts here, still not properly catalogued and many needing careful repair. Binding sacred texts, fishing and gardening seem a better way of ending my days than worrying about the two-thirty at Thurles.

Would you do me a great service and wind up the Killowen yard? Michael Molloy has been running things for two years now; I suggest he takes himself and as many of his owners as he can persuade (that will, I think, be most of them, as he's patient and knowledgeable) to Dan Herlihy's yard on the Curragh. Dan will welcome Michael if he comes with a dozen decent horses. You should decide what to do with the house. I think most of the mortgage is paid off. Once I am a monk I must give up all my worldly possessions, and I have made arrangements with our Dublin lawyers to transfer everything into your name.

What I have found here is, by definition, hard to explain; it is what St Paul calls in his Epistle to the Philippians, "the peace of God, which passeth all understanding". I know this is the right way for me. I also know that I will see less of you as a result, and nothing of Linda, and I regret that. I have been at best a fitful father, although one who loves you and is proud of you, something I've never found easy to show. Please come and see me soon. We welcome visitors.

Your loving father,
John +

'He's gone mad,' says Linda when James reads the letter aloud over breakfast. 'A retreat for a month is eccentric enough. But living there as a monk? And we can't keep Killowen going.'

'I don't think he's mad at all. He's had a turbulent life, father killed on the Somme, mother executed by the IRA, ten years of war in Spain and Europe. He killed nineteen Germans with a Sten gun when he won his MC.'

'Goodness.'

'He's a curious mixture, my dad, you think he's only interested in horses and then he surprises you. There's more to him than your average Anglo-Irish racehorse trainer – Ma wouldn't have stayed with him else. I realized that at Ma's funeral. He believes. And now he's decided to do what he believes in. I agree it's odd, but I admire him for it.'

'You should go out and see him.'

'I will. But it won't be a mission to change his mind. He's about to become Brother John, he's not Major Burke, MC, formerly of Derriquin Castle, any more.'

James makes the trip out to Mount Athos in early September. His father has arranged his permit and sent careful instructions on the route across the peninsula to Stavronikita. James needs a little more than the four hours he had been told to allow for the journey, and he is impressed that his sixty-nine-year-old father had made the trip on foot. John meets him on the hill above the monastery, and they embrace. Then James pushes his father away, looks at him and laughs.

'I like the beard. I'm not sure they would approve in the Kildare Street Club. You've gone quite grey.'

'It saves on razor blades, and I do trim it. Most of the monks let their beards run amok.'

They walk down to the monastery and James is shown to his room by his father and the guest master.

'There's supper at seven, bread, cheese and some fish I caught this afternoon. No meat here, but plenty of raki. It's strong stuff; I find half a glass plenty. After supper there's a service in the main church. I've told them you are orthodox, and so you are, at least without the capital O. That means you can come into the church.'

The church is small, much of it in shadow, as hanging oil lamps provide the only light. The air is heavy with incense. James watches, copies his father's movements and listens as he joins in the prayers. Now and again John takes James's hand in his. Tired after the journey, James finds it hard to concentrate, and the exotic surroundings, the ritual and the language emphasize how far his father has come from the simplicities of the Church of Ireland.

'It's very strange to me,' says James as they walk back to their rooms. 'I've been to Catholic services, but this is quite different, Byzantine.'

'That makes it mysterious,' says John. 'I don't think your great-grandfather would approve, although he'd understand the search for peace.'

The next day they go out together in the little boat, and James helps John put out and pull in the net. They catch half a dozen red mullet.

'Quite good for this time of year. They'll be kept for the feast day on Thursday. We've many saints to celebrate.'

That evening they sit and talk in John's room, where James notices on the table beside the bed three pictures – one of Kate taken in Spain, one of James and Linda on their wedding day, and one of a young girl on horseback.

'I don't recognise that. Mum when she was young?'

'No. The daughter of an old friend.'

'Anyone I know?'

'They live in Maryborough. Don't think you've met.'

Later, fortified by a full glass of raki, James asks his father, 'Dad, why are you staying here? It's as if . . .'

'I have to unburden myself. I'm sixty-nine, I've spent my working life with horses, and that's not a great preparation for the afterlife. Until I was in my twenties I was unformed, and what happened to Eileen and to me during The Troubles somehow froze me. Marrying your mother began a long thaw, but that's still incomplete. Kate's death was a great shock. She always seemed indestructible. And there's been a lot of violence in my life, in Ireland, in Spain, in Normandy. All that presses heavily on me, and the load is lighter here.'

'I've read the citation for your MC. You killed a lot of Germans.'

'I feel worse about Spain. That was a vicious war.'

The next day James leaves the monastery to return to Ireland.

'I'll come with you up to the watershed,' says John.

'Dad, I can find my way back.'

'I want to come. For the company, not as your guide.'

They reach the top of the pass, embrace, and James swallows hard as they part. John makes a sign of the cross on James's forehead, kisses him again and walks down the hill. James watches him until the track curves out of sight through an olive grove. John doesn't look back.

IV.
Northumberland and Ireland
1993 and beyond

32.

J AMES BURKE LOOKS into his grandfather's leather-bound
shaving mirror. It is big enough to frame his face. The silvering
has gone in a couple of places, revealing the leather back; the
stitching still holds on all but one side. The leather border is
scalloped to conceal the jagged edges of the glass. On the back
his grandfather has written in faded black ink, 'Glass taken from
a shelled estaminet, Rue des Puits, near Croix Barbe, Pas de
Calais, Feby 1915,' and his initials, HB.

The mirror had been put together by a regimental saddler
with no horses left to saddle. Artillery, machine guns and Flanders
mud turned the Royal Irish Dragoons from the flamboyant
horsemen who charged alongside the Scots Greys at Waterloo
into poor bloody infantry. It had been sent back to Derriquin,
together with a few letters, photographs, four medal ribbons and
a worn signet ring, all that survived of Henry Burke after the first
day of the Somme.

The mirror is a talisman. It holds James, through years of
daily use, within its frame; if it breaks, more than glass would
break. It has watched him change from a pink-cheeked optimist,
just beginning to shave, to his present lean, cautious reflection.
He sometimes turns and looks as he leaves the bathroom to see
whether his reflection is still caught, is watching him go.

As he shaves on the morning of his trip to Scotland, for the
briefest of moments James seems to step sideways, away from
and out of his body, while the world stops turning. And as he

rejoins himself, and the world begins to move again, he is enter-
ing the body of a stranger. He knows the stranger's history; he
decides in that moment to leave it behind.

On the slow train to Edinburgh, James struggles with the
Guardian, then sleeps, woken at irregular intervals at
Peterborough, York, Darlington, Durham. His carriage is almost
empty apart from a businessman tapping at his laptop two seats
away. The slowness of the journey heightens his feeling of escape.
He looks at his reflection in the carriage window. You're the one
I'm escaping, he says to himself.

Outside Durham the train stops altogether – in a field that
stretches out to a housing estate James sees a young couple lying
on the grass watching their small child kicking a red football
with clumsy determination. It is a reminder of his own childhood, his early married years, his daughter, years of optimism
and hope.

Disjointed images along the journey lodge in his half-awake
memory – an angler under a green umbrella, a field with half a
dozen piebald ponies, a giant yellow digger idle in a gravel pit,
the great towers of Durham Cathedral, a wall of graffiti-ed initials in red, yellow and blue, all using the same bulging capitals.

He has brought his great-grandmother Burke's diaries and
letters with him, an archive of County Kerry in the middle of the
nineteenth century, handed down by his great-aunt. A long train
journey had seemed an ideal opportunity to sort through them,
but he soon realizes that he needs a bigger table and a more
settled mind for the task, and he puts them away.

Beyond Newcastle the train edges gradually towards the coast,
the balance between land and sea shifting until the track is separated from the North Sea by less than a mile of well-cultivated
fields. The train is behaving oddly, stopping at intervals for no
apparent reason, waiting a few minutes, and then starting up
again. James dozes off until a violent stop jerks him awake to a

landscape that he has dreamed before. He is looking across ploughed fields to a narrow river estuary. On the far side a little town crouches under a castle- and tree-topped hill. Curving towards him is the enfolding arm of a harbour wall guarding the estuary mouth and twenty or thirty boats against the winds of the North Sea. The sun has come out; the water of the estuary gleams.

His waking dream is interrupted by the gloomy voice of the ticket collector.

'Complete electrical failure. Next carriage doors opened, won't close – can't go on – relief train in half an hour from Newcastle.'

The businessman sighs.

James looks again at the town, the river, the estuary, the sunlit sea. He stands up with a sudden purpose, picks up his bag and walks into the next carriage. It has been cleared; the doors, as the ticket collector has warned, are open. After a moment's hesitation James jumps down to the low embankment, climbs through the hedge and sets off across the fields towards the town. He has a feeling of escape, of shaking off pursuers.

There is no path. He skirts the ripening wheat and makes slow progress across the fields, damp clods of earth clinging to his black shoes. Gripped by a sudden feeling of childish folly, he looks back, turns and goes on.

Between the second field and the edge of the estuary the land merges into the water through a long reed-covered margin. A brace of teal rise up and circle inland, and as James watches their flight he sees what had been his train move cautiously across the viaduct spanning the river a mile upstream. There is no obvious alternative crossing. A rough path leads in two directions, inland between high hedges to the viaduct, outwards to the estuary mouth and the coastline. He turns inland, unhappy at the thought of clambering up to the viaduct.

'Why couldn't the train have given up the ghost on the other side of the river,' he mutters, realizing as he speaks that it is the enfolding arm of the harbour wall that has pulled him out of the train and towards the town. Without that view he'd still be on his way to Edinburgh.

He walks slowly along and takes a right fork towards the river, which narrows in a final constriction before splaying out into the estuary. The river is spanned by a rickety footbridge, half a dozen railway sleepers resting end to end on wires suspended either side from two overhead cables. It has been built for fishermen and, judging by the rusting cables and weather-beaten sleepers, not very recently. The bridge sways with each step as he makes his way across.

At the halfway point he stops, looks upstream and sees a fisher in the final stages of playing a fish. The distant figure – it is hard to tell whether it is a man or a woman – beaches the salmon, bends to unhook it, and then nurses it gently in the shallows before letting it go.

On the other side he follows the path downstream; it curves away from the river to open up a full view of the town and its little harbour. His pace quickens, bringing him to a road flanked by houses on the landward side and on the right by the sprawl of the estuary.

A green bench gives him a chance to sit down and think about his surroundings and his erratic behaviour. His disengagement began in the morning in his shaving mirror; even so, leaving a train in mid-journey was out of keeping with his measured, rational approach to life. You're a retired Permanent Secretary, he tells himself, due in Edinburgh for a Trust dinner tonight and a Trustees' meeting tomorrow. Sitting there, he unrolls a mental list of memorial services, silver wedding anniversaries, regimental reunions, seminars on funding the arts, college Gaudies, godchildren's twenty-firsts, farewell parties for barely remembered colleagues, all of which he has converted into duties. The clubs need a separate list – the Garrick, the Other Club, the Saintsbury. He feels suddenly liberated from these self-imposed obligations. And without guilt.

He leaves a message on her mobile for his deputy (a brisk forty-year-old who calls James 'Chair' even over dinner, and is longing to display her chairperson talents). He blames family complications for his sudden absence, presses 'Send', and drops his phone into the litter bin. As he walks away, he imagines its ring-tone calling, calling in vain.

The path joins a small road leading into the town. 'Welcome to Allenmouth', the sign says, approving James's decision to abandon the train. In smaller letters below it announces, 'Twinned with Lippspringe (Germany) and Castéra (France)'. Passing an old-fashioned red telephone kiosk and postbox, James sees with pleasure that the latter is marked 'G VI R'. Perhaps he is changing his decade as well as his destination.

His road is now flanked by shops and houses, an engaging mixture of the architecture of the last three hundred years, stone, brick, render, the tallest a half-timbered Edwardian/Elizabethan building with an unglazed gallery on the top floor. The street looks like the miniature rows of houses that accompanied his Hornby train set when he was eight. The saltings are tamed by a low wall that gradually increases in size to form the harbour. The tide is coming in; the wall's granite blocks change from dark to light, marking high tide fifteen feet above low water. Twenty or thirty boats, mostly day-fishing boats with one bigger trawler and an incongruous fifty-foot ketch, bob at their fendered moorings or on buoys further out.

On the corner of the road there is a four-storeyed, red-brick, Victorian building, taller than its neighbours, with a first-floor bow window and a swinging heraldic sign, the Allen Arms. A small card in the window says 'Bed and Breakfast'. James goes into a large, cheerful bar with two or three men nursing their drinks in the guarded way of low-spending regulars. The barman, busily polishing glasses, becomes animated and friendly when James asks for two Scotch eggs, a pint of bitter and a room for two nights.

'Sally,' he shouts, in a broad Geordie accent. 'Gent here wants a room,' and to James, 'She needs to get the room ready – the holiday season's beginning.'

James takes his pint and his eggs – he is thirsty and hungry from his walk and his change of plan. Or, to be precise, the abandonment of planning in favour of an uncharted future.

Twenty minutes later he is shown up to a room overlooking small narrow gardens to the backs of houses. Half a dozen pigeons wheel around a loft tacked on to the middle storey of the house opposite. The room is clean and simple.

'Facilities on your right at the end of the passage. Twenty-nine pounds a night, in advance, including breakfast.'

Unpacking his briefcase takes a minute. He has a sponge bag, clothes for his Edinburgh day, and his great-grandmother's diaries and letters. The papers for the meeting he shoves into the wastepaper basket.

He sets off to explore Allenmouth. In the harbour, somebody on board the ketch is coiling ropes; a man sitting in a dinghy is wrestling with a reluctant British Seagull outboard motor, a defunct brand that had tested James's patience and tortured his hands on Irish seaside holidays. A couple are embracing at the end of the harbour wall, which is rounded off with a small battlemented tower. James walks out to the tower and back towards the town, turning inland up a steeply sloping street past the row of houses he had seen from his room.

A sign points up a grassy lane to 'The Golf Club – Visitors Welcome'. The clubhouse is a small building surrounded on three sides by a generous verandah. Twisted iron columns support a red shingled roof. The building is locked; a notice in the window says 'Ring Jack Pearson, Professional, for a lesson or access to the clubhouse'. James makes a note of the telephone number, finds a teak garden seat and sits down. The course is spread out before him, a perfect nine-hole links, four holes out, one on the turn, four more back.

Below the course the coastline stretches out in the sun. Sand dunes fall away to a long stretch of white beach marked at regular intervals by wooden breakwaters, untested by the waves of the incoming tide. A lighthouse blinks on a distant headland.

Oystercatchers wheel along the shore; a few waders pick away at the darkened rim of the sand. The red flags marking the greens flutter in the sea breeze. James feels a sudden surge of pleasure. This could give him something to do.

By the next morning he has decided to stay. A trip to the gentlemen's outfitters he'd seen the day before produces corduroy trousers, half a dozen Viyella shirts, some woollen socks that remind him of his prep school, a brown herringbone jacket, stout brogues. Looking at himself in the shop mirror, James realizes, with a curious feeling of filial duty, that he has become his father.

He walks back towards his hotel and notices in the window of the junk shop a clutter of sporting equipment. He goes in, surprised by the loud clang of the doorbell that announces his entry, and asks about the golf clubs.

'All yours for a tenner,' the young man in charge suggests. James picks through the assortment and winds up with a modern steel-shafted driver, a miscellaneous collection of irons including 'the Harry Vardon Mashie Niblick', a number four wood, a beautiful hickory putter and a canvas bag.

Saturday morning is bright and clear, sharpened by a wind off the North Sea that pushes James at an angle along the quayside towards the newspapers. The smaller fishing boats knock against the harbour wall; two nets are laid out to dry in long coils, adding the tang of fish and tar to the salt of the sea air. A few seagulls hang in the wind and a lonely seal shows his disappointed face above the harbour's water. An orange fisherman's glove, fingers and thumb inflated with air, bobs on the surface and points to the sky.

As he walks on, he hears loud, throbbing music from a side street leading off the harbour. The sound, out of place on an Allenmouth Saturday, draws him towards a low green Scout hut whose corrugated-iron roof amplifies the steady beat inside.

The double doors are open. He walks up to the entrance and looks in. Now he can hear the words, 'The Lord, Lord reigns, The Lord, Lord reigns, The Lord, Lord reigns,' sung over and over again by a group of around twenty men and women. A priestess in a purple robe holds a microphone. Framed by a screen showing the text 'The Lord reigns' over an image of a tumbling mountain stream, she dances from side to side, leading the song and the singers. The congregation are dancing or swaying on the spot, from time to time lifting their hands aloft. They are all smiling as they sing.

At the back, a tall young man is dancing in counterpoint to the priestess at the front of the hall. He is strikingly handsome. Both his arms are raised; his eyes are closed as he dances and sings, 'The Lord, Lord reigns'. James takes a step forward. The young man opens his eyes, gives a warm smile, moves towards James and folds a friendly arm around his shoulder. 'Join us, brother, join us.'

'It's not . . . I'm late,' mumbles James, and as he turns to go is caught by the hurt look on the young man's face.

How can they be so bloody happy? James wonders as he walks away, feeling a mixture of guilt and cowardice as sharp as the sea air.

On Monday morning he wakes, disoriented, and tries to get out of bed on the side next to the wall. He turns left instead of right to find the lavatory at the end of the corridor and, the final, painful indignity, stubs his toe bloodily on the projecting foot of the bed. This bad start is redeemed by a sunny, blowy morning and a walk along the seashore; by lunchtime he decides to move out of the pub.

After inspecting three dreary B&Bs masquerading as flats on the newsagent's cards, the fourth, 'Top floor studio flat, separate entrance, bathroom/kitchen, sea view', turns out to be more promising, located above the antique shop he passed when he first walked into the town. Over the shop is a sign, 'Campaign Furniture'; inside there is a large tent hanging from the ceiling and opening towards the door, showing off a collection of nineteenth- and early twentieth-century military gear, teak chests, canvas chairs, mahogany tables, telescopes on tripods, camp beds, washbasins, everything that a young officer might need before setting out for India or Africa a hundred years ago. He'd need a dozen porters, thinks James.

The shop's owner introduces himself. George is wearing an un-military outfit of black trousers with an evening stripe down the sides, a green cashmere sweater, a pink woollen scarf and a suspicious expression. He takes James round the back through an arched alleyway and up a wooden external staircase, doubling as a fire escape, to the top of the three-storey building.

The room is fifteen feet square, with wide oak floorboards and bare white walls. There is an iron fireplace in one wall with a surround of blue-and-white Delft tiles. A step up to small glazed double doors, through which the afternoon light is streaming, leads out onto a railed balcony. James looks down on the harbour and sees the floating rubber glove still pointing its orange fingers to the sky.

He inspects the tiny kitchen-bathroom, separated only by a screen from the rest of the room. The bath is an odd shape.

'It's a sitz-bath.'

George demonstrates by sitting in the bath on its built-in step, then swivelling round and dropping his bottom into the deep half while resting his calves and feet on the shallow end.

'You wash in position one, then soak in position two: very green, very economical with the water.'

'Green is good. But where's the lavatory?'

George looks uneasy.

'Outside. But it has a wonderful view.'

James follows George through the double doors outside to the balcony; what was once a small pigeon loft juts out at the far end. 'WC' is painted in faded dark blue letters on the door. There is a ledge near the top of the door, above it a dozen large holes, formerly for pigeons, now for ventilation.

'Not ideal when it's raining,' says George, opening the door. 'But it's an original 1899 Thomas Crapper double-syphonic-action water closet, mahogany box and seat, floral decorations around the inside of the bowl. And with the door open you over-look the harbour.'

The double-syphonic action and the view clinch it for James. He takes the flat on the spot.

They complete the transaction downstairs. James looks around at the collection, which matches his sense of adventure. He buys a brass-bound teak desk/chest of drawers marked 'Army and Navy Stores', a folding campaign chair with leather seat and back that once belonged to Captain Andrews of the 9th Lancers, a steel-and-wood architect's adjustable standard lamp, an umbrella globe that opens to reveal an 1890 world of Imperial red, and a five-foot-wide mahogany bed.

'Will we ever get the bed up the stairs?' James asks.

'Of course. Everything here is demountable; it's all designed for the back of a mule, a camel or a pack-horse. I'll throw in a modern mattress; you wouldn't thank me for the horsehair original.'

A week later James has filled his bookcase with a random collection from the second-hand bookshop – Donne, Hopkins, Eliot, Browning, Nabokov, Mailer, Updike, Tolstoy, Kipling, Trollope, a near-complete set of Gibbon and sixteen volumes of the 1914–1918 edition of *Punch*. There is a Samuel Palmer print, *The Early Ploughman*, above the fireplace, anemones in a Wemyss beehive mug by his bed, a threadbare Persian rug on the floor and a brass eight-day ship's chronometer with Roman numerals on the wall.

James thinks the room perfect; for the first time for many years he has consulted no one's taste but his own. He has become, he recognizes with guilty pleasure, a bachelor again.

*

As a boy James had played golf all over the West of Ireland, at a time when golf courses were neither expensive nor crowded. Kiltimagh, Ardnacross, Derryboy, Carrickmannon – little nine-hole courses with sheep as the green-keepers, where the greens were like English fairways and the fairways like English rough – had taught him to get out of trouble as easily as he had got into it. His cousin Fred had been his golfing companion, gentle, uncompetitive, relaxed as James's game outstripped his own.

At first they played at the local course halfway between Killowen and Burke's Fort. This had been carved out of the demesne of a neighbouring estate whose big house had been abandoned during The Troubles. A local builder had bought the estate, cannibalized what was left of the buildings, and built a golf course in anticipation of a demand that never came. He'd run out of money after twelve holes, but the six missing holes didn't seem to matter. There was no clubhouse. Beside the first tee on a straw bale there was an old Quality Street tin with a slot punched in the lid and a little notice saying '2/6d a round'. A pleasant air of melancholy hung over the course and the ruins of the house; an ornamental lake, taken over by rushes and guarded by a pair of swans, acted as a natural water hazard and stored mis-hit golf balls that gleamed in its shallow margins.

Later, when James had inherited his mother's Ford Prefect, he and Fred spent a week in the summer touring round Galway and Mayo, as much for the new freedom of their motor car as for the golf. Here James discovered the glory of links courses and the wild flowers of the machair for the first time. The sea acted as a clear and limiting boundary for his wayward swing on the outward nine; skipping the clubhouse, if there was one, he and Fred would seek out the bar in the nearest village after a round and each order a glass of stout. These bars were mostly front rooms with a turf fire as the only concession to comfort. The air was heavy with cigarette smoke; there was sawdust on the floor and a fixed corkscrew on the counter. Outside the bar's name – 'Byrne's', 'Mullen's', 'O'Grady's', 'McGrath's Spirit Vaults' – was painted in fading letters above the door. The Guinness still came in corked bottles; the conversation between the two or three other regulars was quiet, and never made the pretence of including them.

At school, golf was an authorized escape from football and cricket; the Winchester club pro had taken James's rustic game in hand without destroying his natural swing and had taught him to putt. In the army, James was the officer selected to partner the regiment's Colonel in-chief, the ex-King of the Belgians, who had turned to golf when his country had turned him out and who demanded a foursome on his regular visits to the regiment. By the time James went up to Oxford he was playing off a 2 handicap.

Oxford golf was altogether different. Every Saturday the university teams visited grand clubs – Rye, St George's Hill, Walton Heath, Huntercombe, the Berkshire. James had to sharpen up his clothes (on his first appearance for the second team, the Divots, an elderly opponent told him sternly to take his trousers out of his socks); he discovered a competitive streak that brought him within striking distance of a Blue in his first and second years, although each time he failed to make the university team.

He arrived at the beginning of his final year unsure whether to pursue a golf Blue or a good degree. He was clear he couldn't get both. Although most of last year's team were up, there were still two places to play for. The question was answered by the arrival of a pair of American Rhodes Scholars, scratch golfers from the University of Miami who had played their way through college. One of them, Roger Tompkins, at Worcester with James, was mildly apologetic when he realized he stood between James and a Blue.

James felt only relief at this clarity. He decided to work, and found a renewed pleasure in English literature that two years in the army and two years of golf had undermined (it was a source of his unease about the game that, with the exception of P. G.

Wodehouse, there was no good writing about golf). And by then James had decided on the Civil Service and a decent degree.

From then on he played for the Divots once a fortnight. To his surprise, his golf improved and his pleasure from the game increased. He didn't lose a singles match all season and was playing close to scratch. Ten days before the Varsity Match James saw a dejected Roger Tompkins at dinner in Hall, his arm in a sling.

'What have you done?' he asked, genuinely concerned and yet, at the back of his mind, feeling a little flicker of excitement.

'Broke my wrist playing touch football in the Parks yesterday. I think they're going to ask you.'

The following morning James went to Vincent's for lunch to meet the captain of the OUGC, a solid Yorkshireman with an inbuilt contempt for someone like James from a soft Southern public school. But he needed a player and said to James, 'I hear you've produced some good results for the Divots recently.'

'I haven't lost a match, and I'm playing scratch golf, I reckon.'

'Are you now? I've got a problem, as you know. Let's have a round tomorrow and see if you're the answer. Cowley, nine o'clock tee-off. OK?'

It was OK. James turned up the next morning with nothing to lose. His driving was long and straight, his approach shots precise, he avoided the bunkers and three-putted only once. He beat the captain two and one.

'That's it. You're our man. You'll get the card this evening.'

The card duly arrived, followed by the Varsity Match a week later. Oxford triumphed; James won one singles, halved the other, and won his foursomes paired with the other American Rhodes Scholar, whose 'Pity you don't take the game seriously' was high praise.

It was an exhilarating climax to James's golfing career. Thereafter he played rarely, put off by the game's aggressive male competitiveness; he recognized some of that in himself and didn't like it. And later in the Civil Service the suggestion that playing against the army, the judges, the House of Commons, the House of Lords and White's might be career-enhancing brought out his mildly anti-establishment streak. He gave away his clubs and didn't think about the game again until Allenmouth.

33.

O N THE FIRST morning in his new flat, James goes outside to his Thomas Crapper double-syphonic action lavatory, then stands on his balcony, looking out at the harbour, the estuary and the country beyond.

The tide is on the turn, the water choppy and disturbed as the flow of the River Allen meets the incoming North Sea. Beyond the water's edge there is dark mud, still gleaming, shading into lighter sand rising up to the edge of the dunes. The marram grass anchoring the dunes to the land is bleached blond by the sun; the green of ordinary grass shows through here and there. Beyond the dunes James sees a patchwork of fields, the bright yellow of oilseed rape, the green of spring wheat, the brown of plough. The only building is a long low ruin in the first field beyond the dunes.

On the left a wide sweep of dry sand is exposed by the tide, broken by the occasional rock pool. A double line of large concrete anti-tank blocks, buried where they begin, gradually emerge as they curve towards the water. They look ancient, left by some long-departed tribe. Above them on the shore a round orange life-ring hangs on a white wooden frame, the white paint peeling. The sign on the frame says 'ANGER'. James shivers as the breeze gets up and goes in.

The next day he has arranged to meet the golf pro; he carries his motley selection of clubs up to the course and buys a dozen golf balls and some wooden tees. Jack Pearson looks doubtfully at his clubs.

'Have you played much golf before?'

'Used to play a bit.'

He stretches a little self-consciously on the first of the nine holes, tees up and begins by slicing the ball wildly out to sea. His second drive goes the same way. He is being watched by a gallery of two – Jack Pearson has been joined by a younger woman with striking auburn hair.

He drives a third ball. This time there is that sweet connection between hands, arms, torso, legs and club head that smacks the ball straight down the fairway for two hundred and forty yards. It reminds James why golf used to give him such pleasure. The woman claps. James turns, smiles and sets off down the fairway.

The rest of the round is mixed. He loses three more balls in the rough, slices half his approach shots and misses several short putts. But he discovers the unfamiliar joys of the number four wood, and muscles that have been long unused, and he knows he will play better. The course is a delight, the rough of the dunes alive with cowslips, forget-me-nots, buttercups, pink sea-thrift and the occasional bluebell. Bounded by the sea on one side, and by coppices and farmland on the other, it reminds James of golf in the West of Ireland. He shares the course only with sheep, rabbits and the occasional seagull.

The last hole, a difficult dog-leg par five, he plays well. A long drive followed by two good shots on the fairway with his new friend, the number four wood, puts him on the green twelve feet from the hole. He sinks the putt.

'Well done,' says Jack Pearson from the captain's bench. 'That looked like par.'

'It was a birdie. Decent drive, two shots on the fairway and you saw the putt.'

'Would have been an eagle if you had decent clubs. If you want a partner any day, you know how to find me.'

James makes an immediate date, goes back to his room, lights a fire and spends a happy and luxurious half-hour in the sitz-bath before supper. From then on he plays golf with Jack Pearson every other afternoon.

'How did you become a professional?'

'Started out caddying at North Berwick when I was twelve. Got some clubs when I was fourteen – not much better than yours – and started to play. Won the North of England Under-Eighteen, and turned pro.'

'On the circuit?' asks James.

'Not good enough to get a card. Most I ever won in a year was nine thousand pounds, barely enough to cover expenses. I met Anna's mother, we had Anna in short order, then this job comes up. I fancy the security, Anna's mother fancies my best friend, who gets his card and makes some money, and she shoves off with him. And here I am.'

'There are worse places.'

'Aye,' says Jack Pearson, and is silent for the rest of the round.

He shows little interest in James's life, only in his golf, suggesting a couple of improvements in his technique off the tee that James gratefully adopts. Their reticence is matched, as is their game.

On their second day James asks Jack Pearson about Anna.

'Sports therapist. That was her by the first tee last Friday. Worked in Newcastle till lately for the Falcons Rugby Club. Came here to get away from her boyfriend. Ever been married?'

'Over twenty years, one daughter. On my own now.'

'There are worse places.'

A few days later their golf comes to an abrupt end. James, who rarely out-drives Jack Pearson, puts in a little extra off the tee and feels a sharp twinge up his right side. He tries to play on, but they have to give up and walk back to the clubhouse; by this time James's back has locked solid.

'Anna will fix you,' says Jack Pearson. 'She's on my home number. Give her a call.'

'It'll be all right in the morning,' says James.

It isn't all right. The next morning he hobbles down the stairs, rings Jack Pearson from the call box and arranges to meet Anna at the clubhouse in an hour.

Up at the clubhouse Anna has set up a folding massage table in a small room next to her father's office. The gas fire is going, the curtains drawn, and the room is comfortably warm. There is a dark blue towel on the table, and an oval hole at its top with another towel twisted around the rim. James looks at Anna uncertainly.

'Take your clothes off, hang them on the back of the door and let's see what's wrong.'

James takes off everything except his boxer shorts.

'Don't worry, I've seen twenty naked men in the Falcons' changing room every week during the rugby season.'

'Not many of them were over fifty,' mutters James, but does as he is told.

'Face the window,' says Anna, and puts her hands on James's shoulders. She clenches her fist and runs it down his back.

'Ouch,' he says.

'Relax, and stop holding your stomach in. Your right-hand side is the problem, it's still in spasm – but you're not in bad shape. On the table, face down.'

Anna rubs oil on her hands and sets about James's back. From time to time she uses her elbow to dig deeply into the large muscle at the base of his spine, following down his thigh to his calf. The pressure is strong, and now and again extracts a groan from James and an apology from Anna.

Through the towelled hole on which his face rests he can see only Anna's legs and feet. She has strong athlete's calves and neat ankles. James tries hard to think of something else.

'That'll do for now,' says Anna after an hour of treatment. 'Tomorrow, same time? It will take four or five sessions to get you right. You'll be quite sore after today. Is thirty pounds OK? That's my Newcastle rate.'

Thirty pounds was fine. James walks down the hill with Anna and turns off to his room.

'I heard you were George's new tenant,' says Anna.

'It's a great room. I came down the hill a lot easier than I went up, thanks to you. See you tomorrow.'

The next morning he walks up the hill to the clubhouse, looking forward to the session with more than just the desire to be healed. Lying face down on the table, James asks Anna about her life.

'I was crazy about sport and the theatre. County hockey, tennis, swam a lot. I studied sports medicine at Newcastle for three years. Acted on the side; there was a good theatre scene at the uni then. Tried my hand at am dram, got a few auditions, played Beatrice in a semi-pro *Much Ado* at the Northern Stage. I did some freelance therapy work around the theatre, but I wasn't going to make it as an actress unless I went to Central or RADA, and I wasn't good enough for that. Can you turn over, please?'

James turns over, closes his eyes, says, 'And then?'

'Then I got a job as sports therapist to the Falcons just as they went professional. Which for five years was terrific. It was a good course at Newcastle. By the time I graduated I knew all about the structure of the body, muscle injuries, osteopathy, Pilates, homoeopathic medicine, and I was good at my job.'

'Isn't most of that homoeopathy stuff faith-healing nonsense?'

James is rewarded by a particularly painful sweep of Anna's elbow down his calf.

Anna laughs. 'Criticism's risky with my elbow digging into you.'

'Fair enough. So what brings you back here?'

'There you are, we're done. Perhaps I'll tell you tomorrow.'

The next morning he is again face down as she works on his back.

'Seems easier today. Your faith and my hands between them are doing some good.'

'Your hands,' says James.

Anna's jeans are cut off above the knee. Her calves are bare, her feet in sandals. She has tanned legs, high insteps, rough skin around the bottom of her heels, fading red polish on her neat toes. James's eyes are only twenty-four inches away from her legs as she massages his shoulders with a steady, near-painful pressure. He watches her calf muscles flex as she leans forward over him, and then shuts his eyes.

'What brought you to Allenmouth?' he asks again.

'It's a long story, but I guess you're not going anywhere for an hour. I had an affair with one of the Falcons. A Western Samoan, inside centre, good player. He signed up after the World Sevens – Newcastle was quite a change from the Pacific Islands. Anyhow, I fixed his hamstring, showed him around Northumberland and we lived together in my cottage just outside the city at Blaydon. Three years we were together. And then we broke up. Zach was a funny mixture, a born-again Christian, looked up and pointed to heaven whenever he scored a try. He was the fastest man on the team, six foot three, sixteen solid stone. I loved watching him play, and he loved the game. Elusive runner, flattening tackler. That got him a yellow card sometimes when he used his shoulder and forgot to use his hands.'

'Did you love him?'

There is a long pause.

'Yes, I loved him. But he wanted me to become a Christian. And he hated my job. Me treating his mates made him jealous, and I guess there were some locker-room jokes. Behind my back, but not behind his. I told him there was nothing to be jealous about, and there wasn't, there absolutely wasn't. He wanted me to give up my job. I said no. And then . . .'

'And then?'

'He knocked me about after a club dance. We were celebrating our promotion, and he had no head for alcohol. He accused me of fancying one of his team-mates. I told him he was a fool, and when we got home he slapped me. Being slapped by a sixteen-stone Samoan is no joke, believe me. He gave me a black eye, a broken nose and a fractured cheekbone. He didn't mean to do that much damage, I know, but he did. I had to drive myself to Newcastle General, I wouldn't let him come, he was crying by then. The police wanted me to press charges. I couldn't do that, or go back to him, or the cottage, or the team. So I came here to Dad. He likes playing with you, by the way – says you don't talk too much.'

'I'm sorry,' says James.

'That's OK. I've never told anyone else. I haven't really told you, have I, only your back. That's it, we're done.'

'Tomorrow?' says James.

'Tomorrow,' says Anna.

That afternoon James walks along the beach below the golf course. Steady driving rain from the sea whips the tops of the incoming waves into white foam. Small crabs sidestep out of his way on hurried journeys. Soaked by the rain, he walks along the wet sand, his shoes making deep prints. Looking back, he sees the tide wiping out the evidence that he has been there.

He wants to think about his writing. Instead he remembers Anna's calves, her hands on his back, the way she bundles up her hair into a tight knot, showing the little hollow at the back of her neck. His forearms still carry the smell of the oil she uses. He does not want his back to get better soon.

When he is on the table the next day it is Anna's turn to ask questions.

'There are some lively theories about why you're in Allenmouth. George thinks you're a closet queen, and you've picked somewhere quiet to come out. Says anyone who likes campaign furniture as much as you do can't be straight.'

'I didn't know there was that much interest in me.'

'That isn't the half of it. Sally in the pub thinks it's sex. Perhaps you've murdered your wife; it's always the quiet ones, she says. She takes the *Daily Mail*, so she'll know when the story breaks. Jack behind the bar says it's white-collar crime. You did arrive with a briefcase.'

'And your dad?'

'He thinks you've come for the golf and forgotten your clubs.'

James tells her the real story. Seeing Allenmouth and the enfolding arm of the harbour wall, climbing down from the train, the need to break out of his life that started with his mirror. He talks about living in Ireland, the army, Oxford, golf. Anna likes the story of his Blue.

Working on his bad side, she takes his arm out at right angles, holds his wrist and hand between her thighs, and probes the knots in his shoulder. Being clasped in this way is intensely erotic, dampened only a little by the pain in his shoulder. He looks hard at the whorled knots in the pine floor below him, feels himself stiffening and has to adjust his erection.

'Is that better?' says Anna.

'A bit,' James says; keen to stop thinking about Anna's thighs, he tells her the story of his Treasury career, the air-traffic control system scandal, his early retirement. Anna is surprised at the outcome of the ATCS row.

'You did well,' Anna says. 'Good for you. But why didn't you talk to the press?'

'Because it wouldn't have had any effect. Half the newspapers love British exports, any exports, guns as much as butter. And the smoking gun, the commission paid to the prime minister's nephew, had no fingerprints.'

'Pity.' Anna pats him on the shoulder. 'That's it. You're a lot looser today, and I don't mean the confessional. Last session tomorrow?'

'Last session.'

James dresses, keeping his back turned. They walk down the hill together, neither talking.

34.

J AMES HAD JOINED the Civil Service not through any great feeling of vocation, but because that was what clever Wykehamists did. It gave him security, a feeling that he was part of an elite, and he liked the sound of 'I'm in the Treasury' more than 'I'm a merchant banker', or 'I'm in advertising'.

Gradually it began to mean more to him than security and status. His analytical mind and ability to write clearly marked him out, and he enjoyed the role of the guardian of the taxpayer's purse against what he had come to see as the hungry, feckless, spending departments. He walked to work every morning via St James's Park, often pausing at the head of the lake just below Buckingham Palace. A large weeping willow on the right and chestnuts, ash and crab apple on the first island framed a view down the lake to a fountain in the middle distance. Beyond the gilded cupola above the Admiralty, the turrets, domes and spires of Whitehall looked as though they were the roofscape of a chateau on the Loire.

He remembered the walk on the morning the ATCS project first landed on his desk; it was a bright spring day, the leaves of the trees freshly green, the piles of mown grass smelling rich, about to decay. It was the only time in his Civil Service career that he kept a diary.

17 April
The air-traffic control system project seemed simple at the beginning – a joint submission by the Department of

Overseas Aid and the DTI, blessed by the Foreign Office (Tanzania is the best of our former colonies – how good is that, I wonder? – and deserves our support, they said), and my Permanent Secretary seems keen to give it the Treasury blessing.

1 May

The technical appraisal of the ATCS has finally arrived – not in the original bundle, as DOA had asked for a review. No wonder – the appraisal, by a panel of three aviation experts, makes it clear that the system is Not Fit for Purpose. Their capitals. What we are supplying is a system designed for controlling and directing military aircraft, at three times the cost of an appropriate civil aircraft solution. Which we don't have.

11 May

Perm Sec asked me to review my minute on the ATCS and queried my conclusion. Which was that this was a clear waste of government money, not a good use of DOA funds, etc., etc. He said I appeared over-reliant on the technical appraisal, warned me against trusting experts, and said how important exports and jobs were in current economic conditions. He wants me to say it's OK. It's not OK.

17 May

I've looked at everything again and come to the same conclusion. Why the enthusiasm for such an obviously bad idea?

18 May

Tripartite meeting – three Perm Secs, three Assistant Secs (one of them me) to talk about how to help the Tanzanians take off and land their aeroplanes. I say the proposal is nonsense, the rest say things like, 'The best is the enemy of the good'. Meaningless, especially in this context. Later the Perm Sec comes to my office, says something like, 'You should know this project is very close to the prime minister's heart,' and leaves my minute on the desk. He's scrawled across it, 'Take another look'.

21 May

I've at last discovered what is going on. Via *Private Eye*. The PM's layabout nephew is a 'consultant' to the government of Tanzania on ATCS and other projects, and will trouser two and a half million pounds in commission if the deal goes ahead. WHICH IT SHOULD NOT.

11 June

Final tripartite meeting, same cast of characters. The Permanent Secretary expresses mild reservations, but 'on balance' gives Treasury approval for the project. I am not asked for my opinion but give it nevertheless. There is an embarrassed silence, followed by a summing-up that gives the green light to wasting £25m of UK taxpayers' money. As a form of outdoor relief for the PM's nephew, it's expensive.

17 June

My original minute has been leaked in its entirety to *The Guardian*. Perm Sec sends for me, plainly believes I leaked the document, says there will have to be an internal inquiry. I go back to my office and write him a note saying: (a) it's a lousy project; (b) the PM's nephew's interest should have been disclosed; (c) I had *not* leaked the document. I feel better immediately.

18 June

Sent for by the Perm Sec, who slaps my note down in front of me, describes it as 'unnecessary and unwise', two cardinal

Treasury sins. He says he has asked the Committee of Inquiry (announced at PM's Questions yesterday) to comment specifically on my role.

27 November

The Committee's report was published today. There is a separate, confidential note on my part in the business. It's now on my file. I have become an ex-high-flyer.

Strictly Private and Confidential

The Committee of Inquiry reached the following conclusions:

1. James Burke, Assistant Secretary to the Treasury, was operating within Departmental guidelines in registering his view that this contract could not be justified in value-for-money terms, and in indicating that, in his opinion, there had been irregularities in the contract award process.
2. The Committee took the view that in reaching his conclusion he had given insufficient weight to the importance of this contract for British exports and manufacturing jobs.
3. The Committee considered that he was wrong in describing certain payments as bribes. These were legitimate commissions payable to a number of consultants providing valuable services to the main contractor and the Tanzanian government. There was no evidence to suggest that any relative of any minister benefited from these commissions.
4. The Committee was unable to attribute responsibility for the leaking of James Burke's minute to the *Guardian*. It has made several recommendations intended to improve security in the department.
5. This note should be placed in James Burke's Personnel file.

Rereading his diary and the weasel words of the Committee of Inquiry, James asks himself why he hadn't resigned. His answer is unsatisfactory. He should never have accepted the *Private Eye* version without corroboration. He should have checked the story. And, given the decision to go ahead with the scheme, he should have resigned. It was the biggest test of his career, and he had failed. The version he had given Anna showed him in a heroic light. Heroic, self-righteous loser, that's what he had been.

35.

THE LAST SESSION on the following day is gentle. They are both uncertain about what is happening between them, still at that point where it is possible to turn back, still curious, still intrigued.

'I'm too comfortable, too conventional, I want the world's approval,' says James. 'No money worries, unlike most people. No one dependent on me any more, no proper job. The Trust doesn't count. My life is on tilt. So what do I do for the next twenty years, look at the fallow deer in the park at Donhead? If I was one of them, the next strong young buck would put me out of my misery.'

Anna laughs. 'You don't seem quite ready.'

James wonders whether yesterday's attempt at concealment had been successful.

'I'm the opposite. I could do with a little more comfort, I don't mean money, although that, too, but I want to stop being restless. You teased me about faith-healing stuff the other day, but it's true, I've been a sucker for yoga, TM, healing, almost anything except astrology and crystals. And I'm thirty-five. I would like . . .' Anna trails her fingers gently down James's back from his neck to the base of his spine. 'Would like to declare you well and truly healed.'

James dresses quickly; there is nothing to hide today. They walk together down the hill. Halfway down Anna takes his hand and doesn't let it go. They stop by the arched alleyway.

'Can I come up and see what you've done to George's room?'

'Of course. It's still quite bare.'

James follows Anna up the outside stairs, unlocks the door and they go in. Anna walks across the room, picks up the beehive mug on the bedside table, puts it down.

'It's all lovely. George's stuff looks good here.'

'It's all designed for soldiers on campaign in India or Africa. Even the bed comes to bits.'

They go out on the balcony. The harbour is quiet; there is a gentle breeze from the sea, and a ray of sunshine picks out the battlements on the tower. James takes Anna's hand, lets it go. She shivers as the sea breeze strengthens, and they go back into the room. Between them there hangs an unanswered question. They are both nervous. Anna inspects the books, takes out a copy of *The Oxford Book of English Verse*, puts it back, walks towards the door, stops by the sitz-bath.

'What an odd bath.'

James explains the principle of the sitz-bath.

'Can I try it? I've only got a shower at Dad's.'

James, his heart pounding and his mouth dry, says, 'Of course. I'll be on the balcony.'

'No need. I've seen you with no clothes on, after all.'

Anna puts in the plug, turns on the water and begins to undress. The bath fills quickly. Anna naked is as James has imagined her. She sits on the step, legs and lap covered in water.

'Can you put the band around this?' Anna says as she gathers up her hair. James fixes the band in place and presses his lips against the downy hollow in her neck.

'Thank you,' and she twists round to kiss him on the lips. The kiss lasts a long time. Then she washes her feet and legs and stomach.

'You scrub my back,' she says, passing James the soap. He begins by running his knuckles down either side of Anna's backbone, which makes her laugh. 'I've taught you my technique,' she says.

'You have. Now swivel and rinse.'

Anna drops down into the bath, the water just covering her breasts, and smiles at James. She soaks for a few minutes, eyes closed, then James wraps her in a large red towel.

'Come here,' says Anna, leading him to the bed, the towel wrapped around her like a sarong. She unbuttons James's shirt, and he slips quickly out of the rest of his clothes. Again he is naked in front of her.

She drops the towel, sits on the bed facing James, strokes him, then leans back, raises her knees and pulls him into her, giving a little moan.

'It's been a long . . . I mean I haven't . . .' says James. He tries to think of anything other than what is happening, realizes this is futile, and comes with a feeling of relief and pleasure.

'It's my turn,' says Anna, her hands pushing James down, then holding the back of his head.

'There, that's perfect, there.'

She comes with a series of gasps as her thighs clasp James's cheeks and then fall slowly away. James leaves his mouth on Anna for a few moments, gets on the bed and wraps his arms around Anna's still-damp body.

'That was lovely,' Anna says, moves her cheek into the hollow of James's arm and goes to sleep. James lies looking at Anna, who has become his reason for leaving the train.

Later they make love again; then Anna leaves for her father's cottage. James asks her to stay.

'I don't think Dad would approve of me seducing a client – and you're his client too.'

'When will I see you again?'

Anna kisses him and doesn't answer.

The next morning James walks down to the phone box at ten and rings Jack Pearson's number. There is no reply. He walks to the tower at the end of the harbour wall, returns to the phone box and rings again. Physical passion, and a longing to see and talk to Anna again, have given him an ache he hasn't felt for many years. You're being ridiculous, he tells himself; she's twenty years younger than you, and you have nothing in common.

Back at his flat he picks up an old edition of Cooper's *Life of Socrates* from his job lot of books; he is looking for a distraction from the thoughts of Anna's kisses, Anna naked, Anna returning, Anna disappearing. The quirkiness of the eighteenth-century language is a partial antidote. He is held by one quotation, 'The unexamined life is not worth living.' With a large marker pen he writes on the whitewashed wall above the fireplace, '*Ho de anexetastos bios ou biotôs anthrôpôi*,' laughing at his own pretension, at the same time pleased he can remember not just the quotation but the Greek lettering. He knows he is showing off, to himself and, he hopes, to Anna, who will tease him about his need to put his knowledge on display. If he sees her again.

In the evening James walks down the harbour towards Jack's cottage, stops short, and goes back to the Allen Arms, hoping Anna will be there. He sits in a corner of the deserted bar, nursing a whisky, wondering why he has built a casual encounter into something much more. He goes up to bed early, the euphoria of the previous day replaced by a black unhappiness.

The next morning he has breakfast in the Harbour Café, walks to Jack's cottage, all the way this time, and knocks on the door. Jack Pearson answers.

'Anna about?'

'Gone to Newcastle. Back still bad?'

'Much better, thanks. I'll be playing golf again any day now.'

James turns away and heads out along the shore beyond the harbour and the clubhouse. The day is overcast, matched to his mood; he walks along the beach until the sand runs into a rocky headland. As he skirts the rock pools a jellyfish reflects a brief ray of sunshine. Five miles from Allenmouth he is forced inland by the cliffs he had seen on his first day. A series of little roads take him first north, and then west in a long sweep back to the river, far above the trestle bridge where he had made his original crossing.

He realizes how little he has seen of the countryside around Allenmouth, and how wild it becomes once the sloping fields above the riverside change from green to the brown of the fells. Small feeder becks, darkened by the peat on the high ground, flow into the main river at intervals, and twice he has to turn up them to find a crossing. Wading through the second beck, he sees the carcass of a drowned ewe, dead for some time, the fleece almost worn away, skin stretched tightly over the protruding ribcage. Occasional flurries of rain soak his tweed jacket; he feels his feet beginning to blister and takes a perverse pleasure in the physical discomfort. By the time he reaches his flat it is almost dark. He climbs wearily up the outside staircase and decides his Allenmouth adventure is over.

Later, lying awake, he hears his door open, the rustle of clothes falling to the floor, and feels Anna's mouth on his as she slides into bed beside him. They light the fire, open a bottle of wine, talk, make love, and Anna stays till morning.

When James wakes up, he reaches over and finds only the warm depression left by Anna's body. He puts on his dressing gown and goes through the open balcony door to Anna, who is looking out to sea. He puts his arm around her and kisses her cheek. Below, the harbour is beginning to come to life. One fisherman has already loaded his nets into a sturdy working boat, with blue sides, a small deckhouse towards the stern, two stubby masts fore and aft; 'ALN 14' is painted on the stern. As they watch, he casts off his mooring and heads out through the narrow harbour mouth.

'I can't make out the name,' says James.

'Neither can I – but it's *Andromeda*. Johnny Pease is always first away.'

'I'd like a boat like that.'

'And live here, and become a fisherman? You may have left it a little late.'

Anna smiles, shivers a little and they go back in together. James makes coffee, squeezes three oranges and scrambles half a dozen eggs.

'I'm not used to such luxury.'

'You should come here more often.'

'Maybe I will,' says Anna as she dresses. 'I'm away; Dad will wonder where I've got to.'

She kisses James, but when he tries to pull her back to bed she puts her hands on his chest and pushes him gently away.

'Let's meet this evening,' says James.

'I'll come round about seven,' and Anna goes through the door and down the outside stairs.

This is the beginning of what James would like to make a routine; Anna's unpredictable comings and goings are the exact opposite. She is reluctant to be pinned down. Sometimes, but not often, she stays the night, sometimes they will arrange to walk together the next day, but it is always left to James to suggest their next meeting. James, although he abandoned the train and deserted his Trust Board meeting, is still a civil servant at heart who likes an organized diary. He finds Anna's attitude to time infuriating. And exciting.

They are at that stage where discovery is a pleasure. James and Anna are both explorer and explored. Anna finds every aspect of his past intriguing, pressing him for stories about his childhood, his marriage, his career.

'You treat me as though you were an anthropologist and I was a member of some unknown tribe in the Amazon rainforest,' says James.

'That's exactly what you are. Everything about you is outside my experience. I like finding out things about you.'

'I talk too much. And you don't talk enough.'

'My life hasn't been as interesting, and it's a lot shorter than yours.'

'It's interesting to me.'

They are walking along the back street towards the Allen Arms when James notices the lettering carved above a double doorway. 'St Elmo' on the left, 'St Valery' on the right, and beside the doorbell a little tarnished brass plaque, 'Allenmouth Ex-Servicemen's Club'.

'Let's have a drink in here for a change,' says James.

'It's for old soldiers.'

'That's me.'

James leads Anna into a small room with a bar in the corner. A grey-haired man in a dark blue blazer with shiny buttons and a regimental badge is drawing himself a glass of beer.

'Ex-servicemen only,' he says. 'Sorry.'

'I am one. 23491332 Trooper Burke, Royal Irish Dragoons.'

'A donkey-walloper, eh? I was REME, kept you buggers on the road. We usually ask for a British Legion card, but if you can still remember your number that'll do me.'

James takes Anna and two halves of bitter over to a table in the corner. She looks surprised by this sudden detour.

'Were you in the army? I've never known a soldier before.'

'Known in the biblical sense?'

'Known in any sense, thank you very much.'

'Well, now you know me. "I 'listed at home for a lancer, Oh who would not sleep with the brave." You would have fancied me in my tight overalls, green velvet waistcoat with gold frog-gings, red jacket trimmed with gold braid and a high green collar with a silver Irish harp. And swan-necked spurs.'

'I'm not sure about the spurs, and besides, I fancy you now. What was it like?'

'It was a different world.'

It was a different world that began with the casually brutal regime of the Royal Armoured Corps Training Regiment at Catterick. James arrived with sixty other bewildered National

Servicemen in a cold Yorkshire autumn and was given a battle-
dress, denims, two pairs of boots, a knife, fork and spoon, a mess
tin, a shapeless black beret with a cap badge – the mailed fist of
the Royal Armoured Corps, 'That's the wanking-spanner' –
pants, vests, scratchy shirts, braces, a tie, sheets, blankets, pillows,
a steel locker and a narrow iron bed in Number Four Hut,
Kandahar Lines, Salamanca Barracks, Catterick Camp, North
Yorkshire. And his number, which he forgot once and, after doubling round the square twenty times, never forgot again.

'Wakey, wakey. Hands off cocks, feet in socks,' the hut lance
corporal shouted at five in the morning, banging his night-stick
on the nearest metal locker and tipping anyone still in bed after
a minute out onto the floor.

The obscenities were as regimented as the drill. 'Trooper
Burke, if you don't wake up I'm going to insert my cock into
your left ear hole and fuck some sense into you.' The living conditions, James had to admit, were no more Spartan than
Winchester.

'Right, line up, you useless articles, tallest on the left, shortest
on the right, move,' shouted Corporal Blinkhorn. 'Now I'm going
to pick out the Potential Officers. I can tell you a mile off.'

He went down the line pointing out the POs, and he didn't
make a mistake.

'You not only talk different, you look fucking well different,
and you've all got names like Peregrine and Humphrey and
Archibald. Christ, we even had a Hilary once. Some of you have
double-barrelled names, but not with me you don't. That white
shoulder flash don't mean a fucking thing to me.'

It did mean something; it singled them out for extra abuse
from the corporal, and some relatively good-natured teasing
from their fellow troopers.

They spent six weeks removing the pimples from their best
boots with spoons heated on candles, then building up carapaces
of black boot polish that shone like ebony; they went on long
route marches, they went on night exercises, they fired World

War Two .303 rifles on the ranges; they learned to fold issue pyjamas into twelve-inch squares so that the stripes on the tops and the bottoms were exactly aligned – 'No, Trooper Burke, those fucking pyjamas are not for wearing, they're for ironing into fucking perfect squares'; they learned to make the unlit iron stove in the hut gleam with Zebo; they learned to blanco the webbing that went over their shoulders and polish their brasses with Duraglit, including the little brass hole at the bottom of the pistol holster, the hole easily forgotten, although not by the inspecting sergeant. And the shiny mailed-fist cap badge.

The wise man of The Squad was Matthew Barrington, an older trooper who had been at Cambridge for the last three years and was destined for the same regiment as James. Partly because of his age, partly because of his temperament, he escaped the worst of the abuse. 'Your fucking BA doesn't outrank these, Barrington,' said Corporal Blinkhorn, pointing to his two shoulder stripes, but quickly decided that there were easier targets in The Squad.

'When they shout at you,' Matthew told James, 'you need the right look. Admiring subservience, impressed but not terrified. Say "Yes, Corporal Blinkhorn" as though in six months' time you'll be giving him orders and you're remembering his name for the future. Or imagine you've just heard a particularly brilliant performance by an operatic villain, Scarpia in *Tosca* for example, and are applauding in spite of your feeling of revulsion.'

James had never been to an opera, but he took Matthew's advice.

Six weeks of basic training were followed by two weeks in the Potential Officers' Wing preparing for the War Office Selection Board.

'Pass WOSB and it's gin and tonics in the Officers' Mess for the next two years,' said Matthew Barrington. 'Fail, it's halves of bitter in the NAAFI.'

WOSB was a three-day ordeal. James and the other POs were given railway passes and sent off to Hampshire for three days of assault courses, lecturettes, written papers, interviews and the culminating test of leadership, the Task.

'It's always the same – a ten-foot river and an eight-foot plank,' said Matthew to James. 'Just shout a lot in a masterful tone of voice, boss everyone about.'

It was an accurate forecast and sound advice. At the end of WOSB the group was lined up and an officer handed out an envelope to each candidate. When James tore his open, he saw to his relief, 'Recommended for Officer Training'.

'Think of this as purgatory,' Matthew told James as they arrived at Officer Cadet School in Aldershot. 'You've been in hell, you've escaped, and after four months here you'll be a second lieutenant, a cornet as our regiment calls us, drinking subsidized gin and tonic in heaven.'

'Gin and tonic is your Holy Grail,' said James.

'Exactly so. Why, did you join the army to travel abroad and kill people?'

'I'm like you, a pressed man.'

James discovered an entirely new pecking order at Mons: the Royal Armoured Corps at the top of the tree, then the Gunners, then everybody else, although he noticed that it was only the 'everybody else' – the REME, the RASC, the Catering Corps – that did anything that could be described as useful outside the army.

'Not all cavalry regiments are the same,' said Matthew. 'We're heavy cavalry, comfortably in the middle. The light cavalry are much grander than us. In the 10th Hussars they won't have you without a private income of at least a thousand a year.'

'That still goes on? In 1958?'

'You have a lot to learn.'

James did have a lot to learn, and not only about the social gradations of the British Army. By the time he left Mons he knew how a car engine worked, how to read a map, how to operate the notoriously unreliable No. 19 set – the Bravo Delta Romeo Mike of the alphabet remained with him for ever. And how to deal with a riot. In the grainy army film ('Amritsar,' said Matthew), they were advised to give one warning on the loud hailer, 'Disperse or we fire,' and then shoot the ringleader. The approach worked on the film.

The months at Mons were crowned by a final exercise, five days and nights on Salisbury Plain, after which 203 Troop, G Squadron, marched up the steps of the parade ground and duly passed out.

The Royal Irish Dragoons were in Malaya; James and Matthew flew out in an uncomfortable Viscount chartered by the RAF that stopped at every colonial and ex-colonial outpost on its round-about route: Brindisi, Baghdad, Bahrain, Karachi, Delhi, Rangoon, Saigon, Singapore. The journey took four days, including an over-night stop in Mrs Minwallah's Grand Hotel in Karachi. In Singapore they transferred to a train to Kuala Lumpur; Matthew was made to sign for a pistol and twenty rounds of ammunition by a harassed quartermaster lieutenant.

'You're in command of the train,' said the lieutenant.

'What does that mean?'

'Only means something if you're ambushed. Hasn't happened for a long time.'

'We are on active service,' said Matthew to James later. 'We're keeping the CTs, the Communist Terrorists, at bay. Luckily we just swan about in armoured cars. It's the infantry and the Special Forces that go into the jungle and do the hard stuff. But we'll all get a general service medal after six months.'

'If spared,' said James, remembering his Ulster nanny's caution about any reference to an uncertain future.

In Kuala Lumpur, where the regiment was based, no one had been told that the days of Empire were over. Race meetings, polo, gymkhanas, golf, cocktail parties, dances were a more sophisti-cated version of life in County Kildare. Without the rain. James was put in charge of Three Troop, A Squadron – two Daimler armoured cars, two Saracen armoured personnel carriers and twenty-eight men.

'You've got Sergeant McLester,' James was told by his squadron leader. 'He won a Military Medal in the Normandy campaign. He'd be an RSM if it wasn't for the drink; busted to private six years ago, climbed back up. You'll not need to boss him about too much, just keep him sober.'

James took this advice, and the regimental duties in KL were not exacting. Vehicle maintenance, regular inspections, the occasional parade, left a lot of time for sport, and the regiment was sport-mad. James rode out every morning at six o'clock on a regimental polo pony, returned in time for breakfast and first parade at eight, watched while Sergeant McLester organized the day's work. The Officers' Mess lived up to Matthew's Promised Land of gin and tonic, although a couple of crusty bachelor captains, one of whom was the adjutant, kept the excesses of twenty subalterns aged nineteen to twenty-four under some sort of control. Once every couple of months one of the regimental bands would beat The Retreat, an evening occasion to entertain local dignitaries with military music and marching.

'Odd title,' said Matthew to James. 'Considering we're meant to be doing the opposite. Still, it's a chance for the ex-pats to blub when they hear "Land of Hope and Glory".'

After a month in Kuala Lumpur, James and Three Troop were sent up-country on detachment to relieve a troop from C Squadron. Camp Gurney, named after a murdered high commissioner, was two thousand feet above sea level at the far end of the Cameron Highlands, two hundred miles and a day's journey from Kuala Lumpur. As they drove north, the landscape changed until all around them the green waves of the tea plantations flowed over the hills and the valleys. The air became cleaner, scented.

'It's the tea,' said Sergeant McLester when they stopped for a brew-up at halfway. 'No shortage of the stuff up here.'

James's first impression of Camp Gurney was of something out of *Beau Geste*. Set in a clearing at the end of a rough laterite road were half a dozen wooden-walled, atap-roofed *bashas* on

CHRISTOPHER BLAND

stilts inside a perimeter fence of barbed wire. The Union Jack flew over a small parade ground of beaten earth that doubled as a helicopter landing pad; an open hangar, the only building with a corrugated roof, housed the Daimlers, the Saracens and the REME. There were Bren-gun posts at each of the four corners of the camp. Outside the wire was a shallow moat filled with evil-looking pointed bamboo stakes at two-foot intervals. A strip fifty yards wide had been cleared of scrub and trees to separate the camp from the jungle and the road. The river was half a mile away, and in a clearing between the camp and the river were half a dozen longhouses, the home of seventy or so Malays. It was all a far cry from the comforts of Kuala Lumpur and the Selangor Club.

On James's arrival he was briefed by the District Officer.

'Your job is to show the flag, escort the food convoys, patrol the roads, cheer up the tea planters and the tin miners, and convince the Malays that we're on top. Which we are, by the way. The Emergency will be over by the end of the year, I reckon. Have they given you any jungle warfare training? Speak any Malay?'

'No and no,' said James. 'National Servicemen aren't around long enough to be worth training. I was given a copy of *The Conduct of Anti-Terrorist Operations in Malaya* and told to read that.'

'Let's hope that's all you need. You'll stick to the road; it's the job of the infantry to look for CTs in the jungle.'

James reported each evening by wireless to his squadron leader and was otherwise left to his own devices. His troop patrolled regularly along the rough, dusty roads that criss-crossed the five hundred square miles of his territory, calling on the five big tea plantations and three tin mines that they were there to protect, and liaising with the Hampshire Regiment's platoon when wireless communications were good enough.

He found the independence of his command both exciting and frightening. He was responsible for almost thirty men, two armoured cars and two armoured personnel carriers – half a million pounds of hardware. And although Sergeant McLester, a tough Ulsterman from County Antrim, took most of the routine decisions and organized the men and the maintenance of the vehicles, he made it clear to the troop that James was in charge.

'Served with your father in Normandy,' he had said to James in Kuala Lumpur. 'Good soldier. Killed a lot of Germans with his Sten gun, so he did.' Some of this glory had attached itself to James.

Each morning at six they moved out on patrol, the air still cool and sharp, the jungle beginning to come to life. After the initial wireless check, Three Alpha, Bravo, Charlie and Delta all on net, at least for the moment, James looked at the lead armoured car from the turret of his Daimler, then back at the two Saracens, and felt the romance as well as the loneliness of his little command.

From the top of an armoured car the jungle looked magnificent. White-, red- and green-barked trees a hundred feet or more high supported a dense green canopy that filtered out most of the light. Their trunks were covered with vines and creepers; mosses and ferns created an aerial garden hung with bougainvillea, hibiscus and frangipani. There were innumerable butterflies, moths and dragonflies, and birds – wonderful birds, James thought, keeping a note of each new sighting in his notebook. Back from the road, and rarely seen, were elephants, tigers, wild pigs and monkeys. The villages were primitive, without electricity or running water unless they were attached to one of the large plantations. The Malays were beautiful, friendly, shy.

'Don't be taken in by the cheerful waves as you drive by,' said the District Officer. 'They are much more frightened of the CTs than they are of us, and for good reason.'

'Who are the CTs?'

'They aren't Communists in any sense of the word, although it suits us to call them that, and they are almost all Chinese, not Malay. But they're terrorists all right; they live off what they can extort – money, food, shelter – from the villages and the plantation workers. They are well armed, but there aren't a lot of them. We've killed some, some have publicly defected, others have just gone home. They've given up any hope of winning. By the end of this year there will be a truce, an amnesty and it'll all be over. And they'll get their independence soon enough. Right now your job is to show them we're here. The armoured cars are quite impressive if you can keep them on the road; the Daimler Mark 2 wasn't designed for the tropics.'

James shared a room with the Hampshires' lieutenant, who was absent on patrol when James arrived. Three days later he returned from fifteen days in the jungle, grey and exhausted. His legs were scarred with angry fire-ant bites and when he needed help to remove a dozen leeches from his legs the jungle lost some of its magic for James.

James and Three Troop soon settled into a routine; stand-to at dawn and dusk, guard duties shared with the Hampshires, vehicle maintenance, machine-gun practice, patrols and escort duty. For the first month it was a welcome change from Kuala Lumpur, although the troopers grumbled about the humidity, the cold nights, the uncomfortable beds and the food.

'Don't you worry about that, sir,' said Sergeant McLester. 'They'd grumble wherever they were, Kuala Lumpur, Catterick or Paradise, not that many of them are likely to get there.'

A week before Three Troop was due to go back to Kuala Lumpur they were on a routine patrol through one of the biggest tea plantations, the twelve-thousand-acre Ladang, when James heard Corporal Dean in the leading armoured car shout over his wireless, 'Three Alpha, Three Alpha, this is Three Charlie, roadblock', then the sound of rifle and machine-gun fire, then, 'Christ, Jack's been hit'.

Jack Mackie was Three Charlie's driver. As James in the second Daimler came round the corner he saw Three Charlie had slewed off the road and into the ditch.

'Close down, close down, fire when you see a target,' James said, although closed down in an armoured car it was hard to see anything but straight ahead, hard to see the source of the bullets zinging off their armour.

James was unsure what to do next, knew he had to do something. He looked down at his hands, grabbed hold of the hatch handle to stop them shaking, felt his mouth dry, tried to speak, took several swallows from his water bottle, then a deep breath, and said, 'I'll go forward and get a tow-rope onto Three Charlie. Saracens, give me covering fire, and don't worry about wasting ammunition once I'm out of the wagon.'

They drove within six feet of Three Charlie, occasional bullets still hitting the armoured cars; the CTs seemed to be in deep brush thirty yards off the road to the left.

'Start firing now, they're on the left of the road,' said James, opening the hatch of his Daimler.

He climbed out of the top, went round to the back and detached the tow-rope, ran forward in an undignified crouch and attached the rope to the rear of Three Alpha and the front of his own armoured car. This seemed to take an age. The machine guns were plastering the jungle edge to the left of the road, tearing up the small trees and bushes. If James was fired at, he didn't notice. He went round to the front of Three Charlie where McKelvey was slumped below the level of the armour, bleeding from the head and unconscious. He pulled him out with difficulty, carried him round to the back of Three Alpha and heaved his body up and onto the engine cover.

'Right, now very gently haul Three Charlie out of the ditch,' he told his driver.

The ditch was dry and not too deep, and after two heart-stopping, wheel-spinning moments Three Charlie was back on the road.

James climbed onto the top of Three Charlie, hammered on the hatch until Corporal Dean opened up, and said, 'Corporal Dean, you drive, you take McKelvey's place.'

There was no reply. Corporal Dean was unable to speak or move, staring down at the empty driving seat spattered with congealing blood.

The covering fire continued, with only the occasional shot in reply; one of the gunners said over the wireless, 'I think I hit one of the bastards.'

Sergeant McLester came up from the rear Saracen and said, 'I'll drive her, sir. Dean can hold McKelvey on the back of the wagon and bandage him up. I've left the first-aid kit beside him,' ran forward and climbed into the driver's seat.

A minute later a reluctant Corporal Dean emerged from Three Charlie to join McKelvey on the back of James's armoured car.

'What did you tell him?' James asked his troop sergeant later.

'I told him the CTs won't shoot you if you climb out, but I fucking well will if you don't.'

'Right, high reverse down the road until we can turn round and see where we are.'

Where they were was in one of the last ambushes of the Malayan Emergency. They drove back to Camp Gurney as fast as carrying Trooper McKelvey and Corporal Dean on the engine hatch would allow. James had already radioed for a helicopter to take the wounded trooper to hospital in Kuala Lumpur, and by the time they were back at the camp the helicopter was sitting on the parade ground ready to take off. McKelvey was still unconscious with a deep furrow along the side of his head from a bullet that had removed the top of his left ear. His bandage was replaced and he was loaded gently into the helicopter.

James and Three Troop were told to return south a day later; at the debriefing the colonel and his squadron leader were cautiously complimentary.

'You did well to get a tow-rope onto Three Charlie,' said the colonel. 'And Trooper McKelvey will be OK. The Hampshires went out the next evening and found one dead CT at the edge of the jungle, so honours were better than even. I'll put you in for a Mention in Despatches.'

James was relieved. Running into an ambush and nearly losing one of his men and an armoured car didn't seem a major military achievement. It was clear the dead CT had tipped the balance.

James's remaining months, all spent in Kuala Lumpur, were uneventful, and he was not sent up-country again. Three Troop, with James in goal, won the regimental seven-a-side football competition, a triumph regarded as more important than a Mention in Despatches, and far more important than James's triumph in the South-East Asia Command Golf Championship.

'Well done, James,' said his commanding officer, who felt that most games were best played from the back of a horse. 'Wished you'd given the brigadier a bit of slack in the semi-final. Five and four was a bit brutal.'

James's journey back at the end of two years' National Service was as tedious and roundabout as the trip out, but without Matthew as company. Matthew had signed on for another year shortly after his arrival in Malaya.

'They'll make me assistant adjutant in October and give me a second pip and Regular pay. It's a change from farming in Northumberland, which is what I'll be doing for the next forty years. And the Emergency is about to come to an end, thanks to Three Troop's heroic exploits in the Cameron Highlands.'

'Bugger off,' said James. 'It's the cheap gin and tonics, you might as well admit it. Not to mention your soldier servant polishing your boots, laying out your uniform, doing your laundry. I'll miss your company on the trip home.'

'We'll keep in touch. The regiment will be back in England this time next year – we'll meet at the regimental dinner.'

*

'It all sounds weird, terrible,' says Anna. 'What did it do to you?'

'Toughened me up, taught me to swear, taught me to smoke, although I never took to cigarettes. It made me tidy; once you've ironed your pyjamas into twelve-inch squares you're never the same again. I'd led a sheltered life, I suppose, in Ireland and at Winchester. I've never been as cold, tired and hungry as during that time at Catterick. Or as scared, except perhaps on a dodgy horse, but not scared of other people acting in a random and often vicious way, people who had real power over you. I was still a boy when I joined the army. I felt grown up two years later.'

'What about the man you killed?'

'I didn't kill him, one of the gunners did; they all wanted the credit, by the way. He was a terrorist, they were trying to kill us, and nearly succeeded with Trooper McKelvey.'

'It was his country.'

'He was Chinese, like the vast majority of CTs. Lim Men Sek, he was called; he'd killed five Malays in Sungai Siput.'

'I see.' Anna doesn't sound convinced.

James didn't add that during those two years he had uncritically absorbed the petty snobberies of a world that was already an anachronism, and he had then shaken them off within days of arriving at Oxford, replacing them with a new set of rules. He felt this made him seem both chameleon-like and priggish, and he continued to need Anna's approval.

They go on a long walk together up the River Allen, retracing in reverse James's journey in the rain when he thought Anna had gone. They are sitting on a bench by the river; the tide is in and the river full.

'Allenmouth must have been a good place to grow up in,' says James.

'I suppose – but it's very small, everyone knows everybody and everything. When I look back it seems strange to have been brought up by my dad. Mum had gone off with his best friend before I was three, so I never knew the two of them together. Dad didn't want to have anything to do with her, so I'd go off by train on my own to Newcastle once a month.'

She got up, picked a cornflower from the bank behind them and tucked it into James's buttonhole, then continued, 'Andy, that was my stepfather, got a job as the pro in a smart golf club just outside Newcastle. He'd made a bit on the European tour, he never won a tournament, but he picked up some decent place money now and again. They lived in a flash villa in Denton Burn, very tidy, no kids, full of my mother's collection of china pigs. I hated going there, went less and less often. Andy tried to teach me to play golf, I thought that was my father's job and told him so, and he gave up on me after that. He probably wasn't a bad bloke, but I couldn't see him straight. I don't suppose Dad was that easy to live with, although he and I get on OK.'

'What about school?'

'I got the bus every day to the comprehensive five miles away in town. Half a dozen of us went there from Allenmouth. We called ourselves the Seaside Gang, hung out together. I couldn't wait to get away, wound up in college in Newcastle for three years. I loved Newcastle, still do – I'm a real Geordie, a city girl at heart.'

'Living with your mother?'

'You're joking. I saw less of them when I was at college than when I was at school. I was in a student hostel for a while, moved out into a flat with my first proper boyfriend.'

'Lucky man.'

'We were both lucky with each other. He was a medical student, but he knew about as much about sex as I did, absolutely nothing. We found out together, and all that was great. After he got sent to Leeds by the NHS we met only at weekends, then I went to work for the Falcons, and he met a nurse in his hospital. We still send each other cards on our birthdays. I met Zach when I was with the Falcons – I've told you about all that.'

'Did you ever think about marrying him?'

'Mum leaving Dad put me off. I did think about it. Zach asked me often enough, swore he'd give up drink, said he was ready to settle down. But rugby's a violent game and he was never able to leave all his aggression on the field. Half the time he didn't know what he was doing; it often wasn't much, a hard push, a slap that he meant to be mild. Sometimes he'd make love to me after a row and it was almost like rape. I found that quite exciting the first time, and later when I tried to stop it I wasn't strong enough, and I suppose he thought it was all part of sex with me. I should have left him then before it got worse. When he beat me up after the dance . . .'

Anna stops talking, takes several deep breaths, starts again. 'I was two months' pregnant, and I hadn't told him. I wasn't ready to tell him, I knew he'd say we'd have to get married.'

Anna buries her face in her hands. 'I thought I'd lose the baby after the battering I'd had. But I didn't. Then I had an abortion, and it's the worst thing I've ever done. I wish I'd kept the baby, it was mine as much as Zach's. But I didn't, and it's gone.'

Anna begins to cry, great shuddering sobs, doubled over, her face in her hands. James tries to put his arm around her; she shrugs him off and moves away. After a few minutes she stops crying, stands up and says fiercely to him, 'No one else knows about that, not Zach, not Dad, no one. I shouldn't have told you – I'm sorry I did. Let's go home.'

They walk back to Allenmouth, not talking. Anna, still angry, stops outside her father's house, ducks a kiss on the cheek from James and leaves him to walk back to his flat alone. James curses his curiosity; they have both been blighted by the story. It shouldn't affect our relationship, he says to himself, but he is aware that logic has nothing to do with it.

That evening he goes to the Ex-Servicemen's Club, knowing that he will see none of his Allenmouth acquaintances there. He is the only customer. He discourages conversation from the ex-REME bartender, whose 'On your own tonight?' is met by a blank stare and a request for a double Scotch. After three of these James walks unsteadily back to his flat; there will be no visit from Anna later that night.

He has no word from her for the next three days, and he doesn't try to contact her, using the time to begin sorting through his great-grandmother's letters and diaries. The north-east coast of England seems a long way from County Kerry in the middle of the nineteenth century, and while he is immersed in them he is able to stop thinking about Anna, at least for a while.

The papers had come from his great-aunt Agnes, in half a dozen boxes containing a miscellaneous collection of letters, rent rolls, commissions, faded photographs and daguerreotypes, newspaper cuttings, diaries and commonplace books, with a covering letter.

'I found these in the stable block, the only part of Derriquin to escape the fire, and thought you would be the best person to look after them now John is away to England,' Josephine Burke had written to Agnes in 1928.

James could smell the smoke that had swirled around the papers and into every corner of every box, and could see the flames roaring up through the stones of his father's, his forebears', house hundreds of miles and a hundred years away on the south-west coast of Ireland.

The earliest letters were from his great-grandmother's father, a prosperous clergyman in County Cork, negotiating his daughter's marriage to John Burke of Derriquin. The Reverend Arthur Hamilton had a practical attitude to the match, emphasizing his daughter Letitia's considerable virtues, by which he meant, 'six thousand pounds in the three and a quarter per cent Consolidated Stock'. At one stage he was ready to call the negotiations off; the fifteen-thousand-pound debt burden on the Derriquin estate brought him to the conclusion 'that the union of our children could not be advantageous to either party, as they would have the prospect for many years of comparative poverty'. There was a gap in the correspondence, then the couple were encouraged to meet in Dublin, 'avoiding the idle gossip of Cork', and finally a letter in which the clergyman praised his daughter for her attitude to the marriage. 'There is no nonsense or romance in Letitia. She is possessed with plain common sense, a quality without which few get on in the world.'

In another box there is a patchwork bag containing letters of condolence after William Burke, a captain in the 57th Foot, had been killed at the battle of Inkerman. The first letter was from an uncle in Cork, who 'is in such a state of anxiety about poor William, watching for the list of casualties to come in by the *Telegraph*', and then, on a more down-to-earth note, saying, 'O'Leary won't pay more than six pounds a ton for barley'. The list of casualties arrived with William's name among the dead; the bag held forty black-bordered letters and a cutting from *The Kerryman*: 'Like an avenging angel, said a brother officer, he dealt death to every Russian within sweep of his weapon. How he escaped so long I know not; he died after a splendid display of gallantry. Ireland may well be proud of him.' The final item in the bundle is a letter from the War Office, confirming repayment of the money that had been used to purchase William's commission.

It is the diaries, letters and cuttings during the Famine years that interest James most. The Burkes were not absentees, and he hopes to find evidence that they were better than most at dealing with the extraordinary misery caused by the successive failures of the potato crop after 1845. His father had told James that the Burkes had been good landlords; a letter from John Burke to *The Times* in 1849 had claimed that there had been no evictions on the Derriquin estate, although in the same box there was an anonymous letter calling him a liar.

One entry in his great-grandmother's diary was so harrowing that James could hardly bear to read it. Letitia had been to visit her father in County Cork; on the return journey her carriage is stopped on the road near Skibbereen:

"by an emaciated figure, his skin yellow and his bones flesh-less, who begged us in a hoarse voice, barely above a whisper, to help his family in the cabin which we could see just beside the road. This was little more than a shed, eight feet long by seven wide. Along the western wall was a newly dug grave in which three of his children were recently buried. Inside the cabin were five individuals, male, female and children, huddled around a fire of a sod of turf and a few sticks, all clearly suffering from a malignant fever; the two children were clutching their mother's old gown and crying for food which she could not give them. I could see on a table in the corner the body of a dead man.

We went back to the village through which we had just passed and returned with tea, sugar, milk and some bread, which were ravenously consumed. I was able the next day to persuade the Poor Law Guardians to take the family into the fever hospital, but by then of the six of them only four were still alive. Both children had died in the night.

There are those who say that the potato disease bears all the marks of Divine affliction. It requires an unquestioning faith to understand the workings of Providence, and to believe that out of such misery good may emerge. I pray that my own faith and that of my dear husband prove strong enough to carry us through these terrible times. Although we have been less badly affected in our corner of Kerry, in the past two years twenty-seven of our four hundred or more tenants have died of the fever, and over thirty have taken the boats to Canada or America, though how many survive that arduous journey is hard to tell. Needless to say the rents cannot be collected, and yet the bank debts on the estate and the Poor Rate must still be paid."

Later there was a brief reference to the religious revival sweeping through the South-West; John and Letitia were converted from the Church of Ireland and became Plymouth Brethren.

Visits to Dublin were more frequent; in 1897 a final entry said,

> My dear John has become increasingly certain that we must look for our salvation not by works on this Earth but through Faith in the life to come. He feels called upon to preach, that in watering others he may himself be watered. So we must leave this earthly paradise to our dear Henry to manage as best he can, while we go to preach the Gospel wherever we are called.

In the scrapbook are three crude drawings over the heading, 'The prospect for Irish landlords'. Each shows a farmer in a tailcoat and billycock hat, saying to the landlord, in 1840, 'Your Honour, there's the rent'. In 1860, 'I think there's time enough'. In 1880, 'Divil a penny I'll pay'. Opposite the drawings there is a threatening letter on blue-lined paper:

> Men of Dunkerron! Anyone who pays more than the Valuation is making his own grave and may expect six balls through the head. Resist the heavy-handed landlords. Ireland Unite! Ordered by Mr Parnell, our chief Adviser of Blood.
>
> The Land League

James is shaken by the cuttings and the diaries. He had hoped to find an exoneration, evidence that John Burke had behaved in a way that had set him apart from and above his peers. Instead he discovers that his great-grandfather had behaved reasonably well, perhaps as well as a man in the grip of such forces could have behaved – but that was all. Not an absentee, not an evicter, not a Souper, but nothing more.

And James finds extraordinary the combination of genuine concern with the belief that the Famine was in some way deserved, or, in the Quakers' words, 'doubtless intended in wisdom for our good'. When James puts the papers back in their boxes, his 'good landlord' hopes are finally extinguished. And he marvels that the disaster of the Famine had turned his great-grandfather towards a God who was responsible for millions of Irish men, women and children dying of hunger and disease.

36.

THREE DAYS OF immersion in family papers and the horrors of the Great Famine are enough for James. He sends Anna a much redrafted letter, worrying about the beginning – Darling? My Dear? Dearest? – as much as the content. He feels like a sixteen-year-old schoolboy writing to a girl for the first time.

> Dearest Anna,
> I am sorry that my curiosity got the better of me on Tuesday. I miss you. Let's go away for a couple of days. Holy Island is within reach and might soothe both of us. I've hired a car for Thursday morning; if you want to come, I'll be leaving the flat at about nine to catch the causeway tide.
> Love,
> James XXXX

He slips the letter under Jack Pearson's door, not anticipating a reply, only half expecting Anna to appear on Thursday morning.

Anna does appear, carrying a small overnight bag. James is unable to control his broad smile; she smiles back and returns his hug and his kiss.

'I'm sorry,' she says. 'It wasn't your fault that I burdened you with all that baggage, and in the end I felt better for telling you. I've never been to Holy Island. And I need to get out of Allenmouth for a while. Zach's followed me here – he's staying with some of his born-again friends in a farmhouse on the Newcastle road.'

An early morning mist has burned away; the sky is blue and cloudless, the sea bright in the mid-May sunshine. They drive up the coast to the Holy Island causeway; the tide has turned and is coming in fast. On the causeway they pass a curious box on stilts fifteen feet above the sand.

'What is it for?' asks Anna.

'It's a refuge box, if you're on foot and get trapped by the tide. The book says the road was built only in 1954; before that you had to follow the guide posts on foot.'

Their small hotel overlooks the harbour; James signs them in as Mr and Mrs Burke. Anna smiles when she sees this. Upstairs in their bedroom she says, 'I've never been a Mrs before. Would they chuck us out if they thought we were living in sin?'

'Not worth the risk. Hotels and guesthouses are the last bastion of sexual morality, especially in the North.'

Anna opens a drawer, empties her overnight bag into it and sits down in a wicker chair to watch James unpack. He lays out his ivory hairbrushes on top of the chest of drawers, puts his socks and pants in one drawer, his handkerchiefs in another, his shirts in a third.

'Goodness, you are methodical; I see what you meant when you told me the army made you tidy.'

James looks sheepish. 'I know, I know. It's second nature to me, has been for thirty years. I still think I'm going to get an extra drill if my hairbrushes aren't aligned.'

In the evening they walk down to St Cuthbert's Island. The tide is out, and they take off their shoes and socks to make the crossing; the island is barely a hundred yards wide.

'St Cuthbert used to come here to get away from the monastery. Otters would play around his feet when he waded in the sea,' says James.

Anna walks over to the ruins of the old chapel. 'No wonder Cuthbert thought this was a good place to meditate. I'm going to do half an hour's yoga. Don't wait.'

James watches as Anna sits down next to the island's wooden

cross. Then he crosses to the main island and looks back at Anna, sitting with her palms flat on the grass, her eyes closed, her breasts rising and falling as she breathes deeply.

They are on the island for three more days, days when the sky is cloudless and the sea blue. James finds living with Anna at close quarters infinitely better than her irregular visits to his Allenmouth flat. He loves watching her dress and undress, take a shower, asleep beside him in the early light; he loves knowing she will be there in the morning when they go to bed. It is a long time since he has shared a bedroom with a woman.

On their second day, James asks about visiting the Farne Islands, and the manager tells him that the boats leave from Seahouses further down the coast.

'That's miles away. Let's go down to the harbour and see what we can find.'

The Holy Island harbour is smaller than Allenmouth, with three lobster boats tied up along the jetty. James asks each skipper in turn about the Farne Islands; the first two say no, the third is encouragingly doubtful.

'I'd do it,' he says. 'But I can carry no more than three, and I need George to help me pull up the pots.'

'I'll be George; I've hauled pots before,' says James. 'And you can pay George to stay ashore.'

'All right – but it'll be twenty pound, mind. And a fiver for George.'

The boat is crowded with spare pots and smells of tar, diesel and fish. They motor two miles off the end of Holy Island and pick up a long line of lobster pots. One in five has a keepable lobster. James shows Anna where to hold a lobster while he puts a strong rubber band around each claw to stop them fighting in the tank.

At the Farnes they see puffins, arctic terns, guillemots, huge colonies of seals. A couple of porpoises accompany them on the return journey.

'I'm impressed you know the names of so many birds. Seagulls are all you get in Newcastle.'

'I've got the book and the binoculars.'

As they walk back to the hotel Anna says, 'That's what I like about you. I would have accepted the Seahouses story and given up. You believed it could be done from here and you were right. It's not easy to persuade a Geordie fisherman.'

Inheriting Donhead from Great-Aunt Agnes came as a complete surprise to James. He had met her once or twice as a child; she had spent the previous twenty years in a home in Shaftesbury, suffering from dementia, and after one visit, when she had no idea who he was or why he had come to see her, he never went again. Donhead had belonged to her husband; although they had no children, it had always been assumed by James and by his father that everything would go to a nephew on John Fuller's side of the family, a nephew who had cultivated his uncle and had become an MP in the European Parliament. So when James was summoned to Lincoln's Inn for the reading of the will he expected to learn of a few Burke possessions that Agnes had felt should be his.

The will was brief. Donhead and its contents, and its deer park and eight hundred acres, and enough capital to provide a substantial income, and a flat in Westminster, were all left to James. George Fuller, the nephew, inherited a thousand pounds, some family pictures and a pair of cuff links.

'Bloody hell,' said George at the end of the session in Lincoln's Inn. 'That was my uncle's house, his flat, his money. I thought the old girl would have had more family feeling.'

She did, but for my family, not yours, thought James. He had taken against George at their only previous meeting, when he had come to the Treasury to lobby James about the importance of reducing the level of inheritance tax on family estates.

'Never mind, Sir George,' said James. 'You've got the baronetcy. Agnes couldn't take that from you.'

Sir George muttered something that sounded suspiciously like 'Fuck off,' and left the room.

The inheritance didn't change James's character, or so he liked to believe, but it did change his way of life. He and Linda sold their small house at the unfashionable end of Fulham, and moved with the children to the country. James commuted from Donhead late on Sunday night and returned on Friday, while Linda immersed herself in Dorset life and indulged her passion for gardening on a grand scale. For both of them it was a translation into a different world, a world all the stranger because neither of them had ever imagined that they would live there.

Donhead was a jewel, a small Georgian house built as a hunting-box for an Earl of Shaftesbury in 1770 that never felt the hand of the Victorian improver. It looked over its own deer park across downland to the beginning of Cranborne Chase.

'We'll have to get rid of the fallow deer,' said Linda.

'Not much point in an empty deer park,' said James. 'They're very beautiful, and they need only a little feeding in the winter.'

James fell in love with the deer as well as the house. The herd was small, a dozen hinds and a couple of optimistic younger bucks that were kept well away from the hinds by a dominant male. James named him Achilles. Achilles' antlers were a powerful contrast to those on the young bucks, and explained why they kept their distance. James left the annual cull to his tenant farmer; there was no shortage of takers for the venison.

In the Treasury, James's good fortune had a surprising impact. It was as though the acquisition of a fortune had brought with it not just independence – he no longer had to hang on for his pension – but an added influence in argument and an enhanced moral authority.

'If this man had not twelve thousand a year, he would be a very stupid fellow,' he reminded himself.

Even the Permanent Secretary, the source of the adverse report after the ATCS row, congratulated him on his good fortune. James thought his earlier censure was completely unfair; he regarded the Donhead legacy as an offsetting unfairness.

*

The next morning Anna suggests they walk across to the mainland and back.

'The pilgrims managed it. Why don't you check the tides?'

They have two hours to make the passage; they set off barefoot on the wet sand along the guide poles; the sand is cold but
surprisingly firm. Anna strides ahead; James enjoys looking at
her calves and ankles.

'That's what made me love you. They were all I could see
when you worked on my back.'

'Your back wasn't too bad.'

They reach the mainland end of the causeway and turn round.
Two-thirds of the way back, Anna says, 'Let's look at the refuge
box. I want to see what it's like.'

It sits on strong piles high above sea level, a wooden sentry
box in grey tongue and groove with a pitched roof; a fifteen-foot
vertical ladder leads up to the opening. There is no door and a
bench around three sides. Anna is first up the ladder. As James
steps into the box, she puts her arms around him, kisses him,
runs her hands down the inside of his jeans.

'Sit on the bench.'

'We can't do it here.'

'I think we can.'

Anna rucks up her skirt, shrugs off her pants, unzips James's fly.

'You said we couldn't do it here. Look at you.'

Anna carefully lowers herself onto James – they are both
laughing, both aroused.

'You planned this from the moment you saw the refuge box;
that's why you wore a skirt.'

'Yes. Come on, come on, we've got to beat the tide.'

Anna and James do beat the rising tide, reorganize their
clothes, climb back down the ladder and walk back to Holy
Island. The tide has come in fast, and they trot through water at
mid-calf level for the last hundred yards.

'Perfect timing,' says Anna. They walk on, holding hands, and then James stops and turns her towards him.

'Anna, I don't want this to end. I want to be with you. I want you to come and live with me at Donhead.'

'Me? At Donhead? I can't imagine . . .' and Anna begins to laugh, stopping when she sees the hurt look on James's face.

'Darling James, that's the nicest thing I've ever heard. But I'd be way out of my depth. Donhead's far too grand for me, you're far too grand for me.'

'I wasn't too grand in the refuge box.'

'That was lovely. But living together at Donhead? That's quite different. Are you sure I'm not just a holiday romance? And I've still got to deal with Zach.'

'You can't go back to him.'

'No, I can't. But there's still unfinished business between us.'

'Well, I've asked you. I love you. That would make it work.'

'You lived there with Linda for years, had your daughter there. I couldn't move in among all that.'

Over breakfast, Linda had told him that she was leaving.

'I've found someone else,' she said. 'I don't want to live with a husband who is just a polite, uninterested companion. You don't love me any more, and you haven't for a long time.'

James thought about persuading Linda to stay; he had assumed that their marriage was much like most other couples who have been together for fifteen or twenty years, and perhaps better than most. They didn't fight, in public or in private; Linda got on with the garden and James with his career. His protestations lacked the conviction that might have persuaded Linda to change her mind.

'That's my point. You're not even angry that I'm sleeping with another man. It's all about the disruption to our – your – domestic arrangements. You can replace me with a housekeeper, and you won't have to make conversation with her.'

Georgia was unsympathetic.

'Dad, all you two have been doing for years is getting along. You don't, either of you, care enough even to have rows. You'll be better on your own, and William loves her.'

'We used to love each other,' James protested, but he realized that Georgia was right. He would be better off on his own.

On their last evening on Holy Island, James has booked a table at the little restaurant next to the priory. The Fisherman's Rest is small and unpretentious. There are two old wicker lobster pots in the window, and a dozen of the green glass balls that were used to keep the tops of the nets afloat. James and Anna study the menu at a table in the corner while they drink their first glass of wine.

A middle-aged couple come into the restaurant; the man looks at James and says with real pleasure, 'Jimmy! Jimmy! What brings you to our neck of the woods? Shall we join you?' He doesn't wait for an answer, pulls up a chair for his wife and sits down himself. He introduces his wife, 'You remember Imogen,' and says to Anna, 'You must be Georgia – I haven't seen you since you were eleven.'

'Georgia's in New York. This is my friend Anna Pearson. We're here for a few days.'

James has known Matthew Barrington, the only person who ever calls him Jimmy, since National Service. They always sit next to each other at regimental dinners, meet for dinner once a year at the Cavalry Club, exchange Christmas cards and have, other than their two years together in the army, remarkably little in common. But James has always liked Matthew's uncomplicated, unchanging attitude to the world, his total lack of political correctness. He is wearing, James notices with a little smile, his permanent casual uniform of yellow corduroy trousers, brown suede chukka boots, a regimental tie and a regimental boating jacket. Anything else would have been shocking.

James and Matthew talk to each other while Imogen cross-questions Anna. Matthew is intrigued by Anna's job.

'Sports therapy and massage, eh? My God, I wished I'd met you before they opened me up for my slipped disc. Are you responsible for Jimmy being in such good shape?'

Anna laughs; it's impossible to dislike Matthew.

'His elegant shape is entirely down to me; he's lost ten pounds since I took him in hand.'

'We're here on a week's retreat at St Aidan's. Imo is a good Anglo-Catholic, and I'm here to lose weight. This is the one night I get out of the Holy Gulag for a decent meal.'

'Not staying for pudding and coffee?' says Matthew later as James and Anna get up to go. 'Imo and I need the calories. I'll get the bill. This is my home turf, not yours.'

As they walk back to the hotel, James says, 'He's one of my oldest friends, although we hardly ever see each other. He hasn't changed an iota since I first met him – dress, opinions, jokes, everything the same.'

'I can believe that; I liked him in spite of myself.'

'The thing about Matthew is he's extremely clever. He got a First in Natural Sciences at Cambridge, he knows a lot about the opera, and he's an expert on British native trees.'

'Imogen is a different matter, she's a real piece of work. Should have been an Inquisitor. I nearly found myself telling her about Zach.'

Anna giggles and says in a good imitation of Imogen's voice, 'Do you know Hugh Northumberland? The Percys have a holiday place in Allenmouth, don't they?'

They walk on, and then Anna says, 'That's why Donhead wouldn't work. I have nothing, absolutely nothing, in common with people like that. They belong in your world, and I don't, I never will. And he thought I was your daughter, didn't he? But you asking meant a lot to me.'

James kisses her cheek and doesn't reply.

They have breakfast in bed the next morning and James tries again.

'I meant what I said about living together. It needn't be at

Donhead. I could pass the house on to Georgia and come and live up here with you.'

'I've heard you talk about Donhead. You might move out, but you'd never forgive me. I'm a Geordie, we're practically Scottish up here; you English seem like foreigners a lot of the time.'

'I'm not English. You wouldn't like me if I was. I'm Anglo-Irish.'

'You had a strange childhood,' says Anna. 'But then so did I. Perhaps that's what we have in common.'

'My upbringing seemed normal enough to me then; that's how you think when you're six, or sixteen.' James is talking about someone he knows, but from whom he is separated by more than time and the Irish Sea. 'Now it feels an anachronism, part of the reason why I've never quite fitted, like trying to force in a bit of a jigsaw that nearly matches but you know is wrong. My memories are an odd jumble of bathrooms, soap, horses. We had two bathrooms for seven bedrooms, quite a respectable ratio in Ireland then. A bath in four inches of water in a freezing bathroom was a weekly duty, not a pleasure. I remember the hierarchy: translucent Pears in the basin, yellow Wrights Coal Tar in the bath, and Cussons Imperial Leather in the guest room. And the lavatory paper was Bronco, totally non-absorbent, you didn't wipe your bottom, you sandpapered it. Our social life at Killowen revolved around horses – Pony Club dances, hunt balls, the Pony Club camp. Brilliant ratios.'

'Ratios?'

'Boys to girls. One boy to twelve girls at the Pony Club, six hundred boys to zero girls at Winchester, ten boys to one girl at Oxford.'

'Well, one to one works best. Let me show you.'

37.

IN THE AFTERNOON they cross the causeway and drive back to Allenmouth through a heavy sea mist. The weather has broken, and they both feel something slipping away. James drops Anna off at her father's house.

'That was lovely, all of it – St Cuthbert's Island, the trip to the Farnes, the refuge box. I loved being with you. You make me feel calm, secure.' Anna leans into the car, kisses him and says, 'You won't be seeing me for a few days. I told you I needed to sort things out with Zach. And then . . .' She goes up the steps, the sentence unfinished, turns and waves, and is gone.

'What does "sorting things out" mean? What's the unfinished business?' James asks himself. He finds Anna's words unsettling after their three days on Holy Island. He knows her response to his Donhead invitation is eminently sensible in theory. In practice he isn't ready to give up and go south alone.

He takes refuge again in his great-grandmother's diaries; nineteenth-century Ireland stops him agonizing over Anna. He spends two days with these papers, going out only for an early morning walk along the beach.

On the evening of the second day, he is out on his balcony looking at the birds on the other side of the estuary when he sees Anna walking past on the street below. She is with a tall, strongly built man; Zach looks exactly like Anna's description of him. He watches until they turn up towards the golf club.

James feels sick, pours himself a whisky and for ten minutes tries to read a book. Then he jumps up, goes down the stairs, and follows Anna and Zach up the hill. He has no clear plan; he cannot bear to sit and think. Perhaps the three of them should talk, although about what is unclear. James reaches the top of the grassy lane; there is no sign of Anna and Zach, no light in the clubhouse. James walks onto the verandah, sees the open door, stands in the little hall. Hears the unmistakable sounds of a couple making love, listens long enough to hear Anna begin to cry out, turns and runs blindly down the hill. Back in the flat, he curses himself. He knows he has become a caricature of a jealous lover. Worse, a voyeur. And he curses Anna. How could she do this after Holy Island? The next morning he gets up early, locks up the flat and catches the mid-morning train back to King's Cross.

That evening he is back in Donhead; there is a thick pile of letters and bills on the hall table, and otherwise no sign that he had been away. What did he expect? Cobwebs? Squatters? His housekeeper comes in, sorts through some domestic details, tells him his bed is made up, and he goes upstairs to sleep.

A day later he begins to be restored to sanity; he had forgotten the glory of the view across the park and over the downs to Cranborne Chase. He remembers an October evening when he and Linda came over the hill, down from London for their first weekend at Donhead. The country to the south-west was alive with the flickering lights of a hundred fires, farmers burning off the stubble after the harvest. 'It's as if the Vikings had landed,' said Linda. They were still in love then, still overcome by their new inheritance.

James sees the fallow deer are at the bottom of the park by the stream; he goes downstairs, makes himself a cup of coffee, lets himself out through the gate in the iron palings and walks down to the little herd.

There is a single stag standing under an oak a hundred yards away from the rest of the fallow deer. It is Achilles, his left antler broken off four inches above the crown, his right antler missing a couple of tines. There is a deep and bloody scar on his flank.

Trotting around the hinds is the cause of Achilles' downfall, the new dominant male, probably one of Achilles' sons. James walks slowly back up the hill, unlocks his gun cabinet, takes out his rarely used .275 rifle, and goes back until he is twenty yards away from Achilles, now quietly grazing. He kills Achilles with a single shot to the heart, returns to the house and telephones his tenant farmer.

'It's been coming for a couple of weeks now; I didn't know he'd finally been kicked out. Doubt there's much meat in him – too busy fighting. I'll take him away. I kept the last set of antlers he cast; I'll let you have them for the hall.'

James cleans his rifle and puts it away. Allenmouth and Anna seem miles and years distant, a dream and – as he remembers standing just inside the clubhouse – a nightmare.

There is more than enough to occupy him at Donhead. He makes a couple of trips to the London Library to do some background reading on his Irish project, and later spends three days in the strange, bunker-like British Colindale periodical library poring over back numbers of *The Kerryman* and *The Irish Times*. His family curiosity has turned into something deeper; he has decided to expand his notes into book form, although he knows his subject is too narrow to find a publisher. He plans a trip to Dublin and Drimnamore; he hasn't been to Drimnamore since he was there as a boy of fourteen on a brief fishing holiday. Derriquin, he knows, is a ruin, and most Irish records went up in flames when the Four Courts were burned, but he wants to get a better feeling for the countryside and the city in which his great-grandmother had spent most of her life.

Dublin Airport is five times the size of the intimate, provincial terminal James remembers. Dublin International, which he used to call Collinstown, has all the retail soullessness of Heathrow or Charles de Gaulle. The departure and arrival boards, which in the old days used to show London, Belfast and Shannon, with an occasional charter to Benidorm, now list Bahrain, Dubai, Abu Dhabi, Paris, Brussels, Prague, Moscow, Shanghai, all new destinations and the source of a transformed Ireland's momentary riches.

Driving into the city centre, James sees new buildings everywhere – offices, hotels, industrial parks, gated executive estates. There are cranes on the skyline, but they all seem to be idle; many of the new buildings have 'To Let' signs offering 'Favourable Terms', and one, a twelve-storey office block, has 'BANK AUCTION' in enormous letters blocking out the windows.

'And none of it's paid for,' says the cab driver. 'The whole country is banjaxed. The politicians, the builders and the bankers have fucked everything up. Your man O'Malley went up the spout for three billion euros last week…'

James stays in one of the new hotels on St Stephen's Green, a hotel like every other five-star boutique hotel in the world except for its eclectic collection of Irish pictures – Jack Yeats, Paul Henry, Roderic O'Conor, Mary Swanzy, Sarah Purser, Louis le Brocquy. In the main room there is a full-length portrait of Eva and Constance Gore-Booth.

> *The light of evening, Lissadell,*
> *Great windows open to the south,*
> *Two girls in silk kimonos, both*
> *Beautiful, one a gazelle.*

James murmurs Yeats's lines to himself and asks the concierge about the pictures.

'Ah well, they're nice enough now, but it's a tax racket – you can write the cost off if you allow public access, and sticking the pictures on the wall of a hotel counts too.'

The next morning James walks to find the hall where his great-grandfather had preached the Revival to the Brethren. The façade survives in all its late Victorian splendour, Corinthian columns, big windows, the roof crowned by a small colonnaded dome. Behind the façade is a charmless, efficient hotel. 'Rebuilt

e' is the receptionist's explanation of the change; she
ed in James's attempt to find out its history. The
interior is unrecognizable. James looks at his old postcard,
mourns the loss of the huge theatrical space with its curious
wrought-iron pulpit, and wonders at a Dublin that in 1902
could fill three thousand seats for John Burke on 'The Coming
of the Kingdom'.

He drives out to Burke's Fort to spend a couple of nights with
his cousin Fred. Fred has kept the Archduke's stud going after his
father's death; horse-breeding seems to be the one area of Irish
economic life that has survived the crash.

'Actually, it was the china dogs that saved us. Dad spent everything he had, and more, on the horses and the hounds,' says Fred.

'China dogs?'

'That's what we called them. You remember those two big
animals that sat either side of the fireplace at the Fort; china
dogs, twenty-five pounds, was the probate valuation. The
Trustees told me I would have to sell Burke's Fort, house, horses,
land and all, to clear off the debts. Christie's came over and
didn't find much to get excited about. The Ferneley of the
Archduke was a copy. Until they saw the dogs. They weren't
dogs, they were Meissen lions, made for Augustus the Strong's
Japanese Palace in 1730-something; God knows how they got to
Queen's County. A woman from the Met in New York came over
specially to see them, and we sold them for seven hundred thousand dollars. That did the trick all right.'

'Good Lord.'

'We're still breeding, but profitably these days. We've half a
dozen good brood mares of our own, a decent stallion, and we
sell everything we breed at Goffs' yearling sales. Stallion fees are
exempt from tax, thanks to Charlie Haughey, though God knows
for how long,' says Fred.

'Haughey was a complete crook, wasn't he?' asks James.

'He was, of course, in a rich Fianna Fáil tradition. But he's our
crook. And you've had a few in England, by the way. We have a

liking for gombeen men; we expect little from our politicians, and least of all honesty. So we're rarely disappointed.'

'We?'

'Yes, we. We're all Irish now – Irish passports, the children go to our local school where they learn Gaelic, and we've been Catholics ever since Dad converted. He was never a Unionist, even ended up a senator for a while. So we've survived, prospered even. The Anglo-Irish don't exist any more, except in little pockets of resistance in the South of England. Anglo-English, that's what they are now. When you toss a coin in Ireland you call heads or harps. We've called harps.'

James doesn't argue. He is disturbed by Fred's hard-headed realism and the unsentimental elimination of the tribe to which he belonged. Why does it matter, why am I unwilling to become an Englishman by default? James asks himself. He doesn't have a satisfactory answer.

Fred and James ride around the estate the next morning. Cantering up a ride, they pass a burned-out building on the edge of a little copse.

'That's the Trafalgar Folly,' says Fred. 'Built by my great-great-grandfather. They say he kept a woman from the village up here. The IRA torched it just after the end of the Civil War. Your father was the stallion man here when it happened, before he went off to train in England.'

'Odd timing, given that the wars were over.'

'Indeed. It was a warning to us that they could burn down Burke's Fort whenever they felt like it, treaty or no treaty, truce or no truce. I was told your father had got across the local IRA man in one way or another. Johnnie Mannion, he was called. My dad thought your father would be better off in England for a while, so away he went. I'm not sure we ever heard the full story. Did your father ever talk about it to you?'

'He wasn't the talkative sort.'

The following day James visits their old home at Killowen in County Kildare. His father's training yard is now in the hands of a thrusting young Irish trainer. John Malone has switched to the Flat from National Hunt.

'The Flat's where the money is,' he explains. 'The Arabs aren't interested in steeplechasing or hurdling. Neither are the men at Coolmore, and they know a thing or two about making money out of horses.'

He shows James around; it is almost unrecognizable from the yard that he remembers. The central yard with forty boxes, the doors gleaming with white paint and black ironwork, is supplemented by a couple of large American-style barns. The staff all wear zipped dark-green jackets with 'Killowen Racing' in white lettering on front and back.

'The barns are new since your father's day. Economical, easy to clean, one girl can keep an eye on thirty horses. And we've ten furlongs of our own all-weather gallops out the back now. We use them all the time, and the horse walker,' pointing to the circular machine in which six thoroughbreds are walking steadily round and round. 'I'm planning a pool so I can swim the horses, great for any kind of muscular problem.'

'It's grand to see the place looking like this,' says James as he shakes John's hand and says goodbye.

He sets out for Kerry on a long drive as strange as the road in from Dublin Airport. Every town he passes through has new shopping centres and new industrial estates. Most look deserted. Further south along the Ring of Kerry, old whitewashed thatched cottages lie abandoned, replaced by hacienda-style houses set closer to the road, all with well-tended rock gardens, wishing wells and wrought-iron gates. On the outskirts of Drimnamore there is a new estate of thirty houses – ten are finished and lived in, the rest are half built, the roads and the landscaping still to be completed. Reinforcing bars stick up out of crumbling concrete blocks and look like rusty, twisted sugar candy. Against a sagging fence there are neat stacks of banded breeze-blocks, lengths of yellow drainage pipes, a six-foot-high cable drum and an abandoned digger. A forlorn sign says, 'New

House Finished to Your Own Specification. Reduced Price. Bank Sale'.

He checks into the Great Southern Hotel, which he remembers as a run-down example of what his father used to call Irish Insane Asylum architecture. There is now a glass-and-steel reception area; signs advertise the Great Southern Spa experience and encourage guests to make reservations for the Kerryman Restaurant or the Ring of Kerry Bistro. The receptionist is disappointed that she can't persuade him to have a massage and detox treatment.

The next morning he drives into the village. Drimnamore is cheerful in the sunlight. The houses and shops, whose universal colour used to be a dreary mixture of browns and blacks, have all been painted or rendered in reds and greens and blues. There is a large modern sculpture in the middle of the green. James sits down on a handsome new wooden bench; a little brass plaque says, 'In Memory of the Volunteers who fell at Staigue Fort, April 1920'. He looks across to the bridge as a couple of buses come by and drive on round the Ring, the occupants, numbed by the four-hour journey, no longer curious enough to look out or take pictures.

James goes into the Protestant church, which is open and empty. As he reads the memorials to his ancestors, he experiences a strong feeling of returning home. He has never lived in Derriquin, never lived in Kerry, but in some strange sense he belongs here. The Burke family pew, with its high sides and private fireplace, has gone, as have all the brass pew plates, which are now glued to a wooden board by the entrance to the church.

In the churchyard he looks for and finds his grandmother's grave; next to it, with an identical headstone, is the grave of William McKelvey. Both graves are badly overgrown, the headstones covered in green and grey lichen, partly obscuring the lettering. Halfway down the slope to the river is the Burke family tomb, a small stone building with a pitched roof and a classical pediment supported by a pair of plain Doric pillars. On the pediment is a cartouche with the Burke coat of arms, worn away by Kerry wind and rain. The tomb is surrounded by a low wrought-iron fence; a couple of sections are missing. James takes a closer look and sees that there is a large diagonal crack in one of the walls. The iron door is slightly ajar. He steps over the railings and pulls the door open; dust, twigs, a scattering of earth and a few small skeletons of mice and birds cover the floor.

On stone ledges that run around three sides of the room there are a dozen coffins, some lead-lined and intact, others crumbling, two totally disintegrated with dry bones and scraps of fabric thrusting through the crumbling wood. Several of the coffins have brass name-plates; his great-grandmother's is clearly labelled, 'Letitia Burke, 1821–1902'. The bones of a hand are resting on the rotten wood; James replaces them alongside what is left of Letitia.

He sits down on an unoccupied lower ledge; perhaps he is reserving his place. These are his forebears, his DNA, or some of it; James is overcome by contradictory feelings of belonging and loss. The sour air makes breathing difficult; he puts his face in his hands and his body is racked with dry, heavy sobs.

After ten minutes he pulls himself together, goes to the general store on the far side of the green and buys a broom, a dustpan and brush, a pair of garden shears, a bucket and a strong scrubbing brush. He trims the grass and cleans the two gravestones, then returns to the tomb to sweep the stone floor clear of years of dirt. He leaves the coffins alone; by lunchtime he has restored the tomb to a state of relative respectability. He is pleased with his work, feeling he has discharged an obligation to both the place and the people. Nobody comes to ask what he is doing. Returning to the general store for the second time, he finds the name of a local builder, goes to see him and together they negotiate a price to fix the crack in the tomb and repair its door.

Back at the hotel, he has dinner in the Kerryman Restaurant, which is comfortable and crowded. The food is excellent. James looks around at the prosperous, well-dressed, confident Irish men and women, and contrasts them with the clientele he remembers from almost forty years ago. Then the guests had been mainly English or Anglo-Irish, the food dreary, the public rooms down-at-heel. On Saturday night the men were in dinner jackets and the women in long dresses, dancing foxtrots and quicksteps after dinner to the music of a four-piece string band. This evening, none of the men wears a tie. James removes his own and puts it in his jacket pocket.

The next day he walks over to Derriquin via Oysterbed Pier. There are now no signs of oyster cultivation apart from a few crumbling concrete pens exposed by the falling tide. Off to one side is a low, half-ruined building; there is a barely legible sign over the big double doors, which are half open and sagging off their rusty hinges. 'Derriquin Oyster Fishery', James reads; the grass has grown around and inside the building, and its roof and walls look as if one more November gale would push them over. He sees an old oyster shell in the grass, bends down, picks it up and wipes it clean with his handkerchief. The mother-of-pearl gleams in the sun.

He walks on around the shoreline, remembering the gaunt, turreted outline of the castle from his last visit with his father. John had been a reluctant guide. He had pointed out his old bedroom window at the top of the central tower, but didn't want to spend much time at the castle.

'Exactly what happened?' James had asked that evening in the hotel. His father had thought for a moment, then told him the whole story. Until then James had heard only the barest of outlines; it was the first time he had seen his father weep.

The path is overgrown with rhododendrons and azaleas run wild from some long-ago formal planting; when James comes round the headland there is nothing where the shell of Derriquin used to stand. For a moment he thinks he hasn't walked far enough, then sees the sea wall stretching towards him and realizes the castle has been demolished.

He walks on, running his hand slowly across, down, across, up the waist-high battlemented wall; Derriquin has been replaced by a car park. Beyond, there is a modern clubhouse instead of the old wooden pavilion, and the nine-hole golf course that used to run through the demesne has been upgraded to, as its sign proudly boasts, the 'Derriquin Castle Championship Golf Course – eighteen holes, seven thousand two hundred yards. Visitors Welcome.' James does not feel welcome. He feels violated by the final disappearance of his father's house, of his house.

He doesn't go into the clubhouse, turning back to the hotel via the old walled garden. That too has changed; a sign on the outside says 'Sullivan Construction – Six Magnificent Executive Homes in a Gated Environment'. He opens the garden door, new and painted red, onto a building site where grass, fuchsias and foxgloves once grew, where crumbling glasshouses used to lean against the wall. The foundations for half a dozen houses are laid out, the building lines neatly marked by wooden pegs and taut twine.

The only sign of life is in the far corner, where a man in a hard hat is standing, smoking a cigarette. Noticing James, he puts out the cigarette, picks his way across the site, holds out his hand and says, 'Mr O'Malley, you're early. I'm Michael Sullivan.'

James explains he is not Mr O'Malley. 'I'm just having a look around.'

'That's fine, help yourself. Here, have a brochure. They're going to be great houses, each with half an acre, each with a great view. Look out to sea.'

James does look out to sea across several islands to the coast on the far side of the estuary and the low mountains beyond.

'It's lovely.'

'If you're interested, you can buy off plan, ten per cent down, fitted out to your own specification.'

'I'm not in the market, but thank you.'

'Ah well. To tell you the truth, O'Malley who I took you for is from the bank in Dublin, and if he doesn't do the decent thing there's no telling when all this will be finished. If ever.' He offers James a cigarette and lights one for himself. 'From England, are you?'

ASHES IN THE WIND

'I grew up in County Kildare,' James replies. 'Tell me, what happened to the burned-out shell of the castle?'

'Pulled down by the County Council. They said children were playing there and might get hurt. They used the stone for the clubhouse and the car park foundations. You've been here before?'

Before James can decide how to reply, they hear a car pull up outside the wall.

'That'll be O'Malley now,' says Michael. 'Nice meeting you.'

James thanks him for the brochure, passes Mr O'Malley at the gate and watches him pick his way across the site to Michael. O'Malley is dressed like an undertaker, and perhaps that's what he is, James thinks. He walks slowly back to the hotel; it has started to rain, and the dripping, wild shrubberies along the path exactly match his mood.

In his hotel room he takes a careful look at Michael's brochure. It has been well designed and expensively produced, and James admits to himself, a little reluctantly, that the architect, or at least the artist, seems to have a good feeling for materials and building design.

This is his last evening in Kerry. He tries the bistro, has a steak and a couple of glasses of red wine, and takes his coffee in the bar overlooking the little harbour below the hotel. The view looks washed and hazy after the rain; the setting sun touches the tops of the Scots pines over where Derriquin used to be.

As he is about to finish his drink and go upstairs, Michael Sullivan comes into the bar and orders a pint of Guinness. He looks around, sees James and walks over.

'Michael – we spoke out at Derriquin. Mind if I join you?'

'I'm James.'

'How was your banker?' James asks as Michael sits down.

'Like they all are, the bastards. All over you to lend money when you don't need it; they pulled the plug on me and my partner the moment times got rough. It's his development now, and he can finish it himself since he won't finance me to do the

333

work. I'm ready to start over. I never pledged my home as security, and I'm back to what I know best, building houses for other people.'

'I like the look of the houses in your brochure. I can't say I admired the new bungalows along the Ring of Kerry.'

Michael laughs. 'I'll buy you another drink before I tell you why you're wrong.'

He comes back with a Guinness and a whiskey. 'You're typical of the Anglo-Irish. You want to keep us in small, picturesque, damp, thatched cottages, and when we try to build anything new you insist we get the blessing of the Irish Georgian Society.' He says this with such good humour that James is unable to take offence.

'Fair enough. It is your country, but it needs looking after.'

'Well, the good news is that there'll be little enough building for a while yet. The Irish recovery is on the long finger.'

Michael stands up. 'I'm away home. I need to tell the wife about Mr O'Malley. Lucky I'm married to a strong woman.'

'Lucky indeed.'

The next day James drives to Cork, catches the midday plane to London and is back in Donhead by the evening. He has laid some ghosts to rest through restoring the family tomb. And the demolition of Derriquin has put an end to his long-harboured fantasy of rebuilding the castle and returning there.

38.

ANNIE SULLIVAN WAS grandmother, mother and father to Michael Sullivan, and the only source of memories of Tomas, for whom Masses were said once a year in the church at Drimnamore. Father Michael said Tomas died fighting for Holy Mother Church, but Annie still had to pay for the Masses. A proposal to erect a memorial to him and other members of the Bandera Irlandesa had been discussed for the last twenty years by the County Council.

She still kept her dead son's Garda uniform cleaned and pressed in a cupboard with the peaked cap of a District Inspector beside it on a hook, ready for a morning inspection or the Last Trump. Annie could hardly remember Kitty, whom she blamed in some unreasonable corner of her heart for Tomas's death. Michael Sullivan had one photograph of his parents taken at a Garda ball in County Clare, his mother beautiful and smiling in a red dress, his father a head taller, serious, looking out beyond the reach of the camera.

At Ardsheelan, Michael was the man of the house. A tall, strong boy, from the age of ten he cut turf, dug drains, rebuilt stone walls, hung gates. Mass every Sunday in Drimnamore with Annie and a match in the afternoon during the Gaelic football season were the fixed points in the Sullivan calendar. Annie plastered the cuts and put ointment on the bruises he brought back from every game. 'It's a miracle you've nothing broken,' she said to him.

*

Only on rare occasions could Annie Sullivan bring herself to watch Michael play, although she knew that football was a good way to get ahead. The Gaelic Athletic Association, the County Council, Fianna Fáil and the Catholic Church were the four corners of power in County Kerry. And while it was known Tomas Sullivan had supported the Treaty and had been Michael Collins's ADC, that was easily forgotten in the light of his son's footballing skills.

'Come to me when you leave school and I'll fix you up with a job,' said Gerry Murphy, a successful local builder, after seeing Drimnamore trounce Cahirciveen 3–8 to 1–4.

Michael took him up on the offer the moment he was old enough to leave school. He was a competent, hard-working bricklayer; more importantly to Murphy Construction, he was picked for Kerry when he was nineteen and captained the side when they beat their great rivals, Cork, in the All-Ireland final at Croke Park two years later.

Annie had been persuaded to make her first and last trip to Dublin for the match.

'Don't let it go to your head,' she said to Michael on the long, triumphant train journey back. 'You'll be the big man in Drimnamore from now on.'

Michael, tired, flushed with success and Guinness after months of abstinence, pulled away from his singing supporters, hugged his grandmother and laughed.

'Drimnamore? The Kingdom of Kerry is mine for the asking,' he said, and was swallowed up in the crowd of happy, celebrating Kerry men.

'It's an amateur game, you can't make a living out of Gaelic football,' said Michael years later to James Burke in Drimnamore. 'Most players barely cover their expenses. But it was the religion, particularly in the South-East and South-West. Rugby didn't have the hold in Cork that it has now. In those days, if you were caught playing rugby or Association football, the Ascendancy games, you were banned by the GAA.

'Anyhow, after we won the All-Ireland I was back to bricklaying on the Tuesday morning; Gerry gave me Monday off. That brought me down to earth all right. Then they tried to persuade me a month later to run for the County Council. "You'll walk it," they said. "I'm not even a member of Fianna Fáil," I said. "We'll soon fix that," they said.

'Thank God I was smart enough to know it wasn't for me. I played for a few more years, we made one more All-Ireland final, then I broke a leg and called it a day. I still go to matches when I can, used to give the Drimnamore and Kerry clubs money in the days when I had plenty, and we always employed a few likely lads in the business.

'It's a great game, plenty of scoring. None of your nil–nil soccer draws. I'll take you to a game one day, open your eyes.'

Michael started courting Aisling; she had bright eyes, long black hair, a good figure and a strong character. She was Gerry Murphy's daughter and Michael wasn't sure how that would go.

'I'm only a brickie, when all's said and done,' he confided to Annie one evening at Ardsheelan.

'You're a brickie who captained Kerry, won the All-Ireland. Don't sell yourself short. Is she good enough for you?' said Annie.

'That's a grandmother talking,' said Michael. 'We'll see what happens. She's a great girl, sure enough.'

One morning Gerry Murphy called Michael into his caravan on a housing project outside Waterville.

'You've been seeing a lot of my daughter. It's time you two did something more than dance.'

'I've not got much to offer. Ardsheelan, six acres and a cottage when my gran dies. It's not enough for Aisling after what she's used to.'

'I started out as a plumber, I was a tradesman for fifteen years. But that's not the point. I'm getting on, she's my only child, it's yours for the asking. If she'll have you, that is.'

'I'm a bricklayer, not a businessman.'

'You know as much as I did when I started the business. You're a worker, with great contacts – I never captained Kerry. Talk to Aisling, but you'd better be quick. She was Miss Rose of Tralee, there's plenty out there after her.'

Gerry, four inches taller than Michael and twenty pounds heavier, stood up and this brought the conversation to an end.

Aisling laughed when he told her about the conversation.

'You're as good a man as he is,' she said. 'But you haven't said you love me.'

'I do, you know I do,' said Michael. 'I'm just not sure about marrying the boss's daughter.'

'That's not who I am. I'm Aisling – look at me, for God's sake.'

Michael held her face between his hands, kissed her, and they were married three months later. Gerry started Michael off as a site foreman, then brought him into the office and taught him about the accounts.

'Listen, it's simple enough. Is more cash coming in than going out? Have you enough in the bank to pay the men, pay the suppliers? Have you kept back enough for the tax man? That's it. Forget what the accountants tell you about accruals and deferrals, and provisions, and reserves. I'll show you my reserves.' Gerry opened the wall safe to reveal stacks of tightly bundled ten-pound notes. 'There's twenty thousand pounds in there,' he said, closing the door with a solid clunk and spinning the combination lock. 'I'll tell you the six numbers when you're ready, but you'll be in trouble if you have to go to the safe. I've used it once in twenty years.'

When Michael took over the business, he knew house-building from the bottom to the top. Sullivan Construction ('Change the name. You're better known in Kerry than I ever was, and

Aisling's a Sullivan now,' Gerry had said) built thirty or forty houses every year for the County Council or small developers who had secured planning permission for a few acres.

Declan O'Donnell was a sharp dresser, a fast talker, drove a brand-new BMW. A bit of a stroke merchant, they called him; in Cork property circles this was a compliment. Not every construction company would deal with him, as he had a reputation for whittling away the final price, but he persuaded Michael Sullivan to build twenty-five houses on a re-zoned site outside Kenmare by sheer persistence and by putting up twenty-five per cent of the construction cost up-front.

'Never done this before,' Declan said to Michael. 'But I know your reputation for doing a decent job and finishing on time.'

Sullivan Construction finished the twenty houses four days early. Declan's quantity surveyor, whom he used as a battering ram to beat the final price down, was unable to fault the work.

'We'll use you again,' Declan said. 'How much did you clear?'

Michael's first instinct was to say 'None of your business,' but instead replied, 'Five thousand euros.'

'Not enough.'

'Per house.'

'That's more like it. A hundred thousand euros isn't to be sniffed at down here. I've got a big project coming up in Cork that might interest you.'

'Twenty houses is the most we've ever built in one go.'

'You need to think bigger. You're Bacon Roll Man; you pitch up at some Spar counter every morning, order a bacon roll and a sausage if they've got one, twenty John Player Blue, the *Daily Star*, a bottle of Lucozade and a Mars Bar. And you're happy driving . . .' he looked out of the window '. . . last year's Rover 400. You don't have to settle for that.'

Michael was stung into looking at the Cork project, a massive development on the edge of the city, two hundred houses, a hotel and a supermarket. A new GAA stadium ('We'll build that last') clinched the planning approval.

'I can't finance my share of something that big.'

'You can, sure. Fifty per cent of the equity will cost you four hundred thousand euros, which you've got in the bank. (Michael's 'How did you know that?' went unanswered.) The Anglo-Irish Bank will lend us eight million and the income from Phase One will fund the rest.'

It worked out exactly as Declan had forecast, except that the prices realized for the houses were twenty per cent higher than the original budget.

'It's all about the marketing,' explained Declan. 'Ardcullen Heights is a great name, fifteen minutes' drive from the centre of Cork, a beautiful show home, three "Sold" signs as you look out the sales office window, and it's all over bar the shouting. Anglo-Irish are eager to lend one hundred per cent of the purchase price to anyone who's breathing, and they bundle the mortgages up and trade them on to the Yanks. When we tell the punters the price will be twenty per cent higher in a year, they can't get their pens out fast enough. And the way property is moving in Ireland at the minute they'll double their money soon enough.'

A few years later, visiting cousins in Cork, Michael decided to show Ardcullen Heights to Aisling.

'You know something,' he said to Aisling as they walked around. 'I'm proud of this place. I know it's a sunny day, and that helps, but we laid it out like a village, not on a grid, the houses aren't identical boxes and we built them well. All lived in, mostly first-time owners from rough flats and houses in Cork.'

They went into the supermarket, busy with shoppers from the city. Michael bought twenty John Player Blue, the *Daily Star*, a bottle of Lucozade and a Mars Bar; Aisling looked at his basket in disbelief.

'What are you doing? You don't smoke any more. And you should put that Mars Bar back, you're not as slim as you were.'

'It's a private joke,' said Michael and didn't elaborate. 'Let's go and look at the stadium. I had to bully Declan into building it. He said it was only ever an aspiration – I said we'd promised it to the planners and it wouldn't make a good headline: "Kerry football star breaks word to Cork GAA".'

Stadium was a grand description for the arena, which had seats for two thousand spectators.

'They'll fill it for a big club game, especially one against a Kerry side,' said Michael as they walked onto the pitch, where a group of young players were being coached at one end.

A ball was kicked towards them; it seemed about to float well over Michael's head until he jumped up and caught it cleanly with his fingertips. He jogged towards the young man coming to retrieve the ball, quickened up, faked with his right shoulder and went left, bounced the ball off his foot back into his hands, then kicked it long and high to sail through the goalposts thirty yards away. There was a little round of applause from the players as Michael jogged back, smiling, to Aisling.

'One point to Kerry – but I'll feel it in the morning.'

Declan and Michael had made ten times their money from Ardcullen Heights in two years; Michael's share was four million euros. They used Section 23 to avoid most of the tax.

'Onwards and upwards,' said Declan. 'I'm looking at a great site down on the Quays. We're going to build Ireland's tallest building there.'

'You'll never get planning permission for that.'

'In Cork they'd build on your big toe at the minute. We'll have an architectural competition, get in the big names, Richard Rogers, Norman Foster, then choose an Irish architect who understands about costs and will design something we can build.'

Michael and Aisling met the movers and shakers of Ireland, to whom Michael's sporting record was as important as his recent share of the Ardcullen Heights development. They went to the Fianna Fáil tent at Galway Races ('It'll cost us ten thousand euros each to watch the politicos lorrying into the wine,' said Declan), they saw the Ryder Cup as the guests of the Anglo-Irish Bank, they went to the Chelsea Flower Show with their estate agents, and Michael bought a villa in Portugal and a new Mercedes. Aisling, who had put on a few pounds after their marriage, lost them and more in order to fit into the smart clothes she now ordered from Dublin and London.

There was a curious mixture at these functions. Most of the men and women were well dressed, confident, talking in loud voices about private jets, Spanish villas and 'blades', which Michael learned from Declan meant helicopters. But there were always two or three couples who looked out of place, the men in brown suits and heavy brogues, the women clearly unaware about the latest trends in fashion.

'Don't be fooled,' said Michael to Aisling. 'That one over there, looks like a Letterkenny cattle dealer, makes half the cement in Ireland and owns six Dublin hotels and the big golf club in Kildare.' He pointed to a large, red-faced man of about sixty, having an awkward conversation with a young banker. 'They say he's worth a billion euros and he looks like he'd need to borrow the price of his next dinner.'

Michael was always sought out for his view about the likely finalists in the next All-Ireland, while Declan worked the room and glad-handed the politicians and the bankers.

'We're on the inside track,' said Declan. 'We're being shown things by the bank not just in Ireland but worldwide.'

They were having dinner in a Dublin restaurant with two Michelin stars; in the previous nine months they had invested together in waste disposal in Holland, hotels in Serbia, a chain of cinemas in Spain, an oilfield in the Niger Delta and a casino in Macao.

'This is heady stuff for a bricklayer from Drimnamore,' said Michael.

'You're not a brickie any more, you'll be in the Irish Rich List next year. You're a hero in *The Kerryman* already; you'll be in the Dublin papers when we pull off the Big One.'

The Big One was the Millennium Tower in Cork, twenty storeys high, three hundred flats, penthouses for three million euros, single-bedroom apartments for three hundred thousand. 'A Landmark Building for a Landmark City,' the marketing brochure said.

'A hundred million to build it. We each put up four million, the bank lends us the rest and rolls up the interest until we start selling. We'll clear twenty-five million each when we're done.'

'It'll take all my cash,' said Michael.

'And mine. But Anglo-Irish have offered us a chance to make a quick two million euros each through taking some of their shares at a friendly price. They need our support, and it gets us the loan for the Millennium deal. We can do it through CFDs, so we only put up ten per cent of the money, and they'll lend us that anyhow.'

'What's a CFD?'

'Contract for Difference. Gives you tremendous gearing when the shares go up.'

'And if they go down?'

'Down? Anglo-Irish shares haven't been this low for years. This stroke will push them up, and we're in good company. All the big men are in.'

Declan and Michael went in alongside the big men. Then the financial world imploded and the Irish property market collapsed. Shares in the Anglo-Irish Bank, which had once been valued at thirteen billion euros, were worthless. The Cork Millennium Tower was never built; the government agency that took over all the bust banks' liabilities sold the site three years later for one and a half million euros, a tenth of the fifteen million Declan and Michael had paid. The twenty thousand in cash that Aisling's father had put away in the safe was long gone.

39.

Back at Donhead, James reminds himself that he is still paying rent for the Allenmouth flat. He decides to make a final visit to end his lease and sort out the furniture; he makes himself a promise not to see Anna again.

Allenmouth and his flat are as he had left them; the weather is overcast and damp. He talks to George, gives him three months' rent in lieu of notice, and resells him the furniture at a substantial loss.

'The difference is my profit margin,' says George cheerfully. 'But I'll leave it all up there. It'll be very easy to let now. And you can always come back as a tenant.'

James borrows a pot of white emulsion and blots out the words of Socrates that he had so carefully written on the wall. They hadn't done him much good. He keeps only the Wemyss beehive mug to remind him of Allenmouth.

He thinks about saying goodbye to Jack Pearson, decides against it, and has a last drink in the Allen Arms. It is a Saturday evening, and the bar is crowded with holidaymakers, the regulars absent or banished to the smaller snug. He is about to leave when a man comes in with a couple of friends, orders a lemonade and starts talking to Sally behind the bar. When the man turns and looks directly at James, he realizes this is Zach; close to, he understands why Anna loved him. And may love him now. He is tall, with golden skin, tight curly hair, a broad smile. And it dawns on James it was Zach dancing with the group in the Scout hut, Zach who'd tried to pull him in, Zach who had looked hurt when James had turned away. He finishes his drink quickly and goes back to the flat.

He is packing the next morning when he hears footsteps on the outside staircase. His heart starts pounding as the door opens. It is Zach, not Anna.

'What are you doing here?'

'I won't stay long. I want to ask you to leave Anna alone.'

'I'm not sure you have the right to ask that question. It's up to Anna; she doesn't belong to you.'

'Look at you, man. You're old enough to be her bloody father. How can you make her happy?'

'That's for Anna to decide.'

'I'm in love with Anna. And she loves me.'

'Beating her up is a funny way to prove it. And she didn't love you enough to keep . . .' James, shocked at himself, doesn't finish the sentence.

'The baby? She told you that?' Zach takes a step forward and punches James hard, knocking him over. 'Keep away from her. Find a woman your own age.'

James, whose nose is broken, stays where he is on the floor and fumbles for a handkerchief; Zach stands over him for a moment, thinks about hitting James again, and then leaves. James gets up slowly and sits in his chair for half an hour, bleeding into a handkerchief, his head still reeling from the blow.

Then the door opens for the second time that morning. It is Anna.

'How dare you say that to Zach? I've just seen him, he told me he'd punched you and why.'

'He turned up uninvited, warned me off.'

'He's been in a state ever since I told him.'

'I wasn't feeling calm. When you said you had unfinished business with Zach, I didn't realize that meant you were going to fuck him in the clubhouse.'

'Who I fuck, and where, is my business. Spying doesn't suit

you. You're a pair of jealous, immature schoolboys. I don't want to see either of you ever again.'

James returns to Donhead with a badly damaged nose and a broken heart. The former he deserves, the latter is harder to handle. He has felt the pain of loss before: when his parents had died; when Linda had walked out of Donhead and their marriage. But he had thought of Allenmouth as a new beginning, a change that meeting and loving Anna had crystallized. He had clung to the belief that he and Anna could have made a life together, even though he also knew that the differences between them made this, as Anna had pointed out, improbable. Improbable, but not impossible. Until now.

He misses her company; he misses her in bed; he mourns the loss of what he had found for a moment in Allenmouth.

He escapes again to the Ireland of the nineteenth and early twentieth century. His great-grandparents' struggle to survive at Derriquin and deal with the monstrous tragedy of the Famine gives him a sense of proportion about his own emotional upheavals. His great-grandfather had decided that preparing for the next world was more important than dealing with the present, and had escaped via the Gospel to the Merrion Hall. His father had also escaped, although to Mount Athos and a more exotic religion than the austere, unforgiving creed of the Plymouth Brethren. Did James have the same melancholic, religious gene? Perhaps his mother's no-nonsense, irreligious Puritanism had cancelled that gene out, or at least watered it down.

Five months later he is sitting at his desk looking out at the park; Achilles' destroyer is busy rounding up his does and keeping off two younger, smaller stags. James hasn't decided what to name him yet.

His phone rings; it is Matthew, whom he hasn't seen since Holy Island.

'Come to lunch at the Cavalry Club next Thursday. I've been

made lord-lieutenant, so you and I can celebrate. And I get to wear my old Royal Irish Dragoons uniform on ceremonial occasions.'

'Will it still fit?'

'It will after another week at the Holy Gulag and a trip to Jones, Chalk and Dawson in Sackville Street. One o'clock suit you?'

Matthew is in ebullient form. He's had an international award for his arboretum, his eldest son has married a good Northumberland girl and presented him with a grandson. He is delighted with his new job.

'Ceremonial entirely, suits me down to the ground. No committees, no fund-raising, no politics, just smile and shake hands, greet the Queen whenever she visits the county. And a KCVO after ten years. Imogen's having her hair done, by the way, lunchtime was the only appointment she could get.'

After lunch the two men go out onto the Piccadilly pavement, where Imogen is waiting by Matthew's car. She ignores Matthew's 'Come on, Imogen, we'll be late,' kisses James and says, 'I bumped into your friend Anna, the masseuse, in Fenwick's in Newcastle last week, and asked how you were. She said she didn't know. We were both in the maternity department; I was buying clothes for our first grandchild.'

'Good to see you,' says Matthew as he bundles Imogen into the car.

'Bloody hell,' says James to the rear of the Mercedes as they drive away. He stands silent on the pavement, trying to understand what he has just heard.

Back at Donhead he continues to turn over Imogen's words and their possible implications. If Anna is pregnant, is the baby his? It was five months since they had parted, and a little longer since they last made love on Holy Island. And there was Zachariah. Or perhaps a new, more recent lover.

That evening he calls Jack Pearson, uncertain how helpful he will be.

'Aye, she's pregnant,' says Jack disapprovingly. 'Gone back to Newcastle to have the baby.'

'Can I have her address, her telephone number?'

'She made me promise not to give them to anyone – not to you, not to Zachariah, not to her mother.'

'Come on, Jack, I need to talk to her.'

'Sorry, can't help.'

'Won't help, you mean,' says James and hangs up.

For two days James thinks of nothing else but how to find Anna. He decides to go north; once in Newcastle he sits in his hotel bedroom making phone calls. He tries to contact Zach through his rugby club.

'Zach's in the South, transferred to Saracens at the start of the season,' the Falcons manager tells him, and Saracens are unwilling to part with Zach's phone number.

He tries the university, but the alumni register has only Anna's Allenmouth address. He goes to the maternity department in Fenwick's, hangs around there for a morning, getting increasingly hostile looks from the security guards, and finds the shop-floor assistants are unwilling to talk about recent customers. Tired and dispirited, he goes back to his hotel, has an indifferent meal and goes to bed.

The next morning he decides that his only remaining route to Anna is through the National Health Service. He remembers the name of the Allenmouth GP who had patched up his broken nose, and thinks it a reasonable bet that he also looked after both the Pearsons. He rings Newcastle General and asks to be put through to Midwifery.

'It's Dr Anderton here from Allenmouth. Can you put me through to Anna Pearson's midwife, please?'

There is a long delay, which James imagines is a security check but in fact is the search through manual records.

'Anna's in our one-to-one midwife programme. Ring back after lunch and speak to Mrs Anstruther.'

James rings back, bolder after this first little success, and speaks to Mrs Anstruther.

'Dr Anderton here, Anna Pearson's GP. You've got her medical records, but I just wanted to confirm that though her blood pressure's pretty good,' James hopes this is true, 'you need to check it regularly, as there's a family history.'

'Thank you, Doctor, that's routine here.'

'I hope she's going to antenatal classes. She's on the old side for a first baby, and she had a termination two years ago.'

'She's booked into the Low Fell antenatal clinic.'

'Thank you, Mrs Anstruther.'

James hangs up, his hands shaking and his mouth dry, amazed at the fluency of his lies and wondering how many laws he has broken.

'Ex-Permanent Secretary Stalks Former Lover in Doctor Dupe Scandal'; he writes his own *Daily Mail* headline, then rings the Low Fell clinic. Their sessions are Mondays, Wednesdays and Fridays.

James sits in a Low Fell café on Monday afternoon opposite the clinic, feeling like a seedy private detective. That's exactly how I'm behaving, he tells himself. A dozen pregnant women arrive, most in their late teens or early twenties, half of them with their partners, but no Anna.

He returns on Wednesday to the café, watches a similar group of expectant mothers enter the clinic – and then Anna, walking as fast as she can manage, goes up the clinic steps.

It's *your* blood pressure the midwife should be watching, he tells himself, as his heart pounds. And now what do you do?

An hour and a half and three cups of coffee later, the class comes out. James crosses the street to where Anna is talking to a young couple and walks up to her; uncertain what to say, he holds out both hands in greeting, or perhaps in supplication. Anna looks astonished, frowns, gives a little smile, takes one of James's hands, and then lets it go.

'How did you find me? Did Jack tell you where I was?'

'You know Jack better than that. I tracked you down – bloodhounds, DNA, police records.' James tries, not very successfully, to sound light-hearted. 'Can we have a cup of coffee? I promise not to be a nuisance.'

Anna softens at the tremor in James's voice; they cross to the coffee shop. Anna looks beautiful, tired, enormous.

'You look as though you'll have the baby any minute.'

'I've three months to go, and I'll be glad when it's over. Green tea for me, please.'

James drinks a glass of water, asks for a second, cannot bring himself to ask the only question he wants to ask.

Anna begins. 'Come on, tell me how you found me.'

James tells her the story, half embarrassed, half proud.

'A senior civil servant impersonating a GP? Jail if you're caught. I *am* impressed. I knew Imogen would talk to you, nosy cow. She didn't quite have the nerve to ask who the father was.'

'Neither do I.'

'Dear James, I don't know and I don't care. This is my baby, I've decided to have it, and I'm strong enough to have it on my own. Jack thinks I'm irresponsible, and perhaps he's right, but that's what I'm doing.'

'I could be quite useful, you know. I've had one baby already.'

'You mean your ex-wife had one. No. Although I'm glad you found me. I hated how we parted. Your nose seems quite straight. Zach packs quite a punch, as we both know.'

James laughs in spite of himself. 'Where is Zach?'

'He's left the Falcons, gone south, but you knew that already. He was outraged when I told him I was pregnant and didn't know, or care, which of you was the father. I thought he was going to hit me again. Called me a Jezebel, a harlot, and stormed off. He'll get rid of his rage on the rugby pitch; I wouldn't like to be the first inside centre he's up against. James, I'm tired, I need to go home – see me to the bus stop.'

'Will you at least give me your telephone number?'

'No, I won't. I know you well enough, you'll keep ringing, and I'm going to do this on my own. Perhaps after the baby is born . . .' She leaves the sentence unfinished.

James realizes there is little point in arguing. He walks Anna to the bus stop, puts his arms around her as the bus arrives, presses her bump against his stomach and feels the baby kick.

Anna smiles. 'It's the excitement; she's lively.'

'Perhaps it's a kick of recognition.'

'She does that all the time. And by the way, I don't know it's a girl.'

Anna gets carefully onto the bus, sits by the window and gives a little wave as the bus pulls away. James waves back, tears in his eyes. Although he arrived in Newcastle expecting nothing, he had hoped to leave with more.

40.

JAMES SPENDS THE next three months writing his book. He alternates between Donhead, the British Library and Colindale; *The Kerryman* is the best single source for background material to his great-grandmother's diaries. For two days he makes a detour and reads the contemporary accounts of his grandmother's execution. The indignation of the *Irish Times* at the murder of an upper-class Englishwoman is matched only by their satisfaction at the execution of the Volunteers after the Staigue Fort battle. James discounts both.

He gives his project – it isn't quite a book, but it isn't scholarly enough to be called a thesis – a name: 'Kerry Diaries 1840–1890 – The Famine and the Religious Revival'.

'Catchy title, Dad,' says Georgia, down from London for the weekend with her husband. 'Bestseller list, that's certain.'

James laughs; he loves being teased by his daughter, whom he adores unconditionally. He is less certain about her husband.

Georgia met Stephen Parker in her last year at Bristol, and they were married, absurdly young in James's view, three years later. James wants to like Stephen, though he knows no one will ever be good enough for his attractive, clever, only child. Stephen has a Mathematics degree, which he immediately afterwards took to Goldman Sachs, first in London, then in New York, leaving after three years to set up his own hedge fund.

James has tried manfully to understand what Stephen does and the place of hedge funds in the grander scheme of things; he has failed on both counts.

'We're a long-short fund, international remit, we take positions in whatever seems to be on the move – equities, bonds, commodities, CDOs, currency. We use all sorts of instruments. Swaps, contracts for difference, puts, calls, simple hedges. Today we like oil and gold, so we're long, hate the lira and the yen, so we're short. Next month it could be different.'

'It sounds like betting to me,' says James unwisely.

'Nothing of the kind,' replies Stephen. 'We use highly sophisticated algorithms to help us make our selections.'

'I've met men who had infallible systems for picking horses.'

'Look, we have 1.3 billion dollars under management, last year we made thirty-three million dollars before tax – and there isn't much of that, our tax domicile is Dublin – and we employ sixty people, mostly graduates, half of them women, less than half born in the UK.'

'How many people do you employ at Donhead, Dad?' says Georgia, ending the conversation.

Later, when he is walking with Georgia, she says, 'You don't like him, do you? It's because he isn't public school and Oxbridge and his parents live in Dorking.'

'That's nonsense,' says James. 'I do like him. I just don't care for what he does. I respect the fact that he works incredibly hard, he's a good provider, and he clearly loves you. As do I.'

'That'll have to do,' says Georgia as they turn back to the house.

A week later James gets a phone call from Anna's father.

'She's just gone into labour. I think you should get up here.' He hangs up before James can reply.

Twenty hours later he is in the Newcastle General, fighting his way past porters, self-important obstetricians, bustling lab technicians, triage nurses and a forest of contradictory NHS signs. He finds the maternity ward, and as he approaches the desk he sees Zach. They look at each other warily.

'We're here to see Anna Pearson,' says James.

'Which one of you is the father?'

'I am,' they reply together.

The nurse laughs.

'Sperm donor and natural father,' says James, without deciding which role he prefers. Zach opens his mouth to speak, and decides to keep quiet.

'She's in Room Fourteen.'

They walk down the corridor in silence. Anna is sleeping; beside her bed is a cot. James and Zach look down at the baby, also fast asleep, and both men smile. James picks up the tag on the baby's cot and shows it to Zach; it reads 'Jack James Zachariah Pearson'.

'I'd like to know one way or the other,' says Zach.

'That's not Anna's plan. She's made it very clear to me that it's her baby, not yours or mine. We'll have to settle for that.'

'Surely you want to know?'

'If he's mine, yes. If he's not . . .'

'I think he looks like me,' says Zach. James laughs; the idea that the tiny, wrinkled, red-faced, sleeping baby looks like anyone, except perhaps Winston Churchill, is wonderfully absurd. After a moment Zach starts to laugh too.

The laughter wakes Anna.

'I'm surprised they let two of you in.'

'It needed a little ingenuity,' says James, but before he can explain, a nurse bustles in and says, 'You can't stay any longer; the obstetrician is on his way,' and shows them out.

James stays in Newcastle for two more days. The first time he visits Anna, Zach is there, the second time he is on his own.

'Where are you going to live? I want to help, and there's plenty of room at Donhead.'

'I'm staying in Newcastle. I can get work here, and there's good support for single mums.'

'You're only a single mother through choice. There are two of us; you should choose me.'

'I think we'll be better on our own,' Anna says as Jack James Zachariah nuzzles hungrily at her breast.

James feels a rush of affection for the two of them. Later he holds the baby, marvelling at his lightness and his warm milky smell. He kisses the baby, kisses Anna and leaves, but not before extracting a promise that she will send him her address once she and the baby are out of hospital and settled.

In Dorset, James finds Donhead has lost the ability to calm and settle his troubled mind. He has lost interest in his fallow deer, and Achilles' successor still remains unnamed. Even the view across to Cranborne Chase no longer holds him, as the fold upon fold of hills stretching out towards the sea used to hold him for minutes at a time.

His Irish project is now finished. Submitted for peer review by two members of the Hibernian Historical Society, it passes their detailed scrutiny with only a few minor amendments. The chairman writes to James, confirming that it is eligible to be published as No. Sixty-Three in their monograph series, 'Provided that, as I warned you, you are prepared to pay for the costs of production'. James is prepared, and has an enjoyable time with the Dublin printers choosing typefaces, endpapers and binding.

'Quarter bound in green leather and green cloth, green marbled end papers, set in Caslon 14 point, which the Cuala Press used to publish poems illustrated by Jack Yeats. Edition limited to five hundred copies, each numbered and signed by the author. Only one illustration, a portrait of my great-grandfather, bearded and looking like an Old Testament prophet, preaching the Word at the Merrion Hall,' he tells Georgia.

'Dad, that sounds wonderful. I look forward to getting a copy and to seeing it in W. H. Smith at Heathrow.'

There is a little launch party at Trinity College, Dublin, where the chairman of the Society makes a generous speech praising 'the elegance of the prose, matched by the elegance of the production'. There is even a favourable, if small, review in the *Irish Times*.

Afterwards, anti-climax. James still thinks about Anna and Anna's son, but no longer with any hope that he might persuade her to live her life differently, with him.

One evening he telephones Georgia and asks her to come down to Donhead alone in the middle of the week.

'Dad, what's the matter? Are you all right?'

'I'm fine, no crisis, but I've an idea to talk over with you.'

When Georgia arrives they sit together in the Donhead library, and James tells Georgia that he wants her and Stephen to take over Donhead.

'You're young enough to enjoy living here, and it's a great place for children, as you know. It's commutable for Stephen, and he's always said he can work from anywhere provided the communications are good. The house needs work, starting with the roof and the attic windows, but the two of you can afford it.'

'Dad, I'd love it. But it's a big step for Stephen. So I'll need to talk to him. And where will you go?'

'I'll keep the London flat. And you'll have me to stay from time to time.'

'Provided you don't bring a hundred knights.'

'Luckily, I have only one daughter. And she a Cordelia,' as he gives her a hug.

Stephen agrees, provided, he says to Georgia, 'We have a free hand – it won't work if your father keeps telling us what to do.'

'Dad isn't like that. He doesn't look back.'

James doesn't look back. He finds leaving easy. The London flat is furnished, and he takes just his clothes, his personal papers and the Wemyss jug from Allenmouth. Donhead had arrived out of the blue; James departs almost as suddenly.

He doesn't look back, but once in London finds he has little to look forward to. His two or three applications for jobs that seem suitable for an ex-Permanent Secretary come to nothing. He resists a suggestion that he should chair a Committee of

Enquiry into the Funding of the Arts; he applies to become Provost of his old Oxford college, gets on the shortlist, but fails to manipulate the internal politics of the Senior Common Room. When they appoint his old boss at the Treasury, James thinks this serves them right.

He has Anna's address; she and Jack have moved to live in Allenmouth with her father. James sends her a short, affectionate letter that avoids any suggestion of getting back together and encloses a cheque for three thousand pounds 'to help with Jack's and your living expenses'.

Anna replies a week later, enclosing the uncashed cheque.

'It's not that the money wouldn't be helpful, and it was generous of you to send it. But Jack and I need to be independent. I don't want to be beholden to anyone other than my dad, and that's difficult enough for me as it is.' She signs the letter 'Love, Anna', but its tone is neutral, and there is no suggestion that they might meet, or that James has any right to see Jack.

James keeps the letter, but pushes Anna and Jack into a distant corner of his mind.

Georgia worries about him. 'Dad, you're not ready for a bath chair. Write another book, or take up golf again. You're eligible to enter the President's Putter, aren't you?'

'I haven't played golf since Oxford,' says James and remembers guiltily that this isn't quite true. 'But I don't like that world enough to become part of it. I've finished my monograph and can't bring myself to write *Memoirs of a Permanent Secretary*. The truth would be libellous, and the bowdlerized version makes me yawn just thinking about it.'

'Well, you need something, you need a project,' says Georgia. 'Wasn't Levin your hero? Don't you remember what he said about work, that lyrical passage about scything? Where's your copy?' She goes to the bookshelves, finds *Anna Karenina*, thumbs through the last fifty pages, and reads aloud:

'The longer Levin mowed, the oftener he felt the moments of unconsciousness in which it seemed the scythe was moving by itself, a body full of life and consciousness of its own, and as though by magic without thinking of it the work turned out regular and precise by itself. These were the most blissful moments.'

'There you are. That says it all. Levin took up bee-keeping. So find some blissful moments, or I'll start looking for a Dorset widow to keep you occupied. Incidentally, you've never told me what you were doing all those weeks in Northumberland. What were you up to?'

Georgia's antennae are good; James gives an unconvincing reply about needing a complete break and deflects further questions by agreeing to find a project.

A month later he is sorting through family papers when he finds an old map of the Derriquin Oyster Fishery, marking the enclosures that he saw off Oysterbed Pier when he last visited Kerry. He is taken by the language – parcs, ambulances, perches – and impressed by the quantities, a total of 9,494,109 oysters in 1883 after 'allowing fifteen per cent for waste or losses'. 'Part of a lot of 1,276,800 bought of Corbigny at sixteen francs, scattered in different places'. And he recalls one of his fellow members at the Dublin launch of his monograph, a man who was writing a detailed history of Irish aquaculture, oyster, mussel and fish farming, saying, 'There's hardly an oyster bed anywhere in the Republic now. It's a tragedy.'

James goes back to Drimnamore and walks again to Oysterbed Pier. He finds one of the Doyles, a man in his nineties, who remembered his father and his grandfather, and who had worked in the oyster beds as a young man.

'It's a crying shame there are no more Kerry oysters. We've beautiful clear water and a great rise and fall of the tide. I'm telling you, our oysters knocked the Galway men sideways when they tasted them.'

James tries to find out who owns the strip of land at Oysterbed Pier and the foreshore, but nobody in Drimnamore seems to know. He contacts the family solicitor in Dublin, who looks into the question and comes back ten days later, rather embarrassed.

'It appears from our records that you do. The property and the foreshore were transferred by your grandfather to the Derriquin Oyster Fishing Company, there were a hundred shares all owned by Henry Burke, and no one seems to have bid for the company in the 1922 auction. We have the share certificates here. They probably aren't worth much, unless you get planning permission.'

James sees this as a sign. He spends the next six months visiting oyster fisheries in Essex, Brittany and Galway, and finds and hires a manager from Galway with a degree in aquaculture to start the new enterprise from scratch.

'You'll have ten per cent of the company; I'll put up all the capital,' he tells Danny Byrne, an enterprising thirty-year-old. 'It'll be worth nothing if it flops, a fortune if it does well.'

Danny laughs. 'Not many fortunes made out of oysters so far,' he says. 'But we'll see. It's a grand place for it all right, big tides, clean water, a good little pier. A bit far from our market, but they seemed to have managed well enough back in the last century. I'll give it a real go.'

41.

'HERE'S THE LIST of what we need,' says Danny Byrne to James. 'My guess is that it'll come to around two hundred thousand euros.'

James whistles. 'No wonder oysters are expensive.'

'That's doing everything properly – new shed, washing and grading machines, purification system, repairing the old enclosures in the water, fixing the pier, buying a decent boat. There's no point chucking a hundred thousand spats in the water and hoping for the best. And EU and Dublin grants will pay for half of it.'

James feels better at the halving of the bill. He and Danny order the equipment and spats for delivery the following spring. He lets his London flat and finds a small cottage on the Drimnamore River half a mile from Oysterbed Pier. It has a good view, no electricity and an outside privy. The owner, Jeremiah Casey, has moved to the new development on the edge of Drimnamore.

'That cottage was built by your great-great-grandfather in 1840. I didn't know when I was well off,' he tells James. 'Now I've got electricity, flush toilets inside the house, no deposit and fifty years to pay. But just look at the state of the feckin' place. A year ago they were guarding the site in case all this stuff got pinched. Now you couldn't give it away. God only knows when the rest of the houses will be finished. The four of us who bought off plan thought we were getting a bargain. We couldn't sell today for the half of what we paid. The eejit banks even evicted the family from Number Three, would you believe it? They shoulda paid them to stay.'

'Wasn't Michael Sullivan the builder?'

'Indeed he was. Financier, developer, builder, he did the lot. And then the banks pulled the rug out from under him. He's bust, God help him, back to being a builder again.'

James signs a lease for a year and spends the next two weeks sorting out Pier Cottage. It is small, three square rooms, the front door opening into a kitchen that separates the bedroom from the parlour, three windows on both sides and one at the south-east end overlooking the river mouth and the Kenmare estuary. It's like going back to Allenmouth, James thinks, remembering his campaign furniture with regret. And I still go outside to the lavatory.

'I had a septic tank installed five years ago that the EU paid for,' Jeremiah had told him. 'Before that it was just a long drop.'

The kitchen doubles as a bathroom, the enamelled iron bath sitting on claw feet, green-stained around the plughole but otherwise serviceable. A wooden cover sits on the bath and serves as a kitchen counter.

'You'll get your kind of furniture over at Tralee,' Jeremiah advised him. 'The craft village there is on hard times, they're giving stuff away.'

James drives the oyster fishery's truck along the coast road past Staigue Fort, past Derrynane, over the Coomakista pass, past Waterville where he had fished with his father on the Butler's Pool and Lough Currane, and into Tralee.

The craft village is a faded glory: café, pottery, jeweller, furniture maker and knitwear shops all wondering at the sudden ending of the boom. The largest shop carries a sign saying:

Kerry Alternative Therapies

Acupuncture, Mystic Healings, Yoga, Reiki,
Thai Massage, Crystal Singing Bowls, Tarot Cards,
Golden Heart Chakra Essence

On the door someone has scrawled 'Going, Going, Gone' in white paint.

James, the only customer, sits in the coffee shop.

'It is late September,' says the middle-aged woman who brings him a pot of tea and some freshly baked soda bread. 'But it's been quiet all summer.'

She sits down with James and shares his pot of tea. James comments on her accent.

'There's lots of Brits in the village – if you count the people from Dublin and Cork we're almost all ex-pats. We came here to get away from it all. We certainly did that, and we seem to have got away from prosperity into the bargain. We're better off than most, my husband has his Post Office pension, you don't need much to live on out here, and there's no need to impress the neighbours. We've all stopped paying rent. I walk to work and we sold the car a year ago. Bought two second-hand bicycles, cheaper and healthier.'

She laughs. 'Our children think we're mad, but we wouldn't go back to Northampton.'

Walking around the craft village, James finds a set of deep-blue hand-made cups and some rugs in the weaver's shop in blues and greens with Celtic knots woven into the fabric. He buys a couple of simple bentwood chairs, and in the antique shop a pair of late nineteenth-century oil lamps with green oil chambers and brass stands. The stock is mostly house clearance junk, although in one corner there is a small Irish Sheraton half-moon table.

'That's the real thing,' says the owner. 'Completely unre-stored.'

James pulls open the central drawer and sees in the top corner a peeling brown label. 'Derriquin Castle, Morning Room, No. 37.'

He shuts the drawer, negotiates a price and the table is his.

Back in Drimnamore, he realizes he hasn't bought a bed, men-tions this to Jeremiah, who nods, and two days later a double bed arrives complete with mattress, pillow, sheets and blankets.

'Eighty euros would do it,' he says. 'Distressed stock. By the by, help yourself to the turf from the stack outside the cottage. I've got underfloor heating.'

James scrubs the stone floors of Pier Cottage down to their original grey, paints the walls white and whitewashes the outside. He installs a Calor gas tank for cooker, fridge and hot water, and when his books arrive from London he feels at home. The Sheraton table looks magnificent and out of place in the corner of the kitchen.

No more out of place than I am in Drimnamore, thinks James, but in reality he has a sense of purpose and a sense that he belongs. After a week's hard work he is tired, satisfied and happy.

Danny Byrne comes to James with a layout for the oyster shed and a builder's estimate. 'Sixty thousand euros, plus VAT, which we'll get back. I've agreed you and I will each work three days a week on the site, and that's to be deducted from the price. At unskilled labour rates. I hope you're happy with the idea.'

'Good. Only one quote, and from Michael Sullivan?'

'He said he'd met you. And they say he's a good builder, a good craftsman. The man from Kenmare said it would be a hundred thousand euros, and he and his team would have to come out from Kenmare every day. Sullivan wants the work, says he'll finish it in three months.'

'Doesn't seem long. What about planning permission?'

'It's a breeze-block shed with a concrete floor, rendered walls, a prefabricated pitched roof and slates from a Cork quarry. Replacement building, so no planning permission is needed. Sullivan can start on Monday week if we sign today. He'll only have to blow on the old shed for it to fall down, and there are lots of hungry builders' merchants around.'

James signs the contract and they start work a week later. Michael Sullivan is builder, site foreman and labourer all in one, telling James and Danny patiently and precisely what they have to do. He is firm with the other two workers from Drimnamore; after four days one of them fails to turn up.

'That's why I hired two,' says Michael. 'I never thought the both of them would see it through. James, I want you on the cement mixer today. Danny and Joe can set up the forms for the floor pouring.'

They work six days a week, ten hours most days. James and Danny decide that their contracted hours are a minimum, and they are eager to see the building finished. At the end of the first week, Michael and James are together in the bar of The Liberator in Drimnamore, drinking pints of Guinness.

'Not as grand as the first place we drank together,' says Michael.

'The Guinness is just as good.'

Michael drinks down his pint, orders two more with whiskey chasers, and says, 'I've found out more about you since we first met. You're a Burke from Derriquin, no?'

'I am.'

'Our two families have a shared history, not all of it good, I have to say.'

'I know my father was at school with a Tomas Sullivan.'

'My father. But that isn't the half of it. My gran told me that Tomas was in the IRA, that he was at Staigue Fort, and then up on the mountain where your grandmother was shot. Your father went to see him in Kilmainham Jail before he escaped. There, now you have it.'

'That's enough to be getting on with.'

'Look, we can fight the War of Independence all over again if you like. But neither of us was there.'

'I've never believed you could right ancient wrongs.'

James finishes his third Guinness and whiskey, orders another round, and asks, 'Does your father live in Kerry?'

'He joined the army, then the Garda, went to Spain with the Bandera Irlandesa after my mother died. Killed in 1938 out there. I never knew him.'

'My father fought in Spain.'

'I don't suppose he was fighting for Franco and Holy Mother Church.'

Both men are silent as they finish their drinks. As they leave the bar, James says, 'I'm glad you told me all that. I'll be glad to forget it.'

Michael looks at him, smiles, says, 'Good man yourself,' and they walk out into the night.

In nine weeks the shell of the oyster shed is up and roofed. 'All we need now is the render,' says Danny. 'And the floor surface. Rubberized paint, hard-wearing, laboratory quality, easy to clean.'

'That wasn't in the estimate,' says Michael.

'No. I've ordered it from France. James and I will put it down. You'll not see us for the next two days, we're off to buy a boat.'

James and Danny drive north to County Mayo. 'There's a bankrupt salmon farm up there that has a likely boat. Maybe other stuff we can use.'

'Pity they went bust.'

'Good thing, if you ask me. They feed the salmon on fish meal. They're full of antibiotics, dosed to make their flesh pink, and their droppings pile up under the cages on the sea floor. I'd ban the lot of them.'

'Oh.'

The offices of the salmon farm have a defeated feeling. There is an old Land-Rover with three flat tyres parked outside, a fourteen-foot dinghy on a trailer with weed growing up through it, and a pile of green boxes marked 'Lough Cutra Salmon – Ireland's Finest Fish'. There is a strong smell of fish in the air, a smell that carries through into the office, where a cheerful young man is sitting at the desk.

'I'm representing the banks,' he says, which explains his cheerfulness. He produces a list. 'Take a look. It's all in there.'

Danny nudges James when he sees what's in the shed. 'Plenty of good stuff. It's been on the market for months.'

They mark off a dozen pairs of thigh waders, a forty-foot conveyor belt, a steam cleaner and the dinghy and trailer outside, then the three men go down to the pier to look at the boat.

'It's not exactly what we wanted, but it'll do,' says Danny.

'Give us a price for the two boats and everything we've marked. We don't need the Land-Rover. And don't tell me that the prices are on the list.'

'Thirty-five thousand euros.'

'Twenty thousand would be nearer the mark.'

'Thirty, and you can have the smoke-house thrown in.'

'Done. Delivered to Drimnamore.'

The young man, still cheerful, telephones Dublin and agrees the price. On the way back James asks, 'You said the boat isn't exactly what we want. And the smoke-house?'

'The boat's perfect, with that big squared-off stern and a new diesel engine. It only lacks a gantry, and we'll build that ourselves. The smoke-house was thrown in, and smoked oysters are brilliant, fetch a good price. We're well below budget.'

Three weeks later the building is finished, gleaming white next to the pier, 'DRIMNAMORE OYSTER FISHERY' in giant green letters down the inland wall.

'I'm glad to be back to building,' says Michael. 'We'll need a party to celebrate. Trestle tables and Guinness for anyone in Drimnamore who wants to come out here.'

Curiosity and free Guinness persuade seventy men, women and children to come to the party. The floor laid down by James and Danny looks pristine until the party-goers tramp in mud from outside.

'It's designed to clean easily, and that's why there's that little slope down to the gutter along the south side. The steam cleaner will see that off in no time,' says Danny.

'Where did you get the oysters?'

'I picked them from out in front at low tide. They're the descendants of the spats your great-grandfather laid down. And there are plenty more out there. We've chosen a good place all right.'

There are a hundred oysters on the table, although most of the guests are cautious about eating them. They are more interested in meeting James. One or two remember John Burke. More than half live in what used to be Derriquin properties.

At the end of the evening one man puts his face close to James's and says, 'Don't think you can buy your way back in here. We got rid of you in 1919, and we could do it again.'

James moves away, but Michael notices and says, 'That was the drink talking. Half an hour ago Tommy was asking about jobs in the fishery.'

The day after the party they bring in the Drimnamore black-smith to build the gantry on the stern of the boat. Its cross-beam holds the pulleys that link two chain-mail purse nets to a winch driven by the boat's engine.

'We let out the purses, tow them open along the seabed, quite slowly, close their mouths when we haul them in, open them up to drop the oysters onto the counter. Chip them clean here, then wash and grade them in the shed.'

'What happens if you lose a purse?'

'Mark the spot and fish it up at low tide. We'll lose a few, that's why we have a dozen in stock.'

Two days later they take the boat out for a trial run in low cloud, drizzle and a choppy sea. The twin purses pay out sweetly, Danny driving the boat while James watches the taut towing wires. On the first pass on the far side of the channel they find only rocks, mud and starfish. The second pass is no better. On the third, closer to the shore, each purse has over a dozen oysters; they slap each other on the back, throw all but six of them back into the inner parc, and return, cold, wet and happy, to the shed. James produces a bottle of white wine; Danny shucks the oysters open and they drink a toast.

'To the Drimnamore Oyster Fishery.'

'*Sláinte*. You'll have to open your own from now on.'

James goes back to his cottage and sleeps soundly. Late in life he has discovered the pleasures of hard manual work. And the perils – he has already sprained a wrist, lost a fingernail and badly bruised his ribs on the building site and on the boat. But his daughter's advice, and Tolstoy's, was good.

42.

SEVERAL YEARS LATER, the Drimnamore Oyster Fishery is beginning to look like a business. Danny, whose caution offsets James's optimism, is pleased.

'We'll sell a hundred and fifty thousand oysters this year, turn over almost ninety thousand euros, close to break even. We've covered my salary and we don't need the bank for working capital any more. Our man in Cork is working out well.'

Their new distributor is based in Cork and travels to London every week to sell smoked salmon to big department stores and expensive restaurants.

'His fifteen per cent is a bargain. All we have to do is to get the oysters to Cork once a week. And he's a Dutchman. I wouldn't trust a Cork man with my money or my sister.'

'There speaks Galway.'

They employ six packers in the shed for most of the year. They cover the oysters in fresh, damp seaweed and pack them in woven baskets with a clear plastic cover and 'Drimnamore Oyster Fishery' stencilled on the side. The baskets are twice the price of cardboard and, Danny agrees, worth every penny. James and Danny work the dredger together and they have hired Tommy, who turns up most days, to chip the oysters clear of barnacles. They start to sell direct to the public at Oysterbed Pier after a succession of summer weekends spent turning away disappointed tourists.

'All we need is a blackboard, a big bottle of tabasco and

hundreds of lemons. We'll make double our normal margin, and it's all cash.'

James has become a fixture in Drimnamore. He is treated with a mixture of curiosity ('Why would you want to come to the end of Ireland, for God's sake?'), affection ('You've brought a bit of life to the place') and suspicion ('What's an Englishman doing making money out of Irish oysters?'). He works hard at the fishery, goes for long walks along the coast and up into the mountains, reads Irish history in the evenings, snug in his cottage. He is making slow progress on expanding his monograph into a longer book about the people of Dunkerron between 1840 and 1900. Once a month he goes to the public library in Tralee where there is a complete set of Kerry newspapers of the period: *The Kerryman, Kerry Sentinel, Kerry Examiner*, and *South Kerry Star*. Only *The Kerryman* survives.

'I know more about Dunkerron in the nineteenth century than I do about the world today,' he tells Danny. 'It was like the Wild West.'

He goes to the Church of Ireland service every Sunday to swell its tiny congregation, never more than ten in the winter. He reads the lesson occasionally, sits in the Burke family pew, helps to weed the graveyard and joins the congregation at the Kerry Coffee Shop after the service. He likes the curious mixture around the table, even the bossy evangelical lay preacher, Sheila Perceval. There is a retired bank manager from Dublin, two Brits making their pensions go further, an elderly American hippy and the woman who started the Kerry Coffee Shop six years ago and is still holding on. Holidaymakers double the congregation and triple the collection during July and August. For the rest of the year, James feels he is part of a dying creed in a colonial outpost.

In contrast, sixty go to the big, gloomy Roman Catholic church outside the village. 'It used to be more like a hundred until they found out what priests and the Christian Brothers had been doing to children for all those years,' says Sheila with a certain amount of satisfaction.

James buys a boat, a Galway hooker that he finds in Roundstone and sails down the coast with Danny as his crew. He can handle the boat alone on all but the roughest days, sailing among the islands in the estuary and when the weather is good as far out as the Bull, the Cow and the Calf. He replaces the British Seagull with a reliable twenty-horsepower Yamaha to bring him home whenever the wind dies away, fishes for mackerel and sets out half a dozen lobster pots close to Rossdohan Island. Occasionally, when there's some water, he tries for salmon in the Drimnamore River. His dog keeps him company. Mick is a Kerry Blue terrier that James acquired from Michael Sullivan.

'That dog is a direct descendant of Michael Collins's famous terrier, Convict 224. My father was given the dog after Collins was killed, and we've bred from the line ever since.'

'He's handsome enough, I must say. Lovely colour, and not small and yappy like a Jack Russell.'

Once a month he has dinner with Michael Sullivan and Aisling in the Great Southern Hotel. After a few attempts to introduce James to merry widows, Michael abandons his hopes of bringing James back to the altar.

'It's not natural,' he grumbles. 'It's a waste of a good man.'

'I've been married, I've got a daughter,' says James. 'I've a dog, a cottage, a boat and the fishery. Quite enough for one man to worry about.'

On one of these evenings Michael tells him the story of the glory days.

'It seemed great while it lasted, and then everyone went bust. My partner Declan shoved off to America with his latest girlfriend and an offshore Ansbacher account. I owed the bank twenty million that I didn't have, so they took Sullivan Construction, took the Mercedes and the villa, took my banjaxed investments, not that they were worth anything, and settled for that. I never pledged the house, only sensible thing I did, and Aisling stuck with me.'

'He had soft hands under a hen, that Declan,' says Aisling.

'And I got carried away with it all, parties, clothes, flying at the front of the plane. I'm only glad Annie and my da weren't alive to see it all.'

Michael takes a deep drink from his pint of Guinness and gives his wife a hug.

'That's all eaten bread now. I still couldn't tell you what a Contract for Difference is, although it blew away eight million euros of money I didn't have. I've done apologizing and I'm back to what I know.'

Georgia comes out to see James without Stephen and stays in the big hotel.

'No, Dad, there's nothing wrong, it's just that the business is going through a rough time. Stephen's sorting it out. And it's lovely to have you to myself.'

James shows Georgia the oyster fishery and takes her out in the boat with Danny, dredging for oysters on a drizzling day. They pick what they need in two hours, and when they land Georgia says, 'That was real work. Dad, I'm very impressed. You've built a good little business from nothing, not bad for an ex-Permanent Secretary. But aren't you lonely?'

'I see people every day, I read a lot of poetry, I do some writing, and I've always got Mick. I'm even learning Gaelic very slowly. If I want company, there's several of them in The Liberator bar who haven't told me their life stories yet.'

'You know something, you're living a different version of the last years of your father's life. Away from home, celibate, fishing, religion . . .'

James laughs. 'Dad was baptized into the Greek Orthodox Church, became a monk, renounced all his worldly possessions. I go to church only once a week, with no incense and not much religion.'

*

A week after Georgia's visit, James is in Drimnamore buying groceries. He has tied Mick to the Staigue Fort bench. When he comes out of the shop he sees a young boy stroking Mick's head and getting his face licked in return.

'He's a friendly dog. His name is Mick. What's your name?'

'Mum says I'm not to talk to strangers.'

'Dogs don't count?'

'Dogs can't talk. Here she comes, anyway. I can talk to you when she's here.'

James looks up and sees Anna Pearson walking towards him. She hugs James, and he kisses her cheek, holding her tight.

'Mum, you told me not to talk to strangers, and you're hugging this man.'

'We've met before. He's the one I told you about, that we're coming to visit.'

'It's lovely to see you. And to see Jack James Zachariah again.'

'How do you know all my names? I'm called Jack. The other ones are spares.'

'How did you track me down?'

'I heard from Imogen you'd moved to Drimnamore. Jack knows Zachariah, and I thought he should meet his other, his other namesake. I didn't think it would be hard to find you in a village this size. She said you were still on your own.'

'Nosy woman. For all she knows I've a string of Irish mistresses. How long are you here?'

'Days, weeks. You know I don't like timetables. We came over on the ferry to Cork. That's my little car outside the Seaview B&B.'

'You'll have to stay till the first Kerry Oyster Festival next weekend. Come down to Oysterbed Pier this afternoon and I'll show you the reason I'm here.'

'Mum, what's a namesake?'

Anna and Jack arrive at Oysterbed Pier and James shows them round.

'At Allenmouth you said you wanted to be a fisherman, and I said you'd left it a bit late. I was quite wrong.'

'We're two packers short this afternoon. You and Jack can make yourself useful at a packing station. Look, I'll fill the basket. Jack, you put on the seaweed and the cover. Anna, you strap the basket round.'

Anna is happy to be put to work, Jack talking non-stop to the other three women on the line as they work. By five o'clock they have filled a hundred baskets.

'That's our quota. Now let's have tea.'

They walk to the new kiosk. James brings over smoked oysters, soda bread and butter, and a piece of cake for Jack. They sit at one of the trestle tables Danny has made from old railway sleepers.

'It's always quiet in the afternoon. When the Ring of Kerry tours arrive in the morning there are plenty of customers. Try some lemon on your oyster.'

'They're delicious.'

They finish the oysters and walk back to the village.

'Join me in The Liberator later, once Jack's in bed. If it's a good day tomorrow we'll go for a sail.'

'What do you say, Jack?'

'Thank you for showing me the oysters.'

James picks Jack up, hugs him, feels his eyes pricking with tears, and puts him down. Anna comes over to the Liberator after half an hour and they talk for a long time in a quiet corner of the bar.

'I hope you stay a while. I do miss you. And seeing Jack . . . he felt like my son when I held him just now.'

'You hardly know each other. And we're not going to have a DNA test. He's your son only if you both agree. But I did want Jack to meet you. He needs a man, not all the time, mind. I can't teach him to sail or fish.'

'I can do both. But I want to be more than just an Outward Bound instructor.'

'That's up to you and up to him. And I have missed you. I'd forgotten how calm and competent you are. Let's see how the three of us get on. I'll bring a picnic for tomorrow.'

'I'll see you both at the pier at ten. We'll sail over to Derrynane if there's enough wind; the races are on in the afternoon.'

James hoists the dark red sails once they have motored away from the pier; the boat heels over as the sails fill and there is a generous gurgle of water under her lee. Jack sits with his arm around Mick.

'Mum, is it meant to tilt like this?'

'Ask the captain.'

'There's a heavy keel to stop it going over. It's called a Galway Hooker. This one is a *leathbad* in Gaelic, a half-boat.'

'I remember you told me Kerry was beautiful.'

'On a day like this. In November, in the rain, with the low cloud blotting out the mountains, it's altogether different. Mind your heads as we go about. We'll anchor on the edge of the channel and try for some mackerel. They've been around since the beginning of the week.'

They each take a line with half a dozen feathered hooks and drop them over the side. Jack has never been fishing before, and shouts with excitement when he pulls up two gleaming blue, black and silver fish. James shows him how to gut a mackerel, and Jack, doubtful at first, manages to clean one on his own.

'That's for your supper. The ones that go in the pots are just slit open. We've got three for supper, six for the lobsters. We'll check the pots on our way back.'

James persuades Anna to take the tiller as they sail in a warm breeze down the estuary and sits beside her as she steers. He puts his hand over hers on the tiller, doesn't take it away. Anna looks at him, smiles, brushes his cheek with hers for a moment as the boat heels over in a gust of wind. It is a rare, cloudless Kerry day, with enough wind to take them to Derrynane, where they anchor off the point. Anna has made sandwiches, James has brought a bottle of wine and some lemonade, and they eat in the cockpit of the boat. They can see the tractors dragging the sand flat for the races and the crowds beginning to gather.

'Can we swim? I'm very hot,' asks Anna.

'The tide's on the turn, there's no current. I'll put the ladder over the stern so you can get back in.'

'Mum, I don't have my swimming costume.'

'Underpants will do fine.'

Anna kicks off her sandals, pulls her dress over her head and before James has a chance to look at her dives into the water.

'It's – it's bracing.'

'It is the Atlantic. It takes a while to get used to it.'

James puts down the ladder, then watches as Jack, very slowly, lowers himself into the sea.

'Aren't you coming in?'

'You always need one on the boat.'

Four minutes are enough. James helps them both up the ladder and they dry themselves on the small towel from the galley. Anna walks forward, her back to James, and slips out of her bra and pants and puts on her dress. She lays the wet clothes on the hatch.

'They'll be dry in twenty minutes.'

'Shall we go to the races? Have you ever been to a horse race? We can take the dinghy over to the pier and walk round.'

'Won't the boat float away?' says Jack.

'This is a safe anchorage in this weather. We can keep an eye on the boat from the shore. Mick stays on board to keep off pirates. He wouldn't be able to resist chasing the horses if we brought him along.'

It's a holiday crowd at the races, determined to enjoy themselves.

'It's the only race meeting in the world on sand under the proper rules of racing,' says James. 'In the Irish Racing Calendar they give the start time as "depending on the tides".'

They watch the last three races, Jack perched on James's shoulders to see over the heads of the crowd.

'This was how my father earned his living, training race-horses.'

James explains the mechanics of betting to Jack, who likes the idea, likes it less when he loses the euros James has given him for the first two races.

'We need a long-odds saver in the last,' says James. 'There's a horse come all the way from Limerick, and that's a fair distance if it doesn't have a chance. Eight to one.'

They look at the horses in the makeshift parade ring, Jack holding James's hand tightly. This time Jack puts on the bet himself. The bookie looks at him, says, 'Are you certain now you're eighteen? Tell you what, I'll give you ten to one.'

'Is that better?'

'It's the best.'

They find a spot close to the winning post.

'Look out for the green and red colours, red cap, that's your horse,' and Jack, bouncing with excitement, shouts his horse home. They collect their winnings, Jack talking about his plans to spend the money as they walk back to the pier. Anna is sitting on a bollard watching them.

'Mum, I won ten euros, that's ten pounds nearly.'

'You've set him on the road to ruin,' says Anna as they sail back up the estuary.

'There's still the women and the drink to look forward to.'

They motor back as the wind dies away, then pull up the lobster pots. Jack watches as James puts a mackerel head-down in each bait bag, draws the top of the bag tight and hooks the door shut.

'If they can get in, why can't they get out?'

'The shape of the door makes it difficult.'

The first four pots are full of small crabs, but the last two each has a good lobster. Back at the cottage James shows Jack and Anna how to kill a lobster with a sharp knife into the brain.

They eat the lobsters in front of the fire, Anna admiring the bitter-sweet smell of the turf. Jack is amazed at the change in colour of the lobsters from deep blue-black to red, but is doubtful about eating them, preferring his mackerel.

After supper, Jack asks, 'Mum, can we stay here tonight?'

'You'll have to ask James.'

Jack sleeps on the sofa, and James shares his bed with Anna. He lights the fire in the bedroom, watches as Anna undresses, her body glowing, then holds her to him the rest of the night. He rediscovers her smell, her taste, the warm feeling of her skin. He thinks about Anna's assumption that they would make love again almost at once after several years apart. Being taken for granted, he decides, has its advantages.

The next morning Anna and Jack are still asleep and James is in the kitchen making coffee when Danny knocks on the door.

'You'd better come to the Pier. We've been burgled.'

James goes with Danny to the shed; the door has been broken open and the stock they had been building up for Saturday's festival has gone.

'They've gone off with two hundred boxes. You can see the tyre marks on the grass. Looks like a small truck or a van. I rang the Garda and they said they'd get a man here on Monday. Once I told them no one was hurt they lost interest. I should have said I'd been beaten up.'

'Bloody hell.'

'You might try your man Michael Sullivan. He knows everything that goes on around Drimnamore.'

James rings Michael, who says he'll ask around. He walks back to the cottage where Anna and Jack are having breakfast and tells them what has happened.

Jack is outraged. 'That's not fair, that's stealing. Can you fish up some more?'

'Not by tomorrow. Never mind. There's not much we can do about it. Let's go and play crazy golf.'

Danny finds them in the coffee shop later that morning.

'Now what?' says James. Danny is smiling.

'We've got them all back. I don't know what Michael Sullivan did, but I got a message to go to the lay-by outside the big hotel, and there were our boxes, every single one.'

The next day, the day of the first Kerry Oyster Festival, is again fine.

'It's a Kerry record, two good days in a row,' says Danny. 'We've work to do. I've put a banner above the road to show we're here, and I called the coach companies yesterday. They said it was the driver's decision where and when to stop. But most of them stop off in Drimnamore. Anna, could you handle the till? Jack, go you and help behind the lemonade table.'

At ten the coaches start to arrive, but the first three pass through Drimnamore without stopping.

'You'd think we'd have got at least one,' says Danny. He looks worried.

'Did you not come to an arrangement with the drivers last time through?' asks Michael Sullivan, who is manning an oyster table with Aisling.

'I did not.'

'Better do something, maybe on the Drimnamore Bridge on the far side of the village.'

The something is a puncture. Danny leaves the fishery van jacked up and without its near-side front tyre on the bridge. No buses can cross for the next two hours, and the passengers are happy enough to make the short walk back into the village. By noon they have almost run out of oysters, the van's puncture has been repaired and the bus drivers made happy.

'It will be bigger and better next year. I can't thank you enough for recovering the oysters,' says James.

He and Anna are having dinner with the Sullivans in the big hotel. Jack and the youngest Sullivan boy are playing in the hotel's games room.

'It wasn't too difficult. It's always the Kellys round here. It would have been a shame if we hadn't had our festival. Anna, James is a good man, and they're not easily found, I can tell you. Here,' he says, embarrassed by his little speech. 'Take a look at this. It's the last letter Tomas wrote to Annie, my gran. I found it a week ago in a box of old letters, Communion cards, exam certificates and my father's commission as a Garda inspector.'

James reads the letter once to himself, once out loud.

> The Ebro,
> Catalonia,
> September 1938

Dear Mam,

A lot has happened since I last wrote from Teruel. We recaptured the town after some pretty fierce fighting. The weather had cleared and our planes did real damage to the Republican troops.

Our section was one of those leading the advance, and we got ahead of ourselves, to be honest we got a bit lost, and were taken prisoner by the Republican rearguard. We were disarmed, sitting waiting to be shot, which is what we would have done if it had been the other way round, when one of the Republicans called out my name.

It was John Burke from Derriquin. He prodded me in the ribs with his rifle and took me round the corner. He's going to shoot me himself, I thought, and, do you know, it seemed fitting, as I'd been one of the men who executed his mother. I told him how to do it in case he botched the job. 'One to the heart, one to the head,' I said. So he pointed his rifle at me, I could see his hands shaking, then he raised the muzzle and fired two shots into the air. 'Your troops will be here within the hour,' he said and walked away.

I heard the shots that killed the rest of my section ten minutes later, and later still rejoined our men as they advanced to the edge of the town.

Mam, I've escaped the hangman and now the firing

squad. There's more fighting to be done at the Ebro, but the war is won. I'm ready to come home and to begin being a father to Michael.

Your loving son,
Tomas

James hands the letter back to Michael, who puts it away. His eyes are moist as he says, 'He was killed a week or so later at the battle of the Ebro, so I never got to see him.'

'I'm sorry. I'm glad my father did what he did.'

Anna and Jack move out of Seaview and into James's cottage. At Oysterbed Pier, Anna takes over the running of the kiosk, while Jack spends most of his time with James or playing with Mick and the Sullivans' son.

Anna asks James to take her over to Derriquin.

'I can see it means a lot to you,' she says. They are sitting on the stone pier. Above them is the golf club car park, the place where the castle, and then its ruined shell, used to stand.

'I have a picture of Dad as a little boy sitting next to his father on this spot, with Derriquin Castle in the background, taken in 1908. Looking at them, you wouldn't think that they had a care in the world, and yet twelve years later Henry was dead and Derriquin gone. That Scots pine is in the photograph, the only thing other than the rocks that still survives. I never lived in the house, never knew it, but Dad was born in Derriquin. He always thought of himself as a Kerryman and was never at home in England. Odd that he should wind up on Mount Athos.'

They stay on the jetty for several minutes, then go back to the cottage. On the way back through the rhododendrons James sees a woodcock sitting unafraid in their way.

'What's that? It's beautiful,' says Anna.

'It's a woodcock. My father would have told you it's my grandfather, Henry Burke. Dad and Josephine, she was my cousin on the wrong side of the blanket and very superstitious, saw one here the night Derriquin was burned.'

James walks towards the bird and reaches down to pick it up. It rises, and Anna feels the beat of its wings as it zigzags away.

'You land on the opposite side of Mount Athos to the Stavronikita monastery,' James says to Anna.

They are sitting in the kitchen late after dinner with the Sullivans.

'It's a stiff walk, rough paths and mule tracks mostly, up and down a series of valleys. The sea is always in sight and the air is scented by the pines and by oleander, "the odour of sanctity", Dad called it.

'He'd meet me an hour above Stavronikita and we'd walk down together. Until my last visit, when he was having trouble with his breathing. He'd been a heavy smoker when he was young, untipped cigarettes and pipes, gave it up too late to save his lungs. He was a reserved man, quite shy, wouldn't talk about himself much, asked about Georgia, whom he hardly knew.

'The monastery was beautiful, although parts of it were crumbling. From the top of the descent it looked like a mediaeval castle, with a big battlemented tower at the centre and an ancient arched viaduct leading into it.'

'What did you do for four days?'

'You get caught up in the routine. Endless, chaotic services at all times of day and night, rushed meals where we were read improving texts in a gabbled Greek, the occasional escape on the boat. Dad was the fisherman, which he enjoyed; it gave him a status among the monks.

'They were an odd bunch, his fellow monks, mostly Greeks, some Russians and Bulgarians, one American. Dad said there were endless squabbles about rituals, about saints' days, but he insisted they were part of ordinary life and to be expected, even in a holy place.'

'Did he die out there?'

'I got a message one January that he'd had a severe heart attack, and I went out as soon as I could. Mount Athos was covered in snow, and it took me five hours to get to the monastery, the paths were so treacherous. I was met at the gates by the Guest Master and the Abbot, who told me that Dad had died the day before. I was taken to see him, laid out in his monk's habit, his eyes closed, his face grey and gaunt, his beard completely white. His hands were crossed on his stomach over a little wooden crucifix. They left me alone with him for half an hour, then took me to the refectory for supper.

'He was buried along with all the other monks in a graveyard that overlooks the Aegean. As beautiful a place as any to finish up, although it's a long way from Kerry.

'I felt incredibly sad that I hadn't got there in time, sad that he and I had only begun to know each other late in the day, sad that I'd never properly told him how much I loved him. I wept when I was alone with him, and again when his coffin was lowered into the ground. The American monk told me as we walked back from the cemetery that death was not the end, but the beginning, and that I should be happy that Dad had found peace at Stavronikita. I wish I believed the first part.

'They gave me his Bible and the copy of Donne's sermons that I had given him. The walk back to Daphne was hard. I remembered how Dad used to walk with me as far as the watershed, holding my hand most of the way. The last time we parted he made a little sign of the cross on my forehead with his finger. I did the same thing for him when I was left alone with his body.

'He didn't leave a will. He'd made everything over to me before he became a monk, and there wasn't much left after we'd sold Killowen and cleared the overdraft.

'He did leave a short letter in which he told me that the girl in the newspaper cutting, the girl I'd asked him about, was my half-sister. He told me how to get in touch with her.'

'What was she like?'

'I've never met her. It wasn't clear from Dad's letter whether they had ever met, whether she knew about him. It did explain, among the family papers and stuff that Linda and I salvaged from Killowen, the raft of cuttings from the *Maryborough Gazette*, about this girl and her family. Looking back, we were remarkably incurious at the time, but there were no clues. And Dad seemed the last person in the world to have an illegitimate daughter.'

James pours himself a stiff whiskey.

'It makes me feel sad for both of you,' says Anna. 'Although there are a lot worse father–son relationships. Zach's father used to knock him and his mother about, and my grandfather vanished the moment my father was born. Dad and I have never talked, ever, about anything important. Perhaps you're feeling too sorry for yourself.'

'Maybe. But it makes me determined, this time round, not to let go of you and Jack. He feels like my son, he looks like my son, he doesn't look half Samoan. Jack needs me and I need him. And I think you need me too. You're so independent, and I love that in you, but you and I would be better together than apart. There, I've said enough.'

'You should get in touch with your half-sister,' says Anna, putting her arms around him.

43.

I<small>N LATE</small> O<small>CTOBER</small>, James gets a call from Georgia.

'Dad, can you come over and see me? I've got a problem and I can't talk about it on the phone.'

They meet for lunch in London.

'Dad, Stephen's company has gone bust. The banks appointed the administrator last week.'

'Good Lord, I'm sorry to hear that. But Stephen's an able man. He can start again.'

'No, he can't. He's been using new money to pay dividends, pay the bank. It was a classic Ponzi scheme. And he pledged Donhead as security without telling me; he'd put it in his name, for tax reasons he said. I think he's going to jail.'

Georgia starts to cry. 'Dad, you were right about him. He's lost all our money, all your money, and he's a crook.'

'Darling Georgia, I never thought he was a crook – I just didn't understand his world. He's obviously got into deep water, didn't know how to get out, did some silly things. He's not the only investment banker to have been caught out. London and Dublin are full of them.'

'But he's my banker, my husband, and he's lied to me and let me down. And you.'

'I've got my oysters, and I bought the cottage in Drimnamore this autumn. You and the boys can live in the London flat if you have to leave Donhead. The tenant gets out in December.'

Georgia lifts her head, blows her nose hard on James's

handkerchief and says, 'Donhead's finished. I can't afford to live there, and the banks own it now. So thank you for the flat – I'd rather be there than move in with Mum and William. I'll try not to be there for ever.'

On his return to Drimnamore, Anna opens the cottage door, pulls James inside and puts her arms around him.

'I wasn't expecting you for two more days. Jack won't be back from school for an hour.'

'So?'

Anna leads James into the bedroom, says, 'Remember the refuge box on Holy Island,' and very soon James does.

They are sitting drinking coffee when Jack comes in; he throws himself into James's arms. Mick is with him, and they sit together on the sofa, Jack's arm around the dog.

'Do you take him to school?'

'He comes to the yard, then he goes home, comes back at three o'clock when we get out.'

'You've taken a shine to each other, that's sure. He's getting to be more your dog than mine.'

Jack looks pleased. 'Only for a bit, I haven't known him that long. He still likes you.'

That evening James tells Anna Georgia's news.

'I've got my pension in a few years' time, and I've got the oysters. But most of my capital has gone and there'll be no rent from the London flat as long as Georgia's there.'

'I always thought you had too much money. Perhaps you need me in Drimnamore now, perhaps I'll be more than the visiting lover.'

'Your description, not mine. Please stay. Jack likes it here and he loves Mick.'

'He's very happy. I'm the restless one. I don't like being dependent.'

'You don't always have to be moving on. It's not a crime to be dependent on someone, able to rely on them.'

'I've got Dad to think about, remember. He's given up the golf club, he lives off his old-age pension, and that's scraping.'

'Well, I'm not rich any more, but I'm not penniless. Let's work out where you and Jack and I, and your father, and Georgia, should live. And how.'

There is no clear resolution to this conversation, but Anna sends for her things from Allenmouth, which gives James some degree of comfort. Jack is now formally enrolled in the Drimnamore school, and James has Michael Sullivan build a little extension on the side of the sitting room that becomes Jack's room, greatly enhanced because the bed is in a gallery reached by a ladder.

James persuades Anna to take over the packing line in the oyster shed.

'They'll not thank you for putting a foreigner, an Englishwoman, in charge.'

'They'll be OK. None of them wanted the responsibility. You're a hard worker, and competent. And I can't manage the line and go out in the boat. Besides, you're not English, you're a Geordie.'

'True – but you've no idea whether I'm competent. I'll give it a try, and we'll see.'

Anna packs more boxes in an hour than anyone else, treading with care the delicate line between giving orders and asking for help. James and Danny dredge oysters three days a week. After thirty years of sitting at a desk, James is earning his living through hard labour for the first time, and he feels his years, particularly in the winter, when the estuary is covered in sheeting rain from the Atlantic and his hands and feet are numb with cold. His back makes bending and hauling on the ropes difficult, and after three hours on the boat he has had enough. Danny doesn't seem to feel the cold.

'You've always got at least one black or missing fingernail,' says Anna. 'I hope you're careful. Danny's half your age, remember.'

'I'm done in at the end of a dredging day. I'm sorry I'm not an ardent lover any more.'

'You've nothing to be sorry about. I get tired after a day's work. We're both calmer than we were about sex, but I still find you exciting. Perhaps in yellow oilskins and thigh waders tomorrow night?' Anna laughs when James looks alarmed. 'Only a fantasy.'

James knows Anna well enough to wonder.

44.

JAMES WORRIES THAT Anna won't find enough in and around Drimnamore to persuade her to stay. They have supper every Saturday in the bar of The Liberator, enjoying the *craic* and leaving before the serious singing and occasional fighting begin. They have dinner with the Sullivans at least twice a month. Anna doesn't share James's passionate interest in birds, but she takes on the oyster shed and the garden around the house.

'Drimnamore is Allenmouth with an Irish accent,' she tells James. 'I don't need a big city any more. I've got something useful to do which I enjoy, I've got Jack, and he likes it here. And I've got you.'

She picks up that week's copy of *The Kerryman*.

'Look, it's just like the Alnwick *Courant*. "Killorglin plans lights for the festive season." "Invite to new Killarney defibrillator course." "Garda stations to be axed – elderly fear for their safety." That's real news. If I want to find out about the Middle East I can listen to the World Service or RTE.'

Jack talks to James about what he should be called.

'The boys at school ask me about my dad, ask me about you.'

'What do you tell them?'

'I say Anna's my mum. I like calling you James, it makes me feel grown-up, but . . .'

'Tell them at school I'm your dad, and that will keep them quiet. And you can go on calling me James at home.'

Jack looks pleased. James reports the conversation to Anna.

'That's an Irish solution if ever I heard one. Next thing they'll be asking me for my marriage certificate. Holy Ireland's a long time a-dying. But if it makes Jack happy . . .'

It does; it also makes James happy when young Tomas Sullivan refers to him as 'your dad' when he plays with Jack.

James begins to feel settled. The hard work at the oyster shed and his research into the Famine years keep his body and mind active.

Anna seems contented with their domestic life and tells James, 'I've never lived like this. With Zach in Newcastle it was a rollercoaster; with Jack on my own in Allenmouth it was hard work with no one to share it. Here I've got Jack, and you, and Mick the dog, and the Sullivans, and my ladies at the oyster shed.'

'If you came to church you could widen your circle, include the ex-pats.'

'I'm not quite ready for God. And I'll never be ready for the ex-pats.'

James has collected little seed pearls from the oysters since he started the fishery; he selects his best dozen, all small and oddly shaped, but with the deep translucent glow of natural pearls, and takes them to the jewellery maker in the Tralee craft village. She is one of the survivors, one of the few Kerry natives to work there.

'They're lovely, quite hard to set in gold, but I'll try. Do you know the ring size?'

James does. He's held Anna's hand with particular care in the previous ten days and knows that her ring finger is the same size as his little finger.

'I'd like an inscription on the inside: "Their hearts shall not grow old."'

'Sorry, you'd need several rings for that. Three short words is the best I can do.'

James collects the ring a month later. On the following Saturday, when Jack has gone to bed and they are sitting in front of the fire, he gives Anna the little red box. She opens it cautiously, sees the ring, frowns and then smiles.

'James, it's beautiful.'

'They're all Drimnamore pearls.'

'They glow. And the gold's a gentle colour. What does it say inside?' She turns the ring over to read the inscription.

'It's Irish gold, the Tralee jeweller said, from an old brooch. Mo *mhuirnín*, it says.'

Anna slips it on her finger and admires it in the light of the fire. 'Perfect fit. It'll be a badge of respectability in Drimnamore.' She stands up and leads James into their bedroom. A pair of thigh waders are draped over the foot of the bed.

'You can choose who wears them,' says Anna.

A week later she asks James if she can borrow the car for two days.

'Of course. Where are you going?'

'Cork. Saracens are playing Munster in the Heineken Cup on Saturday. Zach's a Saracen now, and he's in the team, so *The Kerryman* says. We'll drive over in the morning, spend the night in Cork.' She sees the look on James's face and adds, 'No, I'm not going to sleep with him. Although that's my business.'

Anna and Jack drive to Cork and return on Sunday. James is relieved; Anna and Jack had reappeared in his life suddenly, and he remains afraid that they could disappear overnight.

'Saracens lost, but Zach scored a try. We met them after the game and Zach gave me this.' Jack holds out a miniature rugby ball with signatures scrawled all over it.

Later Anna says to James, 'I'm glad they met again. Jack loved seeing him play. He still looks up and points to heaven when he scores, and he did ask Jack whether he was saved and then tried to explain what that meant until I stopped him. He's probably got no more than a year or two playing top-class rugby, and I can't think what he will do after that. I told him the three of us were living together here.'

'Why did you tell him that?'

'Jack talked about you, and Zach asked. And he saw my ring. He may be drinking again. He had only one pint in the clubhouse bar after the game, but with Zach it's always been all or nothing.'

Anna prods James at regular intervals to get in touch with his half-sister.

'I don't know her. It might disrupt her life and she probably won't want to meet me.'

'Why don't you let her decide that? She's hardly a child, she can make up her own mind.'

James agrees but does nothing. The demands of the oyster fishery are his excuse, until in early spring a sudden bloom of algae in the Kenmare River means they cannot harvest oysters for at least three weeks.

'Now's your chance,' says Anna.

James, nervous, rings the Maryborough number his father had given him and asks to speak to Cathleen McCann.

'She lives in Dublin,' says a man's voice. 'Who shall I say called?'

'I'm James Burke. John Burke's son.'

James hears nothing and wonders whether the phone is about to be put down.

'I'm Diarmuid McCann, Cathleen's brother. If you give me your number she may call you back at the weekend. That's up to her.'

James is surprised at how pleased he feels when Cathleen returns his call on Sunday evening.

'I know who you are, of course,' she says, and agrees to meet in Dublin in a week's time.

Dublin hasn't changed since James's last visit. The 'To Let' and 'For Sale' signs are everywhere, and James sees only one hopeful 'Under Offer' above an office block that he remembers from his earlier trip. As he drives around St Stephen's Green there is scaffolding on the front of one of the new financial palaces;

workmen are dismantling the Anglo-Irish Bank's sign. 'Go Irish', the remaining letters read, in a strange injunction to the bankers, property developers and estate agents responsible for Ireland's boom and bust.

Cathleen and James meet for supper in an Italian restaurant near her flat; she had vetoed James's suggestion of the Gresham: 'Too grand for me.'

He recognizes his half-sister at once when she comes into the restaurant, unmistakably his father's – her father's – daughter. She is tall, white-haired, handsome rather than beautiful; he had in his mind the image of a much younger woman, the girl in his father's photograph. James feels a sudden surge of affection for this unknown older sister. He wants to embrace her, but she offers her hand and he shakes it.

She declines a glass of wine, 'We're a Pioneer family,' and they sit in silence until the waiter takes their order.

When the food arrives, Cathleen begins to talk. 'I was seventeen when I was told that I was a Burke. I sometimes wonder whether I would have been better off not knowing.'

'Dad left me only the briefest of notes when he died. Until then I didn't know you existed. Did you ever see him?'

'My mother wouldn't meet him, said it would upset Eamonn too much, but she was happy enough for me to make contact. It took me a while to get used to the idea that Eamonn wasn't my natural father. He was a good man, thought I had a right to know and he didn't want me to find out by accident.'

Cathleen takes a drink of water and picks at her risotto. 'Grania told me she was frightened of her father, a hard, unforgiving man. He said that unless she married Eamonn her baby would be given to the laundry nuns. They could do that in those days. And he swore he'd kill John Burke if he didn't leave Ireland. When he came over to the farm, trying to see Grania, Mannion and his men nearly destroyed John. Our father.'

She stops as she says the last two words and looks at James as if for the first time. 'They were children; she was twenty-two, John was twenty-four. He was great with the horses, a shy man, very handsome, Grania said. And she must have been quite something then. They used to ride out to the Trafalgar Folly to meet, which I suppose is why Mannion burned it down. She cried a lot the night she told me, said they were in love, said it never would have worked. "I've been happy enough with your father," she said.'

'I'd love to have known what Dad was like then, and your mother. It wouldn't seem earth-shattering today, but Ireland then wasn't like Ireland now.'

'I was a typical Irish girl from a small country town, in love with horses till I was sixteen, then I thought I had a vocation. "Oh Mary, I give thee the lily of my heart, Be thou its guardian for ever." Eamonn encouraged me, said the McCanns hadn't had a priest or a nun for a generation.'

James laughs. 'I doubt the Burkes have ever had either.'

'And then I found out I was half Prod, half a Burke. I began by feeling sorry for myself, finished by being angry. There was a terrible row when I told them, "I don't feel the same about Our Lady now. Perhaps I'd have been better off in the Magdalene Laundries." I'm ashamed now at how fierce I was.'

'I see you're not a nun.'

'Nuns come in different guises these days, but I'm not. I became a nurse, spent the whole of my career at the Mater here in Dublin. Never married, but I lived with another nurse for twenty years. She died two years ago, and now I live on my own.'

Cathleen blows her nose, takes another long drink of water. 'Anyhow, after several years and a great deal of heart-searching I went to see John. Three times in all, always at the yard among the horses, and we got on well. Partly because he'd found his calling and understood how I'd lost mine.'

'He died in his monastery on Mount Athos.'

'I spent most of a day with him before he went out to Stavronikita for the last time.'

'I never fully understood that, although I went to see him there several times.'

'It was the burden of Spain, he told me. He saved one prisoner outside a place called Teruel, but at the cost of not stopping the shooting of a dozen. Including a boy of seventeen or so. That stayed with him all his life. Do you know the Jesus prayer, do you know about Hesychasm?'

'I do not.'

'"Lord Jesus Christ, Son of God, have mercy on me, the sinner." Repeated many times, like a mantra. John said that inner prayer, the blocking of the senses, was the only thing that brought him peace.'

James orders a second glass of wine and tells Cathleen about his life at Drimnamore, about the oyster fishery, about Anna and Jack. At the end of supper and after three cups of coffee they stand up, and this time they do embrace.

'I'm sorry I've put off this meeting for so long,' says James.

'I'm glad we were both brave enough. Strange that the tug of blood is as strong, don't you think?'

'Strange and strong. I would like to meet again.'

'Let's think about that. We've both got a lot to digest.'

They exchange telephone numbers and addresses and then part, Cathleen to her flat, James to his hotel.

The next day James drives back to Kerry via Burke's Fort and the Trafalgar Folly. He doesn't call on his cousins; instead he parks on the road below the folly and walks the muddy mile and a half through fields and woods to the ruin. He looks at what is left of the folly with a different eye. Only three of the incised names of Nelson's ships – *Victory, Mars, Temeraire* – are visible on the connecting walls, the rest blackened out by the fire.

In the first-floor wall he sees, out of his reach on the surviving chimneypiece, a white enamelled mug streaked with soot. He pokes among the debris on the ground floor in the main building, turns over the remains of some cushions with his foot and sees a little book ruined by fire and rain. He picks it up, leafs through a few battered pages, then reads out loud, 'I thought, O my love, you were so – As the moon is, or sun . . .' The rest of the words are burned away. He puts the book in his pocket, walks slowly down to the road and drives back to County Kerry.

When James gets back to Drimnamore, Danny produces the latest accounts and bank statement for the oyster fishery. They have become a regular stopping point for tourists on the Ring of Kerry, and their Cork distributor cannot keep up with demand. The Kerry Oyster Festival now takes place over a three-day weekend and Drimnamore's bars are enthusiastic sellers of oysters alongside pints of Guinness. Danny is paid a respectable salary and James takes a dividend for the first time.

Although *The Kerryman* comments favourably on this success, there is also some resentment that the profits from Kerry oysters should be 'lining the pockets of a man from Galway and a Brit'. When Anna hears this loud aside in the bar of The Liberator, she reports it to Michael and Aisling when they next meet for dinner.

'Typical,' says Michael. 'But nothing to worry about. Everyone knows who put up the capital. It wouldn't exist if it wasn't for James and Danny and you.'

This reassurance lasts for a week. Danny comes to James with a large envelope and some papers, saying, 'The chancers have served a writ on us. They claim we have no rights to the seabed, that anyone can dredge for oysters in the Kenmare River.'

'We put the spats there in the first place. They belong to us as much as if they were potatoes we'd planted or heifers we'd reared.'

'Much harder to prove.'

'Anyhow, who are "they"?'

'Two of the Kellys and a County Councillor from Tralee.

They're calling themselves Kerry Organic Oysters, and they say any profits should go to the community.'

Michael and Aisling are outraged. 'They're pulling a stroke, so they are. It's all a fantasy. They want to be bought off,' says Michael.

'The writ is real enough. And I had thought about putting half my shares in a trust for Drimnamore,' says James.

'Do no such thing. It's Danegeld. They'll only be back for more.'

Anna is less robust than Michael and Aisling. 'It makes me feel unwelcome, a foreigner.'

'Come on, it's three people, that's all. They'll go away in the end. Ask your ladies on the packing line.'

Anna's ladies are as angry as Michael. They dissect the characters of the two Kellys and the County Councillor in lurid detail, then decide to invite them out to the oyster shed. 'We'll try them with a few dead oysters that've been left out in the sun. That'll get them running.' And for a while Anna cheers up.

The legal formalities drag on, and James has to make a brief trip to Dublin to get the deeds to the land around Oysterbed Pier. He goes up by train one evening and comes back twenty-four hours later.

When he returns to the cottage, Anna is sitting in an armchair in front of an unlit fire, and doesn't get up when James comes into the room. She is shaking, her eyes red with tears, her left cheek swollen, both legs bruised and scratched.

'My God, what's happened to you?' he says.

'Zach came back. He'd been drinking. Tried to get me to leave with him, and when I wouldn't . . .' She cannot finish the sentence and starts to cry, burying her face in her hands.

'Where's Jack?'

Anna is unable to answer for a minute, then says, 'He's with the Sullivans. It's Tomas's birthday today and he's spending the night there.'

'You need a doctor, and I'll call the Garda. When did Zach leave?'

'He's been gone two hours, back to Cork and the ferry. Please don't call the police, that would make everything worse. I need a bath, not a doctor.'

Anna cries out as James helps her into a hot bath. Her ribs are painful and there are purple bruises on both thighs. In the bath, still crying, she looks up at James, sees the unasked question in his eyes, and says, 'He didn't just knock me about.'

Anna spends the night curled up on her side of the bed, moaning occasionally when she changes position. The next morning she is silent, and it is difficult for James to find the right words of comfort. When he suggests again that he should call the Garda, her reply is clear.

'I don't want that. And some of the fault is mine.'

'What do you mean?'

'I should never have gone to Cork, never encouraged him.'

'You said—'

'—I wasn't going to sleep with him. And I didn't. But he put his arm around me in the clubhouse bar after the game, kissed me on the cheek and I didn't push him away. He behaved to his team-mates as though I'd come back to him, tried to persuade me to return to England.'

'None of that justifies what he did, morally or in a court of law. You told him you and Jack were with me, you came back to Drimnamore.'

'I know. But I completely mishandled him.'

When Jack is dropped home from the Sullivans', she hugs her son, winces as he hugs her. 'I had a fall while you and James were away,' she says, managing a little smile. 'I'm not safe on my own.' Jack is happy with the explanation.

It takes Anna most of a week to recover, to walk without limping, for her swollen cheek to return to normal. She doesn't want to talk to James, and his attempts at the gentlest of touches are pushed away.

'Have you talked to Aisling?' James asks.

'No. And you're not to tell her.'

'You need some help, some comfort, and I don't seem to provide any.'

'I need to deal with this myself. It's my problem, not yours or Aisling's.'

Maybe, thinks James, but it affects us all.

He spends the next week on the packing line, explaining Anna's absence as gastric flu. On Friday, Danny drives him over to Kenmare for a court hearing, which lasts all of a frustrating day in which an earlier case drags on so long that theirs is postponed for a further two months.

'That's typical of the Irish courts at the minute,' says Danny as they drive back. 'They're up to their oxters in repossessions and bankruptcies.'

When James arrives at Pier Cottage his car is gone. There is a note on the kitchen table.

Jack and I are on the way to Farranfore to catch the afternoon flight to Stansted. I'm sorry I've stolen the car. You'll find it in the airport car park – I'll push the key into the exhaust.

Please don't come after us. It's all too much for me to handle at Drimnamore, and I haven't been able to share my troubles with you. That's my fault, not yours, dear James. It seems we weren't meant to be together for very long.

Anna

Below there is a message from Jack.

Dear Dad,
Mum said we had to rush to catch a plane. Sorry not to say goodbye,
See you soon,
Love,
Jack XOXO

James crumples up the note into a ball, then smoothes it out and reads it again and again. He looks for comfort and affection and finds little, apart from the 'dear James' at the end of the letter. Jack's letter gives him some hope. He knows enough not to pursue Anna and Jack or to try to contact them straightaway.

He goes over to the Sullivans and tells them all that has happened. He finds himself speaking of Anna in the past tense, as if she were dead.

'She was great on the packing line, didn't talk much, worked really hard herself. She knew not to boss the ladies about.'

Michael pours out three glasses of whiskey.

'She's gone for good; they've gone for good, haven't they?' says James.

'I'm sure she'll be back,' says Aisling. 'She fitted in here, she was well liked.'

Michael says nothing.

James doesn't stay for supper. He hasn't yet been to Farranfore to collect his car; as long as the car is at the airport, Anna and Jack seem more likely to return. He walks home via Derriquin and sits on the rocks where his grandfather and father were photographed together in 1908. Once he had thought of getting Anna to take a picture of Jack at his knee on the same rock, but that moment has gone.

He recalls Cathleen wondering whether she was better off knowing about her real father, and asks himself if he would have been happier if he'd never met Anna. He curses the independence that made her think she could manage Zach. He picks up half a dozen stones and throws them into the sea one by one, then realizes that he is close to blaming Anna for what had happened. That way madness lies, he says to himself. It was Anna's independence that had brought her and Jack back to Drimnamore. And then taken her away again.

His sense of loss is far greater than when Anna had first moved out of his life. This time she had brought Jack, and while the three of them had been together at Drimnamore James felt that Anna's restlessness had gone. He remembers a verse of Auden's, stands up and says the lines to the rocks and the sea:

> *That later we, though parted then,*
> *May still recall these evenings when*
> *Fear gave his watch no look;*
> *The lion griefs loped from the shade*
> *And on our knees their muzzles laid,*
> *And Death put down his book.*

Then, as the light fades, he walks back to his empty cottage, his lion griefs alongside him.

Before he makes his supper he walks around, looking for traces of Anna and Jack. She had always travelled light; her chest of drawers is empty, but on top of it he finds the red box, opens it and sees that she still has the ring. Otherwise nothing, apart from a single blue sock at the bottom of Jack's bed, to show that they had ever been there. He picks up the sock, holds it to his cheek, then puts it in his pocket.

When James's mother had died, it was as sudden as Anna's departure, but then he had most of his life ahead of him. Now most of it lay behind. Kate's death was final; Anna and Jack's departure has left unanswered questions. Might they come back? Might he follow them? Neither seems likely, either that evening, or through a troubled night when he dreams of Anna stroking his cheek, or when he wakes up.

The next morning James looks into his grandfather's shaving mirror and remembers the moment twelve years ago when he had set out for Edinburgh and left the train for Allenmouth. And Anna, and Jack, and the oyster beds. The face he sees framed by the worn leather is lined, tired, his hair one-third grey. He hasn't shaved for three days. Perhaps it's 'shiva', he thinks, perhaps

Anna might as well be dead. He runs his hand over his face, whistles for Mick, then leaves the cottage.

He goes down to the pier where Danny is repairing one of the oyster purses.

'I need to clear my head,' James says as he steps into his boat.

It is a grey, blustery day. He uses the outboard to get past Rossdohan, then hoists the sails. The boat heels over sharply, and James realizes he should have reefed the mainsail, decides to leave it be. He sails out towards the mouth of the estuary in a series of tacks, Mick at his feet, from time to time whimpering his disapproval.

James concentrates on the boat, trying hard to banish the images of Anna and Jack. The wind has risen, making the rigging hum, and he sees the dark line of a heavy squall just in time to turn for home. The estuary now has lumpy, white-capped waves as its rivers fight the tide, and James has to use all his strength to keep the boat straight and avoid a jibe. He is still a mile away from Oysterbed Pier when a violent gust sweeps the boom across, striking James's arm as he ducks and protects his head. He hears the mast snap off two feet above the deck and the boat tilts sideways. As the water comes over the coaming, he is thrown clear of the sinking boat, which drifts away from him in the current and the wind.

The cold water knocks the breath out of James and clamps his chest – he is forty yards from the shore with a damaged arm and no lifejacket. For a moment this seems as good a way to go as any, then Mick's nose pushes into his neck. Mick is paddling strongly and James is shamed into survival. He can only manage a clumsy, one-armed side-stroke, but Mick keeps him company as the wind and tide take them gradually towards the land.

Mick scrambles out and waits while James pulls himself pain-fully over the rocks onto the springy grass of the foreshore and lies there, listening to the wind and the waves, his cheek pressed into the earth. His left arm is badly bruised, he is soaked through and shivering, his physical pain increased as he remembers Anna and Jack are gone.

After ten minutes Mick shakes himself vigorously, which persuades James to get to his feet. He stands for a moment, then, waterlogged and tired, walks with his dog along the road and past Drimnamore. As they turn together into the lane, Mick starts to bark, then trots down towards Pier Cottage. James looks up, sees a car parked outside the cottage, looks again and breaks into an awkward run towards whatever the future may hold.

ACKNOWLEDGEMENTS

I want to thank Michael Sissons, who volunteered to read an early draft and agreed to become my agent; Rosie de Courcy at Head of Zeus, my publishers, who bought the book and made many important editorial suggestions; and Celia Levett for help with the chronology.

Several people read my manuscript at various stages and gave me encouragement and help; Xandra Bingley, John and Kitty Fairlie, Michael Abrahams, Godfrey Bland, Thomas and Val Pakenham, Richard Eyre and Sue Birtwistle, Norah Perkins, Tony Gibson (who was a Troop leader during the Malayan Emergency and was Mentioned in Despatches), Simon Barrow (who put me in touch with the Colchester Oyster Fishery), and Patrick Perceval (who told me about Mount Athos). Archie Bland gave me a detailed and invaluable edit, and Jamie and Elizabeth Byng were generous with their advice on the text and on publication.

My teachers at Birkbeck were Claire Collison and Lois Keith, and at the Faber Academy, Gillian Slovo; I am very grateful to them and to my fellow aspiring writers for their encouragement and constructive criticism. Our Faber group has had a continuing and enjoyable existence during the two years after our formal course finished.

I used a number of sources as background for the novel; in particular *On Another Man's Wound* by Ernie O'Malley, who escaped from Kilmainham Jail in February 1921, and *Lady Hostage* by Tim Sheehan, an account of the abduction and execution of Mrs Lindsay after the Dripsey ambush in County Cork.

Ashes in the Wind is a novel, not history, but I have used some real characters, Michael Collins and Emmet Dalton in particular, and some real events. I gave Michael Collins an ADC at Béal na mBláth, but the Big Fellow was the only casualty in that tragic skirmish. Michael O'Hanrahan was executed after the Easter Rising, but had no daughter. Lord Midleton was the leader of the Southern Unionists from 1910 to 1922; his sister Albinia Brodrick, who is buried in the churchyard in Sneem, Co. Kerry, was an active supporter of Sinn Féin. I moved Laytown Races to County Kerry. And I used my author's prerogative at the end of the book to compress time and allow Michael Sullivan to rise and fall with the Irish property boom.

Finally, I owe an immense debt of gratitude to my wife Jennie, who has encouraged and supported me during the years of writing this book, as she has throughout our life together.